I0762033

True
Wings

CLAN OF THE ARCHANGEL SERIES

BOOK 1

GRACIE
MITCHELL

Copyright © 2019 Gracie Mitchell.

All rights reserved. No part of this publication may be reproduced, distributed, or transmitted in any form or by any means, including photocopying, recording, or other electronic or mechanical methods, without the prior written permission of the publisher, except in the case of brief quotations embodied in critical reviews and certain other noncommercial uses permitted by copyright law. For permission requests, write to the Author, addressed "Attention: Permissions Coordinator," at the address below.

ISBN: 978-1-7354575-0-5 (E-book)
ISBN: 978-1-7354575-1-2 (Paperback)
ISBN: 978-1-7354575-2-9 (Hardcover)

Any references to historical events, real people, or real places are used fictitiously. Names, characters, and places are products of the author's imagination.

Cover Design and Illustrations: Jessica Slater
Editor: Connie Dowell | Nichole Heydenburg | Anachal Jain
Book Design and Typesetting: Enchanted Ink Publishing

Printed by IngramSpark, Barnes and Nobles Press, and Kindle Direct Publishing in the United States of America.

First printing edition 2021.

To my husband for encouraging me to
follow my dreams.

My amazing, eccentric family and friends
for the unending support.

Lastly, to my sister Brittany who watches
me from above and always encouraged me
to reach for the stars.

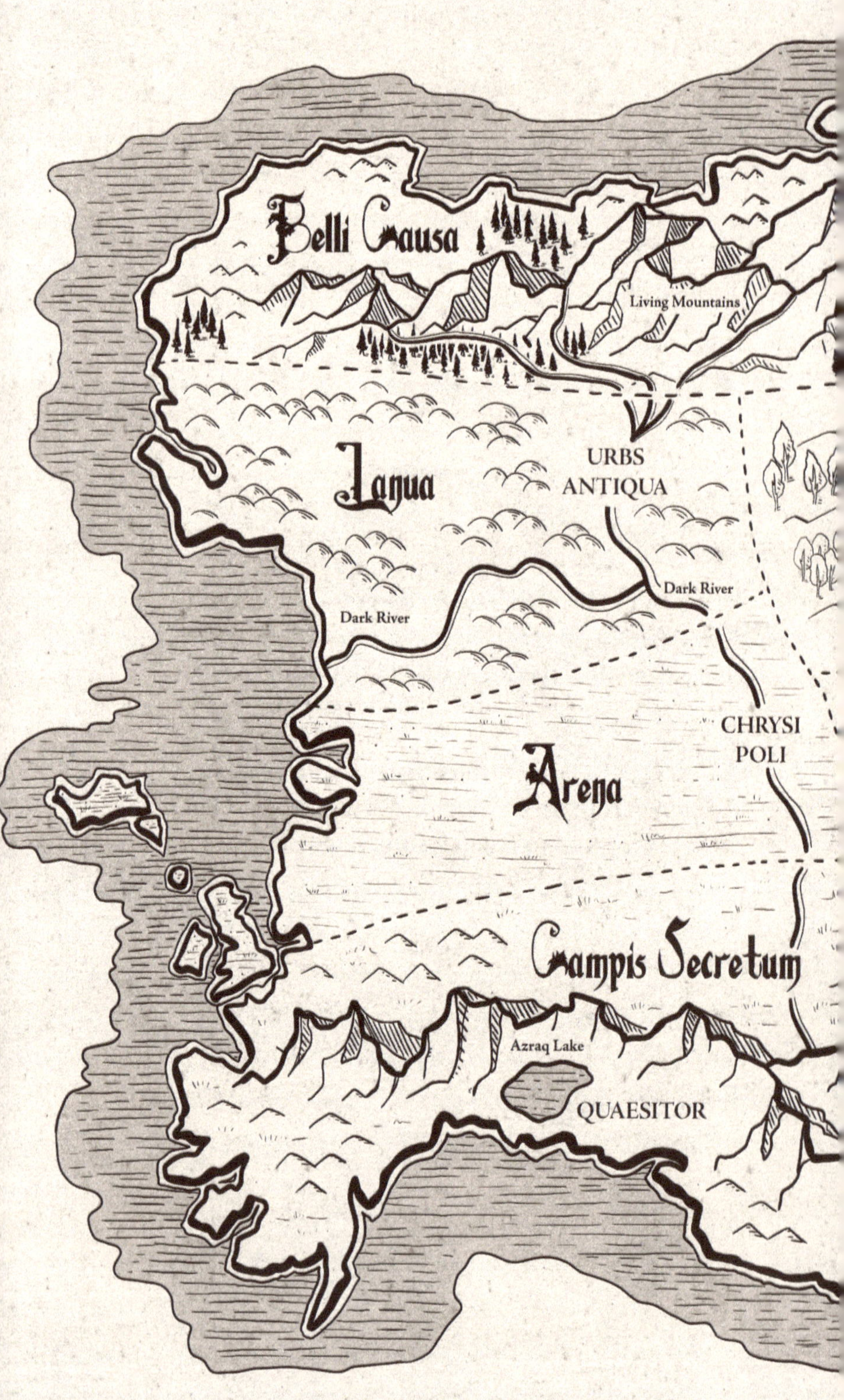

Belli Causa
Living Mountains
Lanua
URBS
ANTIQUA
Dark River
Dark River
CHRYSI
POLI
Arena
Campis Secretum
Azraq Lake
QUAESITOR

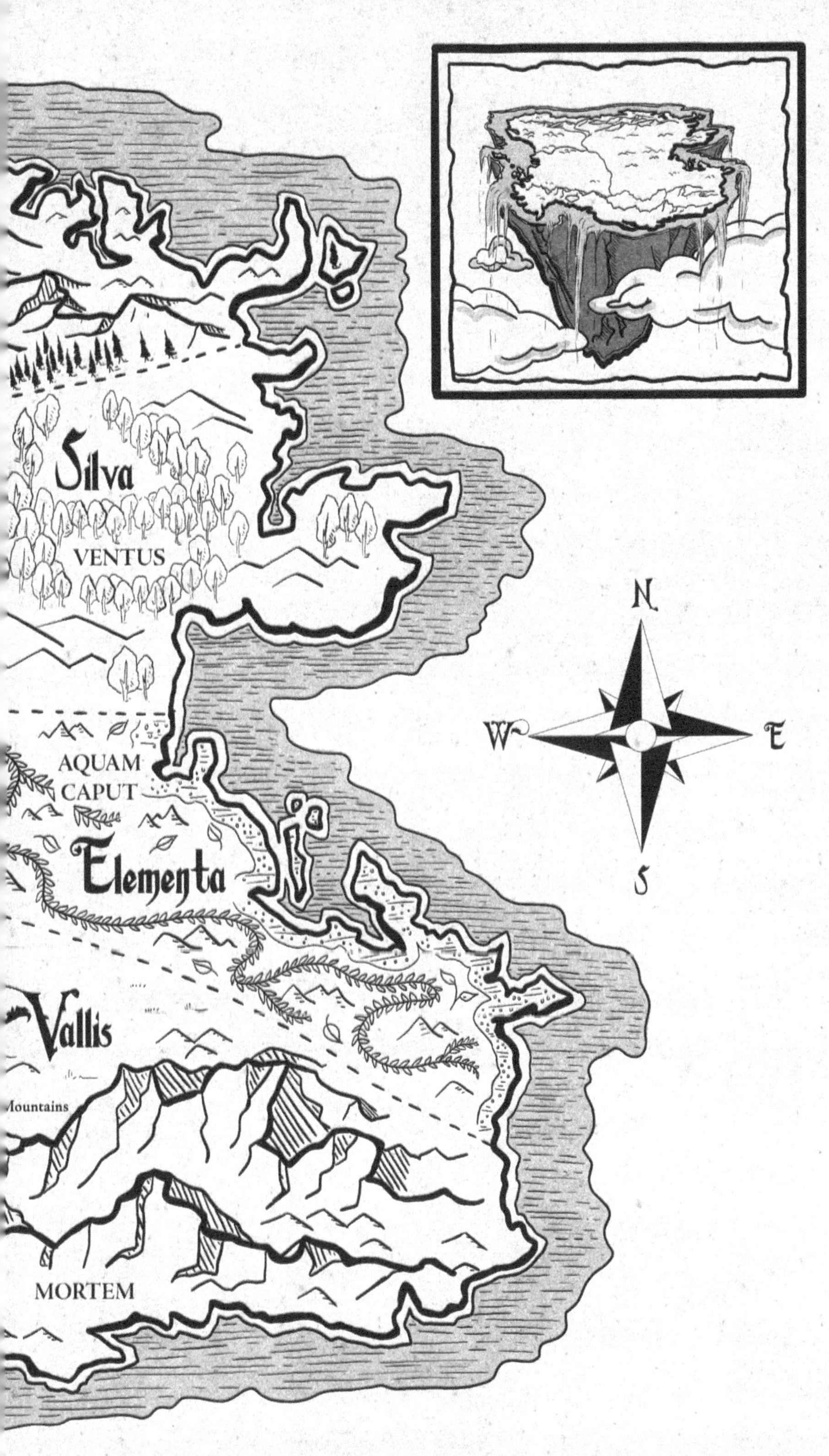
Silva
VENTUS
AQUAM
CAPUT
Elementa
Vallis
Mountains
MORTEM
N
W
E
S

Chapter 1

Atarah

The sun danced along the horizon as if teasing the day's end. The rays of light took away the last bit of warmth, letting the chilly night ascend. The Faroe Islands were truly stunning. Standing upon the steep cliff gazing out at the Nordic Sea, Atarah contemplated her life.

Nothing put one's existence into perspective like standing next to something as vast as the ocean. The ocean made Atarah feel tiny, but this was nothing new. Growing up in the Michael Clan, she had always felt minuscule. However, now it was time for a change.

This summit meeting was the perfect chance to no longer be the weakest link. In her youth, she had always been the tiniest of the Michael Archangels. Even normal angels, ranked beneath Archangels, could often beat her in strength, speed, and agility. She trained harder than everyone else to keep up with her peers.

Now she intended to change all of that. She would gain as much power as she could while meeting with other Archangels. The summit meeting called forth all of the Archangel Clan Heads. Seven clans, derived from the seven original Archangels, oversaw different regions in the Spirit realm. In their realm, angels had a hierarchy, and she wanted to go to the top. The Head Archs ruled over the regions to maintain peace. Or tried to.

Due to the conflicts between the clans, Atarah's life outside of her region and family had been limited, until today. Atarah's stomach flipped with nerves and excitement. She was thrilled to be able to learn from other archs, but apprehensive because of the past rivalry and the fear of being in the human realm.

The humans' dimension filled Atarah with dread. While in this realm, she had to consume the horrid serum. This agent was a bitter liquid that concealed their powers and wings from humans and other spiritual beings. If a demon looked at her, it would think she was a normal human. She shuddered at the thought of those monsters.

"Atarah!" a familiar deep voice called out to her.

She turned her head to see her older brother Arick, waving his hands. He was striking in the best of ways. He stood tall, nearly 6'7", almost as big as their father. His ebony skin was smooth and flawless, going well with his golden eyes. He, like other Michael angels, kept his hair short, nearly shaved.

While she wore the "human" clothes their father had ordered them to don, Arick still dressed in their black and indigo uniform. A black circle on the right shoulder outlined their home mountains, blue in color. The black combat boots were loud as he approached, almost like he didn't care about being caught.

He stopped a few feet behind her.

"We are being summoned. In the Library," Arick said dryly.

He glanced back at the cottage house they were staying at for the summit meeting. The cottage was a ruse to keep humans from looking too closely. Once one entered the house, the illusion lifted to reveal an expansive estate. Dozens of rooms led from the main meeting area. The central room was composed of a large, round wooden table lined with broad chairs. The table stood before a large fireplace that spanned nearly the entire back wall. An enormous luxury wooden cabin would better described where they were staying.

Dismayed, she started back to the building. She didn't want to play peacemaker for her brother and father today. *Two bulls butting heads,* her mother said throughout the years.

Her brother followed after her through the front door of their residence and down the north facing hall. They passed by a few other Archangel heirs, but she ignored them. They would make full introductions tomorrow anyway. Arick gave a cocky smile before winking at a female angel as they walked. She heard giggling and almost rolled her eyes.

She pushed the carved door leading into the small library. Books lined the walls, while a desk sat in the center, with a few chairs in front. *Like children being called into the office,* Atarah thought. She sat in one of the chairs and sank almost immediately. Her father didn't even glance up at them from his book. Their father, Mikael Viribus, was the current Archangel Head of the Michael Clan. He had broad shoulders and stood taller than everyone. His golden eyes were stern, and his voice was commanding and deep. He wore his "human" clothes, composed of black dress pants, a white button-down shirt, and an unbuttoned black jacket. Mikael glanced up and then returned to whatever he was reading. Though Atarah noticed his jaw clenched in frustration when he looked at Arick.

Once Arick sat down, Mikael addressed both of them. Slowly. He set down his pen and closed the book before him. He cleared his throat, regarding them with mild annoyance.

"The Raphael Clan will be here in a few hours. They are the last to arrive. Once here, we will finally begin this meeting." Mikael narrowed his eyes slightly. "The Raphael family will give us the hardest time." He sighed and murmured something about old wounds. He turned to her with a frown. "They will probably insist upon an arranged marriage for you, Atarah, just to spite me."

"I understand our need for allies," she said carefully. She didn't want to get married, but she also didn't want to cause another fight between clans.

"I will not force you into any marriage," her father said vehemently. "Both of you." He glanced at Arick, who smirked. "Do not lower your guard. Each of these families have their own agenda. Mercifully we only have to deal with four Head families instead of seven, but that doesn't lessen the severity of the situation."

"Danger everywhere. Got it," Arick said sardonically.

Mikael narrowed his eyes at his son in irritation.

"Silence," Mikael said harshly. "Only speak when spoken to."

Arick gave a small smile, but Atarah wasn't fooled. Both male angels were irritated.

"Is there anything you can tell us about the families to prepare us for what is to come?" Atarah inquired, more to change the subject than out of actual curiosity.

Mikael frowned slightly at her but answered. "The Uriel family is undecided, whereas the Gabriels are more or less an ally." Mikael mused for a moment. "Do you remember Malachi Ignis' daughters?"

"You mean Clarissa and Isabella?" Atarah said with disdain.

An old memory of one of the girls lighting her dress on fire came to the surface of her mind. Malachi Ignis, Head Archangel of the Uriel Clan, had brought his heirs to Sanctum on a diplomatic visit upon her father's insistence. Mikael had thought meeting other female Archangels her age would help her make friends and break out of her shell. Oh, how wrong he had been.

"Yes. They will be in attendance. Try to learn what you can and befriend them. I know you were acquainted years ago."

Atarah nearly scoffed. She still saw Clarissa's satisfied smirk and heard Isabella's giggles as she frantically patted the flames from her dress all those years ago.

"As for *you*," Mikael said as he turned to Arick, "Keep your focus on Gabriel Fores the twentieth—not the nineteenth—and Noah Salutem. Those two heirs should keep you busy enough."

Gabriel Fores XIX was the current Archangel Head of the Gabriel Clan with Gabriel Fores XX as his heir. They were the only clan that still passed on their familial name to the next in line. The rumor was that the head family nicknamed the males by the birth order number. Their clan had the power to travel through the different realms easily.

Noah was the son and heir to Elijah Salutem, Head Archangel of the Raphael Clan. The Raphaels were known as healing angels. They could regenerate their own wounds faster than others. Her mother told her that if a high-ranking Raphael angel trained diligently, they could heal anything.

Two heirs to deal with for each of them. Atarah wanted to groan at the prospect, but she kept her composure.

"Your wish is my command, Father," Arick said dryly. He added a mocking bow of his head, further pushing their father's patience.

"My wish is for a competent son. Make that your command," their father said scathingly. His gold eyes seemed to shine with annoyance. If his wings had been out, they would be flared in irritation.

Mikael waved a hand in dismissal. Atarah was grateful to escape. She thanked her father and grabbed Arick before either of them could say another word.

Once out in the hallway, she released a deep breath. Her shoulders relaxed and her jaw loosened, while Arick still appeared tense. She patted his arm.

"Come on," she said softly. "Let's get a drink."

Arick simply nodded and turned left, down the hall, toward the kitchen. She sighed. When their father was out of the equation, her brother and she were the best of friends. However, when Father came around . . . things changed.

She followed after him. The kitchen was not far. Pushing through double doors brought them to an industrial size kitchen. Stainless steel seemed to shine everywhere. The appliances, countertops, and shelving were all made of the same material. The kitchen crew was busy and moved all around. The staff barely paid them any attention, too busy preparing the dinner for all of the Head families expected for tonight. Off to the side was a small wooden bar with a polished top and a few tall stools. Arick made a beeline toward the bar without hesitation.

"The largest glass you have on the shelf," Arick demanded of the bartender. He didn't bother sitting down, but she did.

She ordered a smaller drink before turning to him. He shook his head and waved her hand away.

"Not yet," he said.

They had been through this before. All throughout their childhood, Father had always treated Arick harshly as a way to toughen him up. Since he was the one to inherit the leadership role of Head Archangel, he received more punishments and scrutiny while she had been treated more . . . gently.

Unintentionally.

Nothing was expected of her, except maybe a marriage to another aristocratic Arch family. Even then, she could put off marriage for several more years.

She didn't have the same strength or speed as Arick or any other Michael angel. While she inherited her father's ability to project one's strength and to crush an opponent, it was one of her weakest skills.

So, she had to strengthen her other abilities. Her hearing, vision, sense of smell, touch, sensitivity, and her intuition. To be able to anticipate her opponent's next move before they took a step. She was hyperaware of everyone around her and their actions. She heard the heart beats of the servants across the kitchen. She felt stomping feet of the angels on the opposite side of the house. She even smelled the horses outside being cleaned. She used all of this, and it wasn't enough. Not for her father or herself. She needed to be more.

Arick sighed after finishing his second drink. "Stop hating yourself, Atarah. You can't help who you are any more than I can help how *he* is."

"I hate how he treats you, Arick," she said gloomily.

Arick laughed and gave her a side hug. "Me too, cricket. Me too. But let's not talk about him,

or else I'll be angry this whole trip."

"You're happy about this trip?"

"Absolutely! Why wouldn't I be? It's not every day I get to see Father boiling with anger at the Raphaels, or fight against other devious heirs trying to prove who's more powerful, and have all the girls of the realm squealing to get my attention." Arick smirked.

Her brother was, without a doubt, strikingly handsome, bearing golden eyes, dark hair, and dark skin. He was built like the warrior whose house he would inherit. Any girl would be lucky to marry him someday. He knew it too.

Atarah shook her head, her father's words of marriage still on her mind. She wondered why the Raphael and Michael houses disliked each other. When did it all start? Atarah gripped her cup with a new determination to find out.

"Don't fret about such things," Arick said, of course knowing what she was thinking. "No matter how much we hate each other's guts, Father and I will never let anyone take you."

"I don't want to be a pawn taken hostage in a game," she said, frustrated. "I want what's best for our people and our region, but I don't want to be a girl in a waiting room. A girl just waiting to be married off. I want to be useful! Powerful!"

"You'd never let yourself be that girl. Despite how small and weak you think you are, you're still a warrior of the House of Michael. You'd never stop fighting."

"You sound like Mother trying to cheer me up after training."

"Mother's right though. There are different ways of being strong."

"Tell that to the girl who kicks me in the face during training," Atarah said, rolling her eyes.

Arick laughed. "You never guard your left side. That's why you get kicked."

"How do you think the summit will go?"

Arick took a deep breath. "Honestly, it'll be a miracle

if everyone makes it out without injury. Only a handful of Arch houses get along with one another."

Atarah nodded, thinking the same. She was going to have to stay safe and get stronger for her family's sake. She chuckled a little.

"What's so funny, little cricket?" Arick asked, taking a sip of his third drink. Cricket was his pet name for her when he was annoyed or teasing her.

"You and Father remind me of eggs sometimes," she said, chuckling.

"Eggs?"

"Yes. You have a hard shell on the outside, but both of you are all goop on the inside." She snickered.

Arick coughed from his drink as she laughed some more. "Never thought of myself as an egg—or any food item, for that matter."

"I never thought of myself as a bug, but you still call me cricket."

"Term of endearment, little cricket."

Atarah rolled her eyes, happy to have her brother back to normal. She felt the all-knowing tug of pain down her back and stifled a wince. She got up and started toward the kitchen exit.

"Where are you off to?" he asked.

"Going to find Mom. I need some more serum. My wings are starting to act up again."

"Grab me some too. My back started hurting before Father summoned us."

Atarah winced openly this time. "Ugh. No wonder you're drinking more than usual."

"I wanted to see how long I could bear the pain."

"Masochist."

Arick tried to smirk, but it looked more like a pained grin. "Baby cricket."

She turned to look for their mother. Once her back

started hurting, the pain would spread until she wouldn't be able to move at all. She was surprised her brother was able to bear this during their father's summons.

The pain came from their wings. The serum they all had to consume to enter the human realm suppressed their powers. It changed them from a spiritual form to a physical one. This allowed them to walk among the humans undetected because it dissipated their wings and abilities. Archs normally were proud of their wings and characteristics and hated smothering them within their bodies, as it caused severe back pain.

Atarah's wings ached and begged her for release as the stabbing sensation continued.

She walked quickly down the halls and up the circular staircase to where her family was staying. She wished the meeting could have taken place back in the Spirit realm, creating no need for the serum. Back in their territory, angels and Archangels could move about freely in their own forms . . . well, until demons started coming through again.

Their realm was above the human realm, while the demon's domain was above their realm. Which meant the demons had to travel through the dimensions to get to their favorite food source—humans. While traveling through the Spirit realm, demons wreaked havoc everywhere—attacking towns, destroying everything in sight.

There were portals or "holes" in between realms that the demons traveled through. Lately, there had been more holes than usual. Instead of a few demons coming through here and there, it was nearly hundreds, sometimes thousands, coming through at once! Hence the need for the summit meeting.

She started for her mother's room at the end of the hallway before the pain could catch up with her.

Once she finally made it, she knocked and entered without waiting. "Hello, Mother. I need the serum quickly. Feels like my wings are about to rip themselves out of my back."

Ava, her mother and Mistress of the House of Michael, looked up from her latest book. Her eyes widened as they took in Atarah's hunched figure.

"Oh my!" She stood and went to the cabinets behind her. "Go ahead and sit down while I grab some."

Atarah sat down but did not lie back due to the pain. The room was a comfortable size for two. The furniture was all made out of oak wood, with a queen size bed, a small sitting area where she sat, and a small bathroom to her right. There was a very cozy feel to the room, however that might have been the effect her mother had on her.

"I swear, this serum affects Archs less and less each trip to the human realm," her mother said with a furrowed brow.

"I lasted six hours this time, and Arick is going on six and a half. He'll need some as well."

Mother sighed. "Those brutes—always the 'pain is good' mindset. Insufferable."

"He and Father got into it a little this afternoon."

Mother looked troubled at that. She'd never liked how harsh Mikael was on Arick. She begged him to change. Father always refused her gently, saying because Arick represented the future of the house, he must be tough on him.

'He will become stronger this way,' Father always said.

Mother sent Arick out of the house on most days to train with different generals so their paths rarely crossed.

"Here you are, Atarah." Her mother handed her a mug that held the serum.

Her body revolted against the serum going down her throat. Her stomach heaved and she nearly gagged as she swallowed. However, Atarah fought back the nausea and forced it down. She knew the summit meeting took place in the human realm to limit fighting amongst houses, but the knowledge didn't help against the taste. Pure bitterness.

"I hate coming to the human realm," Atarah said, trying to keep the serum down. Vinegar would taste better.

"A necessary evil, my dear. The council doesn't want any fighting to occur, and coming here discourages that," she said, confirming Atarah's thoughts.

Mother still looked worried. There was something more in her expression that Atarah couldn't place. She decided to be straightforward. "What else is going on?"

"Nothing for you to fret about. But I think you should know something for your own protection." She sat down beside her in the small sitting area. She sighed. "The House of Raphael will most definitely try something, but I'm not sure what they're plotting."

Her mother was a gentle spirit with a kind heart no one could resist. Her curly black hair framed her face nicely. However, what struck most people about Atarah's mother was her petite frame, healing hands, and stunning eyes. Atarah wasn't sure exactly what color her mother's eyes were. Brown? Green? Hazel? She was never sure, but the moment she looked into them, she couldn't help but feel at ease.

Many of the angels in her region said Atarah took after her mother, and Arick, to his chagrin, took after their father. Even their wings mirrored their parents'. Arick's wings were like their father's—hard, leathery, and bat-like. Or more like dragon wings, Atarah thought. They were powerful, hard wings, specifically designed for battle. Atarah's and her mother's wings were made of ivory feathers, wings used for swiftness and gentle gliding, and most certainly not to be used for battle.

"Aren't they always plotting something against us?" Atarah asked.

"This isn't like any of the usual jabs they throw at us." Mother looked away. "But something bigger."

"Does Father know about your suspicion?"

"No, I don't want to make your father any more tense than he already is at the idea of being in the same room as them." Mother looked dazed, as if her mind was far away, then shook her head slightly and looked back at Atarah. "You should probably go back to your brother and give him some serum. He'll need to stay on his guard and rely on his physical strength while we're here. I loathe that the heirs were called to this meeting, and your father agrees. This does nothing but put all of you in danger."

Atarah laughed a little. "We're not necessarily children, Mother. I'm seventeen, and Arick's going on nineteen. We can handle ourselves among the heirs."

The ages of the heirs ranged from fourteen to thirty years old. Relatively young, but by no means defenseless children. Most of them had been learning how to fight since they could walk. Even if all of them didn't have their powers under control, they still had advanced fighting techniques.

However, in the human realm their loss of powers was a needed detail for today. Many angels did not fully develop and control their powers until they were well into adulthood. Which was usually fifty years or more.

Well, except for a few cases, Atarah thought grimly.

"Atarah, are you listening? Hello?" Mother asked, walking over to her.

"I'm sorry; what was that?" Atarah needed to keep her head clear.

"I said you need to get going to your brother. He's probably passed out from the pain by now."

"Oh! I forgot. Goodnight, Mother." She hurried out the door.

Atarah scurried down the hall and down the stairs. *Tomorrow,* she thought, *tomorrow I will be ready for anything.*

At least, she hoped. She raced toward the kitchen to give her brother the serum.

Chapter 2

Atarah

Atarah walked beside her family along the wide hallway. Lined along the wooden walls were lanterns, giving barely enough light to see ahead. They reached the end of the hall, under an arched doorway to see the large dining room. An enormous round oak table sat in the middle of the room with chairs along the edge. Behind the table, a vast fireplace was ablaze and crackling.

Turning away from the table, she took in her other surroundings. The House of Uriel seemed to have arrived already. Malachi Ignis, Head Archangel of the Uriel House, and his two daughters, Clarissa and Isabella, stood by the table. They had been the first to arrive.

"And here I thought you got lost." Malachi nodded towards Mikael. "Getting a bit slow there, Mikael. The children slowed you down?" Malachi said with a chuckle.

Malachi had a jovial personality. Even though he was looking up at her father, his confidence made him seem taller. His long, red hair, which usually hung past his shoulders, was up in a messy bun. The bun oddly suited him, with his chiseled jawline, straight nose, and full beard. Despite his lighthearted spirit, there was a tightness around his hazel eyes that Atarah noticed. A stress response.

Atarah and her family moved closer to the table. Mikael and Malachi grabbed hands in greeting, her father smiling slightly. The Houses of Uriel and Michael were not enemies, but she had never heard her father say they were friends.

We'll need as many non-enemies as possible in this meeting, Atarah thought.

Against whatever legends humans wrote about angels and Archs, they did in fact age, although it was at a significantly slower rate than humans. Despite her father's age of ninety-six years, he didn't look older than thirty to human eyes. This age difference could be quite inconvenient. Especially when an angel might be forty but look to be in high school and treated as such. Angel children grew at the same rate as humans until they hit puberty. Once puberty began, the aging process slowed dramatically. Humans would think she was seventeen for the next three decades.

Malachi turned to look at her and Arick. His eyes widened a bit when he took in Arick, more so when he regarded her. Father stepped back from Malachi and stood in front of them, blocking them from Malachi's view.

"They have grown much since the last time we all met," Father said coolly.

"Indeed, time flies. One day they can barely walk, the next day they're ready to take over!" Malachi said, indicating his daughters. He smiled proudly.

"You remember my daughters, Clarissa and Isabella."

Atarah did unfortunately. *Last time I sat down to make friends,* she thought.

"Hello, how do you do?" Clarissa, the oldest, said politely.

They'd inherited the red hair and pale skin of their father. Supposedly, they'd inherited their green eyes from their late mother.

"Well. Thank you for asking," Atarah replied, staring them down.

"I suppose we should go ahead and sit down, while we wait for the others," her father said, pulling a chair out for mother.

Malachi and his daughters relaxed in the chairs closest to the door, while the Michael Clan sat farthest from the door. Mother sat to father's right and Arick to his left. Leaving her sitting next to Arick.

"So far away, Mikael. One would think you want nothing to do with this meeting," Malachi called out. "Though I wouldn't blame you. Your region hasn't taken nearly as big of a hit as others."

Father tensed. "I'm very fortunate to not have to deal with the demon filth that tries to prey upon this land," he stated. "From what I heard, these holes like to appear more in some regions than others. I wouldn't be surprised if some of the houses were to blame me for these holes." He leveled his gaze at Malachi, who smirked.

"It only makes sense for the warrior angels to take on more demons than the rest of us," Malachi said smoothly.

Atarah froze. Was this what mother had been trying to say last night? Was the summit called to demand that father take on more demons?

Before father could reply to Malachi, a door behind Malachi opened. The Archangels of the Gabriel House walked through the arch doorway.

"Good evening, household heads and heirs," said Gabriel Fores XIX of Gabriel House. Behind him stood his wife, Rachael, and son, Gabriel Fores XX.

Atarah vaguely remembered Rachael and Gabriel Jr. from her past. Their black hair and ice blue eyes were the signature look of those from the Gabriel House. Their house and her own had a long history with one another, but were nonetheless allies.

Gabriel Sr. and his family sat at the middle of the table to her father's right. This left only the space beside Atarah open for the last family to arrive. Her stomach dropped at the thought. *Only the Raphael family is left.*

Sure enough, once the Gabriel family sat down, the same door opened to reveal Elijah Salutem, Head Archangel of the Raphael House.

Atarah immediately noticed his eyes. His eyes were a mixture of colors: green, brown, and hazel. He wore a green and amber uniform with a tree insignia on the top right shoulder. He was taller than other Heads—but not as tall as her father—with dark, curly hair. His broad chest and built arms gave Atarah the impression that he knew how to fight. Elijah's gaze went straight toward mother and stayed there for a moment too long.

Her mother, Ava, paled under his scrutiny.

"Hello, everyone," Elijah said, still looking at her mother. Father stiffened in his chair. "House of Raphael has arrived." He broke his gaze and glanced to the vacant spots next to her. Behind him stood his wife Elizabeth, son, Noah, and daughter Charlotte. Each wore a similar outfit as Elijah. Dressed in green and amber colors, they all wore large dark orange scarves with the same tree insignia embroidered on the front.

Elizabeth was tall with dark, wavy hair that came down to her waist. Her round face and hazel eyes gave her a look of effortless elegance. Noah bore the same curly hair as his father but acquired his mother's hazel eyes. He was built athletic and lean. Charlotte was the last to enter. She stood hesitantly in the back, as if trying to hide from everyone's gaze. Her brown, wavy hair fell around her shoulders and face. Atarah could barely make out her heart-shaped face and small nose through her hair. She attempted to shield herself as much as possible.

It seemed the Raphael House didn't get the dress code memo, for they didn't dress in human attire. Everyone else wore a variation of jeans, skirts, T-shirts, and button-downs.

Elijah took a seat next to Atarah; his family followed after him. As his gaze passed by her, she could've sworn his eyes widened a little, but she wasn't sure.

"Seems you take after your mother," he said to her. "How very fortunate for you."

She narrowed her eyes at him. "I am fortunate for both of my parents."

He ignored her. Instead, he turned to address the rest of the table. "Now then. Shall we begin?" Elijah spoke to everyone, but he looked directly at her father.

Father leaned forward. "Yes. Let's begin."

Chapter 3

Elijah

Elijah clenched his fists. It would give him no greater pleasure than to punch Mikael in his smug face. However, he glanced at his eldest daughter, Ava, taking in as much detail as he could. She looked pale but healthy. Scared but determined. He turned away, struggling with his emotions. He wished he could whisk Ava back home and tell her everything would be alright but knew he couldn't.

He needed to be smart about this if he was going to bring his family together. He peered at the young angel to his left, Atarah. She nearly knocked the wind out of him when he saw her. She was the spitting image of Ava when she had been that age. He had heard Mikael had a daughter but had never seen her. The last time he had a chance to see them, Mikael's son had been no more than a year old. Now Arick sat there looking so much like his father, it was uncanny.

"What are your thoughts, Elijah?" Gabriel Sr. asked, watching him closely.

Cautious little fairy, Elijah thought. He had been so consumed with his plans that he nearly missed the question.

"This is in regards to Mikael's forces moving to the southern borders?" he inquired. He sat forward, resting his elbows on the table.

"Yes," Mikael spoke. "It has been kindly pointed out to me that all of the holes in our realm are concentrated away from my region and in the south."

"The southern regions aren't defenseless," Elijah chimed in.

Malachi grunted in disapproval.

"Yeah, but we're nowhere near as . . .equipped compared to Michael angels," Malachi countered. "That's probably why the holes are opened in the southern regions."

"But most of the Houses in the southern region would burn any soldier Mikael sends, let alone allow them to help," Elijah argued. He looked at Mikael. "You burned many bridges in the south, and peace will not come easy."

"I don't want peace. I want tolerance," Mikael said firmly. "That is why I need you to back my forces to show the others that we come as friends, not as enemies."

"Why not Malachi's stamp of approval? Or Gabriel's?" Elijah inquired. He was reluctant to align his name even further with Mikael's.

"They do not have the same history as us." Mikael spoke as if his words were not salt on an open wound.

Elijah gripped his chair so hard the wood groaned. Anger coursed through him at the bitter memories of the past. Ava visibly paled, which made him pause. He had to be smart about this, for his eldest daughter, for his whole family.

"I'll agree on one condition," Elijah said softly. Mikael tensed at his words while Elijah moved his eyes to the young girl beside him. Atarah, his granddaughter. "She is to marry one of our high-ranking officials."

"Absolutely not," Mikael spoke harshly.

It doesn't feel good to have your daughter taken, does it? Elijah thought cynically.

"It's about time she learned about this side of the family, don't you think?" Elijah said.

Atarah's eyes shot up to meet his in surprise. Now she took in his features with a new interest, realizing their relationship.

So, she didn't know, Elijah mused.

"I won't allow this," Mikael said firmly. "Pick something else and leave *my* family out of it, Elijah."

At the word family, Elijah lunged at Mikael, unable to control his anger. He got one good punch in before surprise was no longer on his side. Mikael countered a punch of his own, not his full strength, but enough to knock Elijah down. Before either of them could attack again, hands were on Elijah dragging him back. Noah and Gabriel Sr. grunted as they tried to pull him away, but it was Elizabeth's gentle hand that brought him back to his senses.

Ava stood for a moment, unsure if she should go to her husband or her father. A dagger went through his heart as she moved toward Mikael, making sure *he* was okay. In all of the commotion, something Elijah did not expect happened.

Atarah stood between them, facing him. The striking resemblance to Ava caused him to pause. She stretched out her hand and poked at him.

"Enough," she said in a gentle but firm voice. "We aren't here to discuss old family wounds. Let's save this family squabble for later."

Elijah regarded her with surprise. He nodded to Noah and Gabriel to signal he wouldn't try anything else.

"Anyone else have any other suggestions?" Elijah said, straightening his clothes.

"Send me as an emissary," Atarah said boldly.

Elijah paused, surprised again.

"Absolutely not," Mikael hissed behind her.

However, Elijah was focused on her. Her eyes, so much like her mother's, were burning with something. Something he couldn't name yet.

"It sends a better message if I go as an emissary of my own volition than under the forced pretense of marriage. The southern Houses will have to see that."

Elijah pondered. He hadn't thought she would be willing to come to Silva with him. Mikael looked as shocked as he did, bewildered to the point of silence.

"She is right," Malachi chimed in. "Allowing Atarah to go willingly shows compromise and vulnerability on Mikael's part. It would send a message."

"I said no!" Mikael boomed. It seemed he found his voice again.

Atarah whirled around to face her father.

"And I'm saying yes," she said firmly. Something passed between them as they stared at each other. Something that softened her face. "I'll be fine. It's not a marriage but a job." Atarah turned to face Elijah. "Do you agree?"

He looked from her to Mikael then to Ava before answering.

"Accepted. I will take you on as an emissary in exchange for my troops and word backing Mikael's forces."

Silence followed for a moment. Mikael and Ava looked worried. Atarah appeared oddly triumphant. Elijah glanced at his wife and younger children and saw expressions of displeasure or unease between them. This would not be an easy reunion.

Malachi clapped his hands together loudly and slowly. "Good show, everyone! Since that matter is out of the way, let's move on. The details can be worked out later."

Mikael gave him an exasperated look.

Gabriel glanced at his watch. "Let's discuss more in the morning. We've all had a long day and need another dose of the serum."

Elijah hadn't noticed how much time had passed. Now that Gabriel pointed it out, he could feel the pull of his back muscles. A reminder to take the serum soon or pain would be inevitable. He resisted the urge to stretch out his aching back, opting to focus on Malachi's words.

"Since I called for the emergency meeting, I'll play host," Malachi said as he indicated the door, left of the fireplace. "Down that corridor are the rooms we will all be staying in. There are barriers around this house and the rooms, so you'll sleep safely."

As they filed out, Elijah was surprised again. Atarah approached him. She looked at him with such genuine curiosity, he almost laughed. Mikael watched them, or really *her*, and immediately came up behind her. He gently placed a hand on her shoulder to draw her attention.

"Atarah, let's head to bed. We all need our rest," he said gently. Elijah had never seen Mikael act so . . . affable before.

Still studying him, Atarah nodded.

Elijah turned to walk away, but Atarah called out. "Don't expect me to call you grandfather or anything."

Elijah chuckled. He looked over his shoulder at her. "I'm too young to be called grandfather anyway." He veered back.

With that, he walked down the hall in search of his family. He liked her spirit. She had a feistiness about her that Ava never had. She dared to speak up, to advocate for herself, when no other heirs dared.

Elijah waited a minute to gather himself. Elizabeth wouldn't be happy about how he'd acted today. Noah and Charlotte would no doubt be pacing the room, waiting to ask him more about his plans and Atarah staying with them.

He took a moment of quiet for himself before walking down the corridor. Stuck with his human senses because of the serum, he didn't hear his family's voices until he turned the corner. His family stood at the threshold of a door in deep discussion.

Charlotte saw him first, then Noah, and Elizabeth. He approached them. "Probably best to talk about this inside our rooms." He strolled into the room.

The spacious room overlooked a gorgeous view of the starry night sky and rolling hills. The bed on the far left side laid big enough to fit his entire family, he was sure. The room was decorated in ivory and accented in green, with a variety of plants all around. A calm and relaxed environment was no doubt what Malachi had in mind when picking this place.

Elijah turned to his family when he heard the door close. Charlotte spoke first.

"She looked healthy at least," she said. Her soft voice tried to sound cheerful but carried too much sadness to be believable as such.

His wife let out a noise between a laugh and a sob. Elizabeth collapsed in a chair looking deflated, no doubt from seeing their eldest daughter. His heart squeezed. He would never forget the devastation that overtook her in that first year after their daughter had been taken. Nor the last time he had seen Ava. She had been so . . . devoid. Hollow was the only word that came to mind whenever he thought of the last time he saw her.

She had been in Belli Causa, lying in bed. Her body was severely malnourished to the extent he could see her bones. Ava hadn't even looked at him when he had walked in. She had stared at the far wall with dead eyes. Empty of any life.

"It doesn't seem like he's mistreating her," Elijah said. "While it's possible he actually cares for her, this won't excuse his deceit in taking her away from us."

The House of Raphael was a close-knit, deeply caring family. When Ava had been taken, Elijah sensed the shift with his whole family, how her absence affected them. Elijah's heart felt torn apart. He was finally able to see his first born after so many years. Yet it seemed as if Ava was retreating from them.

"What about the girl?" Noah asked stiffly. "You're not really going to bring her with us. She's still his daughter."

"She's just as much her daughter as well, Noah," Elijah replied. Then an all-knowing, painful tug pulled at his back. He winced.

Elizabeth started on the serums, sensing the growing pains within their family. One thing he could do without in the human realm, he mused, was this pain and the disgusting serum itself.

"We won't know what she's like until we spend more time around her," Charlotte said.

"She shouldn't be trusted until then. We have to be careful of her," Noah said.

Elijah looked at his wife when she handed him the serum. "What do you think of the girl, my love?" He gulped down the vile serum.

Elizabeth thought for a minute. "I think she has much potential to bridge the divide between us and our daughter. She could be very useful to us if we plan carefully."

Not the response he'd been hoping for. His gentle wife had taken Ava's kidnapping the hardest. Since then,

Elizabeth became reclusive and inhospitable toward anyone outside of the family. She had locked Charlotte and Noah away for years before Elijah finally convinced her to let them venture beyond the walls of their home. She improved over time, even let Noah join their army, but she never returned to her carefree self.

It seemed his family was either seeing Atarah as someone not to be trusted or someone to be used. Elijah rubbed his face and sighed. He was tired and ready to get this summit over with to return home. However, before the end of the meeting, his whole family needed to be on the same page. He stood.

"I know there's much hurt and distrust within us, but nonetheless that girl is part of our family, whether we like it or not. We will welcome her. We won't share everything regarding the region with her"—he looked at Noah—"nor will we try to manipulate her." He glanced at his wife. "I want to unify this family more than anything in the whole realm, and that starts with the girl."

While everyone looked solemn, they still nodded in acceptance.

"All right. Now let's go to bed. We'll need our strength for tomorrow," Elijah said.

Charlotte and Noah rose to head to their room, adjacent to Elijah and Elizabeth's. Elijah took his wife's hand and headed toward their bed. As he changed, his wife wrote in her journal. She had once told him she felt better writing her feelings rather than speaking them. He gave her the privacy she needed to compose all that happened today. He felt tempted to see what she wrote but decided against it. She needed a way to process her own emotions without someone else looking through her thoughts.

He took a moment to think back on what happened today. His mind went to the girl. He wondered if she was like her father and was scared to know the answer. She looked so much like her mother that a part of him couldn't resist the pull on his heart. The boy—well, boy no longer. Arick was as tall as Mikael and probably as powerful. He seemed more reserved, like Ava. However, Elijah didn't want to bring him into the mix. Arick looked too much like his father. Elijah feared he would project his hatred of Mikael onto him, so best not to have him around. Atarah was his best option to bring his family together again.

"She cannot replace our daughter, Elijah," Elizabeth said gently. A simple reminder he couldn't change the past.

Of course she knew what he was thinking, he thought with a smile.

"I know, but I can't help but hope for a relationship with her. I know she's not our daughter, but I'm selfish. At least we can have a part of our daughter back in our lives again," he muttered.

Elizabeth got under the covers, and Elijah moved to join her. They lay close to each other, enjoying simply being in each other's presence.

"She won't fill the hole Ava left, but she may give us something else, Elijah. Only time will tell," Elizabeth said before falling asleep.

She was right, of course, he thought, before he too gently fell asleep.

CHAPTER 4

Arick

Arick wasn't happy with his sister. The morning sunrise peeked through his curtains as he prepared for the last day of this accursed summit meeting. His mind raced as he showered, trying to rinse off his irritation and worry over the change that was about to happen.

How could she think it was a good idea to go into a region where everyone would hate her? Of all the idiotic ideas the Heads of Houses could come up with, this was it? Arick shook his head, getting water everywhere in the bathroom. The bathroom was pristine white with green and blue accents. His room was similar, but with more green tones and an amazing view of the rolling hills. *No doubt trying to set a calm mood,* he thought, wondering if anyone else had caught on. Arick got out of the shower and dressed for the final day of the summit.

He'd just finished putting his shirt on, back again in his homeland uniform, when he heard a knock at the door. He went to open the door but his sister had already barged in.

Despite his irritation with her, he couldn't help but smile at the gift she had in her hands. Two cups of hot coffee.

"I thought you'd want some coffee," she said with a smirk.

She handed him a cup and sat on the vanity. Arick took a big gulp of the dark coffee, savoring the rich, bitter taste. Atarah took small sips of hers before setting it down. She was back in her human clothes: an indigo long-sleeved shirt with black leggings and boots. She seemed different today. The only time she didn't go after her coffee was when she was anxious.

Arick had a good idea of what that something was. He furrowed his brow. "You can always back out. It's not too late, Atarah."

Even as he said those words, he realized how unrealistic they were. She sighed, looking so small to him. His chest tightened at how helpless he felt and how helpless she looked.

"I'm going to miss our mornings like this," she said.

Arick rolled his eyes at her dramatics. "This isn't going to be our last morning, Atarah," he said as he took a sip of his drink.

She didn't seem to hear him. "I have so many questions about Mom and what Dad did in the Southern Region. And I won't get a chance to ask them."

Not that Dad would give her a chance to ask them, he thought. Right after the meeting yesterday, Mikael had ordered all of them straight to bed with no discussion. Their father hadn't even rebuked her for her outburst at the meeting last night. Arick was curious too, but if anyone could question their father and live, it was Atarah, who was leaving at the end of the day. He decided to sit down next to her to listen.

"I'm not going to lie. I'm afraid, but not for the reason you think. I'm afraid of messing this opportunity up. Afraid I'll keep getting swept to the side if I don't stand my ground," she said.

"Why do you care? There's no pressure in being swept aside," he replied.

"There's no purpose either."

Arick debated arguing with her but smiled sadly instead. She didn't need another voice to fight with today.

"I really am going to miss you, little cricket."

She grinned back. "Me too. Maybe I'll learn how to heal others while I'm there."

"Maybe you can heal our broken souls while you're at it," he said sarcastically.

They both chuckled as their parents walked in, taking in their relaxed appearance with a grimace.

"Your sister is to be taken away from us today and you find it funny," Father said quietly.

Irritation sparked within him, but he refused to show it to his father. He would never give him that satisfaction.

"Most things are funny when you find the humor in it," he replied with a smirk.

"He did nothing wrong." Atarah tried to defend him as their father's face became thunderous.

"Quiet! Not another word from you today, Arick." Father angrily paced the room. Arick had never seen his father pace before.

"Atarah's leaving doesn't give you the right to treat Arick as such," their mother snapped at Father.

All of them looked at her, a little surprised. She wasn't one to be quick to anger. She would reprimand Father but not usually in that manner. Arick guessed her outburst came from the stress of one of her children being taken away.

"We have much to tell both of you, and now we're running out of time," Mother said.

Why didn't you tell us last night? Arick thought, irritated.

"Did Father kidnap you and force you into marriage?" Atarah asked with the boldness of a younger sibling.

"No. Well, not at first," Mother began. Her hands shook slightly. "I was to be married to someone who became very cruel. At first, I thought I loved him, but after a while, plans changed. Before long, he was someone I didn't know." The shaking extended to her whole body.

Father went to her and took her hands. "We haven't told you or spoken of it because it brings up painful memories for your mother. We wanted to protect both of you from what happened in those days. However, Elijah will no doubt tell you only the story he knows."

A knock at the door interrupted him.

Malachi popped his head in and saw them all standing together. He looked exasperated by what he saw. "Everyone is getting tired of waiting for you. Hurry up with whatever family meeting is going on."

"We'll be out momentarily," Father replied. He continued only when the door was shut. "Please trust us when we say there's another side to the story. One we can't quite tell yet."

"Why not now, before I go to a foreign region?" Atarah insisted.

"Because the knowledge may put our region in danger in more ways than one," Father replied pressingly. His brow furrowed and lips turned downward as he continued to pace around the room. He was genuinely worried.

Mother took hold of Atarah's hand and said to Father, "We must go now."

Father took a deep breath. "All right."

They walked out of the room. Arick also took a deep breath and followed them. They entered the main room they'd been in the day before. Malachi and his daughters were the only ones in the same seats as yesterday.

Gabriel moved his family to where the House of Raphael had been the day before. An effective swap.

"Please take your time sitting down. It's not like we've been waiting for you," Elijah said dryly. No one acknowledged him as they took their seats.

"Now, how about we begin with you, Mikael? What can you contribute?" Malachi asked, his hands folded together in front of him.

"I'll give Joshua Scio, House of Raziel of the Southern Region, thirty thousand of my soldiers in the effort to fight against the demons . . . and my daughter, Atarah Viribus, to the House of Raphael as an emissary," Mikael said.

"Very well. I'll send word to the Houses of Azrael and Raziel vowing that we are a united front. I'll send a couple of troops down south as well for reinforcement," Malachi said finally. His voice was cold.

Arick's apprehension didn't ease in the slightest. Arick didn't trust the Raphael House. While Atarah might not remember much, he remembered every time his mother clutched his hand at the mention of their name. How tightly she held him while trying to hide her tears.

Malachi turned to Gabriel. "What can you contribute?"

"Since my soldiers have been disappearing at an increasing rate, I can only contribute a few thousand soldiers. The House of Gabriel is not built for battle *per se*, but we're useful with communication, transportation, and information."

"We could use every bit of help in the Southwest Region," Malachi said. He looked around until his gaze settled on Elijah. "Your region currently has few holes to deal with. However, the specialization of your people's healing abilities allows for fewer casualties. Are there any major healers you can spare for the other regions?"

"All of my major healers are currently on the front lines. Nonetheless, I can offer a few minor healers to aid the south."

"That's excellent. How many can you give?"

"Six."

"Six thousand isn't as many as I hoped for, but if that's all you can give, we all understand."

"No. I mean, I can only give six healers to help other regions," Elijah said firmly.

An uneasy chuckle left Malachi.

"Are you serious? Only six? That's one healer for each region. That's pathetic," Isabella said from where she sat beside her father, incredulous.

"Do you have any mass-specialized healers?" Elijah asked with mild sarcasm. "Our healers don't come in multitudes like a common angel. They come from special family lines of archs and principalities, taking decades to cultivate their powers."

"How can you expect me to work with six healers, Elijah?" Malachi said irritably.

"You're lucky to have one healer in your midst, because now you'll probably save one or two hundred soldiers," Elijah said angrily.

"What? What do you mean, one or two hundred?" Clarissa asked with interest.

"Each individual healer is trained to heal multiple injuries at a time. Their training includes how to increase that number over the years. A minor healer has cleared the one-hundred injury mark, and a major healer has passed the one-thousand injury mark," Elijah explained.

Everyone seemed surprised, except for Mother and Father.

"How are we just now hearing of this?" Gabriel asked. "I know there are famed healers in your region and have heard legends, but I've never heard of such an amount."

"Because for hundreds of years, our numbers have stayed drastically low. In our hierarchy, only archs or a few principalities have enough power to heal others. I can count on one hand how many major healers we have and maybe two hands how many minor healers we have. They've always been low and therefore not common knowledge," Elijah retorted.

"The legends?" Malachi began, still seeming amazed.

"Raphael angels have the ability to heal faster than others. However, this by no means makes them invincible. If the injury is severe enough, then yes, they can die. However, the major and minor healers are exceptional healers who come once in a blue moon. Which is why they're so valuable," Elijah said.

Arick looked at Atarah and wondered if she would be able to learn from such gifted masters. She appeared to be thinking about the same thing and looked excited at the idea. Arick glanced at his parents and saw worry in their eyes.

"I can send a shipment of healing serum to Arena and Campis Secretum, since I cannot spare any other healers, but that's it. Now that you're done trying to degrade my healers, I say let's get back to the matters at hand," Elijah said.

Malachi coughed. "When can we gather the forces?" he asked everyone. "While Elijah's region has a few holes, he doesn't bear the heaviest of casualties."

"I can have my men in the Southern Region in a week's time. I suggest they camp at the base of the mountain range bordering the other regions so they may travel swiftly to other areas," Mikael said.

"I can send my healers and troops out once I return, and they'll probably reach their respective regions within a few days. However, the forest and mountain ranges are difficult for anyone to travel through, let alone with an army. We should think about having them base along the river that goes through most of the regions," Elijah said.

"The river is in a wide-open space, easy to ambush and, like you said, doesn't cover all of the regions," Malachi stated.

Gabriel paused before responding. "My soldiers will probably get there within a few days as well. However, I agree with the mountain suggestion, especially with Mikael's soldiers who've trained and thrived in mountain environments. Their wings are designed for those rugged winds to carry and navigate them through mountainous passageways."

Elijah and Malachi pondered the idea, then both nodded in agreement.

"That was the easiest agreement we've had this whole summit," Malachi said, smirking.

"What about you, Malachi?" Gabriel asked.

"What about me, Gabriel?"

"Are you going to contribute to any other region's efforts?"

Malachi laughed out loud. Gabriel stiffened.

"Malachi's forces have taken the second biggest hit since the appearance of the large hole in the south," Elijah said softly.

Arick could've sworn he saw a bit of shame in Gabriel's eyes. However, it was gone in a flash, and his face was stone.

"My apologies, Malachi," Gabriel Sr. said stiffly.

Malachi continued to laugh and looked at everyone. "I think we need to get together more often. It's surprising, all the things you can learn in one summit meeting about one another."

Indeed, Arick thought, ashamed he knew so little about the different regions. However, the regions barely interacted. There'd hardly ever been a reason to, except demons moving through the holes in the realms.

Arick tried to think back on his tutoring to see if he remembered much about the other regions. He couldn't think of many times where the other regions interacted, except when necessary. The lessons of the different abilities came to mind, as well as the hierarchical order. Even understanding the mechanics of the spirit realm versus the human realm. Their realm sat on top of the human realm; however, no human would ever know. Humans cannot see spiritual forms but could sense them. Whereas their spiritual forms can influence physical forms but they cannot directly touch the humans. This is why they needed the serum to turn their spiritual forms into physical ones.

Strange still, he thought. *I would have thought more interaction would have occurred between the regions in our realm throughout the years I've been alive.*

Malachi was about to speak further when a messenger burst through a door, with a frantic expression, and panting from running. All attention turned to him.

"Overrun . . . Southwest . . . Region," the messenger managed to get out.

He continued breathing heavily; however, everyone knew what he meant. All of the Archs were on their feet. Elijah paled. Malachi grabbed the messenger by the shoulders and shook him.

"What else, Bart?" Malachi said urgently, his eyes wide. That region was within his border. How had they gotten there so soon?

Bart got his breath back. "They're nearly overrun by demons and need help now! The demons are starting to filter into the realm and the cities."

Mikael and Gabriel were already out the front door before Bart finished his sentence.

Arick was about to follow his father when Mikael grabbed him by the shoulder and whispered to him.

"Arick, go with Atarah and Elijah for now. We'll meet up in the Southern Region. Stay alert."

Fine with me, he thought. *I'll take any reason to not be around him right now.*

He was almost out the door when Atarah and their mother ran after him.

Gabriel was already outside with his family, gathering enough energy to send them all back to the spirit realm. Malachi walked out as well and practically dragged his messenger behind him. Malachi, for once, looked shaken, Arick mused.

Arick made it outside to see Father embracing Atarah and their mother crying nearby. He understood now why she'd run after him. This might be the last time she saw them for a long while. He looked away to give them privacy.

"I guess we'll all be seeing one another very soon," a high-pitched voice called out behind him.

Arick turned to find Clarissa, Isabella, Charlotte, and Noah behind him. Clarissa was the one who'd spoken, not looking too happy at the prospect of all of them spending time together. Isabella, who stared at Arick, blushed when he looked at her and glanced away.

He turned to Charlotte and Noah, ignoring the Uriel sisters out of pure indifference. He studied the Raphael Archs for a moment with mild interest.

"Seems like we'll all get to know one another a little better. I hope, at least." Arick gave a grin that seemed to irritate Noah.

"Why should we bother?" Noah snapped. He shifted the weight between his feet as if he wanted to move away from him. While Noah was not taller than him, he held a lot of confidence.

"We can always stay back and watch the regions get destroyed and realms trampled on," Arick said facetiously. "The demons haven't been a bother to us."

"I wonder why that is." Clarissa looked at him suspiciously.

"Call it Divine favor," Arick purred with sarcasm.

"I think your family has had enough Divine favor," Noah said heatedly. "I think it's time your family is held accountable for the crimes committed."

Before Arick could reply with a sarcastic comment, Elijah coughed loudly behind them all.

"Clarissa and Isabella, I suggest you go with your father this instant before he leaves without you," he said.

Clarissa and Isabella bowed their heads quietly and left, but not before Clarissa shot him a fierce glare and Isabella gave him a shy smile. Arick wanted to roll his eyes at them both but kept his face composed. Bored.

"As for the rest of you, come with me," Elijah commanded, studying Arick cautiously.

Arick felt a familiar bump on his arm. He turned to his sister and asked, "Are you all right?"

"I will be," was the only reply Arick received. Her eyes were downcast, and her hands shook by her side. She was putting on a brave face for everyone.

Before them, Gabriel Sr. opened the portal between their realms. A large blazing oval opening hovered before them. The Gabriel house was the only house that could travel more freely between realms. This portal would have cost a lot of energy for their father to create, yet Gabriel was able to do it within minutes while looking perfectly fine.

"It's time, everyone," Gabriel Sr. called out. "This

portal will send you just outside of your regional border. Each family goes one at a time."

Malachi and his group were the first to go through. The opening engulfed them easily as they ventured back. The serum should wear off within the hour or so, Arick judged by the mild pulling in his back. *Finally,* he thought. He couldn't wait to stretch out his wings and his back. He hated feeling so confined.

Their parents and court were next. They both turned to look lovingly at Atarah. His mother looked briefly at him; only fear shone in her eyes.

Goodbye to you too. Hope you travel safe, Arick thought bitterly. The Michael court vanished through the portal with no words of goodbye.

"I'm grateful you're coming with me, if only for a little bit," Atarah said, walking toward the portal. Along with the Raphael Clan, they were the last ones to go through. Elijah and his family walked through the portal without looking to see if they followed.

This is going to be great, Arick thought.

Atarah started after the House of Raphael quickly, leaving Arick to follow. Thinking back on the heir's comment on his family's crime, Arick was happy to be going along as well.

He followed them, determined to keep an eye on the House of Raphael.

Chapter 5

Atarah

Leaving her parents was not as hard as Atarah anticipated. However, she truly was grateful to not face this strange family alone. While she knew right away that she liked Elijah, she wasn't sure about the rest of the family. Except for Elizabeth. Atarah felt uneasy whenever their eyes met. The blank look in those hazel eyes chilled her.

She shook her head slightly and followed them through the portal. Venturing through a portal was never difficult, more so disorienting. One minute she stood on earth, surrounded by grass and ocean, the next engulfed in bright, hot light and a rushing sound of wind. Like learning how to fly for the first time, it was awkward. It never lasted long, like waking up from a dream. Suddenly, they arrived.

Wow, Atarah thought as she took in the scenery.

Upon a coastline surrounded by large trees stood a small town. Atarah was stunned by the beauty of it all. The sunrise came gloriously slow, as if calling everyone's attention, announcing that it had arrived. In awe, she felt weightless. Breathing was easy and hard at the same time. Despite the silence, she heard the fluttering drum of her own heart.

She felt at peace.

Atarah stretched out her hands as if she could catch the sunlight itself and preserve it somehow. She noticed the serum wore off as her wings came forward. She didn't even mind the sharp pain. Her ivory wings vibrated to life, as if having a will of their own, reaching for the sun. She took in a breath, and the air descended into her body. When she breathed out, she was in the air.

Her wings took command of the winds as they lifted her high. She was weightless, she was strong, and she was the wind. The sun, as if sensing her joy, joined her and lit a path before her. She took in the small mountains and the dense surrounding forest. The forest seemed to stretch on forever. The mountains weren't like the mountains in her father's region; they were smaller but seemed to welcome the autumn forest that surrounded them. She took in as much as her eyes would allow, breathing in the trees and gliding under the sun's guidance.

The town close by was something out of a fairytale. The roads were made of cobblestones of all different colors. The buildings along the road—Atarah wasn't sure if she should even call them buildings—were part of the trees, interwoven as if to enhance rather than weigh down the tree. The trees were some of the biggest she'd ever seen, with thick trunks and large branches spreading wide. All were of a different color. Some had bright red leaves, others orange or yellow, and some green.

The buildings consisted of the interwoven branches, along with the variety of leaves used as shelter. The architecture was unlike anything Atarah had seen. When she thought of homes in trees, she didn't imagine how sophisticated everything would look. The leaves seemed to sparkle and reflected the sun to give light to the houses.

Atarah's wings vibrated with excitement. She could only imagine nighttime with all of the lanterns lit, illuminating the houses further. The cool breeze of the ocean, along with the heat of the sun, made the climate comfortable. She wanted to explore every part of this region.

"Atarah!" a voice yelled.

She glanced back down at the shore to see Arick looking at her disapprovingly. She reluctantly landed. Not everyone had their wings back yet.

"Get a good look at Silva?" Elijah seemed amused by her reaction.

"A little," Atarah replied, her gaze still toward the small town.

"Would you like a tour sometime?" a soft, timid voice said.

She turned to find Charlotte. Her long, dark brown hair was up in a neat bun with a few curls framing her petite face nicely. She was still in her Raphael attire. A fitted, long green dress with a thin amber scarf. The tree insignia was on her top right shoulder.

Her posture was one of hesitance, as if unsure of how they were going to react to her. Atarah's heart softened toward Charlotte.

"No, than—" Arick started.

"Yes!" Atarah fired back.

Charlotte tried to hide a small smile as she looked between them. She opened her mouth to speak when a grimace marred her face. Soon, her wings shimmied from behind her. Atarah gaped at her. Charlotte's wings were like her own. Ivory, soft, and feathery. Grunts and groans began in a chorus as wings sprouted amongst Elijah and his court. Out of the corner of her eye, Elijah ordered a servant to get horses for them. As the servant flew away, Atarah studied Elijah's wings.

His wings were by far the largest out of the Raphael angels. She knew she took after her mother in her wings, but never realized it was the Raphael wings she had inherited. She glanced at Arick to see his wings emerge. His wings were large, larger than Elijah's, and leathery. With black talons at each joint, his wings were definitely Michael wings. Made for battle and destruction.

"I'm glad to see you enjoying the scenery. Did your mother never talk about Silva?" Elijah said, drawing her attention. His wings relaxed. He directed his question toward her, not Arick.

"Sometimes," Atarah hesitated, unsure of how much to share. Elijah had been kind thus far. She decided to open up a little. "She starts to tear up any time we've asked about her upbringing."

Elijah kept his gaze forward. His short, curly, dark hair fell before his face, creating a sad shadow. His wings slumped at her words.

"I was afraid of that." Elijah sighed. "Ava was always the type to silently endure. She never wants to cause anyone else pain, so she bottles up her own." His eyes were downcast.

Atarah's heart pulled, as if she sensed his hurt.

"Whenever she did speak . . . about her childhood," Atarah continued, "she only had great things to say."

Elijah looked at her with a faint smile on his face. His eyes were so much like her mother's, it eased the last of Atarah's apprehension. "The responsibility of being a Head Arch of the Raphael clan is a great honor but—" He paused. "I always struggled and tried to give my family the best I could offer."

Atarah felt more understanding of Elijah. He reminded her of her own father.

"Horses will be on their way soon. Once they're here, we'll all travel to Ventus, the capital," Elijah explained. He addressed her and Arick now. "There will be a lot to learn from one another."

Noah scoffed from behind Elijah. His wings were slightly flared in agitation.

"What? You have a hard time learning new things now, Noah?" Arick goaded him. He finds it amusing to get under someone else's skin, she thought.

Noah's eyes flashed and his wings flared completely.

"Now, now!" Elijah scolded, opening his arms to keep distance between Arick and Noah. He looked to say something further when another shout cut him off.

"Horses! We have the horses!" one of the servants called out.

Charlotte and Atarah blew a sigh of relief. Arick smirked.

"Until next time then, Arick." Noah sneered.

Elijah narrowed his eyes. "There will be no next time. I want everyone to learn how to get along. All of you," he chided them. "There's a lot to be done and I don't want to have to break up any fights, understand?"

There was silence between them all.

"I said, do you understand?" Elijah said firmly.

"Yes," Noah said reluctantly.

Arick gave a salute. "Sir, yes sir."

With one last glare between them, Elijah left to talk with the angels of his court. Noah glared at Arick before taking his leave as well.

"I think we'll be best friends with him," Arick said sardonically. His eyes twinkled with mischief.

"Ignore him," Charlotte said, shuffling on her feet. "Change is hard for Noah sometimes."

Arick moved to claim a horse.

As Atarah was about to walk on her own, Charlotte said, "Despite whatever you hear about our family, I'm glad you're here."

Atarah stood stunned for a moment. She'd never thought of them that way exactly. They were related, but Atarah was just now processing that they were family. She wasn't sure how the others felt about this. She wasn't sure how she felt about this.

Charlotte turned on her heel and walked toward her mother hurriedly. Atarah went to her brother who now held the reins of two horses. Both wore dark green reins with the Raphael insignia on the saddle. The one Arick had was light brown all around, but the one he handed to her was white with large brown spots. They were both mares.

"What do you think?" Arick whispered as he petted his horse's neck. No one was close by enough to hear, but plenty were around.

"I don't know yet," she replied honestly. She patted her own horse, trying to gather her thoughts.

"Do you think they're being genuine?"

"I think Charlotte and Elijah are. However, I don't trust Noah or Elizabeth, and they don't trust us."

"Should we trust them?"

"I think we should give them a chance. They love our mother dearly and are our family."

Arick looked at her, his face impassive. Then he sighed.

"What do you think about them?" she asked.

Arick ran his hand over his head before mounting his horse. He answered her seriously. "I think we should be careful. This is an old wound that's never fully healed between them. I think there's a chance that the wound festered all of this time. I also don't like us being caught in the middle of everything."

Atarah nodded, again grateful Arick was there with her. She mounted her horse.

"How long will you stay here?" Atarah asked, surveying the others.

Arick shrugged. "The plan so far is I move out with Elijah's forces and head south. Meet our father there and go berserk on some demons until further notice." Arick glanced at Elijah, who was helping Elizabeth up onto her horse. "Depending on how fast he gathers his troops, I won't be here for too long." He looked at Atarah. "You have a plan in place?"

Atarah pursed her lips. "A rough one," she answered reluctantly.

Arick snorted. "The money our father spent on tutoring you went to waste if you can't solidify a plan." Arick chuckled. "Taught everything about the vast realms and its inhabitants, yet you're still indecisive."

"I'm not indecisive!" she whispered indignantly. "I know what I want. I'm figuring out the how, and I don't plan on anything getting in my way."

Arick looked at her with a raised eyebrow. "All right, little cricket. Just be safe."

Atarah wanted to roll her eyes. "You sound like Father and everyone else back at home. Doubting me."

"Unlike Father, it's how you will get things done that worries me, not that I don't believe you'll get it done."

A shout from Elijah told them it was time to move on.

"Nothing is bleaker to me than a woman who doesn't know her own strength." With that, Arick spurred his horse forward.

At a loss for words, Atarah tucked her wings and pushed forward.

They began down a large pine pathway covered in shade by the tree village within the canopy. The path turned into cobblestone as they went through the village.

Silva was vibrant, warm, and dulcet in its atmosphere, whereas back at home it was harsh, cold, and stark.

Atarah nearly gasped as a bright red squirrel scurried along the tree canopy above them. The birds sang morning songs as they traveled. The birds were different in this region: smaller and more colorful than the birds back in Belli Causa. She couldn't help but compare the different regions.

Charlotte giggled at her reaction and indulged her in some knowledge about their region—how the design of their houses had taken almost a century to perfect, how they maintained the health of the trees and the land. Apparently, the trees grew autumn leaves year-round due to the special properties of the soil. She listened as they rode on. The trees encased them more as they traveled deeper into the forest. Branches reached out in every direction, as if trying to grab them.

"We feed off the trees' nutrients and use them for shelter. It's imperative to keep them in strong health in order for our society to manage," Charlotte explained.

"What about in a drought? How does everyone manage?" Atarah asked, unable to get enough of this beautiful region.

"Over the centuries, the trees have grown so big and strong. The roots reach far down into the underground water reserve, so droughts aren't a severe problem. We don't normally have to endure droughts anyway."

"There are so many trees," Atarah said in awe.

Charlotte laughed. "You should see some of the trees in the other regions. While these have red, orange, yellow, and green leaves, others bloom flowers. The colors range from pink to blue to violet. Even the Head Trees can get exotic."

"Head Trees? Oh right, I forgot almost every region has one," Atarah commented.

Elijah had slowed his horse down to join them.

"Do you not have a Head Tree in Belli Causa?" Charlotte asked, surprised.

Atarah shook her head.

Head Trees were large, ancient spiritual pinnacles that provided a barrier around each city within a region. Every city had a tree, but the largest was known as the Head Tree, which normally resided in the capital. The Head Tree had the most spiritual power and connected to other Head Trees in different regions through vast root systems. Or so the ancient scripts said. Archs used to have the ability to join their spiritual forms with the Head Trees, but it had been many years since the last Arch was able to connect.

"Why can the Archs no longer connect to the Head Trees?" Atarah asked Elijah.

He sighed and rubbed a hand over his hair. "No one knows for certain. But every Head Arch has tried to no avail."

"Will we see the Head Tree in Silva?" Atarah inquired. Her wings hummed in excitement. Elijah grinned at her. "Definitely," he replied.

Ahead of them, Noah scoffed. "It'll be hard to miss."

"I hope both you and Arick"—Elijah gave a backward glance at Arick riding behind them—"feel at home here in Silva."

A shout from the front drew Elijah's attention. Elizabeth was studying them. He gave a sheepish grin before moving up toward his wife. Atarah let her attention wander to her surroundings.

She had a hard time not feeling at home in this place. As she looked on, trying to capture every detail, she noticed even the markets were up in the trees. Woven baskets kept the fruits and vegetables from plummeting to the ground, and a variety of clothes and jewelry hung from the branches as well.

She turned to Arick to point out the market. But when she looked at him, she thought better of it. Arick's face was a mask of dislike and wariness; even his wings were tense and flared. She wondered why he was uncomfortable when this region seemed to be so peaceful.

Never mind him, she thought.

She wasn't going to allow Arick to ruin her fun with his mood. They continued through the forest at a comfortable pace for several hours. Soon enough, the houses became sparse and eventually disappeared from sight. The deeper into the forest they traveled, the more Atarah heard the animals and birds. They only stopped once for a few snacks before mounting again. They traveled for hours with few breaks. During one of the breaks, Charlotte extended some water to Atarah. Another offering of friendship.

"What is all of Silva like? What is Ventus like?" Atarah asked Charlotte.

Charlotte mused for a moment, while she munched on her apple. Her face appeared flush from exertion. She was lighter in complexion compared to the rest of them.

"I wouldn't know much about the rest of Silva, but Ventus is amazing! The trees and architecture are truly something to behold."

"Have you not explored outside of Ventus?" Atarah asked. She had finished with her snack and mounted her horse again.

Charlotte blushed and her wings slumped. "After Ava . . . I was rarely allowed to venture outside much, but I can tell you more about Ventus. I can even give you a tour if you like. I know the library, the best parks, and shops to visit. Also, the best textiles are in Ventus!" she exclaimed excitedly.

Atarah nodded and grinned at Charlotte. She was much easier to get along with than her brother Noah, who ignored them most of the ride or flat out glared. Arick, to his credit, always grinned back at him and waved, which seemed to annoy Noah even further. Soon, they were mounted and on their way again.

Eventually, they entered a clearing, and Atarah gasped. A large waterfall greeted them on their right as they came across the large field, with stunning orange flowers blooming in it. Elijah trotted toward the waterfall and dismounted along the edge. Noah, Elizabeth, and Charlotte followed Elijah. Atarah and Arick approached more skeptically. Elijah continued along the water's edge until he seemed to pass through the waterfall with his mount behind him. Soon, Noah and Elizabeth followed him through the falls. Charlotte indicated with her hand for Atarah and Arick to follow before disappearing through the waterfall herself.

Atarah and Arick gave each other a pointed look before dismounting.

"Do you think it's a trap?" Arick asked.

"Pretty elaborate to fake a waterfall if it is," Atarah replied.

She went ahead of Arick. She slowly walked along the water's edge, careful not to touch it. Her mount followed her, unfazed at traveling through a waterfall. As she rounded the edge of the fall, she felt a little gust of cool air and then she was on the other side.

What she thought she'd see was a dark, wet cave of some sort. However, this wasn't the case. She entered what seemed like more woods. The cobblestoned path ended as they reached the field. What laid before her now seemed like a city in the trees. Rivers flowed along the trees and bridges woven from branches connected them. There seemed to be no beginning or ending to this place. Lanterns were placed everywhere, luminating the entire city with a soft, firelight glow.

Atarah felt a small bump on her shoulder, which told her Arick made it through the waterfall safely. He stared up at the city before them and seemed to be in dismay. His wings slumped in displeasure.

A sound caught Atarah's attention. She turned to see Charlotte waving to her. Her family handed their horses off to a caretaker in what seemed more like a stone castle than stables. Atarah and Arick brought their steeds over to the caretaker before following Elijah into the city.

"Welcome to Ventus, the capital of my region," Elijah said. His wings expanded to their full length, then he took off with a gust of air so strong the wind almost knocked Atarah to the ground.

Elizabeth, Noah, and Charlotte expanded their wings and took to the sky.

Atarah's wings hummed.

"Come on. Let's show them how the House of Michael can really fly," Arick said, for the first time acting enthusiastic about their circumstances. Even he couldn't resist the excitement of flying.

Atarah took to the sky first, stretching her wings as far as she could, enjoying their length like the first stretch out of bed. She soared, knowing Arick would be close behind her in no time. She tried to focus on Elijah and his family before she lost herself in the feeling of flying again.

She maneuvered her wings to follow them. A shadow overcame her, but she wasn't afraid. She knew Arick was flying above her, causing the shadow.

Showoff, she thought with a smile. Anything to flaunt the expansion and power of his wings. Atarah rolled her eyes. While she couldn't look at her brother, she knew he was happy to finally stretch his wings.

Atarah tried to stay focused on Elijah's wings to not lose sight of him. However, she couldn't stop her gaze from wandering around the vast city before her. The sight was as stunning as the one she'd seen from the boat that morning. Houses were interwoven with one another and within the trees. Markets flourished all around them, selling a variety of items from clothing to food to weapons. The sun was setting, so many of the businesses were lighting more lanterns, causing an almost magical effect with the colors of the trees and the dim golden light of the small flame. Atarah was so enraptured with what was going on around her, she almost lost sight of Elijah. She raced forward to catch up with the others.

They came upon a mammoth tree. A mansion had been built in the center of it. The mansion's exterior was elaborately carved with vines and flowers. Large pillars colored in green and russet red on the front. Tall, branch-like towers spread out, giving the mansion width and height that almost matched the tree's size. Lanterns lined the branches, which had intricate sculptures. Some were of small leaves, others were of angels flying off into the sky, or of ancient scrolls. This must be the Head Tree Elijah told her about.

They each landed gently and tucked in their wings. Atarah landed, then noticed the absence of rushing wind usually accompanied by her brother's wing flaps. She looked around her. Her brother was not there. She looked behind and above her, sure he had been right behind her.

"Has anyone seen Arick?" Atarah called out. She looked to Elijah, but ended up locking eyes with Noah.

"Don't look at me," Noah scoffed. "I could care less what happens to that overgrown bat."

Atarah's wings flared in frustration at his apathy. Elijah came over as her worry for her brother grew.

"What's going on, Atarah?" Elijah asked.

"Arick is missing, and he was right behind me as we entered the city."

A laugh escaped Noah's lips, drawing their attention.

"Do you know something about Arick's disappearance, son?" Elijah spoke slowly.

Another chuckle left Noah. "Ha! The Intercity guards must have swarmed him once he came into the city. I gave them orders to attack anything that wasn't a Raphael angel."

"Why would you order such a thing?!" Atarah asked, outraged. She could tolerate his snide comments and glares, but she wouldn't stand by while he hurt her brother.

Noah rolled his eyes. "I gave the orders because we've had demons wandering just outside of the city barrier, attacking our citizens. Of course I'm going to give out those orders! I didn't expect to come back with a muscled pterodactyl."

Elijah stepped in between Noah and Atarah as she clenched her fists.

"That's enough, son." Elijah sighed. He pinched the bridge of his nose in frustration. "Charlotte, come here, please."

She walked toward them hesitantly. Noah glanced at his father and sister in confusion. Genuine concern showed in Charlotte's eyes, and her presence made both of them relax their wings.

"Charlotte, you and Atarah are going to retrace the path we just flew from the front gate and search for Arick. If neither of you can find him, both of you are to come back here safe and sound."

"And if we don't find him?" Charlotte asked wearily.

"We'll call for a search party."

Atarah spread her wings and soared to the sky, scanning the surrounding trees from where they'd come.

Charlotte looked sheepishly at her father and nodded, then flew up to join Atarah and quickly caught up to her, pointing at some of the trees. "We came from over those structures."

Atarah moved through the trees Charlotte indicated, scanning everywhere she could. She forced herself to scan the area slowly to ensure she caught any suspicious behavior. Her anxiety grew with each passing minute. What could have happened to Arick? Was he hurt? Was it an ambush? So many thoughts went through her mind she almost missed an important detail.

She started back at the front gate and looked around. A broken branch hung off to the side. The oddness of a broken branch, off the side of the city caught her attention. Atarah's power flowed through her body as she prepared herself.

She silently prayed that she had inherited large amounts of spiritual power from her family or else she would be doomed. Atarah would have missed it if she hadn't had her powers. She flew over to the broken branch and landed gently on the branch beside it. She closed her eyes to see if she could sense Arick nearby. She waited and waited for a sign. She extended her reach and waited for any kind of pulse or indication of a living being. A rustle of leaves and ragged breathing, beyond the city.

There.

Atarah opened her eyes. She locked onto the sound's location and took off from the branch. She vaguely heard Charlotte calling her name but ignored her. She maneuvered through the trees with the wind on her side, giving her speed. She was almost there. Just a little farther.

A vicious twist in her back sent Atarah careening toward the ground. The ground was unmercifully hard as she landed, leaves flying all over her.

Ouch! Pain radiated up her arm. *Ugh, can nothing go right today?*

Her whole body protested as she got to her feet. She was pretty sure her wrist was broken, but that seemed to be the most serious injury. She looked around for what had hit her and saw Charlotte frantically flying toward her.

She landed nearby and looked at Atarah with concern

and guilt. "I'm so sorry, Atarah. I didn't know how else to stop you," she panted sorrowfully, trying to regain her breath.

"What do you mean?" Atarah groaned, trying to keep her frustration at bay.

"I tried calling your name over and over, but you didn't hear me. Then you kept going, so I thought I would cause a muscle spasm to blow you off course. I never wanted you to get hurt!"

"Why were you trying to stop me?" Atarah asked, irritated.

"You weren't flying to Arick—"

"And how do you know that?" she interrupted.

"That's not a creature you want to be near. I can tell by its physique. Healers have the ability to sense how a living body is feeling. This body isn't one of an angel."

Atarah was about to ask for more information after learning that Charlotte was a healer, but heard a deep rumble. They froze, and didn't dare to breathe. Atarah slowly put a finger to her lips. The wind suddenly felt stagnant and stale.

Atarah took in her surroundings for the first time. There were no birds or small animals scurrying about. The trees seemed to be weighed down with something, and the branches hung low. There was an oppressive force in this area, she realized, one that was now heading toward them.

Atarah couldn't see anything, but she sensed when the creature was by them. Charlotte stayed frozen with terror, beads of sweat threatening to cascade down her face in her effort to stay still. Atarah followed her example as the creature slithered through the area. The creature seemed to be looking for something—possibly the ruckus Atarah had caused.

She hoped Arick wasn't around, for this creature promised a slow and painful death. They waited, taking shallow breaths for seconds that turned into minutes, as the creature roamed. After a long while, the creature passed.

Atarah finally let out a breath—and instantly regretted it.

A vicious roar told her the demon had turned back and zeroed in on her. She stood still, confused that she could sense the demon but not see it. She waited until she knew where the creature was before striking, but she was too slow. Something pierced her arm in a matter of seconds. She screamed at the pain and felt the creature trying to inject something in her as searing heat entered her arm—venom.

Quickly, she concentrated her power into her other arm and punched the demon as hard as she could. The force of her hit knocked the creature back, enough for her to scrabble to her feet. She readied her powers to strike. This time, she would be fast enough. She relied more on her other senses, since sight was doing her little good. She paid more attention to the creature's breathing patterns and the sensations on the ground.

The creature didn't give up easily. It wasted no time before attacking again, this time going for her wings. She crouched low and dodged left, keeping her wings tucked back tight. Unfortunately, the creature was quick to adjust. She saw the change in its direction based off the rustling leaves on the ground. It ducked low and latched onto her right leg.

Atarah screamed from the pain, so strong she could hardly think. Nonetheless, she gave a strong kick to knock the demon off her again. She got back into her fight position and moved to strike. She knew she needed to finish this demon off fast. The venom would affect her soon.

She heard Charlotte grunt in effort and saw her hands stretched out. Atarah felt lighter as the wound in her arm began to heal. Charlotte looked fatigued and obviously not used to combat.

The creature doubled back and went after Charlotte.

"No!" Atarah screamed and used as much strength as she could gather and outwardly pushed it out of her body as a condensed pressure. Slamming it into the creature, bringing it to the ground.

It screamed in pain, but she didn't dare let up. She continued to add force onto the creature, determined to crush it. The earth splintered under the weight she pressed onto the creature, but it wasn't enough, for the creature still lived, injured and in pain, but fighting to get free. Atarah struggled to maintain the amount of power she exerted onto the creature, but it waned. It felt uncomfortable to expand her strength outside of her, stretched thin. Which was why she seldom used this power. Now more than ever she regretted not training more on force exertion.

She tried to think of another plan of attack, for her hold wouldn't keep the creature at bay for long. As it started to wriggle free, lightning struck, sending Atarah and Charlotte careening backward. Her wings flared out instinctively to catch her.

She looked up to see what caused the explosion. A strikingly handsome angel stood where the creature had once been. His hands swirled with electricity and power, explaining the explosion. Arick stood next to him, looking irked.

Atarah sighed in relief. Her brother was safe, though he seemed to be injured by the way one of his wings hung off the side, as it unlatched at one of the joints. She glanced at Charlotte, who was also alive and uninjured. She limped to her brother and the stranger to assess the damage. Arick turned to her, and she used her abilities to analyze his injuries. In times like these, Atarah was grateful to have inherited the small amount of her mother's healing abilities.

Or I guess the House of Raphael's powers, Atarah thought grimly.

Healing was her weakest power. She could only heal small cuts and bruises, one at a time. Pathetic compared to a true Raphael angel. She changed her eyesight to see if there were any broken bones or inner hemorrhaging.

A few broken ribs and a tendon tear in his wings seemed to be the worst of Arick's injuries. She lifted a hand to heal him. Arick smacked it away.

His face was unreadable, and his wings flared defensively. "Heal yourself first before you start on me."

Atarah narrowed her eyes at him, irritated. "Care to explain what happened to you?"

"As long as you explain what you're doing out here in the woods challenging a drude demon."

Drude demons were demons that preferred to roam at night and fed upon people's fear. They infiltrated people's dreams through their venom and fed off of their nightmares. Their forms showed better in complete darkness; however, it was usually in a form people feared the most. Given that it had been dusk when they'd stumbled upon it, Atarah hadn't been able to see it fully and was certain the demon wasn't too happy at the early wake up.

"Do you have any idea how dangerous they are?" Arick continued irritably.

"Well, we do now," Atarah replied sardonically. Her pride stung. She didn't defeat the demon by herself.

"There was no need for you to be so reckless," Arick insisted.

"We didn't know there was a drude demon out and about. We were looking for you."

Atarah crossed her arms. A sharp pain shot down her right arm at the movement. She looked down to see three nasty gashes on her upper arm, oozing black and red. Some venom was still in her body. If she didn't get it out soon, the venom would continue to spread through her bloodstream until it reached her brain. If left in the body too long, the venom could cause hallucinations.

"Arick's right. Your wounds need to be healed," a deep voice said. The voice came from the angel who flew in with Arick.

Atarah looked up to regard the mystery angel. This time, she saw a round, attractive face with the muscular build of someone who trained regularly. His light brown eyes, tan skin, and dark hair gave him an almost intense demeanor. His large, light brown wings seemed relaxed and friendly.

The small grin he gave Atarah made her heart flutter strangely in her chest. She put a hand on her chest, confused as to what was going on.

"Sorry to meet you under such circumstances, but it's a pleasure to meet you, nonetheless. My name is Benjamin Doctrina." His voice was smooth, but his eyes were intense and he gave a small bow.

"I—" Atarah was at a loss for words until Arick nudged her. Then she shook out of her daze as recognition registered. "Doctrina? As in the heir of Selaphiel Archangel Clan?" she asked, amazed.

The Selaphiel clan resided in the desert region of Arena. They were a reserved civilization that prided itself on prestige and prominence. The angels with the most powerful bloodlines were known to read minds.

He gave a small chuckle before nodding. While she was baffled and left gaping at him, Arick's wings tensed as he looked around the woods.

"Come on, let's get somewhere safe and tend to those wounds."

"Wait. Let me help, Atarah," Charlotte pleaded.

Atarah remembered where they were and her injuries when Charlotte came into view. Charlotte was able to stand and didn't appear to have any significant injuries that prevented her from moving. The large lacerations on her arms were closing quickly.

Atarah relaxed her wings as the pain eased. Charlotte walked over, keeping her eyes down, and began to heal Atarah's wounds.

"If I warned you earlier, we could've avoided the drude," Charlotte said mournfully.

"It's not your fault, Charlotte. I charged ahead without taking the correct precaution. You tried your best to stop me," Atarah replied, as shame came over her. She couldn't even hold her own against a single demon. How pathetic she felt wearing the Michael insignia.

"But I only added to your injuries. I wasn't any help at all."

"Do you know how to fight?" Atarah asked.

Charlotte shook her head. "Females don't have to learn how to fight in Silva."

Atarah didn't say anything further, but grunted in pain as Charlotte moved on to her leg. She was lucky her leg hadn't been torn off entirely. Desperate for anything to distract her, she asked Arick once again what had happened to him and why Benjamin was with him.

"I was following you when several angels crashed into me. They wore green uniforms and had their faces hooded. I was able to get them off me with no problem until they called in reinforcements. Then that's when this guy helped me." Arick indicated Benjamin. "We were able to shake them and take off, but we got lost a little bit in the city because I wasn't sure where we were heading in the first place," Arick said. "It wasn't until I heard Atarah screaming that I flew as fast as I could and found both of you."

Atarah punched him in the side and smirked. "Took you long enough."

Arick chuckled. "I got here as fast as I could with a torn wing."

"I'm surprised you could fly at all with a torn tendon in your wing," Benjamin said in amazement.

"They train us for that," Arick replied nonchalantly. "They train all Michael angels to fight, even under immense pain." He seemed to embrace the pain, while Atarah always tried to ignore it by distracting herself.

"Both of you have trained to fight," Benjamin said more as a statement than a question.

Atarah nodded.

"Both of you fight amazingly!" Charlotte said enthusiastically.

Atarah laughed. "Trust me, I'm nowhere near as great of a fighter as Arick or my father." She was practically pathetic compared to them. Part of her nickname that Arick gave her came from her tiny punches during their combat training. No one in training ever felt her punches.

"She never gives herself as much credit as she deserves," Arick stated. "She's in denial of her own strength." He rolled his eyes.

Atarah was about to contest Arick's statement when Charlotte chimed in.

"No, trust me, Atarah, you were amazing. You had much more endurance than I did. Could you teach me how you keep up your strength during battle?" she implored.

Atarah was surprised. No one ever asked her for training advice, and she'd never considered herself the best for battle advice. But their powers were similar, so maybe she could help Charlotte.

"All right. I'll try to help as much as I can," Atarah replied.

Charlotte hugged her excitedly.

"I hate to break up the little party we're having here, but I think it'd be best if we head back now. These woods will fill up with more demons soon," Benjamin said.

It was almost pitch black, especially without the lights from the city. Benjamin had a point. Atarah gingerly moved her arm and her leg, testing them, and they moved practically painlessly.

"Thank you, Charlotte," she said.

She turned and saw Charlotte trying to heal Arick's wing injury. He waved her off, tending to his other injuries.

"I'll be all right with the others."

"Why not heal them now while I can?" Charlotte inquired.

"Don't bother, Charlotte," Atarah said. "In our region, men value their injuries like badges of honor, and they see healing the wounds as coddling."

"We only heal what needs to be healed in order to move again," Arick added. He stretched out his wings, testing them. Satisfied, he thanked Charlotte.

"All right, let's go," Atarah said, then stretched her wings and took off.

"Oh, Benjamin. Thank you for helping my brother," she said oddly, feeling bashful.

Benjamin looked at her, his wings seeming to hum. He gave her that mischievous grin again.

"Please, call me Ben." He lifted into the sky.

Arick followed suit as well as Charlotte. Charlotte led the way back to the city, while Arick positioned himself above and slightly behind Atarah, not showing off this time, instead probably trying to make sure no one attacked her from above.

This wasn't what Atarah imagined her first day in the city would be like. Battered and on the defense wasn't how she wanted to mend the rift between both regions and families. She flew out of the woods and back into the city with them. The guards stopped them soon after they left the woods and attempted to apprehend Arick, whose wings instantly flared in anger.

Fortunately, Charlotte and Benjamin stepped in and explained he was there as a diplomat and a guest of the Archangel House family. The police didn't seem too pleased. Atarah was certain if Charlotte hadn't been there with them, diplomat or not, they would have attacked them simply for being foreign. However, she wondered if Arick had told Benjamin he was a diplomat.

They continued their trek toward the mansion without any more interruptions. Atarah's anxiety only worsened with each passing minute.

CHAPTER 6

Arick

Arick wasn't just mildly annoyed anymore with this family; he seethed with resentment. Were it not for Charlotte, he would've already beaten them all into the ground, especially Noah.

The little runt, Arick thought bitterly. Outwardly, he appeared unbothered.

They finally came into view of what appeared to be a giant mansion on the side of a huge tree trunk. Arick was briefly impressed by the red-and-green design of the mansion before masking his amazement. He didn't want to appear easily impressed.

His sister, Ben, and Charlotte landed with ease before he did.

"I'm afraid this is where I have to leave you," Benjamin said.

"Wait! Why is an heir from Selaphiel even here?" Atarah said right as Ben lifted off.

Arick was also curious about Ben. What was his role in all of this?

Ben simply bowed. "All will be explained in time. Just know that I'm a friend." He smirked. "And we have to get together for dinner sometime soon."

Atarah seemed frustrated by his response. Ben winked at her and flew off into the sky. Arick didn't completely trust him but preferred his company compared to others. The angel had helped him escape the guards and navigate through the massive city.

He quickly surveyed the scene before following Charlotte into the mansion. Once inside, Arick was indeed impressed. Not because of the vast wealth the house seemed to have, but because of its ordinary appearance. The interior was designed more for an everyday family than royalty. While the foyer was open, there was a dark, wooden coat closet that held a variety of jackets and shoes. The foyer led to an open living room with warm, rustic colors, comfortable furniture, and a large fireplace. The interior design of the house was exactly how he would have imagined a house in the middle of the woods. A cottage. He wanted to shudder at the timber-wood beams. As if Arick hadn't had enough of these trees.

He longed for the mountains, where he didn't feel so closed in for wing space and the rugged terrain invited rougher winds to fly with. He couldn't place his finger on it, but Arick felt almost claustrophobic being in the forest.

He looked at Atarah to ensure she was close by and safe. He frowned at her awestruck expression. Arick didn't like that she seemed so at ease in this environment. She practically welcomed the change. How could she not sense the walls closing in around them? He felt so cramped. The dark wood was almost choking him. He missed the openness and massiveness of the mountains. His wings wanted to stretch out but couldn't.

As they continued through the tour, he paid attention to every exit. After the living room, they went into the modest kitchen that seemed to mix the theme of a small cottage or farmhouse. It wasn't anywhere as contemporary as their house back in the mountains.

They ventured up a decorative spiral staircase that led to the next level of the house. The floor seemed to be more circular than a square structure, as most houses with various hallways and doors. Charlotte showed them a workout studio behind one door, an art studio behind another, while another room seemed to be a classroom. She explained how this floor was used mostly for their studies and each room had a theme based on the lesson they had. One room was composed of maps of places around the human and angel realms. Others were for combat. Charlotte told them that they used the room to train to control their powers.

Most angels, even Archangels, took years to master their given powers. There were a few prodigies who mastered their powers within their youth. His late uncle, who died an untimely death, had been a prodigy. However, rumor had it that there were two prodigies amongst the Archs currently. One in Raphael and one in Selaphiel house. He glanced at Charlotte while she showed Atarah the library.

According to legend, each house had been granted a power from the Trinity when Archangels were first created. The House of Michael had been given the power of battle, so most of their powers stemmed from that root blessing alone. The House of Uriel had been given the power to control various elements. The House of Raphael had been given the power of healing. Each house had a unique power. The original intent had been for all the houses to come together with the powers. However, this hadn't happened. Arick had always thought this to be an old legend to coerce the Archs to get along with each other. None of it was real.

He briefly wondered about their parents' marriage and

how it had only further divided the houses. He wondered what the whole story was behind their marriage and how it happened. He didn't trust Elijah or Noah yet to believe a word they said about it. However, now was the best opportunity to dig around.

Charlotte led them up one more level to show them their rooms. Arick didn't particularly care how fancy or nice his room was. He didn't want to remain here long. He barely listened to her as she told them about the house and their rooms. Only when she spoke up about dinner did he tune in.

"What was that?" Arick asked.

"Dinner will be soon. It's not normally so late. But what are you to do when a drude attacks?" Charlotte asked rhetorically, tactfully not mentioning they'd been searching for Arick.

"I'm so hungry," Atarah said. "We haven't eaten a meal since yesterday."

He had been starving this entire time, but refused to mention it. He kept his face aloof.

"Are we all supposed to eat together like a big family?" Arick asked, full of sarcasm.

Charlotte's face faltered a bit, but she continued walking. He felt a little tickle on his side. Atarah had elbowed him again. He patted her head to irritate her. Sure enough, her wings flared.

"We'll at least give them a chance. This could bring the family together," Atarah whispered firmly and swatted his hand away.

Arick resisted the urge to roll his eyes. Family by blood hardly meant much to him. Just because they were blood didn't give them an instant spot as family members. Nonetheless, he simply nodded.

Atarah turned back to Charlotte. "Where will the dinner be held, and what time?"

"Probably in half an hour. Just make your way back down to the kitchen and you'll see everyone."

"Thank you very much, Charlotte," Atarah said.

"No problem at all" Charlotte walked down a white, clean hallway. The walls seemed to be made out of all different types of crystals, while the floor was made out of simple white marble. The doors that led into their rooms were a light brown wood. Their rooms were once again directly across from each other.

Atarah entered the door on the right.

Well, I guess I'll take the room on the left then, Arick thought.

Charlotte followed her into the room, and Arick's distrust rose. He entered and looked around, making sure to focus on whatever Charlotte was doing. Just because she wasn't an enemy didn't mean Charlotte had earned his trust yet.

The room, sure enough, was splendid. It incorporated a large white bed with light green décor. The room had a whimsical, woodland theme. Arick wanted to roll his eyes again but resisted.

"It's beautiful here." Atarah looked around.

Charlotte smiled shyly. "I can show you the gardens around the Head Tree after dinner. But now I have to wash and change before we eat. I'll see both of you at dinner."

Once Charlotte left the room, Arick's wings dropped. He turned to leave. "I'm going to clean up as well."

"Arick?"

He paused. "Yes?"

"Are you really all right?" Atarah sounded concerned.

Arick's heart flickered. His irritation and distrust of the Raphael Head family fell away, and he patted Atarah's head again, but this time with affection. "Yes. The police caught me off guard. Learn from my mistake and don't let your guard down, little cricket."

He ventured into his room. Once the door closed, he

allowed the anger to return, and his wings flared. His mind turned as he wondered what their parents hadn't told them that could have caused such animosity. He thought of a plan to approach the topic at dinner. If there was anything he truly hated, it was secrets.

Arick quickly went into the bathroom to shower as he thought over the layout of the house and the city. It was more intricate than his home. Arick finished dressing when he heard a knock at the door. He quickly suppressed any emotion that might show before he opened the door. His hidden anger dissipated as his little sister came in. She wore a simple black shirt and jeans. Arick smiled; he donned jeans and a plain gray T-shirt. Neither of them felt the need to dress up for their newfound family members, it seemed.

"I'm ready whenever you are," Atarah said, lounged on his bed and looked out the window, deep in thought.

"Let's go. Don't let your guard down."

Atarah took a deep breath before they left his room. As they traveled down to the first level, Arick took notice of the house's small details. He made notes of which doors they hadn't been through yet.

They made it to the dining room and were the only ones not seated. The table wasn't as large as the one at the summit meeting, but it wasn't small either. The round table comfortably sat eight.

Arick and Atarah briefly nodded hello to everyone before taking their seats. They all wore green tunics with burnt orange scarves with the tree sigil on the upper right shoulder. Elijah regarded Atarah first, then Arick, before signaling for the food to be brought out. The silence in the room gave away to the tension. Inwardly, he probably wouldn't relax for the rest of his stay here. Outwardly, he kept his face impassive and bored. As if he could care less.

"Sorry for my lateness."

Arick froze at the new voice. Ben entered behind them and sat down beside him and Noah just as the food was placed down. Atarah's wings twitched in surprise at the new addition. Ben grinned at her.

"Told you we would grab dinner sometime soon," Ben said smoothly.

"Why are you here?" Atarah asked, the surprise fading. "I mean, what's your role in all of this?"

Elijah coughed to catch everyone's attention.

"Everyone eat first, then we'll get into it," he said tiredly.

Arick debated about arguing, but wanted his dinner more. There was a variety of food made up of mostly vegetables, nuts, fruits, and a couple of fish dishes.

They look like they're mostly salad people, Arick thought as he surveyed the food display. The salads held a variety of colors from the different foods mixed together. Arick had forgotten how colorful berries could be. They passed items around in a family style dinner. It was in stark contrast compared to the food he was used to. There was more meat on the table back at home. Fish, chicken, or lamb with a small mix of hearty vegetables that could withstand a colder climate like potatoes, squash, carrots, or brussels sprouts. Rarely any fruit or leafy greens, like the spread before them.

For a while, they ate in an uncomfortable silence. Arick didn't see the need for small talk in this situation. Food was the main priority, so he could keep up his strength. Arick adjusted to the atmosphere when Elijah turned to him.

"I truly am sorry to hear of the attack. I assure you; no one anticipated our police would attack you upon entry."

Seems someone has a conscience, Arick thought. Out of the corner of his eye, he saw Noah suppressing a smirk.

Well, not everyone.

Arick smiled back. "No harm, no foul, I suppose.

However, I'd love to help with their training. I saw much room for improvement."

Noah's wings flared slightly.

Elijah gave him a stern look. "I think that's a good idea."

"What?" Noah said, surprised, looking at his father.

"You heard exactly what I said, Noah. Training is exactly what we all need. Charlotte, you too shall take part in the training Arick has so generously offered."

Charlotte regarded Arick nervously, then nodded.

"Might as well come along too, Atarah," Arick said, not wanting to leave her alone.

"Done. Given my new role, I need to learn as much as I can about this city and its soldiers." Atarah replied. Her wings twitched every now and then, the only clue to her discomfort.

Charlotte nodded enthusiastically.

"Glad that's settled," Elijah said.

"Why must Charlotte participate in this training?" Elizabeth inquired.

Arick glanced at Elizabeth. Her face was expressionless, but more importantly her wings were flared. Her dark brown, soft curls bounced around her face as she turned her head to direct a question to Elijah. He wondered further about her and noticed she'd been quiet since Arick and Atarah had arrived. Arick could see glimpses of his mother in Elizabeth's face, but her face held a coldness that his mother never had. She had the same thick, curly hair their mother had, but her eyes were greener than their mother's. Arick turned his attention back to the conversation.

"Charlotte needs more combat training, especially since she and Atarah were all by themselves when they faced off with a drude demon. Demons plague our land by more numbers each day. We've neglected her training for far too long," Elijah finished firmly.

Arick stole a glance at Ben. It appeared Elijah had a little informant on his side. Did he work for Elijah? If so, why? Out of all of the regions to work with, why Silva?

"Charlotte's fine in combat. You said it yourself—they defeated the demon," Elizabeth continued.

"No, they didn't. Ben defeated the demon. The girls merely fended it off," Elijah retorted. Atarah flinched at the last part.

"Charlotte can take lessons from Noah if she needs to fine-tune her combat." Elizabeth was not going to relent on this issue, it seemed.

"Why wouldn't we use Arick's expertise, especially since he specializes in combat?" Elijah replied.

Arick could tell he didn't mean that as a compliment, but was simply stating a fact.

He was mildly irritated that Elijah hadn't included Atarah. Arick peeked at her. Atarah's face was blank, almost bored. Arick was proud she kept her face impassive, but wished she would speak up more on her own ability and power.

"Why would we allow someone from the House of Michael to see the inner workings of our forces?" Elizabeth shot back.

Elijah's eyes narrowed at his wife. He clearly didn't like where the conversation was going. "Because the point of them being here is to establish trust and peace. How else should I treat them, Elizabeth? Do you have any suggestions?"

"Have them sleep outside," Noah said under his breath.

"We never did get to live a sheltered life behind a Head Tree. Maybe we should," Arick replied, looking at Noah.

"Beats still living in Mommy and Daddy's place I'm sure. Right, Noah?"

Noah looked infuriated.

"How does the Head Tree work actually?" Atarah inquired of Elijah. "Everyone seemed very alarmed when hearing the breach of the Southwest Region. Does that have to do with the Head Tree there?"

"Yes it does," Elijah replied, sounding exasperated. "The Head Tree in Aquam Caput was breached."

"How is that possible?" Atarah said. "We were taught that breaking the Head Tree barrier was impossible because of how much energy they produce."

"See, the Head Trees in each region are like a connected water system. Always flowing water. A constant flux of energy that every region uses as a shield for their people against attacks." He looked at Ben briefly. "Now, imagine that water flow becomes weaker and weaker as each year goes by."

Atarah and Arick shared a glance before looking back at Elijah.

"How are we just now hearing of this?" Atarah asked.

"We haven't exactly been on speaking terms lately," Noah said dryly.

"The spiritual energy within the Head Trees has been gradually getting weaker for nearly twenty years. None of the Archs have been able to connect to a tree to see what's wrong," Elijah explained.

"That's why the summit was called," Arick said, realizing the full picture. Nearly every region was losing their only defense.

"Demons like the drude we encountered are only going to grow in number and in power. The rumor is that the demons have a high-ranking demon on their side," Ben said. "While our shields are intact, every region has been bringing in their citizens from the countryside to the capital and making preparations for battle. Meanwhile, more powerful demons are traveling through the portal in the south."

"Which is why right after this meal we have to go straight to work. Ben, Noah, you will join me after dinner to enforce the city entrance," Elijah said, looking at everyone. "And in the morning, Noah and Arick head out with half of our forces to Mortem." He looked to Atarah. "Charlotte will travel to Chrysi Poli to help with healing, and Atarah, I'll need you to accompany her, since Charlotte's combat training isn't up to par quite yet. Ben will lead straight to the city."

Charlotte grimaced and tried to hide herself behind her own hair.

"Let this be your first test as an emissary." Elijah finished. He looked at Ben and Noah before nodding.

All of them got up and headed toward the door.

"Excuse us for now. All of you will gather here in the morning before the sun rises. We have much work to do preparing for the reinforcements. We'll need to send them out at first light to help the Southwest Region," Elijah said, then walked out.

"When will both of you be back?" Charlotte asked.

They ignored her as they walked out of the room, and her wings slumped.

"Don't be discouraged. While they're off doing whatever, at least we'll be in the library with a warm blanket, some tea, and good books around us," Atarah said to Charlotte.

Charlotte and Arick couldn't help but chuckle at that idea. Elizabeth had quietly left the room during their banter. Arick had to keep resisting the urge to roll his eyes.

Well, at least she didn't have any more lasting remarks, Arick thought.

Now that she was gone, Arick's best bet for answers was probably from Charlotte.

"Charlotte, what happened between our families?" he inquired.

Charlotte froze at the question, and her wings flared in defense. Interesting. "Are you always so forward?"

"I just prefer to get to the point."

Charlotte shifted in her seat, uncomfortable. Her hands shook. "We're not really supposed to talk about what happened with Ava. There's so much that happened."

She seemed so young now. Arick had to remember this was his aunt, instead of a close-in-age cousin. "What's the age difference between you and Mother?"

"Fourteen years. I was five when everything happened."

She was only six then when I was born, Arick thought. *Very young.*

"You spoke of something happening earlier. Did our mother do something?" Atarah asked.

"No! Not at all. If anything, she's the one who should be most angry."

This took Atarah and Arick by surprise. *Angry? Angry about what?* Their mother always seemed relaxed and happy around them, including Father. Granted, Arick always wondered how she could be married to such a horrible man, but Father always treated Mother with adoration.

"Angry because of what exactly?" Atarah asked as a door slammed shut behind them.

They all turned as Elizabeth entered the room again with so much fury her wings flared to full expansion.

"Charlotte, go to your room now," Elizabeth said quietly, her wings vibrating.

Charlotte paled at her mother's demeanor and quickly scurried out of the room.

Atarah stood up to follow her, but then fell to the ground. Withering in pain. A mere half a second was all

Arick had before a sharp pain spread all across his body, dropping him to his knees. He felt as if his own blood was coiling and attacking him, twisting his insides, trying to tear them apart. His stomach curled, threatening to upheave everything he had just eaten. Arick struggled against the stabbing pain across his body. It was a blood attack. An ability only a Raphael angel had. Instead of healing cells in the body, the angel disintegrated them. Destroying them on a cellular level.

He threw a chair at Elizabeth to stop the attack. From the surprised cry and thump he heard, Elizabeth had been pushed back. He lifted his head to look at Atarah. She waved her hand to signal she was fine before getting up.

"Using a blood attack is hardly imaginative, Elizabeth," Arick rasped as he regained his footing.

Elizabeth regained her posture, her wings still flared. "You had no right to corner Charlotte like that," she hissed.

"What do you mean? All we did was ask her a question," Atarah answered, back on her feet.

"You shouldn't be questioning her is what I mean! If it weren't for you and that boy"—she pointed at Arick—"we could've gotten our lives back on track."

"What's that supposed to mean?" Atarah's patience seemed to be wearing thin quickly.

Elizabeth scoffed at her. "Ask your loving father," she sneered. She turned to leave. "Don't try to corner Charlotte or anyone else in the family again, or else I'll leave both of you out in the forest." The door slammed as she left.

Atarah's wings relaxed. "Don't throw that, Arick."

Arick froze. Of course Atarah noticed. He'd been about to throw another chair at Elizabeth. This time with enough strength to bust down the door.

"We don't need any more fighting than what has happened so far."

"Why not? Keeps it fun around here," Arick said lightly, while he imagined curling his hands into fists. He wanted to unleash his power. His wings vibrated with fury.

"You've been in almost three fights today. One actual battle on our first day here!"

"Nothing we can't handle."

Atarah sighed and slumped in the chair she'd been in earlier. "How are we to help them when they don't want us here in the first place?"

"Didn't you say we have to earn their trust?" Arick said, sitting down as well. He reached for his drink, wishing for something, anything, other than water.

Atarah rubbed her face with her hand. "I'm trying to find a way to earn their trust, but I don't know how."

Arick wished he cared as much as Atarah sometimes. There were few people he genuinely cared about, and the House of Raphael definitely didn't make the cut. He couldn't have cared less if the whole forest was ravaged by demons at times.

However, he did need answers.

Atarah tried to stop pacing around her room, but failed miserably. After the disastrous dinner, they went to their rooms and changed their clothes to rest for the night. However, she couldn't stop the burning desire to know the truth. What was the reason behind Elizabeth's anger? Atarah quickly changed out of her jeans and into her black trousers and a form fitting, indigo tunic that bore her family insignia on the back. The insignia was a simple one of the rugged mountains that she called home.

While Noah and Elijah had gone off to fight the demons, this gave Atarah enough time to explore. She walked over to Arick's room and knocked gently. He was there instantly, wearing his tunic as well. He must've been thinking the same as her.

"Want to explore a little bit?" Atarah grinned mischievously.

Arick grinned back and opened the door further. His weapons were out, and he'd already started to pack his favorite daggers in various spots around his body.

"Hell yes."

Atarah turned and started down the hallway, excited with anticipation. Arick quietly followed her. They ventured down to the floor below and came upon the main floor. Arick went ahead of Atarah to scope out the area. While her brother scanned the kitchen, Atarah went through a door on the far-right side of the kitchen. If the door on the left led to the dining room, then Atarah wondered where this door led. She reached to open it. Heat consumed her hand, burning it. She jerked away. She'd barely touched it, and the door handle had almost scorched her hand. She was going to have to find a way to open this door.

Atarah saw Arick out of the corner of her eye and turned to him. He silently held up his hand and showed it was burned as well.

"Seems the doorknobs have a spell on them. Someone doesn't want us to go exploring," Arick whispered.

Atarah nodded, already knowing who that person might be. However, there was one door she knew would open for them. She walked through the house with Arick behind her, until she reached the door she wanted. Arick looked at the door then at her, as if inquiring if she was sure. She nodded.

They stood before the front door, about to venture out into the vast wooded city before them. She knew no one would stop them from walking out the front door. She reached for the handle and sure enough, the door opened easily. She was about to step out, but Arick took hold of her shoulder.

"Remember, cricket, stay on guard. This door will most likely lock once we leave."

Atarah nodded, then expanded her wings and took off in flight. There were few lanterns shining in the night, making visibility difficult. The large city trees swayed gently as a breeze blew by. The light from the moon and stars glittered on the forest floor through the leaves. Ventus was stunning at night.

Arick flew above her. They circled the massive Head Tree to spy any entrances. Thankful for little rays of light, Atarah felt her way along the tree to find any crevices, while Arick scanned the area, on the lookout for police or demons. If demons were infiltrating the outskirts of the city, how were they not already within the city? Wouldn't they be aiming for the tree at the heart of the city? Elijah said no Archs had been able to connect to a tree in twenty years, but that didn't stop her from wanting to try. Michael angels did not grow up with a Head Tree, so maybe she would have some luck.

Atarah thought about the positioning of the tree at the center of the city and got an idea. Atarah placed both hands on the tree and extended her powers into it. Back at home, she could use her powers with trees or even the mountains to sense other spiritual beings. Surely, this tree would be no different.

She thought wrong. Atarah felt like she was pushing against tar to get any sort of feeling.

She backed away from the tree, panting heavily. Arick looked back to check on her. Atarah gave him a thumbs-up to indicate she was fine, but she barely managed to keep herself in the sky as her exhaustion spread to her wings. Expanding her senses had never been difficult for her, even with the mountains. This reminded her of the water analogy Elijah had used earlier. A huge flow of energy pushed against her like a river, preventing her from looking within.

Atarah signaled to her brother. Not taking his eyes off of the surrounding, sleeping city, he came closer to her.

"Let's go to the border of the city," Atarah whispered.

"Did you find anything?"

"There's still a strong enough flow of energy around the tree that I can't get through."

"Let's try something else then."

"What do you mean?" Atarah inquired.

"Follow me."

Arick flew down to the ground. Atarah followed quietly to make sure no one had spotted them. Where were the guards? Surely, there would be guards around the ancient tree. They landed gently on the ground, each scanning the area.

"Try against the roots," Arick said, still on the lookout.

"The roots?"

"Yes."

"I don't think this will work."

"Give it a try. Now you can focus on just the tree without having to make sure you don't fall from the sky."

Arick had a point.

Atarah faced the tree once more and placed her hands on it. This time, she focused solely on one point of the tree and extended all her powers onto the point. She pushed with all of her strength into the tree, trying to break through. She felt like she was fighting against a whole current to get through. A small amount of her spirit got through some of the tree, but not enough. Her wings dropped weakly.

No, I'm not stopping now.

She pushed even harder. Though it still felt like moving through tar, nonetheless she was moving deeper. Her senses and her spirit were slowly getting through the tree.

She could hear and feel the crackling of the tree bark as she worked hard to get through. She dropped to her knees, shaking.

Not yet. I'm almost through, she thought, taking deep breaths. She gave another push—and got through. However, what she experienced wasn't expected. She had no physical body as such, more so just her spiritual essence. Atarah felt shocked as she realized that she didn't just expand her sense or her powers—her very spirit left her body and was now within the tree itself. It was like when one's consciousness slipped into a dream, except it was her soul going into the depth of an ancient spirit. This was beyond her powers. She had connected with the tree's spirit. She quickly looked up to get her bearings as a way to utilize the adrenaline pumping through her now. She had no idea what to do anymore, never having done this before. No angel had connected with a tree for many years now, but she did!

She was part of an intricate system of currents all flowing from the ancient tree. She felt all the roots and how they connected with every tree within the city and beyond. Atarah sensed the barrier surrounding the city, and more importantly, she felt a pulse pushing her so forcefully she was almost pushed out of the tree. The barrier was being attacked.

Atarah didn't fight the current pushing her out. She pulled out of the tree and her body collapsed to the ground, completely exhausted. Arick was by her side instantly, lifting her up. Atarah struggled to stand but managed somehow.

"What happened? What'd you sense?" Arick fired off questions furiously.

Atarah took a minute to catch her breath. "I . . . didn't see . . . everyone in the house," She finally caught her breath. "I saw what was within the tree itself."

Arick looked at her again. "You connected with the Head Tree? How? I thought—"

"The tree's barrier is under heavy attack and is weakening," she interrupted.

"Where's the barrier being attacked?" he inquired.

"The location of where we fought the drude demon earlier today."

"Let's go check it out." Arick flew into the sky.

"Wait!" Atarah hissed in a whisper. "We need to awaken the others and get help."

"I think we'll be fine. Two Archangel Michael warriors, especially with your abilities. We'll be fine. Besides, we're on the other side of the barrier." Arick's wings vibrated with excitement.

"What happened to the person who told me not to be reckless?" Atarah retorted.

"That was before when you didn't know how to spiritually connect with the tree." Arick waved his hand nonchalantly. "Even though I don't fully understand it, I have an idea we could try."

Atarah couldn't believe his confidence and shook her head. He was never hesitant when it came to battle. She rolled her eyes at him.

Arick chuckled at her. "Come on, little cricket. Let's check the area out, and if it's bad, we'll wake the others for help."

Atarah took a deep breath. "All right, we'll go check it out." She expanded her wings and lifted off the ground to join Arick in the sky.

"We'll have to follow the moonlight to find the same area."

"All right. Let's go."

Arick took off toward the city to get to the edge of the border. Atarah followed suit, keeping an eye on their surroundings. Arick slowed down, so the noise of his wings wouldn't be heard. With his large size, ducking around branches made flying quite difficult for him. They weaved around the trees and homes quietly and strained their eyes, on the lookout for the familiar branches.

Atarah knew they were headed in the right direction, as the air changed. The air felt more and more oppressive as they flew closer. She worried the barrier had been breached by the surroundings. Atarah noticed this time around the area didn't have as many houses or as much activity.

They probably relocated the people in the area, she thought grimly.

They reached the broken branch she had spotted earlier; except this time, she sensed the force itself pressing in along the branches at the border that protected the city.

Arick's wings were fully extended, and he was ready for a fight. Atarah scanned the branches, yet didn't see a single demon. She crept closer but couldn't see anything—physically, at least. Nonetheless, Atarah knew better than to go any farther than where she was now. She felt the demons staring at her like prey, even though she couldn't see them. She slowly backed away and looked at Arick.

Arick was looking thoughtfully at the hidden barrier. He glided forward, staring out into the vast, dark woods. Then before she could blink, Arick pulled out his dagger and threw it into the night.

Atarah waited, anticipating the dagger to strike something. She was surprised to hear the dagger drop to the ground with a quiet thud. A moment of silence—and then the dagger flew back toward them straight from the ground to Arick, except with more force than what he'd originally thrown it with.

He caught it easily enough and put it back in the sheath at his side. "Just as I thought."

"What is it?" Atarah asked, intrigued by Arick's little experiment.

"We can't attack them from this point. However, they can attack us," he explained.

"The barrier only prevents the demons from coming through here. That doesn't mean they can't launch attacks," Atarah concluded.

"That's probably why the branches are broken around this area."

"But not everywhere within the city?" she asked.

"I think the city is actually surrounded by demons. At night when they're strongest, the demons concentrate on one area to try and break through. Not a bad strategy, and it's actually working. The barrier's weaker here than anywhere else."

"But when we were out there earlier, there weren't many demons around," Atarah pointed out.

"They were probably waking up at the time we were leaving. So, I'd say we got very lucky."

"Do you want to use your other sight to see them, through whatever spell they're using?"

"No, there's no need to know when we can sense them from here. We'll have to figure out what spell they're using, so we can directly attack them next time."

Atarah nodded, wondering if the barrier would hold for tonight.

"Atarah?"

"Yes?"

"Try to extend your powers toward the barrier, like before with the tree."

So, that was Arick's idea. It seemed Atarah was not the only one worried. She nodded and placed her hands in front of her. She focused on the barrier and nearly got swept away again like at the old tree. Atarah stood her ground, miraculously, in the barrier and her power stretched out around her. The pain of feeling stretched out nearly caused her to throw up all of her dinner. She had to withstand it if the city was to sleep tonight. She tried to detach her stretched-out form and attach it to the barrier itself. Atarah had to try three times before succeeding.

By the time she pulled away from the barrier, she realized two things. The demons were roaring and growling in anger at them from the other side. Ghost-like limbs reached for them in anger as they were pushed back even farther. Lastly, Atarah was no longer holding herself up.

Arick was holding her in the sky to keep her from falling to the ground.

I'm going to have to work on flying and using my powers at the same time, it seems, Atarah thought weakly.

He had one of his arms right under her armpits, below her collarbone. Causing the rest of her body to simply dangle, limp.

"You did good, little cricket."

Atarah could barely hear him over the roars of the demons. She groaned in response and Arick chuckled. She could barely do a single job and it took this much out of her? No wonder her father had wanted to coddle her. She needed to get much stronger if she was ever going to prove that coming here wasn't a mistake.

"All right. Let's get back to the main tree."

Atarah thought she would pass out as Arick started to fly back to the main tree when she saw lanterns coming their way. She became more alert and tried to fly on her own, but Arick wouldn't let her.

"Calm down. They probably heard the roars and thought they were under attack. We'll just talk with them."

Atarah scoffed. "How do you think that'll go?"

"Hopefully well, because right now I can't fight with them and keep you safe at the same time. You're still too weak to fly, let alone take them on."

Atarah snorted, but didn't argue with him.

They flew closer, and Atarah saw Elijah and Ben first and was almost relieved. Almost—until Noah flew into view looking furious, along with about a dozen guards.

Well, dang, I wonder how this will go, Atarah thought sardonically.

"I knew it!" Noah hissed. "They're spies. Arrest them!"

"Wait!" Elijah called, but he was too late. Two guards had already flung themselves toward Arick.

Fools.

Arick swung his wings around them. When the guards got close, he flung them out, swatting them like flies. Elijah and Noah looked a little surprised at the ease with which he dismantled their guards.

"We're not spies," Arick called out calmly. She could tell he was trying hard for his wings not to vibrate with anger.

Elijah finally reached them, close enough to look at Atarah in her limp state. "What happened? Why are you both out here?"

"We went out for a night flight and came across a barrier—a barrier weakened from attacks by demons."

"Lies! Lies, all of it!" Noah cried, flying by Elijah's side. "Why are you really out here?"

Atarah regarded him. He was looking for an opening to attack Arick as he questioned them.

"We were tired of all the secrecy in this family, so we went out to escape it for a moment," Arick replied nonchalantly.

"Is Atarah hurt? Why are you carrying her?" Elijah interjected. He waved his hand back to call off the guards that were slowly creeping around Arick. Atarah was surprised once more by the sincerity in Elijah's tone. Like earlier when they arrived in Silva, he had been gentle and understanding. Now he sounded genuinely concerned, two incidents where he appeared to care for her.

"When we came across the barrier, demons were attacking it, trying to weaken it. Atarah used her powers to strengthen the barrier, so the city could sleep another night," Arick explained. A hint of pride came into his voice as he said her name. As if he was bragging about her accomplishment.

Atarah wanted to sigh at that. Why should she be proud? Using her powers like she did weakened her so much that she couldn't even fly on her own! Her pride stung at her dependency.

Furthermore, Atarah was surprised at him telling most of the truth so far—minus the snooping around the main tree, of course, but now wasn't the time to divulge that bit of information.

Noah regarded them suspiciously.

Arick shrugged at him. "If you don't believe us, you can always go back to where we came from and see the border yourself."

Noah gave Arick one last look of animosity before nodding to a few guards, indicating they should check out the border. Three guards took off onto the path they'd just flown from to inspect.

Atarah turned back to the situation at hand and tried to hover on her own once again.

"Atarah, are you sure you're strong enough to fly?" Arick asked, this time allowing room for her wings to expand.

"I should be all right," she replied, a slight shake in her voice. She was relieved she was able to fly by herself without plummeting to the ground.

"I thought you'd be happy we were outside of the house, Noah," she said sarcastically.

Noah rolled his eyes at her. "I won't be happy until both of you are out of this region."

"You won't be happy very often," Atarah replied.

Before she could blink, Noah lunged for her. He couldn't even touch her, Arick was there—and so was Benjamin.

Arick was right in front of her to block any attack and Benjamin was behind Noah, holding him back.

Seems a bit awkward with the wings in the way, Atarah thought at the sight.

"You can't attack her simply because she stated the obvious, Noah," Ben grunted, trying to keep Noah in place.

"Shut it!" he replied. "You can't even read other angel's minds. So, why should I listen to you?" He tried to shake Ben off instead of going after Atarah.

"Let him go, Benjamin," Elijah said calmly. He flew in between them and looked at Noah.

Noah's wings relaxed at his father's gaze, and he stopped struggling. Atarah was able to get a better look at Benjamin when he let go. They'd just seen each other hours ago, but he seemed to have changed attire. His wings looked darker and flared in the lantern light. Atarah could see his uniform fine. His outfit was similar to the guards', but the colors weren't from this region. While Noah and his guards wore green in their uniforms with their insignia being a large tree outlined in amber coloring, Benjamin wore white and gold with a different insignia, the gold outlined what looked to be large sand dunes along the upper arm. He caught Atarah gazing at him and his wings relaxed from their battle position as he gave her a small grin.

"It appears the border has been strengthened," one of the guards said in awe.

Noah turned back to them, giving them a suspicious look, while Elijah and everyone else looked shocked at Atarah.

"You were able to strengthen the border all by yourself?" Elijah asked her in surprise.

"Yes," she replied.

"How?" Elijah said with wonder.

"I don't know," Atarah said hesitantly.

All of their faces looked at her in wonder and a few in awe. They were looking at her in a way she had never been looked at before.

"No one, not even the Head Archs have been able to make a spiritual connection to a Head Tree in many years!" Elijah said fervently. "So, I ask again, how were you able to strengthen the barrier?" He stared at her.

Atarah pursed her lips, deciding to trust Elijah with the full truth. Her wings relaxed. "I pushed some of my power into the barrier. Exuding some of my strength into it. At first, there was a lot of resistance, but I was able to make a connection."

Genuine surprise came onto everyone's face at Atarah's explanation, except for Arick.

"Do you know how the other regions are doing?" Noah demanded, but was no longer trying to accuse them.

"I felt the other Head Trees and the roots all connecting together. While they're far away from one another, the barriers are all still connected. Though it was a distant feeling, I still felt the tearing of some of the roots. As if they're on the verge of breaking," she explained.

Elijah nodded. "All the barriers were created at once and interconnected. Each barrier protected each region for each Arch family. When one falls, it's safe to assume others will as well. Starting tomorrow, all civilians will be relocated to the capital in every region. To ensure they are safest around the Head Tree."

"Please, both of you go back to the estate. You're both going to have a long day tomorrow, so will you, Noah. You've taken on too much tonight," Elijah implored. "I'll think more about this tonight and let everyone know in the morning."

The exhaustion on Elijah's face was evident. Atarah nudged Arick to indicate they should follow his plea tonight. Arick nodded and turned in the direction of the estate. Atarah went to follow her brother, until Ben caught her eye.

"What's your role going to be?" she inquired again. She was getting very irritated by his elusiveness.

Ben turned to look at her as Noah and the guards all started back to their base, wherever that was. "I'll be everywhere a little bit, I suppose. Stay out of trouble, Atarah." He grinned at her, then flew off with Elijah.

Atarah studied the insignia on his upper arm for a moment and turned to catch up with Arick. She pondered what an angel from another region, another clan, was doing in the Silva Region. Moreover, she wondered why she hadn't seen him at the summit meeting.

Chapter 7

Noah

Noah woke in his bed, not remembering going to bed the night before. He sat up dreading what the day entailed. He got up to peer out his window.

Probably a few hours before the sunrise, he thought groggily. *Might as well get ready.*

He fixed up his room and dressed for his training. He donned his gray workout shorts and a loose-fitting white shirt. He stretched his wings briefly before heading out.

The training grounds weren't far from his family's house. It was easier to assemble troops at the big tree because it was hard to miss. Noah always wanted the troops to see his home as their home, should they need anything. He entered the training building, the second biggest structure in the city, other than his home. As he ventured toward the main room, he heard movement inside one of the rooms. Noah stopped outside the door. His wings flared defensively as he leaned forward to listen.

A loud bang, right by his ear, rocked him onto his backside. A laugh from the other side of the door boiled his blood. Noah got up and jerked the door open to find Arick on his knees laughing, his wings relaxed. Arick wore black athletic shorts with a fitted long-sleeved shirt. His horned wings had metal attached to the edges, making them look deadlier. Even in his jovial demeanor, Arick's strength and power intimidated him. Arick's golden eyes settled on Noah once more, still twinkling with laughter.

Noah clenched his fists and gritted his teeth, wanting to hit him in his smug face. "What in the hell are you doing here?"

Arick tried to speak, but Noah couldn't understand him between the chuckles. "What? Speak up!" He yelled.

Arick finished laughing and rose to his feet, still holding his side. "I said, I always train for hours before dawn. If that's not something all your troops do, that needs to change immediately."

Despite his irritation and reluctance, Noah needed help with training new troops. His damn curiosity was piqued. "Does every citizen in Belli Causa train like you?"

"Yes, training starts when a child first walks. Not that anyone minds. Strength is all that matters in our region."

"What does each soldier do for training?" Noah crossed the floor of the training room to regard the tools Arick had grabbed.

"It depends on the soldier's age and the amount of aggression they have. Because of our design, we can pack on more muscle than the average angel. Our goal is to always increase endurance in our power."

Noah picked up a weight Arick had grabbed. He grunted and put the weight down. "So, you start with weight training."

"Well, really, these weights are my warm-up. Then,

I start with heavier weight training, then target practice with various weapons, specialized weapon training, and of course hand-to-hand combat."

Noah nodded, wondering how these troops would fare in Arick's training.

"Nervous for your troops?" Arick inquired.

Noah's temper and wings flared. Something about this angel got right under his skin. *You have to make this work*, he told himself.

"What's it to you?" he sneered. *Very mature*, he berated himself.

"You should be nervous for them."

"You don't know yet."

"Noah, my region doesn't have a Head Tree barrier. Never has, and demons still avoid it when they come to our realm."

It took a moment for those words to sink in, and Noah's wings and heart slumped with the realization. They were powerful. The Michael Clan never needed a Head Tree.

"That's right, Noah. You need to be nervous for these troops." Arick moved around Noah to go back to his weights.

Noah thought he'd seen Arick's power in combat, but now he realized Arick was barely trying. Yet there was a whole army of angels like him, sitting on their asses, Noah thought cynically.

"When do our new punching bags come in?" Arick asked, going back to his "warm-up."

"What?" Noah asked, pulled from his thoughts.

"I mean, our new recruits."

"In two more hours, probably." Noah looked around the room to start a warm-up of his own. He reached for some weights, determined, and took a seat across from Arick.

"That may be too much for a warm-up," Arick said with a raised eyebrow.

"You don't know what I can do," Noah snapped.

Arick held up his hands in peace. "All right."

Noah did a variety of exercises with the heavy weights he had chosen and regretted it. *Come on. Push through.*

"What does your normal training routine look like?"

"Normally drills. Mainly flight-maneuvering drills," Noah grunted.

"Why are your men not out here when you are?"

"I tend to get up early and come here." Noah would normally be irritated at the questions if it weren't for his weights drawing his attention. He was getting winded.

"The men in our region are on the training floor before the general, usually. By the time he gets on the floor, the men are already warmed up and ready for training," Arick said, not even breaking a sweat.

"You suggesting to sleep-deprive my men?" Noah panted.

He immediately knew what he'd said was stupid. Sleep-deprive his men? This was war, not naptime. Noah waited for a snarky response.

"What do you think is best for your men?" Arick asked, his wings relaxed. He seemed to have no ill intentions.

Noah put down his weights and looked at Arick sitting opposite him with more weights. His wings relaxed for the first time since coming into the training room. "I think we need to prepare them for reality and train them to the point where they're strong enough to face it," Noah answered honestly.

Arick nodded and handed Noah a lighter set of weights.

"I can do more than this for a warm-up," Noah countered. His pride stung.

"I have no doubt you can, but these aren't for the exercises you think you'll be doing. Don't worry, they'll feel like a ton in a minute."

Arick got up with a small set of weights as well and proceeded to do various sets of strange exercises.

Noah looked at his weight. "What exactly are you doing?"

"Try this and tell me what you think," Arick replied, still not breaking a sweat.

Noah copied Arick's form and did the same exercise. For a few seconds, he thought it was silly doing this exercise and then immediately felt what the exercise was targeting. A slow burn quickly spread throughout his shoulders and back. How was this possible? The weights were incredibly light. His arms trembled in the second set, as well as his back. Noah completed the third set and dropped his weights on the ground.

"I've been doing that exercise almost all of my life, and I still feel the burn," Arick said, done with his own sets.

"I felt it though," Noah said, surprised with himself. He was intrigued. Even now, his back and his wings stood a little taller. "How'd you know about that exercise?"

"Your clan may know a lot about the body and healing, but we study the body to learn how to strengthen it, as well as how to destroy it."

Noah nodded and couldn't help but be slightly impressed. Arick noticed and gave a sly grin. Noah scowled at him.

"Kiss my ass, you smug bat."

Arick laughed. "I'm going to wake up the new recruits. It's time for training."

Atarah walked downstairs to venture outside once more. She'd heard Arick get up and leave for the day. She hadn't been able to go back to sleep. Arick had probably done that on purpose, so she'd get up to train as well, she thought grumpily. She decided to start her own little training session, since she couldn't go back to sleep. Atarah rounded the corner into the foyer and ran right into Charlotte.

"Ow! Oh my goodness, you Michael angels are hard as stone!" Charlotte whispered. She held her nose in pain.

"What in the realms are you doing up this early?" Atarah whispered. She didn't want Elizabeth to see what she was up to.

"I could ask the same of you! What're you doing up? Dawn is still hours away." Charlotte's hand came away from her nose. A bruise might form, but Atarah knew she'd heal it soon enough.

"I'm about to start my training. What about you?"

"I . . . Well . . ." Charlotte started.

Atarah crossed her arms. She fidgeted with her dark green long-sleeved shirt. She wore long black leggings that closed around her ankles. *Perfect for flight drills*, she thought.

"All right, I woke up early to join my brother in training, but I'm a little nervous. Well, I've been nervous ever since Father mentioned I'd be training with Noah and his men. So, I was hoping to train with just you instead." Charlotte said, all her words in a hushed tone.

Atarah understood her hesitancy, but was she really the one to train Charlotte? Wouldn't she want the best warrior to teach her instead?

"All right, that's fine by me. But my training is probably different from what Arick's and Noah's training will be."

"That's fine!" Charlotte said quickly. "I have a feeling I'll do better training with you, instead of with them."

Atarah nodded and indicated Charlotte should follow her and keep quiet. They walked out the door, and once outside Atarah's wings relaxed. Humming in anticipation of flying, her wings begged for release. Charlotte also seemed to breathe easier once outside.

Atarah stretched her wings and took off in the direction she and Arick had gone yesterday. Charlotte followed her.

"Where are we heading?" she inquired, keeping up with Atarah easily.

"To the tree canopies."

Despite Atarah's lack of clarity on their training, Charlotte seemed perfectly fine with following her lead.

They ascended toward the thick bunch of branches and slowed before settling on a branch.

"What do you do here for training?" Charlotte asked, weaving around the branches carefully before landing.

"Well, this is the perfect place to do flight drills."

Charlotte squinted at all of the branches that crowded around them, the question clear on her face. With the sun still not up, this made the exercise perfect for them.

"Yes. We'll dart through all of the branches. Imagine the branches are demons attacking us."

"Shouldn't we be practicing more offensive moves against demons?"

"We will, but remember when we fought that drude demon? We were at a severe disadvantage because I didn't dodge fast enough and got injured. It's harder to go on the offensive when you have a weak defense."

Charlotte nodded and started toward the branches, but Atarah held her back.

Charlotte looked back at her. "What's wrong? Shouldn't we start already?"

"Hold up a second. This is just a little bit of the training. It'd be too easy if we floated across these branches as they are now."

"What are we waiting for then?"

A gust of wind blew Atarah's hair forward. "That! Now, let's go!"

Atarah and Charlotte darted forward with the wind on their backs. The wind moving the branches to and fro added an unexpected dynamic. Much like an enemy's attack, the branches jerked and swayed against the wind. Atarah bobbed and weaved through the branches, determined not to touch a single one.

Concentrate, Atarah thought.

She tried to imitate the fluid-like movements of the wind with her wings to dodge the branches.

Flow like wind, and if you hit something, relax your body to continue with the current. There.

Atarah entered a small space between the tree canopies. She looked back to see how Charlotte fared. She didn't see her anywhere close to her.

The wind stilled, and Atarah took off back into the tree canopy to find Charlotte. When she did, Atarah couldn't help but burst out laughing.

"Stop laughing and help me out of this." Charlotte scowled.

She was upside down and entangled in the branches. Her usually neat hair was trapped in branches. Her clothes were snared as if she had been caught in a spider web.

Atarah subdued her laughing to small giggles and helped detangle Charlotte's limbs and wings. The branches were everywhere. She'd gotten an arm and a leg trapped, and her wings—Atarah concentrated like she was solving a puzzle trying to get Charlotte out of the branches.

"I guess this means I would've been dead a long time ago if these branches were all demons."

"That's why we train," Atarah murmured as she finished freeing one of her wings.

"It's so hard to see when they're all moving and the sun isn't even up yet! How do you do it?"

"Timing and following the current is really what I do, and it helps," she explained, freeing the other wing.

"Shouldn't we wait until the sun's up?" Charlotte tried to wiggle free.

"No, because demons mostly like to attack at night. So, we need to adjust to fighting in the dark."

Charlotte finally shook free of the branches just in time for the wind to pick back up.

"Bring your wings closer to your body and try to anticipate the movement of the branches in front of you. Hear and feel the wind more than you see it," Atarah encouraged.

"When I bring my wings in, I go faster, and I feel more out of control."

"Perfect. That's what you need to be more comfortable with. In a battle, you won't always be in control."

Charlotte nodded and took off into the canopy once again. Atarah followed suit, going back into her mindset. Flow, listen, adjust, tuck, and float. She tried to remember her previous training and allowed her body to move. Before she knew it, she was back in the small clearing and saw Charlotte there as well, with a few cuts and bruises from the branches but otherwise doing fine.

She glided her way over to Charlotte, who was still panting.

"I didn't . . . get stuck . . . this time," Charlotte huffed. Her wings trembled with effort to keep her afloat.

Atarah grinned at her and gave her a thumbs up, also catching her breath. "You're a very quick learner. Each time it gets easier and easier."

"How many times before you got through with no problem?"

Atarah pondered for a moment.

"It depends on the day, but if my focus isn't right it becomes much harder than it's supposed to be."

Charlotte nodded. Suddenly, a red glow appeared on her face. Atarah turned around and flew above the canopies to see the sunrise. Her breath caught in her throat at the sight before her. She would never tire of the sunrise. The sense of a new day and possibility awakened her. She sensed Charlotte next to her.

"You really love sunrises."

"When you live in the mountains, you learn to appreciate the small things."

Charlotte and Atarah took a moment in silence to enjoy the sunrise. During that one moment of peace and tranquility among the trees in the quiet morning, Atarah's spirit calmed. They both simply enjoyed each other's company, while they watched the sun rays peak over the horizon. She felt grateful and relieved that Charlotte didn't feel the need to fill the silence with talk. As if Charlotte felt as much peace as she did from the quiet morning. Her wings not only relaxed, but hummed with happiness. Charlotte's wings did the same.

A horn signaled in the distance. Just like that, the moment was gone.

"They need to know where we are before they worry too much," Charlotte said, already sitting up.

Atarah followed suit, glancing one last time at the ascending sun. They both launched themselves up into the sky, turning around and diving toward the large Head Tree. As they glided through the air, Charlotte got curious about Atarah.

"Do you usually train by yourself, instead of with your brother and the others?" Charlotte asked, not unkindly.

"Usually, yeah. I do my own kind of training. I need every advantage I can get, to be honest."

"You're not as bad as me, trust me," Charlotte said gloomily.

"Everyone has advantages and disadvantages." Atarah remembered what her mother said to her after practice. She felt so at ease talking with Charlotte. "How about a trade?" That caught Charlotte's attention. "I teach you what I know about combat and fighting, and you can teach me what you know about healing others. Deal?"

Charlotte's face lit up. "Deal!"

They navigated below the tree canopies and flew toward the large main tree, passing by a couple of markets and shops that were opening for the day. A few lanterns lit up as the morning progressed. The city was awakening. Birds began to chirp, signaling the day had started.

"Haven't you learned any self-defense measures with Noah?" Atarah asked, curious with her own questions.

"Not any combat training, no. My specialty is healing. I'm one of the advanced healers in the region," Charlotte said with pride. That was something to be proud of; there were only a handful of them in Silva.

"When can I get a lesson from you?" Atarah asked with eagerness. She needed to practice her other powers desperately.

They reached the main tree and landed before Charlotte answered. "Have you ever tried before?"

"Not really." Atarah hesitated with embarrassment. "My mother usually heals everyone. She taught me a few things about healing, but I've never tried to fully heal someone. Just myself."

"The hardest part is when you first start trying. But once you master the basics, the skills become easier," Charlotte said as they walked through the front door of the house.

Atarah's wings tingled. She quickly pivoted to see who was watching them. Elizabeth looked at them hauntingly from the stairwell on their far-right side. They stared at each other for a while until Charlotte grabbed her arm and hurried her to the dining room.

"Do you have a death wish?" she whispered. Her wings trembled with fear.

"I won't back down from her—" Atarah couldn't finish her sentence at the sight in front of her. They had walked into the dining room just in time for breakfast.

An array of food lined the table in an incredible arrangement of muffins, scones, fruits, and eggs, but that wasn't what caught her attention. Noah and Arick were practically inhaling their food at the table. Gone was proper table etiquette. Arick and Noah grabbed food left and right and shoved it into their mouths without bothering to finish chewing.

Arick looked up with his mouth full of food. "What?"

Atarah couldn't stop the laughter bubbling up. Only when Noah looked up with the same expression did she burst out laughing. She doubled over in laughter. She was nearly in tears, laughing at how they looked. Charlotte, despite running into her mother, coughed to hide her own laughter. Arick and Noah both rolled their eyes and went back to their food.

"What are you doing?" Atarah said between laughs.

"What does it look like?" Arick said, again with his mouth full.

Noah looked at her like she was simpleminded. Atarah couldn't have cared less, compared to how they looked.

"She makes a good point. What are you both doing here? Eating . . . together?" Charlotte said, giggling a little.

Noah looked ready to leave the room in that moment.

Arick scoffed. "We trained earlier and happened to end at the same time for breakfast." He slid a mug over to Atarah.

She reached out instinctively and caught the mug, then

looked down and smiled when she saw the steaming coffee. "Tha—" she started.

"I know. I'm the best," Arick said cockily, already returning to his food.

Charlotte walked over to Noah and flicked him on the back of his neck. "Why don't I get any coffee after training?"

Noah rubbed the back of his neck and looked at her incredulously. "You don't even like coffee! You only drink tea, and you're very picky about it. Also, you were training this morning?" He looked between the two of them in question.

Atarah shrugged. She settled into a chair and piled food onto her own plate. It somehow didn't feel right to speak to someone else on something that was new to Charlotte.

"We started training earlier this morning with some drills," Charlotte said with pride. She started her own plate of food and prattled off to Noah about how much she'd improved in her flight skills.

While Charlotte talked, Atarah's thoughts drifted back to the barrier. How would the day go? Would Elijah be back soon to discuss the troops again? She was wondering briefly about going back to the barrier spot where they'd seen demons when someone else came into the room. She froze when she realized who it was.

Ben smiled at Atarah as he strolled into the room, his soft brown wings completely at ease behind him as he settled into the seat next to her. He wore tan riding pants with a long white tunic. They were wrinkled as if he had been riding all night. His tousled hair curled around his deep brown eyes nicely. Despite the disheveled look, he looked devastatingly handsome.

"Good morning," he said, still grinning at her.

Atarah tried to keep from blushing under his grin. She tried to pull her eyes away from him but couldn't. She dared another glance along his body to see, then felt a kick from under the table. She looked up to see Charlotte eyeing her.

Unfortunately, Noah wasn't as gracious in his modesty. "Does every female angel in the mountains ogle their males like that?"

Arick and Ben choked on their drinks in laughter, while Atarah was certain her face was in a full blush.

"I don't mind being ogled by a beautiful angel," Ben said, winking at Atarah.

She resisted the urge to put her head down in embarrassment. Instead, she said, "You have yet to answer any of my questions."

Ben gave a sly grin. "Forgive me. I am usually more forthcoming, but I can't explain why I'm here quite yet," Ben said with ease as he ate some fruit.

Atarah glanced at Charlotte for a clue, but all she did was shrug. "We actually don't know why he's here anymore than you two. Father brought him here about a week ago."

Noah didn't seem too happy about this and seemed to regard Ben with suspicion.

Atarah looked back at Ben, still determined to get answers. "What can you tell us then?"

"I can tell you anything and everything you want to hear," Ben said, amusement in his eyes.

Atarah's curiosity burned, but she knew she wouldn't get anywhere. She resigned herself to eating her breakfast instead. Perfect timing, for Elijah walked through the doors.

He looked at them in surprise and approached cautiously. "All of you are here . . . eating together?"

Noah gave a look of disgust at Arick and Atarah, as if their momentary peace was about to end.

Arick shrugged. "We all had some bonding time by the fire, while we sang songs of love and harmony." His voice dripped with cynicism.

Noah flashed a small grin, as if he couldn't help it. Elijah regarded everyone at the table with amazement and it almost looked like relief to Atarah.

I suppose hungry stomachs can bring anyone together, Atarah thought, bemused.

Elijah settled into the nearest chair, but didn't start to eat. "I'm happy you're here early, Benjamin. We have much to discuss."

Benjamin nodded at Elijah.

"What's the action plan today?" Arick asked Elijah.

"First thing, Noah will lead our forces to Mortem with Arick accompanying him. Charlotte will go to Chrysi Poli, for they still need healers with Ben as a guide." Elijah looked at Atarah. "Atarah, I need you to travel to Chrysi Poli to strengthen their Head Tree like you did ours, as well as keep Charlotte safe. I know this is a lot to ask, but I can't spare any more soldiers."

Arick stiffened. Noah narrowed his eyes in distrust, but neither objected.

"You have better combat training, and Charlotte has better healing training. I think both of you ladies can help each other—if you look after each other," Elijah finished.

Atarah, at first startled, quickly composed herself. She'd never dared to think of herself as a warrior like Arick or her father. She glanced at Charlotte and saw hopefulness glowing in her eyes.

Atarah grinned at Charlotte and nodded. "Let's do it."

"You'll have to leave fairly quickly," Elijah stated. "All of you will have to leave within a few hours."

Atarah had finished strapping the last of her belongings to her horse, Midnight. Her mare was all black and silk to the touch. Midnight had a gentle spirit about her that gave

Atarah confidence for their long journey. She was petting her mane when Noah approached her. Her wings flared in defense but relaxed when she saw his wings were relaxed and hanging low by his ankles.

Strange, Atarah thought, *he is normally feistier and not as . . . calm.* She stroked her mare's black mane as Noah seemed to try to gather his words. Atarah took the time to assess Noah, her . . . uncle, she supposed.

Upon further inspection, Noah seemed older than she originally thought. Worry lines marred his face, aging him, but nonetheless he seemed to take after his mother. Soft brown hair with strong curls accented his face. His eyes looked more hazel today than green as he squinted, deep in thought. He was fairly tall—nowhere near as tall as Arick, but nonetheless taller than her. His build was slender but toned with muscles, and he had several knives and daggers strapped around him that made him look quite deadly. Despite this appearance, his eyes seemed almost warm.

"I . . . hope you both travel safely," Noah said hesitantly.

Atarah paused. For him to take so long to say this small sentence, Atarah wondered if this was the beginning of him trusting her. *He said, 'you both,'* she thought hopefully.

"If you fly off by yourself again and leave Charlotte defenseless, I'll personally rip off both your wings and set them on fire," Noah said with deadly calm, staring her down.

She held his gaze, but grabbed the mare's mane tightly, so he wouldn't see her hands shaking.

"You can trust me," she said with as much calm as she could muster.

Noah looked at her for one moment longer before nodding. He turned and walked away, right as Charlotte walked toward Atarah. She had finally brought her horse around the stables. Her horse was beautiful, with brown and white patches.

"What was all that about?" Charlotte inquired, looking at Noah's retreating figure.

"Just some small talk," Atarah said, giving Charlotte's horse some pets along the neck.

Charlotte looked like she wanted to say more, but shrugged it off.

Atarah climbed on her mount, and Charlotte followed suit. The agreement was that Arick and Noah would venture to Malachi's region, Elementa, with Elijah's forces first before heading to Mortem. They would report the status of the city of Aquam Caput before moving on. After Elijah explained the missions, everyone quickly dispersed to get ready for their journeys, except for Ben. Elijah asked Ben to stay behind and told them to go west without Ben for now.

Ben assured her that he would catch up with them and guide them. It would only take an hour or so before he would catch up. At least, that's what both Elijah and Ben said to her and Charlotte.

She had packed her favorite lightweight knives and daggers. She loaded up her clothes more suitable for battle. She chose her gray pants for today with a black, long-sleeved shirt to keep her warm against the cool, morning breeze. She looked at the edge of the border from which they'd come two nights before and urged her mare closer to the waterfall gate. The journey was to be a long one.

They were about to leave the walls of the city when Atarah heard the pounding of hooves beside them. She turned to see her brother and Noah at full gallop. Their troops followed closely, almost stampeding. Noah and Arick had more to travel with, but Atarah didn't doubt for one moment they'd get there by tomorrow night. *Normally a three-day journey*, Atarah thought with a grin. They'd make it in two.

Arick looked in Atarah's direction, gave her a brief nod, and turned back to focus on riding.

That was all the farewell she'd receive. This didn't bother her because she had confidence in her brother's return. Goodbyes had a finality to them that they took seriously. To say goodbye meant there was a permanent understanding that there was no return. They were going to see each other again.

His salute told her that Arick had confidence in her ability to return—that she could handle herself. She vowed silently she wouldn't hurt that confidence. Once the last of their forces passed through the gate, Atarah and Charlotte took off on their own journey. The beautiful leaves that surrounded them glistened as the sunlight bounced off of them. The autumn colors of red, orange, and yellow danced around them as they galloped down the trail that would take them to the Selaphiel Region, Arena. Atarah took in the beauty of the leaves while she could before they went into another strange region.

They galloped for hours until the landscape started to change slowly. She had never been to Arena Region, so she became curious.

"What is the region like, Charlotte?" Atarah inquired.

"I've . . . only been there . . . one time . . . and I was very young," Charlotte puffed, already looking tired from horseback.

We've only been riding for about two hours, Atarah thought in amusement.

"Want to teach me about healing now, Charlotte?" she teased.

Charlotte gave Atarah an annoyed look, which only made Atarah giggle more. With her red face, frantic panting, and slumped body, even her annoyed expression looked exhausted.

"When . . . you're tired of . . . healing practice . . . I'll get you back," Charlotte squeaked out.

"All right, then let's take a quick break," Atarah said with a grin.

"No!" Charlotte exclaimed. "I don't want to slow us down."

Atarah nodded. She knew exactly what it felt like to be in Charlotte's shoes. She took the time to observe her surroundings.

The landscape is starting to truly shift into something else, Atarah thought. Unease grew in the back of her mind. She was once again charging into unknown territory to aid others who might not want her help. It was starting to unnerve her, but she didn't want to acknowledge her fears. Instead, she focused on the landscape around them and the fact that she wasn't hiding at home. She was doing something unexpected of her and didn't want that to stop now.

The trees were shrinking and seemed to have fewer leaves as they traveled. The ground slowly turned from dark brown to a light sand color. As they traveled, the decline in tree coverage offered little protection for them against the now blazing sun. Atarah didn't mind the sun, but looking at Charlotte's red face, she didn't want her to overdo things. As they rode on, the afternoon sun got less and less forgiving, especially on Charlotte and her lighter skin.

Atarah formulated a plan as she passed Charlotte her water canteen. Charlotte gulped greedily as if the water were air.

"Let's stop up here, so we can refill the water," Atarah suggested.

Charlotte simply nodded, too tired to speak.

Atarah pulled her mare over to the side of a now widening road before them. She looked ahead and realized how the landscape would affect them. Charlotte stumbled off of her horse and moved closer to one of the few trees around them. She collapsed and sprawled out, basking in the cool shade the tree provided.

Atarah quickly ventured to another tree to track its water source. She placed her hand on the tree and concentrated.

Breathe, listen, and wait. Breathe, listen, and wait. Wait. Wait. Now.

Atarah struck one of the roots and pulled the water the root extracted from the soil. As the water was pouring into her container, Atarah went to scout the area. She placed her hands on the ground and reached out through her hands, pushing her power forward, to see if she could sense anything, any vibration of other creatures scurrying about. It was almost like sonar, giving her the location of anything and everything around her. She waited. Her wings flared wide. She felt something . . .

Footsteps!

Atarah whipped around and slammed her dagger into the tree Charlotte had collapsed by.

Charlotte jolted up in alarm. "What's going on?" she shrieked.

"Ben has caught up with us apparently," Atarah said without taking her eyes off of the tree. She had been hoping to get further without help, to prove they were strong enough to make it on their own.

Charlotte looked at the tree in suspicion. A whistle blew out from behind it, and their late guide came out. Charlotte's eyes were still wide in surprise, but Atarah simply put away her dagger, undeterred. Her wings relaxed.

Ben stepped out of the shade and removed his head covering. He was wearing something slightly different now. He wore loose-fitting cargo pants with a white, long-sleeve shirt. The shirt looked quite light and breathable, with a bundled up, lightweight scarf.

He held up his water canteen, punctured by her dagger. "I believe you owe me a container now."

"You shouldn't have been so mischievous, trying to pour water on Charlotte's head."

Charlotte looked incredulously at Ben.

He laughed. "She was just lying there, and it was too much of a temptation. Also, I expected you to sense me much earlier than this. Been lazy, I see." He grinned irritatingly.

Atarah resisted the urge to roll her eyes, but silently berated herself because Ben was right. If it had been a demon or something else sinister following them, they would've been in real trouble. She reminded herself to do a perimeter check before they let their guard down next time. She needed to stay vigilant and strong.

"Apologies for not catching up sooner. Elijah kept me longer than anticipated," Ben said as his explanation.

"I don't suppose you would tell us why he kept you behind?" Atarah asked dryly. He hadn't answered any of her questions thus far, and she didn't expect him to now.

"What I can tell you is that Elijah is a very concerned father," Ben said softly. He looked at Charlotte. "He wanted me to gather these for you." He handed her scrolls with ancient writing on them. "He said this should be a refresher from your studies, since this is your first healing mission."

Charlotte clutched the scroll with shaking hands. "Thank you," Charlotte said sincerely.

Well, that answers everything, Ben, Atarah thought sardonically.

She moved to retrieve her water container from the tree root, while Charlotte tried to ask more questions. He danced around the truth, but he wouldn't give all of the truth if he didn't want them to know.

Atarah divided the water into three containers before capping them and returning to the back-and-forth chatter between Ben and Charlotte. Charlotte attempted to get answers from Ben, while he grinned at her attempts. Atarah passed them each their own container. Ben winked at her when she gave one to him.

A prank of her own came into her mind. The temptation was too great. As Ben went to take a drink, Atarah tipped the container, causing water to run down his face. Ben sputtered and coughed water as Atarah and Charlotte nearly fell on the ground laughing.

"That's what you get for sneaking up on us and trying to prank us," Charlotte got out in between laughs.

She patted Atarah on the back as Atarah tried to regain her posture from laughing. Ben glared at them for a moment before his own lips quivered into a grin, then he started to laugh with them.

"All right, we need to get a move on before it gets too dark," Ben said as he packed his water and mounted his horse.

Atarah and Charlotte followed suit onto their horses, still grinning. Atarah thought it would be dark soon and they would have to set up camp. *Hopefully we can get a few more hours of riding in before camp.*

They set off on their path, recharged from the brief rest, their pace faster than before. Ben rode ahead of them swiftly.

Not surprising he was able to catch up to us so quickly, Atarah thought.

She wanted to ride ahead as well, but didn't want Charlotte to fall too far behind. Charlotte put on a brave face as the pace quickened, determined to keep up. Atarah looked ahead as the last couple of trees fell away from their path. Now they entered into a new desert terrain.

Ben covered his head and face with his scarf, resembling a shemagh, protecting against the sun and sand. Atarah thought it smart to do the same but had no scarf. She reached back into her pack and tried to mimic the same with her shawl. She had worn some gray riding pants with a black, long-sleeved athletic shirt for Silva's climate, but now wished she could change into something different. She turned and saw Charlotte struggling with the same predicament. Atarah slowed to give Charlotte one of her lighter shawls to work with.

"How does he deal with this kind of stuff?" Charlotte puffed as she tried to keep up, while covering her face from the flying sand Ben's horse kicked up.

"It comes naturally to him because this is his region."

"Not quite," Ben called from the front. "We're about one or two hours from the Selaphiel border. You'll see the difference when we get there."

Is this not already enough of a change? Atarah thought.

She focused on the horizon and spurred her mare onward. As the sun dipped lower in the sky, Atarah decided to look into their surroundings. She expanded her reach and tried to get a sense if any being was around them. Something was off. Atarah couldn't get a clear picture of their surroundings. The shifting sands made it difficult to discern anything clear underneath them. She tried to concentrate, but everything seemed unstable or muffled in an odd way. *I'll try again when we make camp.*

Atarah turned her focus back to her horseback riding. Ben faced forward as her head came up. He slowed his pace slightly, so he was closer to Atarah and Charlotte. Atarah became more watchful and signaled to Charlotte that she should do the same. Charlotte, red-faced, gave her a brief nod.

"I think you're going to love Chrysi Poli, the Golden City. It's where I grew up," Ben said, drawing her attention from Charlotte. "The statues are larger than any tree or mountain, and the city's architecture is unlike any other city I've seen so far."

"Do you travel very often? Is Chrysi Poli the capital of Selaphiel?" Atarah's curiosity was piqued.

"Chrysi Poli is the capital, and I've traveled more often in recent times around Selaphiel and other regions."

"Why do you travel? Is it difficult for you?"

"It's only truly difficult for me when my country is struggling on the front lines. My brothers have been holding down the front line, while I have a more foreign role to play in this war."

"What's your family like?" she asked. She wanted to get to know him more.

"My brothers aren't as direct as I am, while my mother and father are not as direct as my brothers are. I believe I take after my uncle more," Ben reflected.

"How many brothers do you have?"

"One too many." Ben grinned. "What about you, little dove?"

"Dove?" Atarah shot him a look. The blood rushed to her face. She turned the other way to hide her blush.

"Seems appropriate given your wings." Ben gave her his charming grin. She struggled to keep her wings from humming.

"I have only my brother. Just a small family compared to others," Atarah said, looking forward. Her blush was still in full force.

"Seems to me you have a much larger family," Ben retorted.

"The family you choose to be around you are the important ones though," she said with sincerity.

He seemed to ponder her last statement with some seriousness. His eyebrows came slightly together as if in concentration. They fell into a natural silence. Atarah's wings relaxed around him, despite her better judgment. She felt she could trust Ben and disliked that because she knew he was withholding information. Why was he already with the Raphael household? Why was he traveling with them, and what was his real role in this battle? So many questions she had for him, and yet something in her said she could trust him. Her heart felt fluttery yet calm whenever he was around.

"Why'd you volunteer yourself during the summit meeting?" Ben probed, seeming to come from deep thought.

"I wanted to work with the other Archangels—"

Ben's chuckle cut her off. "Sorry. Why in heaven would you want to do that? They're not all that pleasant to work with."

"Because we need to. Our power increases when working together. We need all the power we can get to defeat the demons flooding into our realm."

"Obviously false. We all have power, whether we work together or not."

"Yes, but we'll never be as strong compared to a combined force."

"I don't know. I get the feeling if the portals had opened in your father's region, our combined efforts wouldn't be needed."

"What are you saying exactly?"

"We don't need to add more forces together. We need to be more strategic about the forces we already have. After all, you don't see the cherubim sweating about an army of demons coming in this realm."

"What do the head Archs think about your thoughts?"

Ben huffed, his wings widening slightly. His eyes almost seemed to glow with passion.

"The only ones willing to half listen to me are my father, Elijah, and Mikael. Only three out of the seven Arch Heads are willing to listen to me," he said vehemently.

The only reason they'd give him the chance to speak was because of his position as heir. Even then, he wasn't the next in line to become the head of his Arch family. So, listening to him was truly out of generosity. Atarah never truly thought her words would matter much to the Head Archs. Nonetheless, she was surprised to hear her father had spoken with Ben.

"When were you able to talk with my father?"

Ben gave a backwards glance, grinned, and pointed ahead. "This looks like a nice place to camp for the night."

Atarah looked and saw a small oasis ahead of them. The palm trees shifted and moved in the evening breeze as if greeting them. The dark blue water glistened in the rays of the setting sun, making Atarah all the more aware of her thirst. Charlotte stared intently at the water, her wings vibrating with happiness. Atarah nodded to Ben, and they spurred their mounts toward the oasis.

"The reason I spoke up at the summit is because . . .I didn't want to sit around and do nothing. Definitely didn't want marriage. Even worse, I didn't want to stay weak or ignorant. All my life, I've been treated as a kid, and I'm tired of it," Atarah admitted. She never spoke about this to anyone. Not even Arick.

Ben nodded. "You have something to prove. Not just to others, but to yourself."

Atarah looked at him, shocked. He understood, truly understood her. That was exactly how she felt. She had something to prove. What exactly? She wasn't sure yet, but she felt certain it wasn't back at Sanctum.

As they came close to the oasis, Ben signaled to Atarah to slow down and stop. Atarah went to ask the question forming in her mind, but Ben put a single finger to his mouth, indicating they should be quiet. Atarah's wings flared and her senses sharpened. Charlotte looked between her and Ben, but said nothing.

Atarah expanded her senses once more to the surrounding area, as Ben dismounted and cautiously approached the edge of the oasis. Atarah focused, trying to feel the pulse of any being near them. She waited, listened, waited, and listened, then sand started to shift.

Atarah looked up at Ben, taking cautious steps around the trees; his wings flared wide. It was the first time she'd seen his wings react in such a way. He went to take a step past a tree, then he froze. His foot was in midair, then he took a step back. Raising his arm up to the sky, a buzzing, crackling sound swirled around his hand as he brought it down.

Suddenly, lightning shot down from the sky, striking the spot Ben had almost stepped on. An eerie screech filled the desert as the sand shifted beneath them in large waves. Atarah's muscles tensed as she realized they weren't alone in the desert. She shifted her mind into her battle mode, by expanding her power and flaring her wings. Atarah quickly dismounted and let her horse loose to escape the area. Charlotte attempted the same, but ended up falling off of her horse unceremoniously as her horse madly raced off in fear. She struggled to stand back up. Concerned for Charlotte, Atarah ran to her, but had trouble reaching her with the shifting sand.

"Grab my hand!" Atarah yelled to Charlotte.

Charlotte turned to her with an outstretched hand, her wings flared and quivering in fear.

Atarah grabbed onto her, expanded her wings as far as they would go, and launched off the ground, towing Charlotte with her. Flying several meters high, Atarah could finally see what was going on. Gathering information was one of the first things taught in combat training. *Where is your team? Where is the enemy? What is the enemy's goal?* All these questions filled Atarah's mind as adrenaline and fear pumped through her. Ben hovered above the ground where the lightning struck as a large, pale, scaly form shifted under the sand. The sand moved in waves as the creature wriggled to the surface. Emerging was a pale serpent with a vile face, unnerving, black pit eyes, and yellow fangs. *The shifting sand*, Atarah realized with clarity. The serpent was the shifting sand she had sensed earlier.

The serpent hissed menacingly at Ben, coiling its body as if ready to strike. Ben continued to lightly flap his wings to stay a little bit off the ground, drawing his elongated, curved sword. A scimitar.

The sun soon disappeared below the horizon and darkness quickly settled over the desert. The serpent moved to attack Ben, spewing a dark yellow liquid. Ben swirled around, causing a spiral of sand and catching the serpent off guard. Another lightning bolt struck the snake savagely, causing it to wail in pain. Coiling up once more to guard its wound, the serpent hissed viciously at Ben, who escaped another attack by soaring higher. Just barely escaped.

She was terrified, but she couldn't stand by and watch.

Atarah loosened her grip on Charlotte. "Stay high up and don't go near the sand."

Charlotte nodded briefly, her eyes never leaving the snake.

Atarah drew her own blade and expanded her senses on the snake, watching its every twitch. The serpent was focused on Ben, lucky for Atarah. She dove as stealthily as she could, swiveling to the side to go for the snake's head.

Unluckily for her, the snake's head snapped behind it, where Atarah was about to attack. The pale serpent hissed and went to strike at Atarah's diving form.

"Atarah!"

Atarah jerked to the left, evading the serpent's strike, slashing as many of its scales as she could. Not the ideal mark, but she was able to cause some damage around its neck. She hovered low to the sand. The serpent launched its venom at her. She evaded it, but she saw the venom melt the sand on the ground.

"Watch out, Atarah!" she heard a panicked voice say.

The serpent attacked Atarah while she was looking away—which was perfect. The serpent reached her. She stepped to the side, turned quickly, and drove her blade as deeply as she could into the serpent's neck. The serpent reared upwards in pain, bringing Atarah with it. Bringing her high into the sky. She held onto her dagger for dear life. She tried to twist, but a steel-like grip dragged Atarah away from the snake and high up into the sky.

The serpent darted away from the oasis and dove into the sand for shelter. Slithering beneath the sand, Atarah's sense of the snake started to disappear. She tried to move to go after it, but Ben kept his grip on her.

"There's no point in going after it. It's leaving."

"Why did you let it escape?" Atarah said harshly, irritated by his grip on her.

"Because killing it will attract more demons to its carcass. What were you doing, being so reckless?" Ben demanded.

"I had a great shot, and you know it."

"Not great enough," Ben said. "Some of its venom got on your clothes."

Atarah started and then looked down. Sure enough, the venom splattered across her clothes, melting the fabric. Atarah gasped and went to wipe it off. Ben grabbed her hands, and gave her a water container, chuckling, which only further embarrassed her. Her face became inflamed by embarrassment and a bruised pride at needing Ben's help.

She blushed as he looked at her with that grin of his.

"You surprised me." Ben gave a short chuckle. "Not many people can do that. I am in awe actually. You're brave when taking down a serpent but bashful at needing help." Ben laughed and shook his head.

Thankfully, Ben turned his attention to Charlotte. He signaled they could land. Charlotte flew over to where they were and noticed Atarah's exposed midriff. Atarah was too busy pouring water all over her clothes to notice Ben taking off in the direction their horses had gone.

"What on earth happened?" Charlotte asked. She grabbed her own water bottle and went to work on Atarah's shoes.

"The serpent must've sprayed me when it went to strike," Atarah said, trying to take in the damage to her clothes. She groaned. Her midriff was exposed and a line from the venom went from the middle of each thigh all the way down to her shoes. She supposed the damage could be worse, or more embarrassing. Atarah shivered as the night breeze blew through her damp clothes.

Why couldn't she do anything on her own? She berated herself. Just like the drude demon, she couldn't lead or defend effectively. *Come on! Pull yourself together,* she chided herself.

"Here, let's try this." Charlotte elaborately tied the scarf they used earlier around her body and down her leg.

Atarah looked down, surprised. Charlotte managed to spread the scarf down evenly to add coverage to her stomach and interwove the rest of the scarf down her leg.

"How'd you do that?" Atarah asked, amazed.

"Mother and I always messed around with clothing while I was growing up. She said Ava started the tradition."

"My mother used to make clothing?"

Charlotte looked up, surprised. "Of course. She was the greatest in the region. She was so creative; she even wove healing properties into her clothing. Soldiers wore her garments and would heal faster because of it."

Atarah blinked in surprise. Learning a new thing about her mother made her feel thrown off for some reason. As if hearing about a completely different person. Just as she was about to ask another question, they heard the pounding of hooves come their way.

Charlotte flared her wings, on guard.

Nice, Atarah thought. She's quickly learning how to be prepared. She wasn't worried though. When she expanded her senses, she knew it was Ben galloping their way. She was getting used to the shifting terrain. Not the best by any means, but better than sensing nothing.

"It's time to make camp. We'll be in the Arena Region in the morning."

Chapter 8

Noah

The wind brutally slapped against the men's faces as they surged forward toward the Southwest Region. The men's morale was strong and determined, especially after early morning training rounds. Combat training was mandatory every night when they made camp and every morning before leaving. Arick saw to their training with amazing attention to detail and patience when he had to modify the training to match the Silva troops.

As much as Noah disliked the smug bat, he had to give Arick credit when it came to helping his troops. Even he had a hard time keeping up with the training Arick provided.

Noah watched as his men packed up from the last night of camp. They would most likely pass the border within a few hours and reach the capital by noon.

"Becoming lazy on our last morning?" Arick taunted.

Noah meant to glare at him, but it ended up looking like a grimace. "We're almost there. Just a few more hours before we're in a possible fray."

They weren't sure what they were going to encounter in Aquam Caput, but he knew in his gut it was nothing good.

Arick grew serious and nodded. They hadn't encountered any demons since their travels, but Noah wondered if this was the calm before the storm. As they got closer to the region, more and more things seemed quiet, reclusive, and somehow sorrowful. The trees grew in width and length as they traveled. The leaves stayed green as they entered the Elementa Region and it seemed more tropical. The leaves expanded wide, providing some shade from the sun. The chilly autumn breeze was no more. Warm, humid air now clung to them. No birds chirped nor insects sang. The forest was quiet.

"My first time in a tropical paradise, and I can't even enjoy it," Arick said facetiously.

Noah gave a brief humorless chuckle. Despite himself, he admired Arick's sense of humor. He expanded his wings to full length, signaling for the troops to finish up their training and be ready for departure. Each morning, they grew more efficient with this process, faster and stronger. Arick went to his stallion and organized his items.

Everyone was mounted, fully armored, and as ready as they could be for battle. Noah pondered what would await them in Malachi's region. His wings hummed slightly.

"Um . . . Commander? Heir?"

Arick turned his head with a raised eyebrow. "Commander?" The astonishment evident in his voice. "That's a new one," Arick mumbled.

A soldier from the ranks steadily approached him. "Heir, the horses are giving the soldiers grief and aren't willing to go any farther. I believe the horses are too scared."

Noah wasn't particularly surprised, but he still had hoped the horses would last a few more hours of riding.

"How many are having trouble with their mounts?" Arick asked.

"Nearly eight dozen or so."

"Tell them to let their horses go and pair with someone else's steed. A little sharing will do us no harm," Arick instructed easily.

"Right away." The soldier promptly turned on his heel and sprinted toward the mass of soldiers to complete his task.

Arick turned to see Noah muttering to himself and giving Arick a sidelong glance.

"Do you have something you want to share?" Arick asked with a sly, raised eyebrow.

"I'd appreciate it if you didn't steal my men's loyalty once this war is over."

Arick laughed and waved Noah off as trivial. He returned to his task of ensuring all the weapons were prepared for battle.

Noah regarded him with disgust before climbing onto his own mount, slighted at being waved away. He tried hard to not be envious of Arick's battle and leadership capabilities, but it was all in vain. Despite Arick's easygoing persona, Noah sensed a struggle within Arick he couldn't quite put his finger on.

Noah reared his horse and flared his wings wide, signaling his troops to move out. They set out at a strong pace, weapons close to their sides and alert to their surroundings.

Arick was probably right, Noah thought. The horses his troops had left would probably be too scared in a few hours. The wind shifted slightly, which caused Noah's wings to flare again. He started to plan out their next move. He signaled to Arick, who quickly moved his horse closer to him.

"What's your plan?" Arick inquired immediately, wasting no time.

The preparation for battle never ceases.

Elijah resisted the urge to pace around the room as he waited for his guest to arrive. He knew what he was doing was a huge risk, but he needed to see this plan through. He looked up as his wife came in with a tray of assorted treats and beverages for the guest. He lightened up as he watched her. Sometimes he truly couldn't believe his luck in falling in love with her, the children she'd brought forth into this world with him, and her continual strength in staying by his side.

Elizabeth smiled back at him as she set the tray down. She walked to his side and encircled her hand around his. "There's no need to be nervous. All will work out."

"I will ensure that it does, my love."

A knock on the door drew their attention away from each other. The door opened to reveal Gabriel Fores XIX of House Gabriel. Elijah stood in greeting to Gabriel, who gave a curt nod to both him and Elizabeth.

He approached the seating area almost cautiously and glanced between the two of them as he took his seat. "To what do I owe the honor of this invitation you've extended to me?"

Elijah and Elizabeth took their seats next to each other, ready to get down to business. "To get right to the point, we have a proposition for you, if you're interested."

Gabriel cocked his head to the side and regarded them. "What proposition do you have?"

"I need your help to transport Atarah and Charlotte to the human realm for safety after all of the soldiers are at the southern border."

Gabriel raised his eyebrows in surprise at Elijah's plan, but looked between them and leaned forward. "Why exactly?" His tone filled with suspicion.

"Your house has the history of being an ambassador to the human realm since the beginning. Your household can transport to the human realm more easily, while the rest of us have to use an enormous amount of power to get there. So, I need you to transport Atarah and Charlotte into the human realm quickly before anything else could hurt them. Keep them there until instructed to do so otherwise."

"Why would I help you with this plan? Why spare a valuable transportation soldier when you could transport your family yourself?"

Elijah knew this was a risk. He didn't want to reveal too much either.

"If you're willing to agree, then a marriage can be arranged for your son Gabriel and my daughter Charlotte. I'm sure she'll bring . . . a multitude of blessings and healing into your family."

"Your daughter, I'm sure, is beautiful and talented, but so are other young female Archs. Why should I risk my alliance?"

"Not many other Archs are advanced healers," Elizabeth chimed in.

Gabriel turned to look at her.

"Even Ava, our eldest, was not as advanced as Charlotte. With Charlotte by your son's side, this would only benefit you and your region."

Gabriel turned to look back at Elijah, as if searching, then slowly stretched out his wings and flattened them toward Elijah. Elijah did the same with his wings, followed by Elizabeth.

Gabriel stood to leave. "Well then, it'll be done. Where will my son meet the female Archs?"

"They will be in Chrysi Poli in the Arena Region."

The glistening sun bounced off the golden sand dunes. The light breeze wasn't too overbearing, allowing them to remove their face and eye coverings. Atarah soaked up the view before them.

"Welcome, Atarah and Charlotte, to the Arena Region and more importantly, off in the distance you'll see the capital. Welcome to Chrysi Poli."

Atarah looked ahead to see an oasis emerge from the desert surrounding them. The Golden City indeed. The buildings seemed to glisten in the afternoon sun, tall, tower-like structures made of sand, gold, and glass. Except the glass seemed to be an array of various colors. From a distance, it was hard to take in the details of the city. Nonetheless, Chrysi Poli was breathtaking even from where they stood. Tall golden statues of wings glistened alongside dome-like buildings. Atarah could see them shining from miles out.

They rode relentlessly all throughout the morning and midday. *Poor Charlotte*, Atarah thought, glancing back at her. She truly could use a break. Charlotte's face was red with exertion, but she gave Atarah a weak smile. Atarah smiled back encouragingly before turning back to face the city.

Ben came up beside her. "We should reach the city in about an hour or so by riding with our group. Then I'll introduce you to my family." Looking at her sideways, he continued, "I can show you around the city if you like. Both you and Charlotte, of course."

Atarah could've sworn his wings hummed slightly. Her wings trembled in excitement as well. She wanted so badly to fly around the city, to explore. She tried to rein in her self-control, and stilled her wings.

"I think we'd enjoy that," Atarah replied, urging her mare forward. Charlotte grunted in effort and prodded her mare forward too. "What plan does your family have in aiding the soldiers on the front lines?"

"We tend to be the ones who gather information during battles."

"What information have you been gathering?"

"Nothing you don't already know or suspect." Another response with no real answer. From what she knew of Selaphiel angels, they made the best spies.

"What have your brothers been gathering?"

"Information," Ben answered with a sardonic smile. "You'd do well in the Selaphiel Region. You ask questions constantly."

Atarah blushed. In other regions, asking too many questions would be a sign of distrust. Apparently, in Selaphiel, questions had a more positive reception.

"How . . . are both . . . of you . . . talking at a time . . . like this?" Charlotte panted.

Ben looked back at Charlotte. "Do you ride horses often in Silva?"

"Only for . . . short-distance . . . traveling. I haven't . . . ridden a horse . . . in a long while."

"With how beautiful Silva is, I wouldn't mind flying around with ease and enjoying the sights and scents. Nothing like a crisp, autumn smell."

Charlotte gave a small laugh and glanced at Atarah. Atarah blushed, remembering her flying escapade when she'd first arrived in Silva.

"I think it's . . . different for me . . . since I grew up in

Silva. The leaves all look the same after a while." Charlotte's panting finally got under control.

"I suppose native land seems boring to natives," Ben said.

"The mountains still intimidate me, no matter how native I am," Atarah said.

"The mountains?" Ben inquired.

Even Charlotte perked up her ears to listen, despite the exhaustion.

"The mountains are fierce and harsh to those who don't know what they're doing. Even growing up in the mountains, if I'm not careful, I could lose my wings, legs, arms, or even my life."

"Is it true the mountains are alive and moving?" Charlotte asked with fascination.

"Where exactly does everyone live?" Ben asked. His eyes glowed with intrigue.

"The mountain passes . . . shift in a way. Only if one grows up in the mountains can they navigate it alone. That's why it's difficult to answer either question." Atarah looked at them. "My ancestors did that on purpose to ensure the safety of the clan."

Ben nodded as if he already knew this, while Charlotte seemed even more perplexed by her explanation.

"The infamous Vivamus Montibus," Ben said with a grin.

"My father said it was like the mountains moved far distances overnight, and he was completely lost within hours of entering the mountain range," Charlotte said. "I was told he was trapped within the mountains for nearly three years before he stumbled out near the border. I believe he returned home once he escaped."

Atarah looked at Charlotte. "When did Elijah try that?"

Charlotte looked away. "It was a long time ago. Are we

going to encounter another giant viper like before?" She changed the direction of the conversation.

"Hmm, we shouldn't now. Those monsters usually have a large territory, but they aren't this far out normally. They don't like the sand conditions along the border. However, it never hurts to double check." Ben glanced knowingly at Atarah.

She had already scanned their surrounding area since they had awoken. Any normal Arch would have been exhausted expending this much energy into their powers. She'd seen full-grown Arch men pass out from exhaustion from just a few hours of using their powers.

Not when you grow up in the Michael Clan. Though judging from the occasional tremors in her body, in another day or so she'd be spent.

Atarah looked sideways at Ben. "What would cause a creature like that to move out of its own territory then?"

Ben furrowed his brow as if in deep thought. "Something bigger and meaner probably," he answered distractedly.

Charlotte's wings flared and slid farther down by her side, showing her unease. Atarah expanded her senses further to underground and aerial surroundings as well.

Of course, she thought, *all of the regions are being affected by demons, but if more regions are receiving an absurd surplus of them, then of course other animals will go into different territories.*

Atarah thought back on her studies of all of the various demons that could pose a bigger threat. She resisted the urge to shudder, thankful she wasn't in her brother's shoes. She wondered how he fared against the swarm east of the Arena Region. Atarah didn't have much time to dwell on her thoughts as they started to approach the main gate to the city.

The city gate was covered in gold and glass in a variety of shapes and sizes. The large wall that surrounded the capital towered over them. *Larger than trees, but smaller than mountains*, Atarah thought. However, that wasn't what perplexed her about the city. She slowly realized there was some type of dome on top of the wall structure. The dome seemed to be made of glass, but also of something else; she couldn't quite guess what.

There was a large golden platform at the top of the dome where guards were stationed all around. Half a dozen guards flew down to meet them from the top of the dome. Atarah and Charlotte's wings flared. Even if they weren't on bad terms with this region, it didn't mean they could let their guards down. Ben's wings stayed relaxed as he raised his hands in greeting. The guards landed and bowed deeply to Ben.

"Welcome back, Arch Ben," a deep voice projected from one of the guards.

Atarah's and Charlotte's wings didn't relax.

Ben lifted his hand. "Go ahead and proceed, Jovan. I want to get inside and wash the sand out of my ears," he spoke with impatience.

The guards moved to disarm Ben and pat him down for more weapons. A few guards moved quickly toward Charlotte, probably to do the same, but Charlotte's wings fully flared. Her face was full of distress and distrust, and she let out a little cry when the guards grabbed her. Out of instinct, Atarah flared her wings fully and side-kicked the guard who grabbed Charlotte. She'd truly meant to make him step back a little, but she'd underestimated her own strength. The guard was flung back, crashing into the other guards. They landed on the ground. The two guards scrambled to their feet; their wings flared defensively.

"Whoa! Whoa! Easy there, Atarah." Ben came forward and stood between Atarah and the guards.

Charlotte stood behind Atarah, still distrustful.

"They're just checking for weapons, Atarah. They do this to everyone. No one in the city is allowed to have weapons, except the guards," Ben explained. His wings were still relaxed.

"We didn't know that. How would we? It's rude for anyone to try to put their hands on another Arch, especially one who isn't expecting it. Let alone another heir. Next time, ensure they explain what they're doing, so they don't frighten anyone else." Atarah's voice rang out a little harsher and with more authority than she had ever used. For once, she felt like a true Michael Archangel.

She expected a retort back from Ben or the guards, some sort of reprimand, but the same deep-voiced angel from earlier spoke beside them.

"You heard her, Archs. Apologize, and explain what you're doing. They don't know our ways, and we can't expect them to."

Atarah turned to regard the guard who'd spoken. He was short but stocky for his build. His voice seemed to carry the weight of many years of military service. He wore a white long-sleeved shirt with the same insignia that Ben wore with tan cargo pants. The golden lines of the sand dunes on the upper right arm. All of the soldiers wore the same outfit.

Atarah's wings relaxed. Charlotte's eyes flickered back and forth between Atarah, Ben, and the guards before she slowly relaxed her wings.

The guards from earlier looked a little sheepish and bowed to Charlotte. "We apologize for the distress we caused you. Please, we need to search along your lower legs and torso to ensure you carry no weapons into the city."

"All right." Charlotte's voice held a slight tremor, but her wings were relaxed.

The guard who'd spoken to Atarah approached her. "I need to do the same to you. We have to ensure no unauthorized weapons enter the city."

Atarah nodded briefly. "What's your name again?" she inquired as he performed his search.

"My name is Jovan, Heir." Jovan removed the knives stashed in her pockets.

"How long have you worked for the guard?"

"Longer than I'd like to admit, but for reference longer than you've been alive." He raised his eyebrow as he found her secret stash of knives hidden along her back behind her wings.

Atarah could only give a sheepish grin and shrugged.

"You must be the Heir from the clan of Michael."

"What could've possibly given that away?" Atarah said facetiously.

Jovan chuckled as he finished taking the last of her knives. He looked her over once before nodding that his work was done. She'd taken the longest to disarm.

Jovan gave a signal, and the wall before them split open wide. Atarah couldn't hold back her gasp of amazement. The beautiful city before them gleamed. All of the tall structures were made of gold and glass and woven into amazing art forms.

Ben navigated them through the city with a high level of patience. Atarah and Charlotte stopped on almost every street, wanting to look around and explore each building. Tall buildings of all shapes and sizes towered over them. It looked like they were made out of glass. However, they couldn't see through the glass. The whole city seemed to be an art piece or a museum in and of itself. Some buildings had a round lower half then morphed into a spiral shape as the building reached the top.

Large fountains were at every street corner. Adorned with elaborate clay sculptures of young angels dancing about, with a golden trim. Many angels gathered around the fountains in what looked to be more socialization than gathering water. The streets were made with gold, arranged in different patterns. The gold pavement felt almost soft against the soles of her feet.

Many people milled around going about their daily lives. Walking through markets, purchasing fabrics, almost normal except the large amount of military present at every corner. Every soldier they passed by was friendly enough, but only after bowing to Ben, who greeted them all warmly. The angels who walked by them eyed Atarah and Charlotte in suspicion. While not unfriendly, they weren't quite welcoming either. Nevertheless, Atarah's breath was taken by the beauty of the city.

Atarah's heart skipped a beat as they passed an enormous, tan stone building with long columns lining the outside. Ben said the building was the library. He had to physically pull her away from the building and promised to take her tomorrow, for they had to meet with his parents tonight to discuss battle plans. The reminder of the battles currently going on brought Atarah back to focus on why she was there. Her brother and Noah could be in the mix of battle as they spoke. She couldn't afford to be distracted at this time.

Ben brought them before a large building, strangely not made of gold, but of white marble that had small hints of gold. The building was square at the bottom, but rounded out into a dome shape at the top where three figures stood.

Atarah focused on the two Head Archs beyond the entrance of the door. There stood Ben's parents: Aesop Doctrina, the Head of House Selaphiel, and his wife Sophia Doctrina. Atarah saw some of Ben's features from both parents—dark brown hair, soft brown eyes, and golden-tan skin, from his dad—but the same light brown wings as both of his parents. Their wings were relaxed at their sides. Aesop had some silver in his hair, speaking volumes of his age. His face was stern and stoic, while Sophia's face was one of gentleness and kindness. She had reddish-brown hair, with beautiful green eyes that stood out against her tan skin. Ben seemed to take after his father a little bit more. Despite the contrast in personality, the reception was welcoming and warm.

Atarah's eyes drifted to Ben. She expected him to be excited at being home, but saw something different. Though there wasn't a drastic change in his outward appearance, Atarah noted a stiffness in his posture. Ben's wings, which had been relaxed since she'd met him, were now flared and alert. Since he was on guard, an uneasiness coiled in Atarah's belly. She looked back at Aesop and Sophia, now unsure. As elusive as Ben was, she trusted him. Ben's wings twitched a little. He glanced at her quickly before turning back to his father.

"Welcome to our region and our home," Aesop said, spreading his arms wide in greeting. His voice was deep and smooth like Ben's. "Please join us in the triclinium. We have much to discuss."

He moved farther into the house and walked up some enormous steps. Sophia followed suit after giving her son a short embrace, while Atarah and Charlotte received an encouraging smile. Atarah thought of her own mother as she ascended the steps after the Heads of Selaphiel.

They entered the triclinium, where there were several settees, as well as a long, thin table in between. The room was adorned with rich turquoise colors along the sides of the walls and accented with the furniture. But that wasn't what caught Atarah's attention. Two male Archangels already sat in the room, calmly waiting for them, and both stood as they entered. One was slightly taller and had lighter colored eyes, green and brown, while the slightly shorter male had a lighter color of brown hair but darker eyes. Another mixture of their household.

"Welcome, daughters of Michael and Raphael. I am Amos, eldest son of Aesop and Sophia," the tallest one spoke, wings relaxed, very military and stone faced.

"Good evening. I am Canaan, the second eldest son." Canaan waved his hand over to the empty chairs across from them. He appeared warmer in comparison to Amos, but neither were anywhere close to as warm as Ben in personality.

"Surely we can clean ourselves up before the plotting begins?" Ben spoke for the first time since they'd arrived at his home. There was a slight hitch in his voice. Atarah could feel herself leaning toward Ben as if to soothe his uneasiness. "I like to be clean when plotting the doom of others."

There was a strange shift in Aesop's eyes before he spoke. "If we had time, we would've most certainly given it to you. I'm afraid no one has the luxury of time."

Atarah and Charlotte walked over and sat down across from the two heirs. Atarah was more than ready as she studied this elusive family. She regarded Sophia, Amos, and Canaan. Out of habit now, she extended her senses to fill the whole room. They were indeed alone, no guards to ambush them. Atarah glanced at Ben and felt his accelerated heart rate. Atarah was concerned by his demeanor. Aesop returned his attention to both Atarah and Charlotte. Atarah sensed Charlotte's heart rate increasing as well. Her muscles clenched, and she was trying her best to keep her wings from flaring. Apparently, she didn't trust this family either.

"Now, let us begin," Aesop said in a grave voice. His tone sounded heavy. "Uriel Region, where both of your brothers have returned from, has been overrun. Last night, the Head Tree fell, and the barrier was broken. Demons have overrun the city of Aquam Caput, and the angels are now fleeing their home region."

Atarah and Charlotte's wings flared as the gravity of his words hit home. The Head Tree fell. The barrier that protected everyone was destroyed, not breached or weakened, but destroyed! Had Arick and Noah made it there in time? The uneasiness that coiled in her belly became ice cold, knotted fear. Her wings shook with anxiety. *A city–a capital city–has fallen!* This gave precedent that any barrier could fall to the demons.

Atarah shifted her gaze back to Aesop, Amos, and Canaan. They all wore grave and serious expressions.

"Since we're the closest region, the Uriel soldiers are fleeing into our capital by the thousands." He frowned. "They will be in dire need of healing and aid." Aesop glanced at Charlotte. "They're injured, hungry, and exhausted. However, they're not our only concern." He sighed and looked at Atarah. "The legions of demons are following their retreat here, killing those who are too weak to keep up with the rest of the retreating soldiers and civilians."

Atarah strained to keep her wings still, but Charlotte's wings flared, her face a mixture of shock and fear. *She's lived her whole life behind a Tree's barrier. To hear one has fallen must be unsettling.*

"The retreating masses will come here—at our estimate, by nightfall." Aesop looked directly at Atarah. "We're not sure how long our barrier will hold out before both of your brothers realize the battle is now here. We may not last one night."

Atarah nodded. She needed to be ready as well. She looked around at all of the Selaphiel family. There was more that needed to be spoken, but no one wanted to say it. In the end, it was Aesop.

"We learned about your ability to enhance border protection, and that's what we'll need help with," he spoke.

Atarah resisted the urge to look at Ben. How had they found out about her connection to the tree? She had yet to speak of it. Was this part of their mind reading powers?

"However, strengthening our border won't be as easy as it was in Raphael's region."

"How so?" Atarah spoke for the first time.

"You were able to strengthen the walls because of your familial connection to the region. You have no connection here, so our tree will reject any offering you give."

"What was your solution to this?" Atarah asked hesitantly.

"You'll need to marry into the family in order for you to establish the connection to strengthen our border."

Atarah looked sharply at Aesop; her wings flared. She was suspicious this was the only solution. Nonetheless, she waited. Female heirs grew up knowing that they could be married to a different house for political gain. Nonetheless, under normal circumstances, marriage was always discussed with the entire family present.

She glanced at Ben once more. She couldn't shake off the unease she felt with Ben's reactions. His wings were slightly flared, and his heart rate was that of someone in battle. Easygoing Ben was now tight with the tension he was fighting.

"Or," Aesop continued, "you could try to strengthen the border, while staying connected to one of our sons. We're not sure how effective this will be, and sadly, we are running out of time. We have at most a few hours." Aesop regarded Atarah with a serious expression, waiting for her response.

"Hold on!" Charlotte said in outrage; her wings flared and vibrated in anger. "We barely made it into this city, the dirt of the road still on our backs, and you're insisting on marrying Atarah to your son whom she's just met? Have you no consideration?" Charlotte said in frustration.

Atarah was mildly surprised by Charlotte's reaction. The quiet, soft, shy Charlotte seemed outraged for her. A warmth spread throughout Atarah's heart as love for Charlotte soared. Aesop didn't react to her outburst, still keeping his gaze on her. This was her first challenge as a diplomat in another region and she didn't want to shame her family. Atarah pondered for a moment before asking.

"What would've happened if we hadn't made it in time? If Elijah had decided for us to go somewhere else?"

"Elijah knew about this, which is why we thought this was the best plan," Ben said from the back wall.

Atarah froze. From her senses she could tell Aesop, Amos, and Canaan gave Ben a withering glare for a half a second before becoming impassive once more. Ben had revealed so much in such a seemingly innocent sentence. She looked at him again. He was tense, and his wings were still flared. As if he was internally fighting with himself. Why would Elijah send her here if he knew Aesop would ask for a speedy marriage? Ben was trying to communicate with her in his own elusive way. He knew she didn't want marriage. Gratitude bloomed in her heart for Ben as she solidified her resolve. She stood, which captured everyone's attention.

She looked at Aesop. "Who else is involved in this?"

"Our family, of course," Aesop said lightly.

"How long have both of you planned this?"

"Amos only found out a while ago," Aesop answered vaguely.

"No," Atarah said calmly. "How long have you and Elijah planned to marry me to your family?"

Aesop paused and regarded her. A ghost of a smile came across his lips. "A while."

Selaphiel angels couldn't tell a direct lie. Charlotte gasped in surprise, while Amos and Canaan looked mildly impressed.

Atarah grinned at Aesop, not at all surprised by either of their actions. "Like you said, we don't have much time. There may be several solutions to the defense problem we're having, but first we need to get to the Head Tree."

"Hmm." Aesop sighed. "You'll make an amazing addition to the family, Atarah. Amos, show them to the tree core to reinforce the barrier. My wife and I will be at the South Gate, giving what help we can. All of you are to join us there when you're finished." He stood, extending a hand toward his wife.

All of them stood to start moving.

Sophia walked toward Aesop and clasped his hand, before turning to address Atarah in a soft voice. "No one knew enhancements could be made on the tree. Please be careful. This is uncharted territory."

She reminded Atarah of her own mother, which caused her heart to squeeze a little. Atarah could only nod in response, before looking to Amos. He quickly led the way out into the hallway. Atarah and Charlotte followed. They walked farther into the main home, each corridor as amazing as the last. White-and-blue marbling accented with silver lined the walls as they walked by. The tall ceilings reminded her of home—Sanctum, the city in the mountains—while the winding hallways reminded her of Ventus.

They all travelled through the hallways in silence. Amos stood tall with his wings set high and lifted away from the ground—military posture. His dark hair was short, and his high cheekbones gave him a harsher looking appearance. His face gave nothing away. Atarah still felt shaky from the encounter with Aesop. She had never portrayed herself with so much confidence and authority. She allowed herself a small victory at being able to evade a marriage proposal, while not making the Michael Clan an enemy of the Selaphiel Clan. Her victorious celebration didn't last long as she focused on the next step, Selaphiel's Head Tree. Demons were able to destroy a Head Tree. Atarah shuddered at the thought of what happened to Aquam Caput when the barrier broke.

She glanced at Charlotte, who looked uneasy. She didn't blame her if she was wondering how Ventus was doing. Was there a barrier still up? How far away was her father? As the questions filled her head, she forced herself to think of solutions. They came to a circular entryway before a sound caught their attention.

"Wait!"

Atarah turned to find Ben running after them. He reached them in no time, glancing at Atarah once before turning to his older brother. "Let me be the one to help with the Head Tree."

"Absolutely not. She needs someone with a strong connection to the Selaphiel Clan."

"I have a strong connection as one of the heirs, and if something goes wrong, the eldest son shouldn't be in the line of fire," Ben argued. "Let it be me, in case something goes wrong."

Atarah hadn't considered the possibility of something going wrong. She remembered how she'd had to fight against the flow of the tree in Silva and grew concerned. What if the tree rejected them? What happened if the current was too strong and they became stuck? Atarah looked at Ben, suddenly unsure.

Amos looked at his younger brother, looked at Atarah, then back to Ben. It seemed as if they were conveying messages to each other. *So, this is what it's like to witness mind reading*, she thought.

Eventually, Amos nodded. "All right. Learn as much as you can to help defend our city." He clasped Ben's shoulder. "Also, take these." He handed Ben long, thick ropes that had hooks on the end. She wondered briefly what the rope was for, but a pendant with a silver circular center caught her eye.

Ben rolled his eyes at the pendant. "I won't need this, Amos."

"Just in case you need your big brother to help." Warmth entered his eyes for the first time as Amos tousled Ben's hair.

Ben gave him an irritated look and ducked to avoid his teasing hand.

"Good luck down there, Arch ladies. If he gives you too much trouble, feel free to press the call signal as well." With that, Amos ran down the hallway to join the rest of his family at the South Gate.

"That's a call signal for help?" Charlotte inquired.

"Yeah," Ben said sheepishly. "They usually try to give me one every mission. It can be very annoying. But let's get going now. The sun's starting to set. Down this way!"

He descended a white marble, spiral stairway with blue accented lines, lined with silver lanterns and an occasional window that allowed in more light. Even with the setting sun in the distance, the stairwell didn't seem as dark as Atarah expected. Ben grabbed hold of one of the lanterns and quickly descended. Atarah and Charlotte followed suit as they ran down the stairs against the setting sun. The tree's core was deep beneath the surface of the Arch's familial home. Charlotte panted with exertion and started to slow.

Atarah grabbed her hand and pulled her forward. "Come on. Just a little bit farther."

Charlotte could only nod and push forward.

"Up ahead!" Ben said.

They came into a wide-open room that seemed to be made of glass. All of the surrounding walls and flooring had a thick sheet of glass with the tree hanging from the ceiling. Through the clear glass, they could see a red, sand-like soil that surrounded them. The glass held the shifting sand in place or else reaching the Tree would have been impossible. Hanging around the Head Tree were dozens of large silver lanterns providing the only light in the whole room. Surprisingly, the Head Tree was as big as the one in Ventus, with a large base, thick branches, and green leaves filling every branch. The base of the tree and the roots dug into the earth, reaching upwards, giving its richness to the city above them.

It was stunning. The lanterns looked like twinkling stars dancing around the massive tree. Atarah's breath was taken. For a second, she wished Sanctum had its own Head Tree. Atarah shook her head. Now was not the time.

"What's your plan, dove?" Ben asked, his deep brown eyes on her for a moment.

Atarah furrowed her brow in thought. Aesop said the connection with this Head Tree wouldn't be simple. She looked at Ben and Charlotte.

"I think you and I need to be touching when I connect with the Tree. Aesop said it would be difficult without a strong familial connection, so we will have to pray for the best." She sighed. "This, or I marry your brother before the demon horde gets here."

Ben's face stayed expressionless, but his wings flared ever so slightly. Charlotte looked apprehensively at the big tree.

"Charlotte, I'll need your help to keep my strength up. The Head Tree back in Ventus took a lot out of me. I'll need all the help I can get," Atarah finished.

They both nodded. They all hoped this would work.

Atarah opened her wings wide and launched herself into the air. Ben and Charlotte were right behind her. She circled the tree before flying high and close to the base and grabbing onto the thick trunk. Ben and Charlotte landed on either side of her. No more than a few inches away. Charlotte and Atarah had a hard time holding on while upside down. They nearly lost hold several times.

"Here, take these!" Ben said as he tossed a rope toward her and Charlotte. Atarah grabbed hold of it. Upon closer look, the rope had a looped hook at the end of it. As Atarah was about to ask how to use it, the rope expanded around the tree trunk on its own. The ends hooked deep into the tree, leaving a loop to go around Atarah's waist. Suspended in the tree now, Atarah straddled the tree and saw the same thing happen to Charlotte, as well as Ben. Ben was suddenly close behind Atarah. Not just close, but pressed up against her backside, suspended and straddling the tree just as she was. Heat flooded her face as she felt his body. Atarah pressed her face to the tree trunk to hide her blush from Ben.

"Um. . .Ben?" Atarah started. "You ready?"

She felt the heat of his body all along her back, and when he spoke, his breath was right in her ear. Ben put his hands around her waist. He wriggled his hands under the hem of her shirt, touching her bare skin. Atarah's wings vibrated, which further humiliated her. They were already under so much stress, with an army on the way, upside down clinging to a tree trunk, and yet her body felt excited beyond measure at his closeness. An electric feeling spread through her body from his touch. She peeked a glance back. She saw Ben's wings were vibrating too out of excitement, but his face looked sheepish and bashful at their predicament. His heart beat almost as fast as his wings.

"As ready as I'll ever be," Ben whispered in her ear, causing her to shiver.

Her heart beat erratically in her chest. Even his scent had an effect on her. Has he always smelled this good?

Since when did this happen? Atarah thought. She shivered at the slightest movement of his hands or body. She normally felt in control of her own body, but with Ben around it was getting harder and harder to hide the effect he had on her.

"Okay, Charlotte, are you ready?" Ben said.

Atarah couldn't see his face, but his body tensed up behind her. She looked at Charlotte, who suddenly seemed very interested in the tree trunk before them. She was blushing too.

"Yeah, I'm ready for anything. Don't worry, Atarah."

Atarah could only nod. She placed her outstretched hands before her on the tree trunk and tried to concentrate. Ben shifted his arms to encircle her waist. His warm arms heated her core, which transferred to her face immediately.

"Whenever you're ready," Ben said when she didn't move. He had whispered into her ear again, causing her to shiver once more.

His arms tightened in response, which made concentrating even harder for her. Thankfully because of his proximity, her wings were pinned down, so they could no longer embarrass her.

Atarah tried to concentrate on pushing her way into the tree, but was met with only the rough bark. She focused again, this time giving her full attention to the tree. She reached out again to expand her senses more. Her powers were nearing exhaustion. She'd been using her expanded senses all day and yesterday. She was tired, plain and simple. As if her very muscles were about to give out on her.

No, Atarah thought. *Push through a little bit longer.*

She strained as much of her power as she could into her arms and into the tree. While the tree core in Ventus had felt like she was moving through tar, in this tree she felt like she was moving a boulder. She pushed and pushed as her power drained rapidly.

She became vaguely aware of Ben talking behind her and a warm presence giving her quiet strength. She wasn't getting strength back, but she was no longer losing her energy. She felt a new sensation around her waist, a burning and tingling sensation. As the tingling sensation grew, she moved the boulder before her. The tingling spread to her arms, and she moved the boulder even farther. As it spread to her legs, she gained more momentum in moving the boulder. She pushed in what felt like an endless trek until suddenly a vastness overcame her. Her consciousness was finally in the current of the tree core. She felt the push and pull of the tree's barrier before her, gentle yet firm. Within the tree, she tried to gather her power once more to give to the barrier the tree created.

Please accept this offering, Atarah thought as she tried to push her powers into the current. She felt heavy backflow from the current, as if the tree was refusing. She pushed harder to get her powers into the tree's current for the barrier, and each time, the tree seemed to shut her off.

Please! Atarah pleaded as she continued to push her way through the current. *We're trying so hard to protect the soldiers and citizens. We only want to keep everyone safe.*

Charlotte, Ben, the soldiers fleeing from persecution, and the other Arch families needed to know the barrier wouldn't fall tonight or any other night. *Other Arch cities will be restored, our enemy will fail, and it all starts with this one,* Atarah pleaded with the tree.

The strength of the resistant current lessened, and her power flowed from her heavily. Atarah realized quickly it wasn't only her power flowing from her, but Ben's and Charlotte's as well. She could feel their power passing through her. Her power felt hot, pulsating, and forceful, while Charlotte's powers felt calm and cool, like a river of water flowing through her. Ben's powers were different. His felt electrifying, sporadic, and wild. Atarah watched with amazement as their powers passed through her arms and into the vastness of the Head Tree's network.

The tree accepted their offer of help with a gentleness she hadn't expected. The current now seemed to hold her, guide her, and showed her how the other cities were doing. It didn't last long. She was shown flashes of other cities and towns within different regions. They were shown so fast Atarah couldn't fully register what she saw. All too soon, Atarah was slammed back to reality, back to Ben and Charlotte. She gasped and collapsed against the tree, completely weakened. Ben also seemed to collapse on top of her, but with shaky knees, he was able to not completely crush her.

Atarah turned to Charlotte and saw she'd passed out from exhaustion, hanging limply from the rope. Ben released both his own rope and Atarah's, causing them to freefall to the ground. She was too exhausted to care about the impact of the ground; she simply clung to Ben. Mercifully, Ben flared his wings wide to soften the landing. He lowered her gently to the ground and flew back up for Charlotte. His flight back seemed to take a lot of effort for him. He released the rope for Charlotte and simply fell from the ceiling like last time, flaring his wings at the last second to soften the landing. He lowered Charlotte to the ground before collapsing in between them, also fatigued.

"I think . . . we should . . . rest here . . . for . . . a minute . . . or so," Ben said in between gasps.

"Yeah, that's a great plan," Atarah said.

"Did it work?" Ben panted.

Atarah turned to look at him. His torso covered in sweat, eyes closed as he laid on his back, taking in deep breaths.

"Yeah, it worked."

Ben looked at her and gave a tired smile. "Ha! Not what I imagined for my first time bringing a girl home. But how much control do we really have in those kinds of things?"

Atarah chuckled. "It's *females*. You brought two *females* home."

Ben laughed and turned to look at her once more. His wings weakly vibrated. "You're right. Not how I imagined bringing two females home." He heaved a big sigh and got to his feet.

Atarah tried the same, but she could only muster strength to roll to her side.

"We're going to feel this in the morning," he groaned.

"How much I would give for a shower right now," Atarah whined.

"Here, here," Charlotte said weakly from where she lay.

Atarah and Ben both let out a cheer at hearing her voice.

"She lives!" Ben yelled joyously.

"Glad to see you made it, Charlotte!" Atarah said sincerely.

Charlotte moaned. "I don't think I can make it up those stairs."

Atarah gave standing another try and was able to get to her feet this time, shaky but not falling down.

"I can help," Atarah and Ben said at the same time. They gave each other a sheepish smile as they wobbled over to Charlotte.

"Did it work?" Charlotte asked with so much hope in her voice Atarah's heart squeezed inside her chest.

She laughed and nodded.

"Ha, thank goodness!" Charlotte said. "Took everything I had to keep both of you afloat for all the power you were giving."

"I felt both of you when I was in the current," Atarah said as she and Ben helped Charlotte up.

"Is that what happened?" Ben asked. His wings seemed to perk up. "I felt like my power and my soul were being sucked out of me while I held onto you."

Atarah blushed a little, remembering his hold. She put one of Charlotte's arms around her shoulders, while Ben did the same from the other side. They made their way to the stairs.

"At first, I couldn't get through or get the tree to accept our power to help."

"The tree refused your help at first?" Ben asked, grunting up the stairs.

Atarah nodded, straining to make it up the stairs. "I tried with my power to help the barrier, but the tree refused. Only when I pleaded and felt both of your powers flow through me did the tree accept it. The tree then added our power to the barrier."

"Good thing the tree core didn't take all of our power," Ben said. "It'll probably take me a full week to recover from this."

"That's not all."

Ben and Charlotte looked at her, waiting.

"It showed me how the other Head Trees were doing throughout each region."

Ben's wings seemed to perk even more.

"How are the other Clan's barriers doing?" Charlotte asked eagerly.

Atarah's wings fell a little lower. "Not good. They're still holding up, but every barrier is significantly weakened."

Chapter 9

Ben

Ben was more than eager to take a shower and collapse in his bed. Muscles he never knew existed quivered, pleading with him to rest. Only when exhaustion set in did Ben feel his body not following his command. His control over his wings and body was something he took pride in. Even his older brothers hadn't fully mastered it like he had.

All three of them finally reached the top of the stairs. They all took a moment to breathe and rest before moving onward. Ben already dreaded trying to guide them to their room. His body protested and demanded he leave them there to find his own solace.

"I wasn't even this tired when we fought that viper outside the city," Charlotte mumbled.

Atarah gave a humorless chuckle.

"Whatever scared the viper away . . ." Atarah trailed off.

Ben paused too, following her train of thought. She looked up at him with those mesmerizing eyes, as his stomach clenched with horror.

"It couldn't be . . .maybe it has nothing to do with the demon horde," Atarah said softly.

He knew better. He could see how it all made sense in her head. She had learned many battle tactics and strategies growing up.

"We need to go now and warn everyone!" he said urgently. Even as he tried to move to a fast walk, his body nearly gave out on him.

"What's going on?" Charlotte asked, now on edge, trying to follow Ben.

Atarah's eyes stunned Ben again, but fortunately she answered.

"The viper we encountered on the outskirts of the region was a big sign for us," she panted, also trying to walk quickly down the corridor. "Ben said those vipers only leave when something bigger and meaner is in the area. Which means there's a huge demon in the area right now!"

Ben nodded. "That demon's waiting for the troops to get here and use the other demons to herd us. It's all a trap to get us in the city. Ugh, damn this! I really didn't want to use this."

Ben grabbed the caller Amos had given him. Amos and Canaan wouldn't let him live this down for weeks—if they all made it through the night.

He pressed the button firmly but still continued to trudge toward the entrance of his home. They needed to be warned the South Gate was about to be bombarded with a nasty demon that had been waiting for this moment. The wheels in Ben's head turned as he strategized what to do next and who they were fighting. The urgency brought life back to Ben's wings.

They made it to the entrance of his home and before he could blink, Atarah soared above his head, flying frantically toward the South Gate. Her usual flying was probably more graceful but with exhaustion setting in, this was as much as she could muster.

"Stay here, Charlotte," Ben said as he took off after Atarah.

"Yeah, right!" she huffed behind him.

He heard a vague flapping sound. However, he couldn't focus on her, especially now that the last of the sun's rays were gone. Nighttime was not their friend in this battle. Atarah was flying so fast she nearly crashed into Amos.

"Head back to the gate and pull everyone back!" Ben called as he flew closer.

"Everyone there's about to be ambushed!" Atarah said, trying to maneuver around Amos.

Amos dove in the air and turned back, flying toward the South Gate. All three of them flew as fast as they could, struggling to fly faster. It almost felt like flying in a dream, trying to fly fast, yet not truly moving.

Atarah gasped in horror, her super-senses picking it up before Ben could—a huge rumbling beneath the surface of the South Gate. It started out small but grew to the ground, sounding like it would explode.

They were within the view of everyone helping the soldiers on the ground at the South Gate. Ben saw his mother, father, and Canaan tending to soldiers and urging others to quickly come through the gate. Ben saw the last chunk of Malachi's soldiers off in the distance running from what could only be described as Hell chasing after them.

The horde of demons of all varying shapes and sizes and malformed bodies let out vicious growls that could be heard well beyond the gate. The distorted bodies of the demons were worse than any nightmare Ben could ever have, like a black-and-gray sandstorm determined to destroy and devour everything in sight. Demons usually had abnormally long limbs, yellow eyes, and blackened mouths with rotting teeth or fangs. Their gray torsos might be covered with scattered patches of unkempt fur or with extra limbs hanging out of their sides. Some resembled other creatures such as goats, goblins, reptiles, and spiders. Right now, their yellowed eyes were focused on the retreating angels of Aquam Caput. The demons would kill every male angel they could and abuse any female angel they could get their hands on. Ben shuddered inwardly as he remembered tales of how demons used female angels for breeding.

His chest tightened as Atarah flew faster than he'd thought she was capable of, and he pushed himself harder.

His parents came into view, flying toward them. They could see them looking confused by the rumbling beneath the ground.

"Run!" he called frantically.

His father and mother looked up. To Ben and Amos's horror, the ground exploded beneath their feet and tore through the entire South Gate. The largest viper Ben had ever seen ripped through the gate and slashed through anyone standing nearby. His mind went numb for a few seconds as the viper tore into every angel around it. The soldiers beyond the gate faltered in their stride as they saw the giant demon before them.

Ben's heart dropped with worry as Atarah charged at the viper.

"Atarah!" he called after her in vain.

The speed with which Atarah charged the viper was fearsome. The viper let out a horrifying sound that seemed to spur on the incoming demons, who were about to catch up to the last of Malachi's forces. The viper turned its head to strike at the struggling angels trying to escape until a cannon-like sound knocked the viper to the ground.

Ben blinked once to comprehend what had happened.

Atarah careened toward the viper, using her momentum and her insanely strong power to collide with the demon. The monstrous viper didn't stay down long, but neither did Atarah. She got up at lightning speed and dove again for the viper.

"Ben, come on!" Amos called to him. He was on the ground, trying to get as many people to safety as he could.

Ben thought of a strategy as he saw the terrified incoming soldiers trying to find a way around the viper. He soared higher and began to draw in his power. From above, he had a better shot. Thunder roared and lightning flashed around him, powering his tired body.

I can't let Atarah take on the monster alone, he thought.

Ben surged as much lightning as he could through his body and aimed at the incoming demon army. The lightning struck hard and true, despite his weakened state. While Atarah kept the viper busy, Ben busied the demon army. The last of Malachi's soldiers and citizens were able to get through the gate, where Amos directed them farther into the city.

Ben heard a scream at the entrance of the gate and knew it was Atarah. He dared a look and the blood drained away from his face at what he saw. Fear, pure crippling fear, rocked his whole body as he saw Atarah's injured body. She was bleeding heavily from her head, but he doubted she was aware. One of her wings was badly twisted and had to be causing mind-blowing pain all through her body. The viper used its large tail and smacked Atarah hard onto the ground outside the gate. They needed to get the viper outside the gate and put up the barrier. Ben heard Amos scream in pain as the viper now turned its attention to those inside the gate.

Stay calm and think logically, Ben thought, fighting the urge to fly to Atarah. *How can we seal off the entrance without the viper?* He needed to think of a plan fast in order to save everyone he loved.

His gaze moved from Atarah, struggling to her feet, to Charlotte below in deep concentration. Everyone who passed by her was instantly healed. That was the power of an advanced healer. An idea came to Ben's mind, but he needed to act quickly.

"Charlotte! Get closer to the gate," he yelled down to her.

Fortunately, she heard him and started to move toward the gate, not breaking her healing concentration. Ben dove, trying to get as much acceleration as possible, while concentrating on the surge of electricity flowing through him. The viper, not to be fooled twice, reared its hideous head at Ben and moved to attack. Viciously sharp, yellow teeth came at him, but didn't deter him in the slightest. He launched himself into the viper's mouth, down into its acidic intestine, and surged electricity all throughout the viper's insides. Thick slime coated the inside and all around him, constricting. The slime almost immediately began to burn as he surged electricity through himself. The familiar icy hot feeling of his powers darted throughout his body. The snake's body shook as it hissed from the outside. It coiled its body tighter, trying to squeeze the life out of him.

Ben pressed on and on and on, not letting up in the slightest with his electricity. Static and thunder roared all around him, building upon itself until suddenly Ben was outside the viper and fell to the ground.

Ben tried to get oriented to his surroundings, but his body had now completely given out on him. All he could do was turn his head. To his dismay, the last thing he saw before drifting off was the bloodthirsty demons charging at him and his beloved city.

"Atarah!"

Atarah squinted through one swollen eye to see Charlotte coming toward her. As she got closer, the blinding pain in her wing subsided. Her powers felt like a cooling cream, soothing against the burning pains and aches of her body. By the time Charlotte was close enough to touch Atarah, she was healed enough to stand and fight again.

She turned as Ben dove into the viper's mouth. *What on earth is he thinking?* Atarah thought, outraged.

Sparks erupted from the viper. Thunder roared above them as if in anger. Atarah understood. Ben was attacking from within.

Lightning surged from inside the demon, causing it to howl in pain. She saw another strike from inside, and the demon howled some more.

He's close to finishing it off! Atarah thought. She looked beyond them and saw yellow, hungry eyes and deformed bodies with rotten, sharp teeth coming for them.

"Charlotte, now's a good time to close the gate," Atarah said, not taking her eyes off of the approaching chaos.

She sensed Charlotte nodding beside her. She took Charlotte's hand and ran to the rubble of the South Gate. Atarah grabbed hold of the crumbled South Gate and extended her hand toward Charlotte, who was looking at the approaching army, terrified.

"It'll be alright, Charlotte," Atarah tried to reassure her. "As long as we get the gate up, we'll manage."

Charlotte nodded, grabbed her hand, and knelt in concentration. Atarah concentrated as well and expanded her powers within the barrier. She reached out, beseeching the Head Tree for its help. She could feel the power of the Head Tree coming from the ground and surging throughout her body. The power was so strong it felt like it was burning her. Another power traveled through her from Charlotte—a cool, healing touch. Charlotte's power soothed, while the Head Tree's power was an inferno, bringing the barrier back together. Slowly but surely, the gate formed itself once again from rubble to a strong, hard stone wall. Just as the demon army closed in, the barrier closed. Blocking the entrance. Atarah released her hold on the power to watch with relief. The dome-like barrier returned, cascading downward around the perimeters of the city.

Atarah and Charlotte screamed with joy as the south wall and gate repaired itself. A loud pop drew Atarah's attention away from the gate to see Ben falling out of the viper. The viper now laid dead outside the gate, and to Atarah's horror, Ben collapsed, Hell's army a mere few paces from where he lay.

Atarah sprinted for him without thought.

"Atarah, no!" Charlotte cried.

The South Gate closed behind Atarah, completely sealing her off from the city. But she wouldn't leave Ben behind to die by himself.

She reached him just as a demon did. Its body was that of a half man, half goat—a faun. Its lower half made up of goat legs was patchy and unkempt. With balding spots of gray fur, scars covered its entire torso, making the skin look hardened, gray, and unhealthy. It had two horns on its head and spikes along its face, giving it a fierce look. Its yellow eyes were fixated on Ben's lying form. It swung high with its axe to give Ben the finishing blow, but it never came.

Atarah dove and jabbed the demon under its arm, disarming it and causing it to fall. The demon growled in anger. Atarah barely gave it a second glance as she took its axe and swiftly chopped its head off. She stood ready for the next demon—a scaly demon with features of a lizard but with as many legs as a spider—and she quickly dispatched its arms and then its head. The next attack came from three demons at once, who tried to use rope to disable her. Atarah had to keep from laughing. She was not the strongest or fastest out of the Michael Clan, but compared to these demons, she was a fierce warrior.

She slashed, dove, maneuvered, and cut down all who came after her. She focused her power and forced it outward, knocking back a few of the oncoming demons. The projection of force she used as she fought grew weaker and weaker with each blow. She needed a way out fast. She knew she could not hold this many off for long. She frantically thought through all of her training to think of something that would get them away from the army.

She had a ridiculously reckless idea.

I have no other choice if I want to make it out of this alive, Atarah thought as more of the army approached.

While she normally pushed out her power in a burst and could get out of most fights that way, it appeared in this instant she had to use her other tactics. Atarah moved her power from an outward path to an inward path. She poured her energy into her muscles, nerves, and skin. She concentrated and absorbed her power within her body to create armor: the infamous Michael Armor. Only the Archs in the Michael Clan had enough strength to call the Armor forth. She had only ever brought her familial armor out one other time, during her training, never in battle.

She hadn't been able to maintain it—until now when her life depended on it. She took a deep breath, bringing in all of her power, then held her breath against the crushing weight of the armor. It felt like trying to hold a deep breath of air in the deepest part of the ocean. The crushing weight of the ocean depths was not something anyone could withstand for long. Nonetheless, the armor covered the entirety of the angel who wore it and strengthened their speed, strength, and power exponentially. Within the armor, the angel was nearly invincible.

Atarah needed to act fast; she couldn't maintain the amount of power she needed to keep the armor on. She grabbed hold of a fallen sword and surged her power into the weapons. She took a deep breath and slashed the demons closest to her. The larger bulk of the army now surrounded her and Ben, snarling and sneering at them. All charged at her, trying to overtake her by sheer numbers alone.

Atarah took another deep breath in and as she let her breath out, she shot her power from her sword and her axe, severing all the bodies within arm's length of her. Surprised by the display of power, the demons were hesitant to approach. Atarah used that as her chance to escape. She grabbed Ben around the waist, launched herself into the sky, and careened over to the gate.

Please work, Atarah thought as they free-fell toward the glass-like dome on top of the wall. She hoped and prayed that the barrier would recognize them as friends and not foes, for she no longer had the strength to fight. Mercifully, the dome opened the passage and closed behind them. Arrows knocked against the dome, almost like falling rain. She released her hold on the armor.

She and Ben crumpled to the ground; her flared wings softened the landing just enough for her to stay conscious. She saw the rise and fall of Ben's chest. He was alive. Atarah sighed in relief and then regretted it. Every part of her body hurt. Even as her limp body laid still on the ground in the middle of the city, the pain was nearly overwhelming. The aftereffects of the armor took its toll on her body. Her head, arms, legs, and back were all in pain. Even breathing hurt!

"Atarah!"

Atarah groaned and rolled over, painfully, to see who called her name. Charlotte ran toward their crumbled bodies. *Poor Charlotte*, Atarah thought. *She was probably worried sick when I ran past the gate.*

Charlotte's eyes were red from crying, and her legs trembled with each step. She collapsed on top of Atarah, causing her more pain, but she didn't mind. Charlotte sobbed on her chest. Atarah wriggled what she could of her arm around Charlotte to comfort her. She felt a little shame from the distress she'd caused Charlotte. She'd already been through so much, from rough traveling, to having almost all of her power get sucked out, to fighting for everyone's lives all in the span of a few hours. A few hours! Had it really been only hours since they'd arrived?

Atarah thought back on all the events that had unfolded today. She couldn't believe she'd taken on almost a whole army by herself, she reflected, amazed. She had done it. *She* had actually succeeded in fighting against demons *and* saved Ben.

Finally, she thought, *that's what I am supposed to do! I shouldn't celebrate!*

The pain in her body was excruciating, but it was a reminder that she had made it out alive. She looked at Ben and Charlotte and was grateful for them. They were good friends to have by her side.

Atarah noticed Charlotte had fallen asleep beside her and stifled a giggle. She was tempted to leave her alone, but their work wasn't done yet.

"Ben, are you up yet?" she asked. She looked him over quickly to see if any major injuries were prevalent. She found nothing, thankfully.

She was met with silence. He was only unconscious, probably from exhaustion. She lightly flapped her wings on top of his head, which startled him awake. "Oh good, you're up now. Did you have a nice nap, Sleeping Beauty?"

Ben gave her an irritated glance and groaned as he sat up, then tried to stand. "Ugh, how am I not dead?"

Atarah tried the same, careful to not wake Charlotte. She attempted to use her power to sense anything around her body. She shook with effort, only able to sense a breath away from her body. Her body was severely weakened. Her muscles ached and the exhaustion was physical, spiritual, and emotional. She had pushed the limit. However, she was thankful that no bones were currently broken. She could move. It would be painful, but it could be done.

"Let's not linger on those details. We should look into how everyone else is doing."

Ben nodded. He was standing, but barely. Both of them were exhausted from the tree core and from the battle. What little of their power remained helped them with minimal tasks until they took some time to rest. They weren't far from the South Gate. Atarah wondered how Ben's family fared. After the viper had broken through the gate's barrier, she hadn't seen them in the madness. She turned to Charlotte's sleeping form and reluctantly woke her up.

Charlotte's eyes fluttered open, red from crying or exhaustion; Atarah wasn't sure.

"We have to get moving," Atarah said gently.

Charlotte rubbed her eyes and struggled to her feet. Her legs reminded Atarah of a newborn calf, shaking and wobbling. After Charlotte's fourth attempt to stand, Atarah tucked her wings in tight and told Charlotte to hop on her back.

"I can walk on my own," Charlotte insisted.

"I know you can, but save your energy for the angels we're about to help. They'll desperately need to be healed," Atarah said. She wasn't the only one who'd been attacked by the viper.

Charlotte grudgingly agreed and climbed on her back. Atarah bit her lip to not cry out against the pain. Once on her back, she could feel Charlotte's cooling power relieve her of the aches and pains. It didn't heal everything, but it was enough relief for her to walk.

"Save your strength," Atarah muttered. "There are many who are worse off than me."

Ben was already walking ahead of them by the time Charlotte was on her back. Atarah trotted after Ben, praying there wasn't too much damage and that his family was all right.

Their progress to the South Gate was slow but steady. As they got closer, they saw more and more injured citizens. Charlotte was tense with concentration, healing those around them. They didn't heal immediately like before, but they healed. Atarah even heard bones cracking back into place slowly as they walked on.

The closer they walked to the South Gate, the denser the crowd became. Finally, they rounded a corner to see the gate. Ben hurried off in one direction as she tried to move to where the most bodies lay. Charlotte started to tremble with effort as she continued to help. As the minutes ticked by, some soldiers were healed enough to walk on their own. Atarah directed them to spread out and help others.

She looked at the South Gate, and what she saw unnerved her. Demons were lined up; their endless yellow eyes stared soullessly at everyone beyond the gate. They varied in shapes and sizes, but they all had gray, mangled, and scarred bodies. They weren't growling or exhibiting hysterical behavior. Now they stood perfectly still and as quiet as the dead. The sight was extremely unsettling.

At least they're not attacking the barrier anymore.

Atarah heard someone call her name in a desperate tone. She turned and saw Ben, who motioned for her to follow him. She grabbed hold of Charlotte and followed Ben. On the far side of the gate, Atarah saw Canaan covered in blood and barely holding onto his life. His heartbeat sounded weak. Canaan's lower half seemed to be crushed, and his wings stuck out at odd angles. Amos and Ben were by his side, imploring him to keep his strength. Amos had a nasty wound on his shoulder, turning his entire arm nearly black. Ben, despite his injuries and exhaustion, looked to be in the best health out of his brothers. Atarah put Charlotte down by Canaan and hoped for the best. Charlotte placed her hands on Canaan and put all of her focus on him. Several minutes went by and, surprisingly, nothing happened. Charlotte didn't break her concentration. A small part of Atarah's strength pulled toward Charlotte. When she realized the tug was there, Atarah gave her energy freely to help Charlotte.

More time passed and Ben became restless. Amos simply kept his head bowed and his hand over Canaan's still chest. Atarah continued to give her power to Charlotte while she worked.

"Why hasn't he awakened yet?" Ben asked, agitated.

"It's not a simple thing to bring someone back from the brink of death," Atarah said.

She wasn't sure it was true, but didn't know what else to say. She worried they'd pushed Charlotte too much. Amos's and Ben's heads popped up suddenly, as if something had caught their attention. They leaned in closer to their brother's still form. Canaan's chest rose and fell slowly. Atarah supported Charlotte as she fell back against her. Charlotte was truly amazing, Atarah thought. After everything, she'd held out until the very end.

Ben and Amos embraced their brother in relief.

"All that's next is to find—" Ben started, but was cut off by Amos's somber expression.

Ben's normally tan face turned white. He shook his head. Amos stood to walk over to where some rubble lay beside them. Atarah's heart hammered in her ears as she watched, helpless to what was to come. Amos moved the rubble with his good arm to reveal their parents, the Arch Heads of Selaphiel. Aesop and Sophia covered in blood; their bodies completely crushed. Aesop's body covered Sophia's protectively. Sadly, it hadn't been enough to save her life. They were both dead.

Atarah looked at Ben's still form and pale, expressionless face as he took in his parents' bodies. Horror and sorrow entrenched itself in Ben's eyes as he looked at his parents. Amos's face was somber and seemed to have aged in the few hours she'd known him.

Amos, now the new Arch Head of the House of Selaphiel, looked at their parents' ashen faces before saying, "We have much to do."

Arick was restless. Even as they rode to their battle, Arick couldn't get a nagging sensation out of his mind. Something didn't feel right. In battle, always trusting one's instincts was what every angel was taught in the House of Michael. His instincts told him something wasn't adding up.

They walked through Aquam Caput, the capital city of the Elementa Region. This was the region of the Arch House of Uriel. Yet not a single soul or demon was in sight. Not a single building was standing, nor a complete boat. The coastal city was burnt down, empty, desolate.

Noah seemed to have a similar feeling and sent two riders to the two neighboring regions before they descended upon this wasteland of a city.

"I never thought Aquam Caput could look like this," he said quietly. "Have you sensed anyone, Arick?"

"No. Not an angel or demon walks anywhere near this city," Arick said.

Noah seemed to be in despair as he looked at what would have been a plethora of ship docks lining the coast. Now all that remained was ashen wood and a blackened sea. Arick couldn't even sense any fish in the waters down below.

"Aquam Caput was one of the most beautiful places I've ever seen. To see it like this—" Noah turned and directed his soldiers not to set up camp for the night, for they would ride out soon.

"Where do you think they went?" he asked, turning back to look out at the sea.

"If Malachi's still alive, he'd want to get all of the citizens out of harm's way," Arick said. "From the looks of it, once their barrier collapsed, they tried to stall for time, for help that came too late."

Noah nodded. "If I were Malachi, I'd head for a city with a standing barrier. However, there were no more active barriers in any city in the Elementa Region, so I'd head to a different region."

"That'd be difficult with young angels. They could fly a good portion away, but after so long, their wings would fatigue."

"If they flew out, which they most likely did, they'd get a good amount of distance between them and the demons."

"The city closest to them with a standing barrier would be in the Arena Region. The next question is, would they go to the capital or simply the closest city?" Arick wondered. If he were Malachi, he'd go to the capital. There, they were the closest to the Head Tree and would have the strongest defense.

"I think Chrysi Poli would be their best bet. We could go there if we want to help Malachi," Arick said with confidence.

Noah looked to be in deep thought. He walked to his horse and grabbed his map of all of the regions and studied it. "Too many ifs to think of. We want to win the war and not the battle, correct?"

Arick looked at him pensively. "Why do you ask?"

"Come and look."

He walked over to where Noah stood and regarded the map.

"All the reports have said that the fight is in the south. How did the demons move north so quickly? And why attack Aquam Caput so hard?"

"I see the strategy here," Arick said thoughtfully. He pointed to the map. "They attacked Aquam Caput and are going across the continent to Chrysi Poli, effectively cutting the continent in half. Cutting off any reinforcements."

"The holes the demons are coming through started here"—Noah pointed on the map to a city named Mortem—"in the Southern Region. Most of the demons worked their way up the land from there. I want to know how to close those holes, so we don't have to keep chasing and fighting them off," Noah said, running a hand through his hair in nervousness.

Well, any soldier would be nervous, Arick thought.

Noah's heart rate sped up, since he'd presented a possible change of plans. Arick didn't blame him. To go see the destruction up close and this close to home—it should make him nervous.

"In the long run, ensuring the holes are closed will help every realm, not just the Arch clans," Arick said, agreeing with his logic.

"Then we shall leave in an hour." Noah turned to inform his soldiers.

"Noah," Arick called. "What are the Houses of Archangel Azrael and Archangel Raziel like?"

Noah paused. "Have you never heard of them?"

"I only know of rumors—that they can be quite difficult to work with."

Noah nodded. "House of Azrael is the one who killed our ambassadors. We aren't sure if it was on purpose or not."

"Are you saying they accidentally killed your angels?"

"Possibly. The House of Azrael is known as the Angels of Death. From what I was told, the Head Arch is calm and patient. I don't know what will happen when we arrive at his capital, Mortem."

"And the other clan?"

Noah mused, "The House of Raziel is known for knowledge, but the knowledge of secrets. They've always had a complex relationship with the House of Selaphiel."

"Do the houses differ in power?"

"The House of Selaphiel cannot tell a lie and seek out truths. The House of Raziel can tell lies, but keep the truth to themselves."

"It's not very nice to keep secrets from your friends."

"They kept their distance from all of the clans. I think Azrael at times will tolerate my house because their power doesn't easily affect us as much. Where do you think we should start?"

Arick looked out at the blackened sea and the damaged harbor around him. "House of Azrael. They're in the southernmost part, where the biggest hole was discovered. Let's see what was going on when it all happened."

"I was hoping you'd say that."

Noah turned to make his way down from the hill they stood on to inform his lieutenants. Arick took this time to gain what he could from his senses. While he wasn't as skilled as his sister, he wasn't completely incompetent either. He flew down to the old harbor to gather as much information as he could. He studied the sand, the burn marks on the docks, and the wreckage of the ships. All of the demons shuffled their feet, making it difficult to tell how many there had been. He picked up a broken canteen to scoop up some water. He sloshed it around the canteen and smelled the dark water. While it was mostly ash, he did smell something else unusual, something he couldn't quite name. The smell was something bitter . . . something . . .

"Heir Arick!"

He turned to see his small group already mounted and ready to head out. He chucked the water out and made his way to his horse. He trotted over to the small group of angels who were slowly becoming a team. At the beginning of their mission, he had asked Noah if he could create a small team for missions that would require more stealth. It would be easier to create a smaller team for scouting or short expeditions. Noah agreed, as long as it wasn't his best warriors.

Each of them stood out the most during all of the training sessions, by their determination. Arick had decided early on to approach them to train them even further. All eagerly agreed, to Arick's surprise. Since entering into Raphael land, Arick hadn't been received well by most Raphael angels. Possibly because of his size or his Arch house, Arick was never sure. They were either uneasy around him, wanted to challenge him, kill him, or feared him. Not these three angels. He gave a half grin at his rowdy, misfit bunch.

Brock, Galvin, and Jared were the most reckless angels of the army or the most stubborn. Who knew? They were some of the few angels who had mixed heritage between clans. While their predominant features were of the Raphael Clan, that didn't mean that they weren't the "oddballs" in Raphaelian culture. Arick couldn't have cared less.

"Playing in the water with your free time?" Brock said sarcastically. He often had a dry sense of humor. Arick had to pay attention to his tone to tell if he was joking or not. Brock was fairly short and stocky, barely taller than his sister. His brown hair was cut short in a military style. His off-white wings were relaxed by his side.

Galvin, to Brock's left, sat quietly waiting, looking around curiously. Galvin wasn't able to speak, but no one knew why. He was a tall, skinny soldier. He was nearly as tall as Arick, but his skinny stature made him appear weaker. His shallow, pale face often made other soldiers uneasy, but none of them seemed to mind. His hair was jet black, but when the sun hit his head just right, one could see streaks of blue. His dark eyes shined with his unspoken intelligence. His cream-colored wings hummed with laughter at Brock. Lastly Jared, the liveliest angel of their group, jabbed at Brock.

"You're just jealous you couldn't join him, Brock," Jared jeered.

Jared was the complete opposite of Galvin in nearly every way. If Galvin was a gray, rainy, and foggy day, Jared was a clear sky, sunny day. He was cheerful, talkative, and overall exuded positivity. His light brown hair was nearly blond and his eyes green. He stood in between Brock and Galvin in height, taking up the middle. Taller than Brock, but nowhere near Galvin or Arick.

Brock chuckled at his response.

They gravitated toward Arick easily. As if they had been friends for decades and not a mere week. Arick got close enough that they could hear him. "We're riding first to the Vallis Region now."

The small grins on their faces faded. They looked at one another, then him in hesitation.

"Should we not give aid to Malachi and his citizens?" Brock asked, not unreasonably.

"I understand wanting to help those who are close by. But if we really want to help everyone, we need to destroy the portal letting all the demons in. Follow the original plan, to travel to Mortem and provide aid there."

Galvin looked at Arick questioningly.

"Maybe, Galvin," Arick replied to the unspoken question. "We might have our own separate mission when the lands are secure."

Brock and Jared's eyes grew wide in surprise. Galvin looked on with curiosity; his wings hummed slightly.

"We will be ahead of the troops and the first line of defense on the way to Mortem, so be ready," Arick finished.

Brock made a face.

"Not fond of the Angels of Death, are you, Brock?" Arick teased.

He gave a small shake of his head to show his unease.

"No one's fond of them. They've always been the black sheep of all of the clans," Jared said.

"I think Arick knows that feeling already, Jared," Brock retorted.

Arick and Jared laughed until their sides hurt. Even Galvin gave several chuckles. Only Brock could get away with making such a jest.

Arick's laughter calmed after a bit, and he became serious. "The only weapon you'll have against Azrael angels is your ability to heal fast. Use it wisely and don't forget the training."

"If we live, we live. If we die, we die. What we do until we die is what matters the most," Brock said.

"Aye, aye!" Jared cheered.

Galvin gave an approving nod.

"Now that we're done with the serious stuff, let's move out!" Arick shouted. He reared his horse and started out on a steady trot heading south. He heard the hollers of his angels and the heavy pounding of hooves behind him.

Noah rode up with the rest of the troops. They caught up and stayed on the upper left flank. From the structure alone, Arick saw Aquam Caput had been lovely. The city sat between the tropical mountainside, giving the city the undisrupted view of the ocean. The potential the city showed had Arick wishing he could've seen it before it was destroyed.

Nothing lasts forever, I suppose.

Their horses ascended the mountain with some difficulty. Even along the roads, the thick brush was difficult to navigate through. The dense forest should have been teeming with activity and life; however, it was dead quiet. No birds chirped. No bugs buzzed. It was as if the forest was completely deserted. The forest was diverse with different plants, all in varying shapes and sizes Arick had never seen before.

There was little sunlight on the forest floor where they traveled because of the large leaves above. The visibility for the soldiers decreased as they went deeper into the forest. The dim light made avoiding the brush even more arduous. Arick heard some troops groaning as they struggled to get the twigs and thorns from their legs and arms. At high noon, this would be the most sunlight they would receive.

"Noah," Arick called. He urged his horse back. Slowing down to Noah, Arick voiced his concerns. "Our visibility will be zero in a few hours. It'd be wise to camp and train before that happens."

Noah didn't even glance at him. "No."

"Why not?" Arick demanded.

"We need to cover a lot of ground while we have visibility."

"Oh, so you know the way to Mortem with the fading light at our backs and the dense brush to fight against?"

"Say what you're not saying," Noah said roughly, finally looking at him.

"We can get lost easily, even with all of the light of noon. I'd rather not test the forest with fading light," Arick said with a raised eyebrow.

Brush in the distance swayed and the lack of sound gave cause for concern. Arick felt the forest closing in on him. He was, normally, the only one who was claustrophobic, but one glance back at the soldiers told a different story.

The angels marched onward as the forest surrounded them. The eyes of unseen forces around them, the echoed cries of terror, the pulling of the leaves, and the fading light—the forest didn't want them to cross. He didn't want other things to awaken from their marching.

Noah slowed his horse to a stop and launched himself into the air. Flying in the air, Noah had a good perception of how far and deep the forest went. Arick wondered if Noah could even sense the path before them.

Noah flew down and mounted his horse. "We'll make camp in an hour. Until then we travel at full speed. We may have to abandon the horses and fly the rest of the way," he said reluctantly.

Arick nodded. The troops wouldn't like having to fly such a far distance, especially with a battle looming ahead. Even growing up in the Michael Clan, young angels were taught to conserve their energy wherever they could. He urged his horse forward at a fast pace, deeper into the invasive forest. Their travels continued at the pace Arick started. The air grew thick and heavy, almost too heavy to breathe. Deep, long breaths were taken, fighting against the weight of the air. The tree line closed tighter and tighter until all of the troops were in single-file line formation. A heavy concentration of brush developed along the trails of the forest. The brush had thorns sprinkled all over its vines. Grabbing onto any article of clothing, the thorns pulled down their feet, while the air weighed down their chests. The troop's pace slowed throughout the hour to a meager shuffle.

Arick couldn't blame them. With the forest fighting against them, tiring them on the first day, the battles ahead would be daunting. However, his attention didn't waver against the eyes in the forest watching them. The eyes waited for them to be too weak to fight back.

"Not getting scared, are you?" Noah taunted.

Arick chuckled, as he glanced at Noah. Noah's face was beaded with sweat and his breaths were labored. "Only of the boogeyman," he said dryly. "What about you?"

"I have only one fear—failure. I suppose any good leader needs that fear though."

"I imagine all the heads of the Arch houses were scared when they first became leaders."

"Not all know they're afraid, apparently," Noah muttered.

Arick looked at Noah questioningly. "What do you mean?"

Noah grimaced. "My father said something to me a long time ago because I said the same thing. He said when you become the Head, fears come to light you never knew about. Depending on which of your fears is the strongest, that will show what type of leader you are."

"So, those who fear failure . . ."

"Will work themselves to the ground."

"But what other fears are there for a leader?"

"Fear of conflict, or a usurper, probably. Those come to mind."

Arick mused. They rode in silence for a while. The sounds of the forest filled the pauses left between them. "Loneliness. Fear of loneliness."

The travels continued past the hour Noah had initially said, much to the soldier's chagrin. Suddenly, the massive trees fell away, revealing an open, high-grass field. Noah finally flared his wings, signaling to stop and set up camp. The soldiers spread out and started to cut down some of the tall grass to make room for the camp.

Arick turned to his small group. Sure enough, they were all covered in sweat. Jared and Brock began the clearing, while Galvin unpacked from their saddles for camp. Arick took out their rations and started on their meal.

Galvin was about to start a fire before Arick intervened. "Don't start a fire. It'll give away our location to any lingering demons in the area."

Jared and Brock moaned in unison.

"Deprived of fire since our first night leaving Silva," Jared groaned.

"Oh, 'my love is like to ice, and I to fire,'" Brock recited.

"'To eat or not to eat. That is the question,' my poets," Arick purred with sarcasm.

Jared and Brock chuckled as they finished clearing the area. Galvin finished laying out the sleeping packs, completing their campsite. They all sat exhausted from the ride as Arick passed out their rations of grain, meat, and a little fruit.

They ate in silence as the darkness started to evolve around them. The lack of sounds from the day seemed to change as night descended upon them. Small croaks and chirps could be heard from their campsite. The sound gave Arick some comfort, knowing that other creatures were surviving. He took a moment to look around and see how the other angels were doing. The effects of the forest weren't as strong as before. The soldiers regained their energy now that they could rest and eat.

Let's see how they do with another day of traveling in the forest.

Arick got up to inspect the perimeter of the camp

and listened for any possible dangers. He walked slowly, occasionally pausing to listen. He made it about halfway around before something caught his senses.

He couldn't quite tell if it was his hearing or sight that became aware of it, but now he focused on the forest. He took a risk and stepped into the uncharted area. Within a few feet, the leaves and brush of the forest engulfed him. Even with all of the sounds and pitch-black darkness, Arick had a sense of where he was going. A humming noise started off low, then amplified as he walked. The noises grew louder, almost to the point where he wanted to cover his ears. He couldn't determine where the sound came from. Nonetheless, he easily evaded trees and thorns despite the darkness, but he was in too much of a trance to notice how odd this was.

Something was out here. Time went on as he walked forward. He tried to figure out what was drawing him closer. It wasn't like something called to him, but almost the opposite. The forest shifted from bleak to pure void. The noise fell away, and the leaves he felt along his sides dipped and withered.

He came to a clearing and the only word that came to his mind was death. There was an eerie silence around this part of the forest. A silence so loud that it made Arick's skin crawl. Even though it was dark, there was another type of darkness that surrounded him. A dark abyss, where all life was taken and there was pure nothingness. It unnerved him. He walked a little farther and nearly ran into a large rock. Arick put up his hand to feel his way along the rock, but when he touched it, he froze.

This wasn't a rock. Arick looked up with dread, but he needed confirmation. It was the Head Tree of the region in Elementa. Broken. Desolate. Forsaken. Arick started to shake. The barrier had been breached in Malachi's region because the tree was destroyed. If demons could destroy the Head Trees in each region, it would leave all of the clans defenseless.

He moved his hand along the trunk of the tree and felt ax marks along the base. He felt the abuse that had been dealt to the Head Tree. The marks went all around the trunk, high and low. He placed both hands on the tree's trunk in sorrow, then leaned in and placed his forehead on the trunk and felt its despair and despondency.

Arick concentrated and fell into the spirit of the tree. He felt no resistance, only bleakness and gloom. Nothing like Atarah described with her experience with the tree back in Silva. The flow of power Atarah talked about was now nothing but a dark puddle before him. There was no flow of power, no stronghold, and no glimmer of life. He could see its once great glory and how strong it would have been. The force of awareness Atarah had explained was nothing but a wisp of a whisper. The whisper was weak, yet carried sorrow and anger. The tree wanted to know what they were doing there.

"I am Arick, Heir to the Clan of Michael. I'm here to help. You aren't alone."

"I . . . am . . . always . . . alone." The anger seemed to be growing.

"Not anymore."

A strong, angry wind came at Arick, trying to push him out. He stumbled back, but held his ground.

"Not anymore," Arick said again with empathy.

A hissing sound came at him, and the wind bellowed. This time, the wind managed to push him back onto the ground. There was much more resistance now. This continued for some time. Arick got knocked to the ground repeatedly, but he didn't dare try to block any blows the tree gave. The tree's sorrow and anger came at Arick for hours. Each time, he stood back up. The only power the tree had came from its anger and sorrow now that it was cut off from the other Head Trees. However, Arick knew anger could only carry one so far. Slowly, as the hours passed, the tree's blows softened against its will.

"Not anymore," Arick whispered, nearly cracking with emotion.

The tree seemed to lose what little ferocity it had and fell silent, broken. "Leave."

This time, Arick knelt before the tree. "I won't. Please forgive me."

The winds moved around Arick in question, seeking an answer.

"We failed you."

The winds fell silent.

"I don't mean our army didn't reach you in time. We, the Clans, failed you a long time ago. Please let me show you we can redeem each other."

Arick was met with silence. He stayed where he was, head bowed upon a bent knee. He wanted to show his sincerity and that he truly was dedicated to bringing all of the Heads of the Clans together.

The wind drifted around him, evaluating him. "No . . . Clan of Michael . . . stands with . . . me . . ."

With that, the tree gave its last powerful push, completely pushing Arick out. He fell back, hurting his wings and groaning in pain. In rejection.

He heard clapping behind him and was alarmed for a few seconds. Noah stood behind him with his wings tucked in tight, but otherwise relaxed. Arick got up slowly to not hurt his wings further.

"Genius plan. Truly genius," Noah said sardonically.

Arick could still only groan in response. He noticed his surroundings and looked at Noah. "It's morning already?"

"Aye, just barely. It's been a long night."

"When'd you get here?"

"I followed you from the campsite last night," Noah said to Arick's surprise. "I followed you thinking you'd get lost, but you seemed to know where you were going. I grew suspicious until I saw the tree."

"I would've heard you if you'd followed me," Arick said with certainty.

"You should have. For the first ten minutes I followed you, I was calling your name. You looked to be in a trance."

"You followed me the whole way here?" Arick was amazed. "I didn't know you loved me this much, Noah," he finished sarcastically.

"Good thing I did," Noah scoffed. "I would've gotten lost, even with the lamp I had. It was too dark to see anything but your backside." Noah indicated a small lamp by his foot.

Now that he had more light, Arick took his time looking around the area. The clearing was still desolate and gray, but the surrounding trees seemed to be withering as well. Death was spreading farther and farther into the forest. As long as the Head Tree remained fallen, the whole area would fall.

"We need to make our way back," Noah said reasonably.

Arick nodded, walking to where Noah stood.

"I hope you know the way back to the camp," Noah said hesitantly.

"Eh, roughly. I have an idea of where we need to go."

"The angels will be up in about an hour or so. That should give us enough time to hurry back."

"We can move faster if we fly."

"Our visibility will be limited."

"As long as we follow the general path and listen for them, we'll be fine. I've also been waiting to spread my wings a little."

Noah looked back at the tree, then at Arick thoughtfully before nodding. They spread their wings wide and launched up into the sky. The wind slapped Arick's face, but he barely noticed. From above, he saw the vast forest before them, but beyond that, he spied mountains in the distance. His wings gave a small hum in excitement, while the rest of him felt numb after the initial sting of rejection from the Head Tree. He flew without any real feeling of his body.

Turning his attention to the forest before them, he retraced the steps he might have taken. Noah followed him. They flew in silence for a few minutes. The lack of conversation helped put Arick's mind at ease. The tree's rejection was something Arick would have to digest later. Until then, they needed a plan to ensure no other Head Tree went down. The Silva tree's barrier had been strengthened thanks to Atarah, but where did that leave the others? The information would be valuable as they made their way around the other regions.

"Is there anything we need to know about the fallen tree?" Noah asked, trying to appear nonchalant.

"Now that the tree is cut off from all of the others, no more power will flow through this region. It'll eventually die."

Noah looked surprised. "Is there no way to help the fallen tree?"

"It's possible only Malachi and his family can save their Head Tree. Even then, there's no guarantee. The tree is filled with despair and anger. If this goes on too long, the tree will become too corrupt to be healed."

"We need to leave the region then as soon as possible."

"It's why the forest is unruly and oppressive. How many days of travel do you think we have? Are we far from the Vallis Region?"

"If we stay at a fast pace, I hope to be there tomorrow," Noah said gloomily, looking at the mountains. "Nighttime is when the Azrael Clan are most active and lively."

"How long has it been since anyone has reached out to the Azrael Clan?"

"From what I suspect, I think by the time they informed us of the severity of the holes in their region, it was probably a month before Malachi reached out to see if the holes were taken care of."

"A whole month of demons!" Arick said incredulously. "Why didn't anyone send aid? Especially Malachi! Now his region is collapsing."

"There's a long history with Azrael, Uriel, and Raziel. The Uriel Clan has a rough history with Azrael. While Raziel has been a close ally with Azrael, it always looks out for the angels of Raziel and no one else."

"Pride goes before destruction."

"But humility before honor," Noah said quietly.

Arick slowed and started to descend closer to the ground. He heard the stirrings of the soldiers. "We're getting close."

Even Noah heard them. "We should probably land and go on foot now."

They both descended into the canopy of the trees. While Noah was able to nimbly navigate through the trees and their branches, Arick was left entangled and breaking every tree limb that got in his way. Noah landed gracefully, while Arick lumbered to the ground, covered in vines, thorns, and leaves. Noah chuckled at Arick's expense but made no comment, while Arick de-leafed himself.

Noah stayed close by Arick for a moment. He seemed hesitant about his next statement. "If you need to talk, I'm here."

Arick looked at Noah surprised, but Noah was facing

away from him. For Noah to express such . . . consideration for Arick it felt foreign to him. Nonetheless, Arick felt oddly relieved that Noah was willing to say such a thing.

He deflected with sarcasm. "Aw, gonna make me tear up and cry."

As soon as the words left his mouth, he felt more like a prick than normal. Noah made a scoffing sound, but he kept his face turned away. They walked back into the camp. While Noah was greeted by his lieutenants, Arick was greeted with his eccentric team.

"We thought our prayers were answered when you didn't wake us up for morning training," Brock jeered.

"Or that hell was about to freeze over," Jared added.

Galvin gave a nod of greeting as Arick chuckled at their banter.

"Did you battle with a beast all night?" Jared asked lightly but also serious.

"No, just battles with a spirit," Arick replied, trying to lift his own.

"More action than we got last night," Brock retorted.

They all laughed, releasing a tension Arick hadn't been aware he was holding. "Let's move out. We can't waste any daylight in this forest."

"No training?" Jared inquired.

"We don't have the luxury of time. We'll need all of our energy to get us to the next region."

"It's a good thing we're not an idle bunch. Our site's already packed up and our horses are ready to mount and go," Brock informed Arick.

He looked to where Noah stood; he appeared to be telling his men to do the same.

"To the Valley of Death, soldiers," Arick said, walking toward his mount.

"I don't fear evil," Jared said, oddly serious.

They all mounted and made their way to the left flank. Arick looked into the forest before them.

Hold on, he pleaded. He kicked his horse into motion as a gust of wind blew past him, urging him onward.

Chapter 10

Atarah

Atarah woke up with a sore and bruised body, but it wasn't as bad as other mornings she'd had. She stretched out along the edge of her bed, despite her body's protest. She grudgingly got up and made her way to the washroom. While it was still dawn, she quickly splashed water on her face and began her morning training.

Even after the battle at the South Gate, helping the citizens in the aftermath took more out of her than the Head Tree. Nonetheless, she wouldn't complain, especially after how much damage the Selaphiel family took. Ben's face was still tense and pale by the time she'd gone to bed last night. The funeral for his parents would take place tomorrow and the viewing would be held tonight. But for now, they all worked on strengthening the structure of the wall and assisted those who were injured.

While Charlotte did most of the work, it gave Atarah time to practice healing with her supervision. Atarah was learning the basics from Charlotte, but she still observed her technique. At times, Atarah couldn't contain her amazement when it came to Charlotte's power. Simply walking into a room, she could heal everyone within minutes. Atarah had practiced on herself and others as much as she could over the past few days. Thus far, she had improved little by little. She also trained hard on her force attack ability. Calling upon the armor took its toll on her, but without it, she would have died. While she had been impressed by her own ability in battle, she still had much she needed to improve on.

Atarah started her normal routine with back and core strengthening for her wings and her fighting stance. Normally Charlotte would join her, but Atarah had told Charlotte to take the day off. She was already expending enough energy reviving the angels in Chrysi Poli. Atarah's thoughts wandered to the demons standing outside the gates.

The demons had moved only once since the attack on the South Gate. Half of the horde moved to the North Gate, while the remaining half stayed at the South Gate. There was no exit the citizens could take now.

The demons stayed still and silent all day, staring at them through the barrier, all in battle formation. Their yellow, empty eyes showed no mercy, sympathy, or soul. Their grotesque bodies gave off the scent of death, enough to make the citizens gag if they got too close to the gate. Soldiers near the gate had to wear special masks to help block their foul smell. The demons didn't eat, sleep, or blink. It was unnerving.

Atarah moved onto a series of attack and defense positions. She built up quite a nice sweat within minutes. She focused on her breathing and expanded her senses. With all that had happened, Atarah needed to utilize her power's full potential.

Her thoughts wandered back to Ben again. She wondered how he was doing, if he was getting enough to eat and sleep. His eyes seemed distant the past few days and his wings were tense nearly all the time. She wondered what she could do for him to help. He was rarely alone whenever she saw him. Either in deep conversation with his brothers, generals, or city officials, he stayed busy late into the night. Amos and Canaan hovered around him earnestly. Whatever their conversations consisted of, it never eased the stress from Ben's face. In fact, from a distance, she sensed Ben grow more stressed anytime his brothers cornered him.

Amos and Canaan seemed like good brothers, she mused. Nonetheless, Atarah couldn't shake the uneasy feeling she had whenever she saw them with Ben. While she trusted Ben, she didn't fully trust Amos or Canaan yet. She must be imagining things. She shook her head and focused on the task at hand.

Satisfied with her training, she stumbled back into the washroom to get ready for the rest of the day. The sun was now completely up, and Atarah could hear everyone in the house moving. She quickly cleaned up, got dressed, and made her way to Charlotte's room, which wasn't far from Atarah's, simply a few turns down the hall. From what Atarah could tell, Charlotte had just gotten out of bed and was stretching by the time she walked in.

"Good morning, starshine," Atarah said, making herself at home.

Charlotte's hair was still tangled from last night's sleep. She made a sound between a groan and a yawn as a greeting to Atarah. "I feel like I could sleep the whole day and still be tired," she grumbled. She looked for a brush on her vanity, which was long with mirrors lining the table.

"I've tried that before. It doesn't feel too good." Atarah

considered her own hair in the mirror. After the battle, she'd left her hair down out of laziness.

I should probably put it up in braids for a while, she thought and started braiding her hair.

"What'd you try?" Charlotte inquired from where she sat.

"Sleeping all day. I got to about fourteen hours and got a bad headache from sleeping too much."

"I'm surprised you were able to do that, with how much training the Michael angels go through."

Atarah laughed, remembering. "I got in trouble. It was after a long training week, where we trained for sixteen hours every day for seven days straight. I begged my mom to let me skip a day, so I could sleep. My father was furious when he found out."

Charlotte shuddered. "I can't imagine having to do that every day."

"You get used to it after a while. In all honesty, since the summit, this has been the laziest Arick and I have been with training."

Charlotte looked at Atarah in surprise. "But you've been training every morning for at least an hour!"

"But an hour is nothing compared to eight hours a day."

"I think I'd die, then throw up, then die again." Charlotte shuddered.

Atarah laughed as she finished wrapping a braid around the rest of her hair. She gathered up the rest of her braids and hair and put it all into a ponytail. At least it was all out of the way. In the Michael Clan, when women didn't have their hair completely braided and out of the way or up, it was seen as indolence. Her mother always got on her about her hair, but she was too lazy to bother with it. Her mother helped with her hair since Atarah had little patience. Times like now, Atarah's heart constricted, missing her mother and father.

She wondered how her parents were doing. Was her father's army already on their way? Arick should have been to the capital Aquam Caput. *Where are they now?* The questions kept filling Atarah's head, and she missed what Charlotte asked her.

"I'm sorry. What was that?" Atarah said, coming out of her thoughts.

"I was asking if you could help me do my hair now. And teach me how to braid? I really like how you styled your hair. It's different from the braids we do in Silva."

"Oh yeah. It's really easy once you get the hang of it."

"Does everyone wear these kinds of styles?"

"Oh no. The female angels in the Michael Clan have much more elaborate braids than me. You're also supposed to braid all of your hair, but I'm too lazy."

Atarah moved onto Charlotte's hair. Charlotte's hair was thick, which made braiding easier for Atarah. *I can use big chunks of hair and get done faster*, she thought. She explained how to braid as she quickly styled Charlotte's hair.

As she finished, a knock came at the door. Atarah went to open the door and the person she never would have guessed came through.

"Good morning," Ben greeted, trying to sound upbeat, but he came up flat. His face wasn't as pale as yesterday, but the good-natured sparkle in his eyes hadn't yet come back. He was making an effort. Her heart ached for Ben to see him struggle to keep a lighthearted attitude.

"Good morning," she greeted warmly. "We were about to come down to eat before heading to the infirmary."

"It's good I caught you at this time then." Ben gave a ghost of a smile as he gazed at her.

"Why's that?" Charlotte asked, standing up from the vanity to come toward the door.

"Because after breakfast, Amos wants us to meet him at the Head Tree downstairs."

Atarah and Charlotte looked at each other in confusion and then at Ben. "Why?" they asked in unison.

"Isn't the barrier strengthened thanks to you and Atarah?" Charlotte asked.

"It is, but there's more we need to know. We need Atarah to go back into the tree and tell us more."

"What else is there?" Charlotte asked politely, but her wings started to shake.

"We need to know how the other regions are doing. The calculation that had to have happened for the attack on the South Gate leads us to believe more will follow. Not just here, but in other regions as well."

Sounded logical enough, but Atarah still dreaded going back into the Head Tree. From Charlotte's reaction, it appeared she wasn't looking forward to it either. They'd been practically immobilized last time. The only shining grace was there was no battle looming over them like before. Atarah and Charlotte reluctantly agreed.

"Well, that went better than expected," Ben said with relief.

"I'd put up more of a fight, but I'm hungry and there's a war to win," Atarah said with a sigh. She looked into Ben's eyes and thought now was her chance. "Would you like to join us for breakfast, Ben?"

Ben's wings seemed to twitch before they went still. A grin slowly appeared across his face that could charm even demons.

"I'd love to join you," he said.

Atarah nodded while Charlotte came up beside her.

Charlotte looped her arm through Atarah's. "Yeah, no point in fighting the offer anyway. We'll need all the energy we can get."

They made their way to the kitchen, where the staff

was at full speed. Atarah grabbed a large serving of food and sat in her and Charlotte's usual spot by the window. Here in the city, there was fruit, coconuts, and vegetables in their meals, and desert hare for meat in most meals, with some desserts. This breakfast was no different. Atarah took some hare meat sausage links, fruit, and a mixed nut salad. Charlotte joined her with a larger portion than Atarah's. Atarah chuckled. If only her parents could see she wasn't the only girl with an appetite in the family.

While they settled in, Ben surprised her once again. He was asleep at the table. His head was resting in his hand, leaning against the window. His wings completely relaxed. His hair curled slightly around his eyes. He looked younger and more . . . carefree.

"Mind if I join you, sleeping beauty?" she said, grinning at him.

His wings twitched and his eyes fluttered open

"Sure," Ben said, suppressing a yawn.

They didn't usually see him in the mornings, and barely in the afternoons. She wondered when the last time he had any sleep was. Charlotte looked at him pensively.

"After everything we've been through, surely me sleeping is not that shocking," Ben said, some sparkle returning to his eyes.

"I don't know. It's like seeing a zombie come back to life," Charlotte said with a grin.

Atarah chuckled. "Where have you been going in the mornings? This is the first time we've seen you at this hour." She dove into her food.

"If I'm being honest, I've been sleeping in," Ben answered with a yawn.

"What?" Atarah said, dumbfounded. Out of everything she could have guessed, sleeping in wasn't one of them. For someone of the Head Clan family, sleeping in didn't seem very . . . royal.

Ben laughed at their expressions. "I've been staying up most nights with Canaan and Amos." His face dropped a fraction. "Plans with the citizens and plans of attack with Malachi."

Atarah had seen Malachi only once when they helped get the citizens to shelter. He'd been badly injured and unconscious. She'd barely recognized him from the summit because of all the blood covering his face. His daughters were in even worse shape. Not that their physical injuries were worse, but the hollowness in their eyes had made Atarah shudder. They'd kept to Malachi's side since they arrived. She wasn't sure if Malachi was still bedridden because they didn't leave the Selaphiel villa often.

"Is Malachi still refusing to be healed by you, Charlotte?" Atarah asked.

Charlotte nodded somberly. "Even his daughters won't let me come near him."

"What's next, now that Malachi and his people are here?" Atarah asked.

Ben sighed. In that moment, he looked older than his years. "We'll be fine for now, but in the weeks and months to come, supplies will get short. We think that's why the horde's waiting outside. They're waiting for us to drive one another insane from food shortages."

Charlotte snorted. "Not just that. Malachi's people are completely different from any other angels in Selaphiel."

Atarah understood what Charlotte meant. The Selaphiel angels were certainly welcoming, but they were also private with their lives. Selaphiel angels were known to be quiet, knowledge-hungry, studious, and reserved. The Uriel angels were known as open, charismatic, rumbustious, and never on time. The two clans had opposing personalities. Even yesterday, when Charlotte was healing an angel's back from the Uriel Clan, the female stripped almost completely naked before the makeshift clinic. Charlotte, used to naked bodies, was only mildly surprised. However, the Selaphiel angels helping her were shocked and excused themselves immediately to work in a different section.

"They might drive one another mad before our food runs out," Charlotte concluded.

"Not only that, but we need to have an effective attack plan. We can't remain sitting ducks for long," Ben said, rubbing his eyes.

Atarah noticed he hadn't touched any of his food this whole time. Meanwhile, the rest of them were already finishing their meals.

"I'll take these back," Charlotte said, giving a pointed glance between her and Ben. She left with their trays, giving them a rare private moment.

"How are you truly doing?" Atarah asked sincerely. "Not Ben the heir, not the diplomat, not the soldier or spy. But how are *you*, Ben, doing?"

Ben looked taken aback by her question. His face softened as he regarded her.

"As well as I can be," Ben replied. "It feels like my parents will walk through that door at any moment though. It doesn't feel like they're truly gone."

Atarah studied him while she listened, trying to understand the warm emotions swarming around within herself and toward Ben. His dark brown eyes looked tired, his hair disheveled, and his face worn, while his uniform was cleaned and pressed. His wings kept twitching every few minutes as if jolted in surprise.

"The only thing that's changed is this sense of urgency. I have so much to get done." Ben sighed.

"What is it you feel so urgent about? What is it you want?" Atarah asked softly. She reached out and grabbed his hand, wanting to comfort him and selfishly wanting to connect with him.

Ben gave a ghost of a grin as he squeezed her hand. His

hand was rough from years of training, but it was warm. He looked up from their hands before answering.

"The same thing you want," Ben replied, barely above a whisper. "To obtain power." Emotions simmered in his eyes that she couldn't decipher.

They stayed that way, studying each other with emotions at the surface, but not allowing them to break the surface.

"Everything okay?" Charlotte asked hesitantly as she reentered the room.

"Everything is . . ." Atarah sighed as she trailed off. Everything wasn't okay, but she didn't want to speak the words. "Let's be done with whatever's to come," she finished. They still needed to see the Head Tree.

They all got up and headed into the hallway. As they walked, Atarah passed a piece of fruit to Ben. He looked at her questioningly.

"You haven't eaten yet, but after the tree you'll want to."

"Looking after me already," Ben said with his charming grin back in place. The brooding persona was gone for now. "If I didn't know any better, I'd say you like me."

"It's a good thing you know better then." Atarah grinned back at him. Enjoying this side of him was back.

Ben laughed. "What will it take for you to admit you have feelings for me?"

"Maybe an army."

He laughed wholeheartedly.

"What about you? Are you ridiculous enough to have feelings for me?" Atarah asked with a raised eyebrow.

Ben's face shifted a little. "I'll tell you mine only when you tell me yours."

She only grinned at him. Charlotte bumped her arm and looked at her. She seemed to be giving her a pointed look. Right. They couldn't forget why they were here and what was going on. Ben bit into the apple Atarah had given him. He quickly ate while they walked.

They started their descent down the stairwell. Unlike before, the bright sun filled the stairwell with more light. The atmosphere felt airier and more breathable compared to last time.

Maybe this time will go better than the last, Atarah thought, trying to encourage her body to keep moving down each step. She thought of all of the training camps she'd survived. Yet despite the memories, her wings, to her horror, started to shiver in small bouts of anxiety. She tried to grab hold of her wings to get them to stop moving completely. But no one was paying attention to her. She wasn't alone in her nervousness. Charlotte's wings quaked so severely that Atarah felt a breeze from the movement. Even Ben's wings shook with unease.

"I guess you're the bravest out of all of us, Atarah," Charlotte said with chattering teeth.

They all released a nervous laugh and walked through the door. The door led them back to the wide, glass room. The Head Tree still hung from the ceiling, seeming to sway in greeting. The tree wasn't the only one greeting them. Underneath the tree stood Malachi, his two daughters Isabella and Clarissa, Canaan, and Amos, the new Arch Head.

Their gazes were drawn to them as soon as they entered the room. A few of the faces didn't look friendly in the slightest. Atarah's smile dropped from her face, and she expanded her senses. She commanded her wings to stay still as best as she could.

You're the daughter of the Arch Head Michael, and you won't be intimidated, she reminded herself. She had fought against the demon army and restored the barrier.

She moved forward and greeted them. "Good morning, everyone," she said stoically.

Isabella, the younger daughter, sneered at her from behind Malachi. Amos looked like he'd slept very little since the attack. Canaan looked the healthiest out of the three brothers. He greeted her warmly, Amos solemnly, and Malachi just regarded her. His gaze was hard and hollow, nothing like the male at the summit meeting days ago. Even though he stood on shaky legs, he looked ready to fight. Oddly enough it was Clarissa, the eldest daughter, who addressed Atarah first.

"We'll only say this once—thank you. Without you, neither our citizens nor the Selaphiel angels would be standing here," she said with an expressionless face.

That was probably the most Atarah would ever get out of them. So, she only nodded.

"Our thanks was to Ben, not you, Atarah," Malachi said harshly.

Atarah's wings flared despite her control, but that wasn't what caught everyone's attention. Charlotte's and Ben's wings flared in response to the cold address. Both looked furious.

"Your gratitude should extend to Atarah especially," Ben said in a dangerously quiet tone. His wings flared wide. "Do not disrespect her again." His voice was filled with finality and promise.

"We're merely addressing the fact that we were almost trapped with a large viper and Ben was the one who defeated it," Clarissa said condescendingly.

"How about the hundreds who were healed, or our ability to keep this barrier standing?" Atarah said firmly and waved her hand at Clarissa, stopping her from talking. She walked forward, getting within inches of Malachi and Clarissa's faces. "Your childish jab aside, yes, we'll continue to help you," Atarah finished.

Clarissa's gaze flamed and her fist curled. *Good*, Atarah thought. Better than the hollow-looking girl she'd seen when they'd first entered the city. She'd rather see something burning in her eyes rather than nothing.

"Help?" Malachi sneered and looked at both Atarah and Charlotte. "Where were either of your brothers in the help that was promised?"

"I think this has gone far enough," Amos said in a voice that reminded Atarah of her father. While his face was worn with grief and lack of sleep, there was a maturity there that hadn't been there before.

"We've all been through enough, and we all want to be back in our homes and in peace." Amos looked at everyone present with a gloomy yet serious expression. "All you have to do is decide right now what you'll do for the future. Will you work now to make it better or not?"

Atarah's wings fell to her side. Amos was right. This was getting them nowhere but helping their pride. She needed to do better.

"What needs to be done?" Ben asked. His wings were also by his side. His relaxed posture reappeared.

Amos sighed. "We need Atarah to go back into the Head Tree and gather any intel she can. We need to see if some other factors are in play or not."

"What other factors are there?" Atarah inquired.

"We're leaving nothing to chance. What you tell me will determine our next step."

"What exactly are you looking for? How are we to look for it as well if you don't tell us?" Charlotte asked. Her wings weren't quite at her side, but not as flared as before.

"Atarah will be looking for anything obvious we need to know. That's all," Amos said.

Atarah paid attention to everyone's heartbeats to see if there was any trickery. There was no lie—only that the whole truth wasn't being shared. The most notable strains were in Amos, Canaan, and Ben.

She debated about pressing them for more information but decided against it.

"Very well, we'll try our best." Atarah looked at Charlotte and Ben. "Are you ready?"

Charlotte looked up at the tree and sighed. "Ready as I'll ever be."

Amos tossed Ben a few hooks and ropes. Possibly the same ones as their first day.

"Thanks," Ben mumbled. He expanded his wings for flight.

With that, they all shot up into the air, aiming for the same spot as last time. They landed and grabbed a hold of the tree's trunk. Ben gave Charlotte the belt hooks once more, while he strapped Atarah and himself down together. Charlotte grabbed ahold of Atarah's right hand, and Ben, on her left, circled his arm around her side.

Let's get this over with, she thought.

Atarah placed her left hand on the tree and reached into it. This time, she expected the boulder that greeted her and pushed with as much power as she could. She immediately felt the power from Ben aiding her in pushing the boulder forward.

Concentrate, Atarah. Push, push, and keep pushing.

Atarah tried to pace her power as best she could, but her power drained away from her.

Keep pushing. When in doubt, keep pushing, she thought.

She felt Charlotte's presence now, aiding her and Ben.

The force of the tree's power demanded sacrifice and diligence. All of their power was the sacrifice and their diligence was in not giving up. Atarah tried to focus her thoughts on reaching out to the tree as well.

I'm here to help. I'm here as a friend. I'm here as a fighter.

Gradually, the boulder moved. This time, the boulder became lighter as she moved it forward. Atarah took this advantage to gain momentum in moving it. Like before, her spirit was in the tree's core. The vast network of power flowing to and from the tree was as mesmerizing as before. She moved along the currents, trying to pinpoint where everything was located. She felt its soft movement push and pull, guiding her. The tree's familiarity with her gave her confidence in asking what she needed to know.

What else is there? she tried to convey. She couldn't speak in her spirit form, only feel and project her feelings.

The current changed in direction as it guided her around the tree's core. Ben and Charlotte's power slipped farther away, as if Atarah was physically traveling away from them. Ben's warmth slowly receded, and Charlotte's reviving touch faded.

Where are we going? Atarah projected worriedly.

A tender breeze moved around Atarah, trying to reassure her. With caution, she continued to venture on with the current.

Despite the lack of normal sight, Atarah could still see everything within the tree, as well as where the tree's power blended into another. Flowing along the current, Atarah sensed another presence around her. Another current joined in with the one carrying her and encircled her. Alarmed at what was happening, Atarah tried to fight against the current. To fight against them was pointless. One current was kind and the other simply seemed . . . enthusiastic about Atarah. Atarah stopped thrashing about and nervously stuck out her hand. The new current wrapped around her hand and warmed her.

Surprised, Atarah stuck out her other hand. The current wrapped around it with warmth and seemed to say hello. That was when she realized this was the current of another Head Tree; the current felt different than the one before. But which one was this current coming from?

The current traveled up her arm and lightly pushed against her forehead. Visions of fall leaves entered her mind. The autumn wind sent them tumbling in a dance. The sun danced with the wind and the leaves, having little care in the world. Towering trees with lanterns hanging from the branches moved in sync with them.

You're the Silva Tree, Atarah thought with wonder.

Warmth spread once again to her hands. Joy bloomed in Atarah's chest, happy to be greeted by a friend. Atarah compelled a question to the Silva current, asking how the barrier was. Another vision came to Atarah's mind, showing the barrier bending, but not breaking. Demons only came at night and the citizens were safe within each town's barrier. Relief hit her hard at seeing Silva safe and sound. The Silva current pulled away as the Selaphiel current continued to carry her along. Atarah waved goodbye, missing the warmth already. Around the tree's core, Atarah understood how each tree was connected, helping and flowing power into one another.

A jolt from another current took Atarah by surprise. This current wasn't as gentle as the Silva one. This was rough and jagged in its movement. Understanding now that this was another Head Tree, Atarah reached her hand out. The current grabbed her hand unforgivingly and seemed to suck all of the warmth from her body. Frigidity overcame Atarah as she came face-to-face with the Azrael tree. The current had little regard for her and wanted her power and life force. From its touch, Atarah felt a black warzone, filled with terror and horror. Fear shook her as she took in what she saw. Her stomach curled in on itself, and Atarah felt a sense of hopelessness from the Azrael tree. She willingly pushed her power to the tree's current. It wasn't much, but it was more help than what they were getting.

Suddenly, the Azrael current pushed her away. The Selaphiel current continued on mercifully. Nonetheless, Atarah looked back at the Azrael current and gave it her sad farewell. It wasn't long before the next current came at Atarah—two currents. While the last one was cold, these two were fiery hot. They blazed across Atarah's hands and legs, burning as they went. She cried out in pain, which the Selaphiel current immediately soothed, wrapping around her protectively.

The new currents then approached with more care. Wanting this to be done with, Atarah stuck both hands out boldly. The two currents grabbed onto her hands. They were both hot, but no longer burning her like before.

With them, she saw two visions. One vision was of an endless graveyard of demons and angels alike, littering fields stretching far along rolling hills. Another vision was of a spring forest. The spring forest had tall, wide trees that bloomed with a variety of colors Atarah had never seen before. The two visions couldn't have been more different. One showed destruction, terror, and no mercy, while the other showed peace, new beginnings, and prosperity in the region. The first vision was from the Raziel tree and the second from the Gabriel tree. While both barriers were up, the Raziel barrier was only held together by a thread. Her heart broke for what she saw in the Raziel region as she gave the last of what she could give to the current. Surprised by her power, both currents let her go on her way.

Weakened, Atarah was close to falling into an abyss of unconsciousness. The Selaphiel current carried her back to where they originally started. Atarah felt the warmth of Ben's powers and the reassuring hand of Charlotte once more. She attempted to raise her hand in farewell, but her spiritual form wouldn't move. Even so, Atarah was sure the tree understood. The current gently pushed her out, and Atarah came crashing back to reality.

"Atarah?"

She heard her name weakly called as arms wrapped around her and unhooked her belt. She started to freefall toward the ground, until two pairs of hands grabbed her sides and flew down. They gently lowered her to the ground, as Atarah fought to stay awake. She heard everyone shuffling around her, murmuring. Her head continued to swim with visions of all of the different regions. She felt the anguish and animosity of the Southern Regions and the strained endurance of the ones to the north of them.

"Atarah."

A gentle hand rested on top of her head, drawing her back. Her vision focused on Ben hovering above her face. His face was the picture of strained worry that transformed into relief as her eyes opened. His wings shook, but calmed down by his sides. Atarah saw Charlotte next, then Amos, and everyone else last.

"What did you see?" Amos asked earnestly. Canaan was right behind him. Malachi and his daughters were drawn in too.

"It's not good," Atarah murmured, turning to Malachi and Amos. "The regions in the south are . . . There's nothing there but chaos, anguish, despair, and suffering. It's a full-on warzone with bodies everywhere."

"Vallis and Campis Secretum, both?"

Atarah nodded.

"What about the other regions?" Charlotte asked. Her wings shook a little.

"Silva and Lanua are still holding their ground with effort."

"But Azrael's and Raziel's regions are about to be conquered?" Ben asked with an expressionless face.

Atarah could only nod, her mind wandering back to the images the Head Trees shared with her.

"What about our region?" Clarissa asked, her wings shaking violently.

Isabella clutched her sister's hand. Their stares pinned Atarah into place with their hopefulness, and Atarah's heart dropped for them. She sat up cautiously, looked down, and gave a small shake of her head.

"Elementa is no longer connected to any of the other Head Trees."

Silence followed Atarah's last statement. Malachi's eyes lost their last little bit of spark and his wings fell to the ground. Gone was the man Atarah had seen at the summit. Now there was a shift in him and his daughters. They looked at one another and nodded. In those few seconds, Atarah saw a change come over Clarissa and Isabella. Something told her that these girls were no longer the girls who'd set her dress on fire so long ago, but they were now true young women. She saw Malachi and his family in a new light, now that their people were refugees and their lands were dying. The hardship that was dealt to them and the hardship yet to come.

Amos pulled a map from inside his cloak and laid it out for all to see. He studied it with a pensive expression.

"The bulk of their armies came through the Azrael and Raziel regions," Canaan said, engrossed in the map as well.

"They started south and are heading north, growing their army as they go along, taking out each region," Ben said thoughtfully. "And with the holes unchecked, they have an uninterrupted supply route."

Atarah stared at her region, the northernmost area on the map. They were going to build their way up to her father's region, her home. They were going to take down all of their possible allies and leave them alone to defend themselves. As much as she wanted to deny it, even with all of their power, knowledge, and training, the Michael Clan wouldn't be able to defeat an army of this size all on their own. The demons' strategy was a good one. Who was the one coming up with all of the plans? Who was their leader?

"What do you think?" Canaan asked Amos, who looked in deep concentration.

"There's still something not adding up yet." Amos pointed at the map. "Our informants say Mikael's traveling to Raziel's region. Then why'd they come to Malachi's region so strongly if they wanted to work their way up the map through the regions? Why not target Chrysi Poli and avoid a possible interaction with Mikael?"

They started discussing the possibilities, but Atarah was too deep in thought to listen.

She thought back to her lessons during those brutal training camps as she looked at the map. If she were the enemy, what would she do? She looked at the layout with all of the different climates and landmarks. At times like this, she wished she had Arick's or her father's brain. They always knew strategy better than her, how to anticipate fights or find solutions. Her father's stories of his past battles, of how he'd failed and succeeded as a commander, and learned how to be a follower and a leader, came to mind.

Come on, think. What would Father do? Atarah thought.

She remembered her own disadvantages in training and how she'd had to overcome them. No one was more aware than herself when it came to her weaknesses.

When the enemy thinks you're weak, be strong, was what her father always said. What strategy did they need to use? What strategy was the enemy using?

Each Arch clan had a unique gift that could be utilized. Clan Raphael's was their healing, and Michael's was their battle prowess, and . . .

Atarah's thoughts stopped, then slowly came together. She picked up the map, drawing Amos's and Ben's attention, while the others were engrossed in debate about what to do next. Warfare was all about deception; that was what she'd been taught.

Ben looked at her knowingly. "What're you thinking will happen?"

"As the one who was raised for battle, what are your thoughts?" Amos asked, drawing everyone else's attention, even Clarissa's and Isabella's.

"If—and I mean, if—I was the enemy, I would draw everyone south." Atarah pointed to Vallis and Campis Secretum.

"Why?" Ben asked, his gaze intense.

"If Noah travels south with Arick, and my father travels south to the neighboring region, it leaves the entire north vulnerable. To attack and defeat the Michael Clan while it's at its weakest would send a damaging message to the rest of the clans. It could kill their morale. As of right now, my region, Belli Causa, doesn't have its leader. An attack would put everyone into too much chaos to attack efficiently." Silence followed Atarah's statement. "It's all a trap. Draw everyone south while they attack from the north, and then attack everyone in both directions."

"They're being herded. It all makes sense," Amos said, amazed. "That's why the holes are almost all in the south. To bring any reinforcements they'd receive south. They attacked Aquam Caput so aggressively that by the time the army showed up, nothing would be there. The soldiers would be ready to fight, especially after seeing the damage to the city. They'll go to the fight in the southern region of Vallis, to the source where all the demons are showing up."

"How would they get all the way to Belli Causa from the south?" Canaan questioned.

"How'd the viper get all the way to Chrysi Poli?" Charlotte countered.

"They knew Malachi and his people were coming here. They knew Noah and his troops were going to head south. We need to know who their key figure is. I don't like having an unknown mastermind in the mix of all this."

"Work with the knowledge you have," Ben said, looking at his brothers. Something passed between them.

"Make the best decision you can," Amos said with a small grin.

"If you fail, that's only more knowledge gained," Canaan finished.

"With that said, where do we go?" Clarissa asked.

Everyone looked to Atarah once more.

"How far underground can you sense creatures?" Ben asked, staring deep into her eyes.

"I never had to test it before," Atarah replied, her gaze trapped by Ben's.

His mouth slowly curved into a grin. "It's time to give it a try."

"There are tunnels that leave out of this room in nearly every direction," Amos informed them.

Atarah was able to pull her eyes away from Ben to focus on Amos.

"These tunnels are old and move to where you need to be, as long as you keep your destination in mind."

"Why hasn't this been brought up before?" Clarissa asked suspiciously.

Canaan looked at her with a raised eyebrow. "The tunnels were built for citizens to escape in case of a breach at the gate. Not for personal enjoyment. Thanks to you two"—he indicated Atarah and Charlotte—"restoring the gate's barrier, we didn't have to use it quite yet."

"Until now," Amos spoke up. "If you travel underground with your ability, can you see if another viper is set to attack the capital of Belli Causa, Sanctum?" Amos asked sincerely.

Atarah looked up at the ceiling and the Head Tree above them. She heard the fuzzy movement of feet above. Her training had paid off. She looked at Amos once again. "Yes, I'll be able to sense it." It would push her abilities and concentration, but she could do it. How she was going to walk and do this at the same time was another story.

Amos nodded. "Very well. It's decided. Atarah, Charlotte, Ben, and . . ." Amos turned around and looked at Clarissa and Isabella. "You two will go together to Sanctum."

"What?" Atarah and Charlotte said in unison. Clarissa and Isabella barely tolerated them as it was now. What was Amos thinking?

"Considering everyone has gone south, we're all that's left to fight against anything coming north," Amos said logically.

Isabella looked like she wanted to argue, but a sharp look from Clarissa stopped her.

"We don't have any armies to spare. However, five highly trained heirs from the top Arch houses . . . that will hopefully be enough," Malachi rasped from behind everyone. His eyes still looked hollow. His figure hunched over, hair draping, tangled, around his face, and his red wings dragged against the floor. Defeated was the only word that came to mind when looking at him.

"Also, if we're wrong, and the attack doesn't happen in the north, then we won't be left wide open in the south," Canaan added gently.

Atarah and Charlotte looked at each other skeptically, but they couldn't deny this was one of the better options.

Clarissa looked from Atarah to Charlotte, then back to Atarah. "I guess we better get a move on." She said the words as if they disgusted her.

Amos nodded and started to move toward the far wall across from where they'd entered. He stopped before a large stone wall and began to speak some strange words.

It was nothing Atarah was used to hearing. Was it even a language?

Then the wall began to move. The sand shifted slowly, revealing a large tunnel door with strange writing along the frame. Beside the door appeared two floating shelves holding a variety of weapons. Daggers of various sizes, large battle axes, a bowstring, and swords lined the opposite shelf. Clarissa and Isabella immediately went to the shelves to pick out their weapons. Atarah stood, thankfully on steady legs, and approached as well to evaluate each weapon carefully. She grabbed the bowstring and tested its strength and structure. Deeming it worthy, she turned to Charlotte and held it out. Charlotte hesitantly took the bow.

"Might as well let that bow be of use to someone else," Isabella jeered as she strapped a dagger to her side.

"Don't listen to them. You're nimble, fast, and accurate. A bow is perfect for you," Atarah said.

"I've never shot a bow and arrow before though," Charlotte said mournfully. She reached out and grabbed onto the bow.

"You'll learn fast," Atarah said confidently.

Charlotte gave her a weak smile and turned to strap the bow down.

Atarah regarded the weapons once more. Meanwhile, Ben came up beside her to grab his own weapon, brushing up against her.

"The lovely Michael angel debates the weapon to skewer her enemies with, when in the end she knows she can just use her own hands," Ben joked lightheartedly beside her, looking forward.

Atarah grinned, still looking straight ahead herself. "Yes, but think of the mess it'll leave on my hands," she mused with a mischievous gleam in her eye.

Ben chuckled once at her, then regarded her up and

down, serious. "Do you feel up to traveling? If not, say the word and we'll wait a day," he said quietly, but with as much authority as an Arch head.

She looked at him and smiled playfully. "Looking after me already, huh? If I didn't know better, I'd think you liked me."

Ben chuckled as his wings hummed.

Atarah nearly gasped at the light that entered Ben's eyes. It caused her heart to clench tight with joy. She realized how little light had been in his eyes before and wanted to keep the light there for him. *This better not come back to bite me*, Atarah thought, feeling ridiculous that she'd fought battles, and a simple bit of laughter made her feel so . . . susceptible.

Ben grabbed a sword and a few daggers before walking closer to Amos. They began to talk quietly.

Atarah only took two items. A pair of gloves and a dagger. The rest, she didn't need.

"Why take those?" Charlotte asked, stepping closer to take a look.

Atarah held out the gloves for her to see. They were brown and looked worn. Some spots were tattered and ragged from use. The fact that the gloves looked so well used drew her attention. From what she could remember from her lessons, most gloves had a magical property that aided the wearer. Maybe the gloves would prove useful to her.

"Oh, good choice. But, of course, that's expected from any angel of the Michael Clan," Canaan said. He'd come closer to them without Atarah noticing.

She was still weakened enough by the Head Tree that she hadn't sensed his approach.

Canaan regarded the gloves with a sense of longing on his face, which surprised Atarah.

Out of this family, it was hard to gauge what was truly

going on in their heads, yet there Canaan was with an actual expression.

"Yes?" Canaan said with a quirked eyebrow.

"I was surprised by your statement," Atarah quickly said.

Charlotte looked at the gloves in confusion. "What's so special about them? Why don't you get new ones?"

"These gloves are powerful. If you touch someone with them and they tell a lie, they give a sort of squeeze and tighten around your hand," Canaan said.

"And if they tell the truth?" Atarah asked.

Canaan looked at the gloves, then back at her, seeming almost bored. "Then you feel no change."

"Then why not wear them all the time?" Charlotte asked.

Canaan flashed a small grin. "Wear them long enough, and you'll see for yourself."

He turned his head as if his name had been called and strolled toward Ben and Amos, where they stood with bowed heads, in deep conversation.

Atarah, despite Canaan's daring remark, put the gloves on. She felt a small amount of warmth seep through her hand and then nothing, as if there were no gloves on her hands at all. She watched her hands in amazement as the gloves truly did disappear. She flipped her hands over, wondering where they'd gone.

"Are you sure that was wise?" Charlotte said reproachfully.

"I don't know, but I'd rather find out now than in the long battle to come," she said, now unsure of what to do with her hands.

Maybe I'll keep them by my side.

"Let's give it a try," Charlotte said boldly. She reached out and grabbed Atarah's hand and was about to say something when Clarissa interrupted her.

"It'd be better if one of us does it," Clarissa said from behind Atarah.

Atarah regarded her for a moment before nodding. She stuck her hand out, which Clarissa grabbed and squeezed harshly.

"All right, tell a lie," Atarah said, surprised slightly at the strength of her grip.

Clarissa smirked. "Oh no. How about you tell me which one the lie is," she purred. "I don't see any of the Arch Clans as useful allies. I'd love to gut you right here and now because the hope in your eyes irritates me. Lastly, my heart dropped when you stood in between Ben and that army of demons, and I admired you for that."

Atarah froze at the last one. She wasn't expecting Clarissa to say that. Clarissa didn't break her cold gaze. The gloves did nothing. They still felt as if nothing was truly there.

Everything Clarissa said was true.

Atarah looked into her eyes, more focused now than before. Clarissa released her hand and walked away. Isabella followed her after looking at them, seeming as surprised as they were by what Clarissa said.

Seeing that Clarissa did have a heart stirred something in Atarah's chest.

Suddenly, Atarah's mind was pulled sharply backward. She must have gasped or made a sound loud enough for Ben to turn to see her start to fall. Charlotte moved to catch her, but she wasn't the fastest.

At lightning speed, Ben was there, looping his arm around her waist before she could hit the ground.

Atarah saw herself in flashes and memories and a wave of emotion whose origin she wasn't sure of. But as fast as those flashes appeared, they left just as quickly.

Atarah regained her footing and stepped away from Ben, disturbed by the emotions that had come up in her memories of him. What had happened? She looked up into Ben's confused face to ask, but she saw Canaan's knowing glance. So, this was the effect of the gloves. Each time she used the glove to seek out truth, a truth would also be sought within her, a truth that she had denied from her own consciousness.

She looked down at her hands. *What a cumbersome weapon.*

The more truth she sought from others, the more truth she'd find about herself. Not many would be that comfortable taking a hard look at their true selves. No wonder these gloves weren't used all the time.

Ben's concerned face still hovered in her peripheral vision. He probably thought she was still weakened by the tree and had a moment of near collapse. Charlotte's hands had already started glowing, healing her aches and pains Atarah hadn't been aware of.

Charlotte put a hand to her head and sighed with relief. "You're all right. Gave us a small scare there though." She eyed Atarah's hands warily.

"What happened? Is it still the effects of the tree?" Ben asked, his wings flared the smallest fraction of an inch.

"It was the—"

"It was the tree," Atarah cut off Charlotte's reply. "But I'm doing much better, thanks to Charlotte." She tried to be as reassuring as she could be.

Ben looked her up and down, not convinced in the slightest. Nonetheless, he gave no argument, just pressed his lips together and nodded.

"Is everyone ready?" he asked, addressing Clarissa and Isabella as well. They gave curt nods, barely looking at him. Not that Ben was even looking at them, but he seemed to register their nods.

"All right. Let's move out." Ben grabbed a torch from one of the shelves and lit it.

"Wait," Malachi called softly.

He looked at his two daughters with an emotion of love so strong Atarah had to look away. Malachi embraced his daughters quickly. It appeared he wasn't the only one saying goodbye. Amos and Canaan quickly embraced Ben in a tight, brotherly hug.

That was when it dawned on Atarah—if they were right, and it was only them who could fight, this might be the last time they saw one another alive. She hoped they were enough. She'd seen Ben fight and he wasn't too bad, but she wasn't sure how Clarissa and Isabella were in battle.

They finished their goodbyes and turned toward the tunnels. None of them looked back. Ben gave a sigh that seemed to say, *here we go*, and led the way down the tunnel.

Eventually, the light from the entrance of the tunnel narrowed as the door behind them closed. The torch in Ben's hand illuminated the passage as their only form of light. Living in the mountains, Atarah was used to dark tunnels and enclosed spaces. She immediately concentrated and expanded her senses all around her. From what Atarah could hear in Charlotte's heartbeat, she didn't like being underground. Her wings started fussing, vibrating and begging to stretch out in the enclosed space. Charlotte wasn't the only one. Atarah heard Clarissa and Isabella's fast heartbeats and their vibrating wings protesting the surroundings. She supposed it was only natural to not like the underground, as it was a natural disadvantage for them. Ben's wings remained calm, cool, and collected as he continued to walk forward. How did he know the way he was going? Atarah wasn't sure, but she trusted what his brother had said about the tunnel. Picture the destination, and the tunnel will lead you there.

"Don't go thinking this is your job," Ben said, his wings flapping and startling Atarah out of her concentration.

"Well, it's my home."

"You're not the only one who's been there."

Atarah looked at Ben questioningly. "When were you ever at Sanctum? No one can come in without the approval or help of the Head Arch."

"Your father held a celebration for your birth and invited some of the other Archs. My family was one of them, so I went along and got to visit Sanctum. Truly a magnificent city. My applause to its designer," Ben said as if they were talking about the weather.

"Wait, how old were you?" Atarah asked, trying to decipher their age difference.

"Oh, I was about four years old or so. But those mountains and that city aren't something you would forget."

Atarah quickly calculated the date of that party and their ages. Ben was three and a half years older than her? "Have you been back since then?" she asked suspiciously.

Ben looked back at her with a grin, then faced forward. "Like you said, it's nearly impossible to get in without someone from the Michael Clan to guide you. I'll bring you up to the forest on the edge of the mountain ranges, which is as far as I can go, probably without your help. But don't forget your real job is to sense if we come across anything that's not our ally. Focus on that, while I focus on where we need to go."

Ben was someone she could rely on, and she was grateful for that.

Focus on what's around us. She doubted it would be another viper like the one at the South Gate. No viper could stand the harsh terrain on the mountains. But whoever was planning their attacks was clever, so she needed to be as aware as possible. Atarah stayed a step behind Ben and put her hand on his shoulder. He turned and looked at her.

"I'll be concentrating deeply. So, don't let me walk into

a wall or anything." Even in the dim lighting, Atarah felt the blush come up along her neck and cheeks.

Ben gave her a grin that made her heart throb. "As you wish," he said quietly.

He faced the front, not breaking a stride.

It took Atarah a few moments to pull herself together enough to use her powers. She was finally able to and sank into a deep state of concentration. She expanded all of her senses as far as she could stretch them, reaching beyond the surface above them. The rest of them became background noise she drowned out as she concentrated on any sound, movement, or malicious energy emanating above. So much of it was hard to truly get a sense of. Everything seemed fuzzy and unclear because of the amount of shifting sand above them. It was no wonder the demon they'd encountered on the way to Chrysi Poli hid so easily from Atarah.

She became enclosed by her own senses, only narrowing in on anything shifting above and below her. She had no sense of her body moving forward following Ben, but somehow it did. She was aware of where they were traveling in the city. Even though they didn't move, she sensed the malice rolling off of the demons that stood above them. They were outside of the gates then—it had only taken a matter of minutes.

Maybe we'll get to Belli Causa in time to stop an attack, Atarah thought, hopeful.

Minutes or hours could have gone by and she wouldn't have known the difference. In this state, Atarah could only sense movement, and whether it was friend or foe. The shifting sand made a small sound informing Atarah where every bunny, lizard, or snake was, but nothing as large as that viper.

In this deep concentration, Atarah completely forgot about the gloves she still wore and realized her mistake far too late. The gloves were active when touching someone else. Whether she posed a question to Ben or not, the effects still came. Her emotions came back full force, only this time, they stayed longer than a few seconds. Feelings she never knew she had about her father, brother, Elijah, Charlotte, and Ben. She felt so much that she couldn't decipher which emotion belonged to whom or why she felt it. The environment around her was forgotten; now Atarah tried all she could to get her emotions under control. She felt anger, she felt sorrow, she felt like she was stuck in the middle, but worst of all she felt love—this love caused the most pressure inside her. Being crushed under all the emotion, Atarah panicked. Would it ever end? She lashed out, hoping an end would come soon.

"Atarah!"

She blinked and realized she was back in the tunnel, surrounded by angels. She slowly realized who they all were, which was difficult because they had all taken a defensive position and were surrounding her like she was a wild animal. Ben was the first to approach. She noticed the tears across his shoulders and that Charlotte was developing a black eye. Atarah looked down at herself and saw the ribbons of cloth from Ben's shirt in her hands. She lowered her hands; her wings started to shake as she realized what she did.

"It's all right, Atarah," Charlotte tried to soothe as she approached slowly.

Atarah couldn't take her gaze off of Charlotte's black eye. She raised her hand slowly, outstretched to Charlotte's face. Ben froze beside her, unsure of what she would do next. Charlotte's face was calm and trusting as she looked at Atarah. Her heart twisted, causing its own sort of pain and comfort knowing Charlotte held nothing against her.

A glow came from her hand that reached Charlotte's

face, but Atarah continued to let the power channel through her. She poured her power into Charlotte until it felt like a cup about to overflow, then she pulled away, revealing Charlotte's face completely healed and glowing from the amount of power Atarah gave. But it was the amazement on Charlotte's face that caught her attention. She looked around to see Ben, Clarissa, and Isabella all wearing the same expression. She had not only healed Charlotte, but healed all of them.

"You did it! You did it, Atarah!" Charlotte said, ecstatic.

Atarah wished she could join in on her joy, but the pain of her black eye was still too fresh in her mind. She had caused the damage because of her own recklessness. She felt arms around her.

Charlotte embraced her. "It's okay, Atarah, really."

Atarah looked at Ben, who stood beside her reassuringly. This time, his hand was on her shoulder, and he was blushing.

"Don't worry. Now we know." Ben's wings hadn't flared. "We know two things now. One, that you can heal—pretty well by the looks of it. And two—"

"Take off those gloves!" Clarissa said, her voice full of venom. Isabella had been shoved behind her. Both of their wings were flared.

Atarah couldn't blame either of them. She lifted up her hand, showing they were bare. This didn't faze Ben. He took her hands gently, pinched the tip of her finger, and slowly pulled at her hand. The glove materialized before them, out of thin air. Then he did the same for the other hand, freeing them completely.

"Thank you," Atarah said sincerely.

"Well, thanks for keeping us on our toes. Exciting stuff always happens when I travel with you."

Atarah blushed and turned to Clarissa and Isabella, wanting to apologize.

"Don't even bother," Clarissa sneered. "But try to attack us again, and I *will* gut you."

With that they moved to the front of the tunnel, leaving the rest of them behind. Isabella gave Atarah a curious glance, but not one of anger or fear, before following her sister.

Doubt we'll be friends anytime soon, she thought sardonically.

"Don't let that get to you," Ben said, drawing her attention once more. His eyes looked sincere and, though she might have imagined it, even a little worried. He nodded when she didn't reply and continued along the tunnel.

He patted his left shoulder before turning and looking at her. "Not too scared to try again, are you?" he teased.

The tiniest smile tugged on Atarah's lips before she reached up and grabbed Ben's shoulder. "As long as you're not too scared."

"Try not to go berserk again. This time, it'll be my other shoulder you'll scratch up," Ben said jokingly. She could hear the smile in his voice.

Atarah looked behind her to see Charlotte giving her an encouraging smile, and they started to walk farther down the tunnel. Eventually, they caught up with the Uriel sisters, at which point Ben took over guiding them through the tunnels to where they needed to go. As they walked, Atarah began her deep concentration again, intensifying everything she heard and felt within the sand.

Hours passed with them like this, traveling down the tunnel. Atarah only knew hours had passed because as they traveled, the terrain above shifted and became more solid. The more solid the ground, the more things rattled with movement and sound, making her job of identifying demons easier. Traveling along the tunnel, they covered more ground than they would have above ground. While most angels traveled by flying, in the deadly times with demons lurking, it would have been too dangerous for them to fly. Flying now would make them easy targets for demons to shoot down.

The terrain became denser and tougher above them. The stretched-out feelings of roots reached out to Atarah, as if searching to see if it was a friend or a foe. The underground became cool and dark as the soil from the ground grew into a new climate. Atarah felt comforted by the darker surroundings, for she felt the life above ground that the terrain provided. The trees steadily grew taller; creatures scurried, all harmless. She felt the forest itself through her powers. The sway of the wind, the struggle of power, food, and safety for the small creatures, the balance their world lived in between death and life. Love and hate, fear and understanding, power and weakness. All there balancing one another in harmonious cycles.

Atarah felt her teammates' apprehension as the tunnel grew darker and smaller, enclosing them, making their wings twitch in panic.

Nonetheless, Atarah knew they were closing in on the borders between Gabriel and Raphael's lands. The lands were similar, but Atarah could feel the difference, even though she couldn't see. She knew from her memory that Raphael's lands were made up of forests with massive trees covered in autumn leaves. From the visions she'd been given by Gabriel's Head Tree, she knew the trees in the Lanua Region were wispier, but adorned with vibrant flowers of spring. So colorful it momentarily mesmerized the onlooker and made one wonder if they'd stumbled into a dream. The forest felt like a contrast of a sunset and a sunrise. Both breathtakingly stunning, yet they represented completely different things.

The border stretch was long, but given how fast the tunnel, somehow, got them out of the desert, Atarah knew they would cross the border in no time. To think it had taken them two days of traveling to get across one region. Now they were about to cross two regions in a single day to get to her home.

While they walked, Atarah had a sense that Ben and Charlotte were talking, but she couldn't focus on what they were saying. Tired as she might be, the moment she tried to focus on one word, her power diminished her ability to feel around their area. After several attempts, Atarah gave up trying to listen in on their conversation and turned to her inward thoughts. She reflected on the mountain of emotions that had come up from the gloves and tried to discern what they meant. While she maintained her attention on her whereabouts, she pulled one emotion up at a time. She had been unaware of how many emotions she had been pushing down until they all came to the surface. The emotions felt like balloons that she had constantly been pushing underwater, until finally they all bubbled to the surface due to the gloves.

The first was anger. Atarah tried to remember the memories that showed themselves when it came to anger. She'd seen her father, and Arick in her mind.

However, anger toward her father and Arick puzzled her. Why was she angry with them? She thought back on her memories. Maybe she was frustrated at not being told everything about what had happened with her mother. Or was she angry her father had tried to hold her back when it came to diplomatic tasks? Was she jealous of Arick? At the moment, Atarah felt no anger or frustration toward anyone and had been surprised when the glove revealed anger to her earlier.

Too puzzled by anger, she decided to move onto the next emotion: sadness. Atarah understood that, especially with everything that happened to Ben's family. It made her reflect on her own family and how much she missed them. She'd felt sadness when she'd left the summit on her own for the first time, and again when she and Arick split up for the first time back in Silva. So much had been going on; Atarah had simply thought it would be better not to address her sadness. Atarah paused; maybe not better, but easier. Sadness lay deep and stayed rooted inside one's soul like a well to be filled with water, and Atarah had no desire to try to swim to the bottom.

The next emotion was anxiety. Atarah shuddered. Examining this emotion felt like something crawled under her skin. She wanted to find a good excuse to not dive into her emotions, but she knew if she didn't reflect on them now, it was because she was running away. Anxiety brought up memories of the summit, her brother and father again, and the Raphael family. Why was the anxiety there, and what was causing it? She didn't have to wonder long before she saw the correlation between each memory. Each memory was from times when there was fighting going on—between her father and brother, between the Head Archs, and when they'd visited Silva with the Raphael Archs. This was easy enough. She decided to look at each memory individually, reflecting on those moments, deciphering them, and deciding why the anxiety was heavier in some memories compared to others.

Slowly, Atarah realized a heavy chunk of anxiety encircled her family conflict more than any other.

No wonder I barely registered sadness when saying goodbye to my family. I felt too much relief at being away from conflict within the family to care about how much I'd miss them.

How odd, the way the two emotions correlated with each other. She moved onto the last one she remembered and dreaded the most: love.

Why was love the most painful? Because it had the most memory, a small voice inside Atarah whispered. One was always told about how powerful love was, but how powerful the memory of love was, was what hurt Atarah.

Her mind went to Ben and warmth spread around her. She had deep feelings for him. Atarah admitted this to herself and was surprised by her own thoughts. The small voice inside her shined through a little more because of her admission. She was about to explore deeper beneath the surface of these emotions, but the change in topography caught her attention. Then a warm hand wrapped around Atarah's, gently shaking her as if waking her from sleep.

"Atarah," Ben said softly, pulling her from her deep thoughts. His gaze was playful as always, but this time there was a sparkle of joy in his eyes that hadn't been there before.

"We're here," he said softly, still gazing at her.

Strong emotions still swam around in Atarah. It was all too much for her to even speak yet. Atarah gave his hand a brief squeeze before letting go. Beyond him was the tunnel opening up above ground, shining a light down upon them, inviting yet daring them to come up and explore.

"We're at the edge of your region. Do you sense any demons underground or above?" Ben asked.

Atarah shook her head, her emotions still close to the surface. Charlotte looked ahead eagerly; this would be the first time she had been to Atarah's region. Atarah prayed it wouldn't be a bad experience.

"This time you lead the way, Atarah," Ben said encouragingly.

Charlotte nodded earnestly. She was still too nervous to go up without Atarah. Atarah spread her wings slightly, then shot for the top. She reached the opening within seconds and flew into the sky recklessly. There it was before her—the mountains, her home.

"Thank goodness," Atarah said breathlessly. The openness and vastness of the mountains used to intimidate her, but now it thrilled her.

The feeling of fully stretching her wings and soaring was nothing she would take for granted. She'd almost made it past the tree line before she heard Ben's worried shout. Sure enough, she looked back to see his face mixed with unease and frustration, and she almost laughed because it went against his usual character. She floated back to him and Charlotte with ease, expanding her senses to ensure they were alone.

"Mind telling me why you get to have all the fun?" Ben teased, but also scowled at her.

"Don't worry. We're well and truly alone," she said back. She landed right beside them.

Clarissa and Isabella cautiously climbed out of the tunnel and looked around, despite what Atarah said. Charlotte glanced at the dark forest that surrounded them, nothing like the light, inviting forest of Silva. The forest that surrounded the mountain range was ancient. Some legends suggested the forest had been around before the creation of angels and humans. The forest wasn't usually kind to visitors and deterred angels and demons alike from traveling this far north.

Atarah took a deep breath, assessing. "It'll snow tonight." She looked at their shocked faces. "Brace yourself for a cold you can only feel up north."

"Could have told us before we left!" Clarissa growled at her.

Isabella and Charlotte were already shivering and trying to warm themselves. They were all still in their desert attire of white long-sleeved shirts and tan cargo pants. While the whiteness of the shirts was useful to reflect the sun rays in the desert, it did little to help absorb the heat they needed. Atarah wished for her black wooled sweater and black, thermal, fleece pants. That's what she would normally wear; however, they would have to make do until they reached her home city of Sanctum.

Atarah shrugged. "If we get moving, it'll help keep the cold at bay."

"Then what're we standing around for?" Charlotte shivered.

Atarah's wings vibrated violently. They looked at her questioningly—or in Clarissa's case, like she was stupid.

She shrugged. "It helps keep my back warm, even if it's exhausting."

It was a technique also used a lot during training to keep the back muscles strong for fighting maneuvers, but she didn't think they'd be interested in that. She walked north toward the mountains, keeping her powers activated in case anything slipped by them. Here, on solid ground she didn't have to work as hard to sense everything. She enjoyed being able to move at ease while using her powers. She heard the others behind her reluctantly trying to keep their wings vibrating to stay warm.

Charlotte pulled up behind her. "Is it supposed to be wintertime here?" Her teeth chattered. Her wings were already tiring from the fast movement.

"It's actually springtime for our region," Atarah said.

The look on Charlotte's face made her laugh.

"Then it'll get warmer as we go along?" Charlotte asked hopefully.

"Yes," Atarah said, still giggling. "We should reach my home by nightfall."

"Nightfall?" Isabella cried in outrage. As if on cue, her stomach growled.

"Oh, right." Atarah was so used to ignoring her hunger, she forgot it had been quite a while since they'd all eaten.

"Do you have any lovely recommendations, Atarah?" Ben asked sarcastically.

Clarissa rolled her eyes at him.

Atarah expanded her powers out, trying to sense if there was any game nearby. "There's a river about a mile northeast. We'll head there for some food, then finish our journey north."

Everyone nodded in agreement for once. They trudged through the forest, following Atarah's every step as if they'd get lost without following exactly what she was doing. She supposed there was some truth to that.

Atarah followed the sounds of the forest, which greeted her. These woods had known her all her life. She escaped to them as often as she could to get away from the frightening mountains. Despite the forest's dark, harsh nature, it always felt safe for her.

For the most part, everyone walked in silence. From their heavy breathing, Atarah guessed that was the reason why they weren't talking as much. Belli Causa was much higher in altitude than other regions, making breathing difficult. Nonetheless, Atarah tried to engage in conversation with Charlotte.

"What did you and Ben talk about while in the tunnel?" Atarah asked quietly, looking at Ben from the corners of her eyes to make sure he wasn't listening.

"Nothing . . . much . . ." Charlotte panted, her cheeks turning pink.

This was going to be harder than Atarah thought. The one time she got a chance to talk was when everyone was too tired.

"What do you think of Belli Causa so far?" Atarah tried one more time.

Charlotte nodded and gave a thumbs-up in approval, too out of breath to use words.

Darn.

"What do you think so far, Atarah?" Ben asked, not as out of breath as the others.

"What do you mean?" Atarah asked as Ben walked closer to her and Charlotte fell a little behind, giving them some privacy.

"What do you think so far about the attack? Do you think your assumption was wrong? Will Sanctum be attacked?"

Atarah was puzzled for a moment. Ben hadn't meant that as a way to doubt her; he simply wanted to know her thoughts.

"I still think they will. I worry that whatever's supposed to attack Sanctum is already there, just like the viper was for Chrysi Poli."

"Are there any helpful creatures that could give us a clue? Like the other one in the desert?" Ben asked.

Atarah shook her head. Most of the creatures in the forest were smaller and only showed themselves when they wanted to be seen. She'd learned that there were larger living beings in these woods, but to never seek them out. She tried to challenge that once, to see one of the legendary creatures and had regretted it since. Behemoths, dragons, Nephilim, even Seraphim, were always told to live deep in the forest and mountains in a dormant state. A few brave angels tried to find them, like Atarah, but to no avail.

"Any ideas on how we should attack?" Atarah asked Ben, who raised a surprised eyebrow. "I saw how you were with both demons we fought. You have a lot of skill in fighting." Atarah fought the blush rising to her cheeks.

"My word. A compliment like that from someone of the Michael Clan? You're going to give me a bigger head than I already have."

"I don't think that's possible," Atarah teased back. "But how'd you learn to fight like that? Especially with lightning?" She'd been meaning to ask him for some time, but it always slipped her mind. Lightning wasn't a common thing to have mastery over.

Ben sighed. "It's a long, old, and embarrassing story. One I don't want to divulge just yet."

Atarah frowned. She wanted to uncover more secrets about Ben. The more she learned about him, the more she craved to know.

"But I can tell you having two older brothers forces you to learn how to fight from an early age," he said, relenting after seeing her frown.

"But you all seem to get along so well," Atarah countered.

Ben laughed. "Not at first. Amos got jealous of Canaan when he was born, then they both got jealous of me when I was born. They love attention," he emphasized with a smile. "They were the biggest, meanest bullies I knew, and none of us liked one another growing up."

Such a strange contrast to her own relationship with Arick, and even more so to how Ben was with his brothers now. "What happened then?"

Ben's smile faltered a little. "We all got into a fight so bad it frightened our mother. She tried to separate us, but by then we were already fully grown, much bigger than her, and sadly not used to our own strength. One of us—we're not sure who to this day—knocked our mother down accidentally when she tried to separate us, and she broke her wing in the fall."

Atarah's eyes widened at the pain that must have caused.

Ben nodded; his face solemn as he thought back on the memory. "She screamed so bad our father heard her from outside and came flying in as fast as he could. All of us, my brothers and I froze, realizing what we'd done." He was quiet for a moment; she wondered if he would continue. "We got her an amazing healer, so she recovered quickly.

But we never forgot. She never blamed anyone for what happened, but after that none of us got into another fight again. Our father didn't say anything to us, which hurt worse than if he had. He probably knew we carried the guilt of what we'd caused and thought that to be enough punishment."

This was the most he'd ever said to her about his upbringing and the most open he'd been. Atarah held onto this little jewel Ben extended to her.

"So then with no fighting, we found out we actually get along with one another quite well. When fighting became off the table, it taught me how much better life can be." Ben gave her another one of his heart-stopping grins. In that moment with his brown hair all tousled and his brown eyes, Atarah thought he was one of the most attractive angels she'd ever met.

She was momentarily stunned at how far they'd come. The river was up ahead past a few trees. The Dark River was what it was called because the dark riverbed gave the illusion the water was black. However, when she pulled the water from the river, it was clear as day. Only those who lived in the forest knew that and dared to drink from the river. So, Atarah wasn't shocked when everyone's expressions were either apprehension or absolute disgust.

Atarah quickly explained the river was safe to eat and drink from and why it looked black. Ben and Charlotte took the news well enough, but Clarissa and Isabella . . .

"We'll eat after all of you have eaten from it first," Isabella said, still wrinkling her nose at the river.

"That works. More for me then." Charlotte looked hungrily at the river, trying to glimpse the fish below.

"The Dark River, huh? The name is a deceiving and yet accurate representation. I like it," Ben mused, dipping his hand in the cold strong current.

The river was large; it came from the mountains and was a safe water source in the region.

"Fishing in it will be hard, and you have to do it quickly or else the current will have no problem taking you," Atarah explained as she took off her shoes. It had been a while since she'd had to swim in this river. "The river's cold even by my standards, which is why I don't like to waste any time getting fish."

"Cold? I'm not even warm yet from our hike over here! I'll die if I fish. Can't you grab one for me?" Charlotte asked in a pleading voice. As much as Atarah's heart squeezed at her plea, she knew she needed to teach Charlotte how to fish. Atarah mused that while Charlotte wouldn't like it now, it was better if she knew how to fish.

"Sorry, Charlotte. This isn't something I can do for you. Everyone has to learn how to fish," Atarah said firmly, as Charlotte's face fell.

"Then teach away, O grand master," Ben said with a dramatic bow.

Atarah resisted the urge to give him a small push and send him into the water. Instead, she smiled and finished rolling up her sleeves. "We're lucky this time of year. Now that it's spring, the fish will be higher up from the riverbed, so we won't have to dive as deep," she explained. "Fishing is really quite simple. You fly up above and try to spot your target. Once you've spotted it, tuck in your wings and dive as far as you can and grab the fish."

"Sounds simple enough," Isabella grumbled.

"Getting the fish isn't the problem. It's getting out of the water with your fish that's the hard part. Once you've grabbed your fish, they'll fight like hell, and you have to use their wriggling motion to gain enough momentum to get yourself out of the water."

"So, the element of surprise," Ben concluded, looking at the water.

Atarah nodded. "When you grab the fish, you immediately have to get it facing upward so it will shoot out of the river. Once out of the river, you can fly over to the shore and eat up."

"Wait, how large are these fish if they can swim us up and out of the water?" Charlotte asked nervously.

"They can get quite big. You need to dive for one that's close to your body size. However, I've never dived for one bigger than my body, if that gives you a reference."

"As big as my body?" Charlotte and Isabella questioned in unison.

Atarah nodded. "It's really not as bad as it sounds."

"How do we hold onto this thing?" Clarissa asked.

"Wrap both of your arms around its body, preferably above its pectoral fins so you have leverage. Then, use your legs to push the tail fin down," Atarah said.

"Atarah goes first, so we can see how it's done," Ben said.

Atarah wondered if he said this more for their benefit than for his own. Charlotte and Isabella looked melancholic, and Clarissa looked annoyed at having to catch her own food.

"If they're so big, why can't we share one?" Clarissa asked snidely.

"Because when they die, they release a poison throughout the inside of their body and only a small portion of it can be eaten. It may be enough to feed one person."

"Ha! Clever fish." Ben laughed humorlessly.

Clarissa looked more annoyed with her answer, to which Atarah could only shrug and get to work on her own fish. She removed her long-sleeved shirt to keep dry, leaving her with just her undershirt. She flew up above the river and glided along it, trying to spot the movement of any fish. She found a spot she thought would have plenty of fish and hovered as quietly as she could. The trick to spotting a fish in the Dark River was to see its scales briefly flash against the sunlight. Once a hunter spotted the flash of the scales, she could lock onto the fish's location. Atarah moved into position now directly above the fish, then tucked in her wings and dove.

The freezing water greeted her, sucking any warmth away instantly, but she had no time to think about that. She circled her arms around her prize, under its pectoral fins, and pushed her legs and her back into the caudal fin, aiming the head upward. Sure enough, on instinct, the fish flapped and bucked to try to knock Atarah off of its back, sending them flying up and shooting into the sky. As soon as Atarah felt the unforgiving breeze, she expanded her wings and flew as fast as she could to the shore. The fish wriggled and fought the whole way there, slipping more and more from her hands the closer they got. To avoid losing her fish, Atarah bent her knees and kicked the fish the rest of the way to the shore. The fish landed on its head with a crunch that made Isabella's face turn green. The fish stopped moving when Atarah landed, wet and shivering. With her fish dealt with, she quickly grabbed the other shirt she'd taken off and flew up to a tree for privacy to change her shirt.

By the time she got back, Isabella's face was a little less green and everyone had gathered around the fish, inspecting it with amazement. The dry clothes didn't give Atarah any warmth, but at least they didn't take any warmth. She made her way and flipped the fish over.

"Well, good luck to whoever's next," Atarah said, taking out her knife to start carving out the pieces she could eat.

They watched as she carved out the lower bit of flesh below the gills. The only safe part that they could eat raw. There were some parts that they could cook, but they didn't have enough time.

"That's all we can eat?" Charlotte asked, surprised. It would be enough, but Atarah could understand her surprise, especially with such a big fish.

"No time to waste then," Ben said.

Atarah turned to warn him about the cold and froze. Ben already had his shirt off, showing his built body. His back muscles rippled as he expanded his wings and in the blink of an eye, he was high up in the sky, looking over the river.

"Show off," Charlotte muttered as she flew up after him.

Clarissa made a sound of exasperation as Isabella looked up admiringly at Ben. They both followed him.

Ben was the first to dive after a fish. For a moment, there was no movement, then the next, Ben flew out of the water riding on the fish's back, pure excitement on his face. He expanded his wings and shot toward Atarah, who still sat mesmerized, watching Ben. He dropped his fish at her feet, bringing her out of her stupor. Atarah quickly stabbed the fish's head with her dagger, and it went still. She became acutely aware of Ben walking up and sitting down beside her, still without his shirt. Even worse, she became aware of Isabella's gaze from above the river, watching them carefully.

"Enjoying yourself?" Atarah said, attempting to make things casual.

Ben grinned at her, still panting from the effort of carrying and flying the fish over.

"This is the most fun I've had in a long time," he managed to get out.

Atarah kept her eyes on his fish, carefully cutting out the pieces he could eat.

"Do you want to show me how to do that?" he asked with a mischievous grin, leaning in closer to her.

This guy, Atarah thought as she blushed, *knows exactly what he's doing*. She flipped the fish over to him. "I think you got it from here, showoff."

"But you're such a good teacher," he whined, still grinning.

"You're such a shameless flirt."

That earned her a carefree laugh. Ben quickly carved up the piece of his fish with undoubted expertise. He still sat close to her. So close their shoulders touched. She resisted the urge to lean into his warm torso.

"How long have you been fishing?" Atarah asked, trying to distract herself.

"The fish travel downstream to Lanua when it's wintertime here. While I was in Gabriel's region, they taught me how to fish there." Ben started to eat his prize.

Arrogant peacock, Atarah thought, smiling anyway.

"Is it wrong to be such a flirt?" he asked, as Atarah watched how the others fared in catching their fish. Charlotte still hadn't found the courage yet to dive, and Clarissa struggled to get her fish's head tilted upward. Isabella struggled with the same issue.

"Flirting is fun and all, but it doesn't show me who you really are," Atarah answered.

"You're very curious for an angel from the Michael Clan."

"I think everyone could use a good dose of curiosity from time to time."

Clarissa finally grabbed hold of a fish and flew toward them, when it slipped from her hands, back into the water. She gave a cry of frustration and dove back in again to retrieve her food. Charlotte and Isabella had finally worked up the courage to dive in for their fish. Now they were working out how to get the fish above the water.

"You never did answer my question," Atarah said, still watching Charlotte and Isabella.

"Pray tell. Which one?" Ben asked leisurely. He put his shirt back on and leaned back, watching the others struggle. He wrapped his wings around her, somehow getting even closer to her.

"How long have you been fishing?" She turned away from the others to look at him.

His deep brown eyes studied her. His gaze was soft. "I've been fishing for as long as I can remember. For many years. I grew up going to Aquam Caput and Urbs Antiqua, where fishing is a popular pastime." Ben's gaze darkened a bit. "It helps me when my mind gets too loud sometimes. To go away to a quiet place and be a part of something . . .different."

Atarah's heart fluttered at this little nugget of insight. A part of her loosened, a part of her that she usually liked to keep hidden. The heat from his body wrapped around her and she melted into him.

"I would go into the forest and try to make friends with the spirits." She looked to the river, as the memories surfaced. "Growing up around Michael angels is very . . . boisterous. So, when I wanted a quiet moment to myself I would sneak out into these very woods and try to find something that was as lonely as I was."

Like a magnet, her eyes were drawn back to his, but this time was different. His eyes seemed to look within her, at her very soul.

"I understand," he said softly. His eyes wide, and amazed.

She believed him instantly. More parts of herself

loosened as she leaned into his shoulder. A shield from within her lowered, and she felt the warmth of sunshine for the first time. She sighed in happiness.

"That's a relief." She turned back to the river. She knew her family loved her, but they never understood how she felt. For Ben to understand her even though he hadn't known her long felt like bliss.

"Oh," Atarah remembered. She pulled away slightly to turn fully to Ben. She nearly regretted it because she missed the warm embrace of his wings. "I forgot the other question I had asked you."

"Hmm." Ben tucked a piece of her hair behind her ear. "What was that?"

"If you have any ideas for an attack plan."

"If it's another large viper, I would try to cave it in the mountains or carve it up. However, there's no guarantee they'll send anything north, let alone a viper. Have you sensed anything?"

Atarah shook her head, wondering if she'd been wrong and this whole trip had been a farce. Her heart and pride sank at the thought. Better for her pride to be hurt than the lives of her clan.

Clarissa flew over frantically and dumped her fish at Atarah's feet. Giving her a nasty glare, Atarah took out her knife and roughly carved out a piece for Clarissa to eat. *Not as neat and clean cut as before, but it gets the job done.*

Isabella and Charlotte were almost done getting their own fish, much to Atarah's relief. They'd already been there long enough and needed to make their way to the mountain passages.

Charlotte cried out with joy as her fish leaped into the air and she made her way to the shore. Isabella, flying close behind her, clutched her own fish. Atarah lifted a hand to wave in congratulations when her eyes widened, and she gasped and froze.

Ben and Clarissa were instantly at her side asking what was wrong, but Atarah barely heard them. Atarah felt rumbling beneath them. Something large was passing by, something full of malice and heading in the exact direction of her mountains. Her face paled and her heart sank with dread. She'd been right.

"Atarah!" Ben said, shaking her shoulders.

She snapped her face to his.

"What's wrong?" he asked urgently.

"It's here," Atarah said hoarsely. "It's passing by us, heading directly for the mountains." She looked at Charlotte's concerned face. "I was right."

Dread slowly spread across all of their faces. A strong gust of wind gave them a brutal reminder of the cold reality of what they must do. They all looked to the mountains before them, knowing the battle they faced ahead.

Chapter 11

Mikael

Mikael walked aimlessly along the mountain trail, deep in thought. The sun hadn't risen, but the glow of it breaching the horizon had started. The wind rumbled through the valleys, carrying with them the faint scent of his family. He turned toward the wind, puzzled by what he smelled. He debated about leaping into the sky to seek out the smell before he heard a shout from far off. Mikael turned around to see a few of his generals. Home must be heavy on his heart today.

The children, Mikael's spirit whispered inside him.

"My Lord."

Atticus, one of his most loyal army generals, called him from his thoughts. Mikael turned to fully address him as well as the other two generals standing nearby, Micah and Jakob. Each was tall with broad shoulders, short military-cut hair, and a gaze that could make any demon quiver in fear. Their sharp golden eyes were tired but aware of everything around them. They wore light-weight black and blue armor and spikes around their wings. Gray and white hair mingled along Atticus's beard, showing his years. Micah showed signs of aging as well, but not as advanced as Atticus. Jakob was the youngest of the generals, but he had an eye for strategy.

Their soldiers were getting into position to march the rest of the way to the large gate of the capital city, Quaesitor, in the Campis Secretum region.

"Sir," Atticus continued. "The Head Arch of Raziel has sent a response to your letter."

"Oh?" Mikael said, mildly surprised.

Joshua Scio, Head Archangel of House Raziel, had always been too proud when it came to accepting help. Mikael reflected on his younger years with Joshua. Joshua was a good fighter because he studied his opponents well. He was proud, intelligent, and charismatic. Back then they'd fought side-by-side, laughed with joy at victories, and even had an alliance between their regions. However, that was in the past, before everything had happened. Mikael wondered how Joshua would receive him—if he was understanding about what happened or if he resented Mikael now. He wasn't sure. But if he knew Joshua, he'd want to know more, which was why he was called for this meeting.

"He said he wants to meet with you first before your armies are allowed to enter," Atticus said, finishing the message meant for him.

Jakob snorted in disgust. "His city is nearly drowning in demons and the dead flesh of his brethren. Is he truly full of so much pride he won't accept our help?" he sneered.

Micah stayed silent, watching Mikael's reaction.

"I'll meet with him. I have a feeling of where he might be," Mikael said grimly.

Micah and Atticus nodded, while Jakob still showed his displeasure at the situation. Mikael didn't blame him; from the outside, he understood how it seemed.

"Stay here and wait for my signal. Whether he invites us within his walls or not, we'll move out to help with the fight," Mikael instructed his generals. They all nodded with some reluctance, but they would obey. Mikael expanded his wings and lifted off into the sky without another word.

Quaesitor was a large city carved into the rocks of an ebony mountain range, the Coal Mountains. Few trees grew on this side of the mountain, but just before the city was a large lake that stretched across most of the city. It was probably why their city had lasted so long against the siege of demons. But no city was perfect. There were only five ways into the city. Two main gates that allowed the citizens and travelers to sell and trade goods. Two gates that led to the Coal Mountains from Azrael lands. The last gate was a secret from almost all public knowledge, the aerial gate. The gate was hidden in plain sight and could only be seen by those who knew where it was. Joshua had shown him this entrance before everything had happened to Ava. Mikael's heart ached painfully at the memories this place brought up. How theatrical of Joshua to want to meet at the very spot they'd seen each other last.

Mikael circled the city once and flew over its turquoise lake, which glistened against the morning sun as it broke past the horizon. The city was made mostly of stone carved from the mountain. A strong fortress and a library dwelled deep within the city and within the mountains, keeping track of all of history. The Selaphiel Clan was the only other clan that rivaled their library. The difference was the Selaphiel library was more trusted but exclusive, with few people allowed to read its content.

Raziel's library was purposefully encrypted, carrying secrets, but everyone was allowed access to their books. If they could read them, that is.

He spotted the tiniest landmark that gave away the only clue to the hidden gate's location. The sun illuminated the smallest of shadows, briefly revealing the curved rock. The only way to access it was by flight, and looking straight at it gave the illusion that it was merely rock and nothing more. Nonetheless, the large, curved rock was slightly hollow and zigzagged around to an entrance. Mikael quickly flew to the entrance, squeezing in between the tight spaces carved into the tunnel that led to the gate. The rocks scraped roughly against his back, arms, and legs as he maneuvered through the tight space. Finally, he entered the wide-open space of the hidden gate. Torches that lined the cavern created the light to see its full glory. The gate was adorned with ancient writing, a riddle that needed to be answered if one wanted the gates to open.

Sure enough, Joshua Scio stood facing the gate, his back to Mikael. His silvery wings reflected the flames from the torches above. His blond hair was sprinkled with gray.

"It's been a long time, old friend." Joshua's voice echoed lightly.

Mikael stopped a few feet from where he stood. Heavy nostalgia coursed through him as Joshua turned around to face him. His strong jawline had a new jagged scar going from the bottom of his ear to the end of his chin. His bright blue eyes looked sunken from a lack of sleep, and his face was slightly hollow from a lack of food and the heavy stress of leadership. However, in his eyes, Mikael saw none of the conceit and arrogance of his younger years, but a man who'd been in the trenches for too long.

"How long has it been since we last saw each other?" Joshua asked, not in an unfriendly way.

"Long enough for our children to be full adults. Long enough for the next generation to shape themselves," Mikael said warily.

Joshua only gave a small nod. His blue eyes sharpened, and his voice turned steely. "We might as well get straight to business. Why should we accept aid from you, the Great Betrayer, and why have you extended a hand now?"

There it was, the name Elijah had screamed at him long ago. The Great Betrayer. A title meant to spew hate and anger, but it had become a term of endearment to Mikael.

"Not everything is what it seems," Mikael replied.

"Indeed. How do I know I'm not letting a poisonous war horse into my city?"

"This war horse carries no poison, but it does carry soldiers. Soldiers who want to keep your walls safe."

Joshua studied him for a bit. "I liked the nickname Elijah gave you back then. The Great Betrayer has a nice ring to it."

"What do you make of the rest? Do you loathe me as much as Elijah does?"

"Many things you are, including a betrayer. But loathsome, you are not." Joshua leveled a stare that would cause others to quake in their boots. But Mikael knew his old friend was simply assessing him. Mikael took some comfort that Joshua may know more than he let on about him.

"How much do you need to know?" he asked.

"I know enough now that you've come here," Joshua answered.

Mikael gave an empty laugh. A moment of silence passed. He regarded the ancient writing as Joshua did when he'd first walked in.

"I've stayed away for many years out of necessity for my family." Mikael looked back at Joshua, who assessed him with no expression and held his stare. "Will you accept us?"

Joshua gave a long sigh. "Even if I didn't accept your lot into my city, you'd just camp outside the gates and attack the hordes that came at night." He paused, and Mikael's lips twitched with the urge to smile. Joshua knew him well.

"As long as you aren't with the enemy, then I welcome any help into my city." Joshua ran his hand warily through his hair. His wings had stayed relaxed this whole time.

Mikael nodded. Joshua had come a long way since the last time he'd seen him. He knew Joshua would have borne the brunt of the fighting, so his city wouldn't have to accept help, but this time . . .

"I'll send the orders," was all Mikael could say. He walked toward the entrance.

Then Joshua called his name. He turned.

"I heard your . . . son . . . may join us soon."

Mikael froze, his wings lifting ever so slightly higher than before. "A new development in the plans?"

"Apparently, Malachi's forces and his people ran for their lives toward Chrysi Poli, with the legions of demons following. By the time the Raphael forces arrived, there was no one there to fight." Joshua paused, seeming to be fully aware of how focused and sharp Mikael's gaze was. "The reports state they are still traveling south to Mortem to help."

Joshua told him this for a reason, Mikael knew, but it didn't help calm the overwhelming fear that gripped his heart. Arick traveling to the City of the Dead. Mikael couldn't stop his flared wings from shaking, with anger and worry.

Joshua looked at Mikael, who willed his wings to stop. "Interesting. You truly do care for the boy."

"Any more reports you receive regarding Arick or Atarah need to come to me," Mikael said through clenched teeth. He turned and exited the cavern as quickly as he could. The cavern started to quake ever so slightly due to Mikael's power, which he knew Joshua would note. His control of his power slipped the tiniest amount due to his strong emotions for his children. The cavern stopped shaking as quickly as it began. Mikael made it to the little sliver of rock leading to the outside and launched himself upward as soon as he saw blue.

A test. It was another one of Joshua's tests, and he obtained all the answers Mikael unwillingly showed. No sense in brooding over it. War came first.

Mikael easily flew down to where his army was lining up, his generals in their positions waiting for the signal. He banked a sharp left, signaling for them to start marching to the gate, for they would be welcomed into the city. His soldiers took flight in order of their ranks, each launching into the sky with swiftness and stealth. Mikael had already started his flight toward the city, leading the way. From his survey earlier, he saw no traps had been laid for them, but he could see the opportunity to lay traps for the demons. He noted blank spots that could use a soldier or defenses they could strengthen. Mikael truly thought the city surviving the attack this long was a miracle. While Joshua was an amazing fighter, his people were by no means fighters themselves. Even Raphael's people stood a better fighting chance compared to the Raziel Clan. Despite it all, they'd held the city. Mikael knew the city from his younger years, and if not much had changed since his last visit, maybe some of his strategies would work. They wouldn't waste the day doing nothing either.

The night before, Mikael had heard the hordes screeching off in the distance. Last night had been absolute silence, while his forces camped a few miles from the city gates.

The demons would be back. Their arrival had only caused a temporary retreat. They would come back tonight with double the forces.

Mikael flew right before the gate and landed in front of the tall stone walls, waiting for his army and for Joshua to give the commands. His generals flanked his left, right, and his back first, confusion on their faces briefly, wondering why they didn't simply fly into the city. He knew their thoughts because he'd once thought the same thing. Quaesitor was a magnificently walled city, but it had developed an aerial defense dome as well, over the centuries of clans fighting one another. Joshua had teased Mikael endlessly when he'd flown right into the dome, like a moth to a flame.

A horn sounded from the other side of the stone wall and a rumbling shook the road they stood on. The wall split open down the middle, revealing Joshua and one of his sons, Barmen. He had striking blue eyes like his father, filled with distrust. His wings flared, despite his father's relaxed figure beside him.

A woman with striking blonde hair stood in front of them; her silver wings were relaxed, but her gray eyes swam with suspicion. She was the first one to greet them, her voice as steely as her eyes.

"Please make your way over to the east bank with your troops. There's room there amongst the rubble for your men to stay." She lifted her hand to the upper right part of the city, which sat overlooking the pristine lake.

Mikael nodded to Jakob to dispatch his group. They all swiftly took off. He turned to Micah and gave his signal to follow and set up on the opposite side of Jakob. Micah and his unit took to the sky in seconds, like a black swarm. Lastly, Atticus stayed by his side, moving his gaze between the female before them and the Head Arch behind her. Mikael gave his signal to Atticus to move his troops into position. Atticus hesitated for a few seconds, but he obeyed. Mikael had no doubt he would circle back to him once his troops were settled. Within a few minutes, only Mikael stood before the Raziel Head Arch family.

"Come." The simple command came from the steel-eyed female. "We have much to discuss."

Mikael did not know who she was, but he knew from her looks she had to be an Arch. "My generals need to be a part of any meeting we have," he replied coolly.

Her face remained expressionless, while Barmen's wings flared at his reply.

"Come now, Farah. They'll need a few moments to get settled in," Joshua said, stepping forward until they were side by side. "Forgive us if we seem a bit strained. It's been a while since we've had guests we liked."

"If this is how you treat the guests you like, Trinity help the ones you despise," Mikael replied.

The sides of Farah's mouth twitched. Barmen stood back. His wings still weren't relaxed.

Joshua chuckled at Mikael's expense. "Indeed. We'll be in the middle of the city, at the base of our Head Tree when you and your generals are ready."

Mikael nodded curtly before expanding his wings and launching himself into the sky. Spotting his troops was easy enough. The east side of the city was all in disrepair. This side of the city was the one that received the brunt of the demon attacks, so this might as well have been the front line for his men. Not that any would have minded, being the only ones that stood between the demons and the angels of Raziel. None of the soldiers cared as long as they could get their time in battle. Nonetheless, Mikael wouldn't ignore that they would rather his men die first before putting any of their men on the front lines. He perched on top of a shattered building overlooking all of his troops stationed along the wall.

Jakob was the first to circle back to him and give him the report of how the soldiers were stationed, the watches that had been put up, and the rations handed out. Micah landed next to him, giving his own reports as well. Last to return was Atticus. As he gave his report, Mikael thought back to older times. Out of all of them, Atticus was his oldest general and the only one who'd been around during the time Ava had entered his life. He'd made it through that time period, so now Mikael prayed all of his generals would live this time.

When they all fell silent, he spoke to them.

"Good. Set the long spikes along the wall facing outward and upward. Once they're done with that, leave instructions for them to set up sparring matches to keep the restlessness at bay."

They all nodded.

"It will be done," Atticus said.

Mikael continued. "We'll meet with the Raziel Arch family and discuss attack plans once you're done giving the troops their instructions."

They all nodded once more in silence as they extended their wings for takeoff. Mikael lifted his hand to them. They looked at him expectantly.

"Tell the captains of their units to train the new soldiers a little extra today. They haven't experienced the chaos of demon hordes yet. The erratic movements and the ghastly sounds will never leave them from this day forth. Let us prepare them as much as possible."

This time, they still said nothing and didn't nod. But the look in each of their eyes gave him the message that they understood and detested this feeling of guilt as much as he did. Over the ages, the guilt and heaviness never dulled as he introduced his soldiers to the horrors of the demons. He knew his generals felt the same. They took off with their instructions, while Mikael took off and surveyed the wall closer than before. He noticed every claw mark and every burn that scuffed the wall in detail. He noted it all—the wall, the damage, the toughness of the dome, and then the looks of the civilian angels that scurried along the street. They were scared to remain outside for too long in case of any demons. The demons could very well attack during the day, but they didn't prefer it. The cover of the night was when they were at their peak, and it was their favorite time to attack. Nonetheless, he knew they would attack tonight. He had carefully studied the attack patterns of all of the cities from the reports he received.

He mused over all of the information he had collected over the past few weeks, when his generals once again came back to him. He pulled himself away from his thoughts and gave them one nod before leaping into the air. They all swiftly followed him as they made their way to the center of the city. As they traveled deeper into the city along the mountain's face, there was a brief dip in the slope, giving it a sunken trench. Within the trench laid the enormous Head Tree.

The tree was a deep burgundy color that would stick out more against the mountain if it wasn't hidden by the sunken trench. There within the mountains, the lone Head Tree stood with Farah, Joshua, and Barmen at the base. They circled the tree one time before landing in front of them. Barmen and Farah's wings flared at the sight of his three generals beside him, but Joshua's wings stayed relaxed at his sides. He offered a small nod of greeting to each of them, the only sign that he remembered them from battles years ago. Behind the tree was the Raziel Court Hall, where most official matters were handled. They all walked up the stone steps. The Hall was as Mikael remembered. Carved out of the mountain, it was one of the oldest buildings in all of Campis Secretum.

It housed all of the books that had every bit of knowledge in their realm, the demon realm, and the human realm. Angels drove themselves mad trying to decipher the texts in the books to gain their knowledge. Sure enough, there were angels in the hall that looked like they hadn't left there in centuries, with their sunken, dilated eyes, hunched over their books, papers scattered, trying to get through the riddles in the books. Some hissed at them and clutched their books tighter to themselves as they passed.

Jakob scoffed at them. Micah looked like he might do the same. Atticus didn't even glance their way and kept walking. Even with demons ravaging their city outside, they wouldn't leave their books behind.

They circled around the Great Hole that dove deep into the mountain's roots, books lining the walls of the hole, supposedly all the way down. However, no one had ever been to the bottom to confirm. If anyone tried, fear of the darkness gripped them so tightly, they raced back up, their eyes dilated, lips bloodless, and shaking so bad they couldn't walk out of the Hall for several hours.

Mikael glanced down there to see the lanterns carried by angels scouring along the wall, looking for their next book. They walked past the Great Hole library and into a wide room with open space, save for one massive, circular table. In the center lay a map of all of Quaesitor. Every hill, house, tunnel, and rock was on the map to inform them of everything that went on with the city. Updated hourly, but by whose power, Mikael had never known. He knew it could be trusted.

Joshua sat down on one side of the table, while Farah and Barmen sat on either side of him. Mikael sat down nearly opposite of him, with Atticus to his right, Jakob to his left, and Micah to Jakob's left. All glanced at the map in the middle.

"So much to cover," Joshua said casually. "Almost hard to decide where to start."

"Start with the night horde and where they usually attack," Mikael said, his face impassive.

"That was part of the fun in battling these creatures," Barmen said for the first time since their arrival. "There's no pattern to them, just chaos."

"Where do they come from? What angle?" Atticus asked calmly.

Farah answered this time. "They attack from almost every angle. They've climbed high along the mountain's cliff to fall down on the city. Tried mining their way through the wall. Tried blasting through the wall."

"Why's the east side so damaged then?" Mikael asked.

Something flickered in Joshua's eyes. "Our shields faltered, and several demons got through the barrier. The east side was where it happened. That was almost a week ago now."

"Have they not tried again? If it's happened once, it can happen again," Micah said logically.

Joshua only gave a grin that was anything but friendly. "Lucky for us, around that time, a certain Arch heir of the Michael Clan strengthened the barrier in the Raphael region. When that happened, the power was distributed between each standing tree. That little bit of power is how we've been able to survive this far after it was breached."

Mikael resisted the urge to flare his wings as his generals suddenly became interested in the map in front of them. "I'm glad we could help you even before we arrived."

"I'm glad your children went to Ventus after the summit," Farah said harshly, her intent clear. Glad they were with the Raphael Arch family and not him. *As long as they're safe*, Mikael thought, *that's all that matters.*

"Come now," Joshua said, playing peacemaker. "Two

young ones traveling is much easier than moving an army. They are hardly comparable."

"However amazing my children are"—Mikael said, looking at Joshua—"we need to get back to what's going to happen tonight when the demons come back with double the force."

"How do you know the demons will come back with more force?" Barmen asked with suspicion.

"If you think we've been flapping our wings out there every day, you're sorely mistaken," Jakob spoke for the first time in the meeting.

"We've been analyzing every attack each city in the Southern Region has faced ever since the summit," Atticus said. "It took us a while to get information, but we've studied every bit of it."

"We have an idea of how they'll attack, especially since you've received reinforcements. I have no doubt the attacks in Vallis have altered." Mikael looked at Joshua. His generals' heads turned slightly toward him. They'd been unaware of this new bit of information.

"The mountain ranges are the only thing separating your regions. The massive hole must be between your regions, allowing the demons passage to each of your lands," Mikael explained.

Joshua looked at him pensively.

"Nothing about this information is new. What point are you trying to make?" Farah asked.

Jakob, Micah, and Atticus's wings flared a little at her tone. Barmen's wings flared in response. Mikael and Joshua ignored all of them.

"The demons have been focused on keeping each city busy with attacks so that you never get a chance to attack back. However, now that you've both received more troops, it's time to strike," Mikael finished.

"What are you proposing?" Joshua said, leaning forward.

"Coordinate with my force and the Raphael force and go after the hole from both sides, killing any demon in our way and closing the hole."

"There are still other holes in the area," Barmen argued.

"Yes, but very few and not as big as the one between your lands. That's where the bulk of the demon army can fit through," Mikael rebutted.

"From our guess, that's probably why they've retreated now to gather more forces," Atticus finished.

"Are we to leave our city completely defenseless, then, while our soldiers are miles away in the mountains?" Farah said bitingly.

Micah was the one to address her, speaking more calmly than Mikael expected. "If we remain here, we'll just continue to be on the defensive. That won't solve the overall problem."

Farah seemed to ignore him and turned to Joshua. "What should we do?"

Barmen sat quietly, still looking between them, his wings not relaxed.

Joshua looked at Mikael with the same pensive face. "What makes you think the Azrael or Raphael forces will comply and agree to this plan?"

"Hopefully reason and logic will win over their disdain for me and my troops."

Joshua laughed. "Do not be so hopeful. Nonetheless, you make a fair point." Joshua turned to Farah. "We need to stop just defending, and we need to start attacking or else nothing will change."

"Why not send the Michael troops out and leave our soldiers here?" Barmen suggested, blind to his crassness.

"Azrael and Raphael definitely won't fight if they know we stayed behind. If we fight with Mikael's troops, there's at least a chance they'll aid us. Neither clan would raise a finger, though, if only the Michael Clan needed help," Joshua said in cruel truth.

Atticus stiffened in the seat next to him. Mikael gave a small wave of his hand, conveying for him to stand down. While Mikael had never asked Atticus how much he knew of what happened, he must know enough for comments like that to anger him. Micah and Jakob didn't bother to hide their anger.

Joshua paid them no mind, however, as he looked at Mikael. "I'll send the message out now. Anything you want me to include for . . . your son?" He was baiting Mikael with the question.

Mikael gave only one sharp shake of his head.

"Very well, that's settled. What's our plan if they don't respond?" Farah asked, not looking at them but at Joshua.

"Give them the biggest greeting we can give from the Michael Clan," Mikael said, his voice hard and commanding. His generals smirked at them—and at the battle ahead.

The burning sensation from exercise consumed Noah's body, but he refused to stop. Arick must have felt the same way, but if he did, he didn't let on. His expression was almost bored as they rode. Closer and closer, they got to the capital Mortem. They had crossed the regional border nearly a day ago.

Finally, Noah thought when they made it through that ridiculously wild tropical forest. *How can anyone stand the summer heat?* He craved the cool autumn climate back in Ventus.

On and on, they rode through the Coal Mountains, and Noah almost wished they could go through the forest instead of the mountains. The Coal Mountains received its name from the black-topped rock peaks and the heat that was so intense, it felt like traveling through burning coal. Whether the mountains truly had coal rock, Noah wasn't sure. Based on the scalding heat, he wouldn't be surprised. Already his water supply ran low because he sweated it all out. The Coal Mountains were a dry desert climate, so traveling through them seemed endless. Noah tried to focus on the next mountain ahead, and then the next mountain, and then the next. Unlike in the forest where the tree coverage limited the amount of sunlight, never-ending sunlight blazed down on them mercilessly.

As much as Noah wanted to take off his clothing, he knew he would cook his skin within a few hours of sun exposure. Most of the soldiers, including him, removed one layer of clothing to use as their shield against the sun, wrapping whatever they could around their arms, head, and neck. Nonetheless, Noah knew this would be one of the toughest parts of their journey. He didn't look forward to traveling through this barren, hot place or being a resident of this region. However, so far each town or village they passed had been empty.

Smart, Noah thought.

Every Head Arch pulled most of the citizens to the main capital city since the demons' rampages. Or else, they would have been tortured and devoured, he thought grimly as he saw the broken remains of a house in the distance. Only the Azrael or the Michael Clans could have lasted this long against a demon army of this magnitude. Since the Azrael angels specialized in the guidance of death, it made any who went against them a fool. While they couldn't outright kill with their powers, they could weaken their opponents significantly.

Noah shuddered, thinking about the last time he'd seen Zewal Adjutor, the heir to the Head Archangel of Azrael. Zewal was tall with stark features. His pale, pasty skin made him stand out, along with his short, navy-blue hair and spiny white wings that bore no feathers, giving hime an unsettling appearance. Most Azrael angels had a similar appearance: pale, pointy wings and either navy or deep-purple hair. It was hard for Noah to put his finger on why, but being around them instantly made his skin crawl and itch as if bugs climbed all over him. Zewal and his family left him the most unsettled. Given their skinny stature, they were by no means warriors of any kind. Noah doubted if one Azrael angel could even lift Arick's sword. Such different clans, one using power and strength, the other completely reliant upon their abilities to do their fighting for them.

Glancing back at Arick, Noah wondered how he'd react seeing an Azrael for the first time, and not just any Azrael, but Zewal, the heir of the Head Arch family. Zewal was the only one who had communicated to the other regions about what went on in their region, and even then, he conveyed little. He communicated when the severity of their situation started to spread to other regions, and other Arch Heads demanded to know what was going on.

Noah was fairly certain Zewal's father was the cause of this reluctance. Sewall Adjutor was a good leader from what Noah had read, but he wanted to do little with the other clans, if he didn't outright despise them. Sewall focused his time and his people on the passage of death for the souls in the other realms—his spiritual purpose. In hindsight, he completed his spiritual duty with such diligence, he neglected his other duty: maintaining balance with the other clans.

Every Arch Head had a spiritual duty and a realm duty. The spiritual duty varied based on the clan and what they specialized in, whereas the realm duty was the simple matter of maintaining peace and balance within the clans. Every Arch Head struggled with balancing these two main responsibilities during their reign. Every Arch heir was raised learning from his or her predecessor's mistakes and how to balance the two when he or she rose to power.

While most heads fell between balancing the two, Sewall heavily focused on his spiritual duty. Noah wondered how Sewall had been coping, since most of his time was taken up with the demon attacks. Secondly, what were the repercussions in the other realms now that less guidance was given?

Noah continued to pant. *Who knows*, he thought, wiping his face for the fiftieth time. *Just get to the capital. We're so close.*

Noah noticed the lack of demons around them and wondered if they'd pulled back just to attack with full force at nighttime. Looking behind him, he saw Arick studying the mountain range, possibly with the same thought. They needed to get to Mortem by nightfall or else they'd be defenseless. He saw how much his troops wanted to stop and rest, but he couldn't risk it. *Just a few more hours.*

Hours continued with them riding full speed ahead. The water supply ran dangerously low and some of the horses, he knew, were about to give out. Just as Noah was about to call it and have them stop, he spotted the snow-white rock peak that signified the capital city of Mortem. Noah yelled triumphantly and gave his signal for his men to halt. They gradually came to a stop and dismounted.

Arick came up to him, no doubt about to ask why they'd stopped. He didn't disappoint.

"Why have we stopped here? The capital is still miles away." Arick was sweating a little, but he wasn't out of breath like Noah.

Noah answered when his breathing had calmed. "The

city can only be reached by flight now. There's no mountain pass or trail that gets closer than this point."

"We'll have to leave the horses behind completely?" Arick said with a bit of surprise.

Noah nodded grimly. "They're trained to travel back to Silva. They'll make it home." He doubted it, though, with how many demons were patrolling these regions. Another reason he had been reluctant to come to Mortem—they'd have to relinquish their horses.

He gave the orders to his commanders for the soldiers to pack everything into a single pack that could be carried in flight. Within a short time, the troops were ready. Noah saw Arick and his little group were ready as well. He frowned at the angels he saw in Arick's group, but he wasn't surprised they'd stuck with Arick.

Noah turned his attention to the rest of his troop and signaled by launching himself into the air in flight. He heard his men taking flight and falling behind him in formation. The only outlier was Arick, who had his own small formation with his men. Based to his large wingspan and idle flaps, Noah guessed he flew slower so everyone else could keep up with him.

"Showoff," Noah grumbled, picking up speed.

The mountain with the white peak was the spot they needed to go to when traveling to the city, so Noah focused on it. The city was positioned at the base of the mountain, which offered a merciful change in temperature. Being surrounded by other mountains casted large shadows across the city throughout the day, making the temperature slightly lower than any other spot in the mountain range. While it was still hot, it would at least be cooler than the temperatures they faced now. Other things to look forward to were the underground homes, providing shade during most hours of the day, so he could stop wearing his sloppily made turban.

Noah had no doubt his men were happy to spread their wings and fly. If they could have, Noah would've had them fly all the way to Aquam Caput in the first place. However, his father had strict instructions that no one traveling should fly. Not that Noah would have argued; an army this size would be an easy target.

They quickly neared the white-topped mountain, close enough to see the city. Noah signaled his commanders to slow, while he surged ahead to scout for a landing. Arick followed him. Just as Noah was about to tell Arick to stand down, an arrow flew at him.

Noah evaded it, understanding its message: they were not welcome.

Ignoring Arick, he made a wide sweep around the mountain then dove straight down. He needed an audience with either Sewall or Zewal. His men needed to land eventually. Noah evaded all the oncoming arrow attacks and finally flashed through where the archers were stationed. Noah stayed low, entering the residential spaces of the city. He hovered just above the ground all the way until he reached the main house. The archers wouldn't shoot him while other angel civilians were around.

As Noah closed in on the main house in the northwest part of the city, Arick landed right in front of him. The overgrown bat threw him off and sent him tumbling along the dirt until he finally skidded to a stop. He coughed up dust, glaring up at where Arick stood.

Arick wasn't even looking at him. Standing before him on the steps of his home was Zewal, watching the entire time. Zewal's eyes had widened briefly at Noah's crash-landing, then he tipped his head back and laughed out loud, a gut laugh that nearly doubled him over.

Never had Noah seen any angel from the Azrael Clan laugh, and never had he wanted to pound Arick into the dirt as badly as he did now. He clenched his fists and tried to gather as much dignity as he could to stand. He rose stiffly and patted the dirt off of his clothes.

Zewal was still laughing, and Arick had joined in, chuckling quietly. Noah vowed to get Arick back for this as he walked over to the base of the steps, trying to ignore him.

Zewal's laughter finally quieted, but it had aroused the attention of other angels in the household behind him. Noah spotted Zewal's younger sister, Tariel, hovering by the door behind him.

"Sorry to intrude—" he began.

Zewal's laughter started up again, cutting him off. Tariel started down the steps. She was probably no more than Charlotte's age. She'd grown taller since the last time Noah saw her. She was now taller than him. Her long, bone straight, navy hair elongated her face even more. Her wiry frame looked awkward with her movements, as if she was still getting used to her own height. Her pale, leathery wings were behind her, completely relaxed. Both Tariel and Zewal wore long, light gray tunics with their family insignia on the upper portion of their arms. The symbol was a sundial, lined out in black against their light gray clothing. They both wore black scarves to help cover their heads and protect themselves against the unforgiving sun.

Tariel walked all the way down to where Noah stood on the first step.

She looked at both Noah and Arick. "Well, both of you know how to make an entrance."

"Noah did all the work." Arick gave one hard pat on Noah's back.

Noah gritted his teeth. *Tonight, I will throttle him in his sleep.*

Tariel's lips flickered in amusement. "My name is Tariel Adjutor, daughter of the Arch Head Sewall. This is my brother Zewal, Heir to the Arch Head of Azrael." She waved a hand in his direction as he seemed to finally recover from the fit of laughter.

Zewal coughed. "Pleasure to meet you, Arick, Heir of Michael."

Arick bowed dramatically.

Zewal turned to Noah. "We meet again, Noah of Raphael." His voice sounded cooler this time. All merriment was gone, like it never happened. "Why are you both here?"

"We were wondering if you had a bathroom we could use?" Arick said before Noah could speak.

Tariel's lips twitched upward again. She blushed as she looked at Arick.

Noah resisted the urge to sigh. *He's all sarcasm*, he wanted to tell her.

"You're in luck," Zewal said, his own lips twitching in amusement. "We have many bathrooms you can use." He paused. "Or your men can use it before you leave."

Subtle, Zewal, very subtle.

"Well, since we're already here"—Arick made a show of stretching—"we heard you have a demon problem in this area. We happen to have some men who've been itching to fight. I propose a trade."

Zewal lifted a hand. "We have no need—"

Arick cut him off, starting up the steps. "Of course, we're going to be fair and square about this. You feed and shelter us, and in exchange for your services, we'll trade you warriors to fight. That sounds like a pretty good trade."

Zewal looked slightly annoyed, while Tariel looked as close to amused as an Azrael angel could look.

"We don't need your services, and you expect too much kindness if you want shelter." His voice was cold, despite their hot surroundings.

Noah stayed on guard and ready. By the sound of Zewal's voice, he might use his powers.

Arick didn't even flinch or look at him. "I guess I wouldn't be friendly either if I had to live in the heat all the time." He paused as if in thought. "Do you happen to know any good shaded areas close by where visitors can set up their own camp? Since locals don't like outsiders."

"There might be a spot in the southeast region of the city. It's vacant due to a high number of demon attacks," Tariel said slyly.

Zewal looked at her reproachfully. He opened his mouth to speak, but Arick beat him to it.

"Perfect. Just what we need." Arick looked back at all three of them. "I knew you'd be some easygoing angels." He turned back and walked straight into their house as if he owned it.

While Noah and Zewal looked appalled by his gall, Tariel seemed amused.

She looked back at Noah. "Would you both like to join us for a quick lunch?"

Zewal looked at her like she'd grown two heads, and Noah thought she had. He gave a sort of gasping response, which she took for a yes.

"I'll inform our father." With that, she hurried off back into the house.

Zewal whirled on Noah. His face had no remnant of humor. "Get him out of our house and leave with all of your men!"

"I would, but I doubt he'll listen to me." Zewal's wings flared. "Also, we have some business with the holes that are allowing the demons through."

"No one's going near the holes, and you're all leaving!" Zewal hissed. He turned to walk into the house but paused.

Sewall Adjutor stood on the top step, looking down at them with an expression that made Noah want to fly away and never come back.

"I was informed we have some *guests* staying in our city tonight."

Snakes would have sounded kinder.

Sewall fixed his cold gaze onto Zewal in irritation as if saying, *why did you let this happen?* Zewal only swallowed and looked down.

Wimp, Noah thought.

Sewall turned to him. It had been so long since Noah felt like a child before someone. "Tell your clansmen to land in the southeast corner of our town. Then, you and your nephew meet us here in an hour."

Arick chose that precise moment to trot down the stairs as if it was any other day. He nodded and waved in greeting to the Head Arch.

"Very well. Thank you."

"Don't thank me yet. You may come to regret it." His gaze swept over Arick with disgust.

Arick didn't seem fazed in the least as he hopped the last few steps to where Noah stood. "All right, we can't keep our men waiting, Noah. It's rude." He smirked at Noah, his back to Sewall.

On the way back, Noah thought. He would throttle him on the way back.

Arick stretched his wings out wide and took off into the sky. Noah gave an apologetic glance at Zewal and Sewall, but the faces he got back were annoyed at best. Noah took off into the sky, flying after Arick.

Once they were a good distance from the city, Noah flew above Arick and dumped the contents of his water. Arick cursed and spluttered in his flight, looking at him.

Noah smirked. "I didn't get a chance to use the bathroom," he said, pretending to adjust his pants.

Arick glowered at him, but he continued to fly toward the troops.

One of Noah's commanders gave him a questioning look at his grin but didn't say anything.

"We'll set up camp in the southeast region of the city. That's where most of the demons have attacked, so guards will be stationed at all times."

They only nodded. Perfect obedience.

Noah flared his wings and led them toward the city. They made it to the section of the city they would stay in for a short time. However, Noah doubted he could call this part of the city. All that remained was rubble from where houses previously stood. At least there was some clearing space for his men to set up camp.

Noah made his rounds to oversee the camp building, guard rotation, ration count, and the training schedule for his men tonight and in the morning if there were no demons spotted. Noah's anxiety grew at the lack of demons in the area. Where were they?

I thought this region was swarming with so many demons that the citizens can't even go out at night.

He suspected the demons pulled back because of their arrival. The lunch with Sewell might confirm his suspicions. Noah's palms began to sweat. How on earth had Arick managed to get a meeting with the Azraels? Noah wondered if they'd use their powers on them and attack during the meal. Noah shuddered and hoped not. He'd felt what their power did one time and never wanted to feel it again.

Arick approached him, drawing his attention from the unsettling memory. "Ready for the fun to start?" he asked as if they were going to a celebration.

Noah looked him up and down. Arick's wings were relaxed, his skin glowed from the shine of the sun, and his gold eyes were at ease. How different could he be from the people they were about to sit down with? Noah scoffed at him.

"Some things we need to go over before we meet with them," Noah said as firmly as he could. "Don't wander off again into their house—uninvited, I might add. Don't go flirting with their daughter, Tariel. Above all else, don't joke around like it's any other family get-together. We're not family or friends with them. We're allies, helping with the demons for everyone's benefit, and that's all!" He emphasized as much as he could.

A strange look came over Arick's face for a split second, but just like that, it was gone, and his annoyingly calm expression returned. "Yes, honey-dear." He smirked. "Also, the bathroom is down the hall and to the right if you need to use it."

Noah rubbed his temples. "Don't use their bathroom again. This is why I never babysit."

"Never babysit something that's bigger than yourself," Arick said, patting Noah on the back.

Noah clenched his fists again and counted to ten before looking at Arick. How was this oversized lizard the same angel who'd communicated with a Head Tree from another region? Noah hadn't spoken to Arick about the Head Tree in Aquam Caput since he'd come stumbling out of it. He wondered what else was said because something shifted ever so slightly within Arick.

It mattered little because Brock, Jared, and Galvin approached, pulling Arick's attention away. Noah frowned once more and decided to refrain from speaking. They all bowed before Noah, respecting him as their leader, but they addressed Arick in a livelier manner.

"How long should we wait for our specialized training?" Brock asked, his eyes shifting to Noah occasionally.

Galvin regarded Noah pensively from the corners of his eyes so as to not seem obvious.

"Ah! Good, you reminded me. As soon as we get back, I have something for each of you to do. As for now, spar with one another once the rest of the troops have started training," Arick instructed.

Noah went to contradict Arick but thought better of it. If they trained with Arick, he doubted they were being lazy.

They walked on to help other troops set up their tents.

"You disapprove of them?" Arick inquired, not looking at Noah.

Noah sighed. "Not disapprove, but I don't find that group to be a wise choice."

"Hmm," Arick mused. "Well, we don't want to be late." He expanded his wings at the same time as Noah and they took off.

They easily made their way back to Sewall's house and were greeted by Zewal once more. Noah landed, this time with a wary eye on Arick. Zewal greeted them with a grimace. That would be the closest to a smile they'd get from him. Arick greeted him with a dramatic bow, while Noah grimaced back. Without a word, Zewal turned and walked into the house as they trailed behind.

Noah took this time to take in the interior design of the house. Made out of white stone, everything looked clean and minimal. Furniture was made out of the black stones that came from the surrounding mountains. The white stone against the black stone made a sharp contrast in every room he walked into. The house had different levels, with wide staircases leading up and down. Noah noted every room, window, and possible exits as they walked through the house. There were no pictures, no plants, or any other signs that indicated someone lived within the house. Just bare white walls and several black bookshelves lined the hallways. There were also no doors of any kind Noah could see around the house, just archways.

Zewal's footsteps were light and soundless, as he led them to the main dining room area. The dining room consisted of one large, round black tabletop with several black stools, leaving plenty of room for their wings to spread. Before them was what Noah thought of as a "neat spread." The spread consisted of cheese, toasted bread, fruits, hummus, olives, and a variety of nuts and sliced meats. The spread was so large that the tray covered most of the round table. However, his eyes weren't really on the food spread, but on the family that all stood and turned to greet them when they entered.

"What a lovely sight this is!" Arick said, his eyes on the food. He turned to Sewall and his daughter and bowed deeply. "Thank you so much for having us here."

Sewall frowned at Arick as his daughter bowed back. They all sat around the table. Arick sat to Noah's right, and to Arick's right was Tariel, then Zewal followed by his father, leaving Noah sitting next to Sewall to his left.

"We have much to talk about, Noah and Arick. Please eat up."

Arick needed nothing else to probe him. He filled his plate quickly, but before he ate, he said, "What do you wish to know? We're open books, Noah and I."

Noah coughed as he drank from his cup of water.

"Why come here? Malachi's citizens would have welcomed your help more than us"

"We were called to aid the citizens of Mortem and report on the angels in Aquam Caput," Noah explained cautiously.

"Oh?" Zewal said, glancing between him and Arick.

"You have the largest hole within these mountains. All of the demons are coming out of here. The lack of management would make this location a priority more than others."

"Management?" Zewal said with ice in his voice.

"Well, maybe not . . . management per say but . . . " Noah struggled to bring his words together as nerves collected within his stomach.

Sewall's eyes froze with fury, Zewal's wings flared, and Tariel looked at him with disgust.

Noah stilled. This whole lunch was a mistake.

Arick raised an eyebrow at him. "What my rambunctious uncle's trying to say is that the city of Mortem is overwhelmed and hurting. If you would share with us what you've learned about the holes thus far, we would love to help." Arick looked at Sewall. "The angels of this city are truly impressive."

Zewal's wings relaxed slightly, and Tariel seemed determined to simply ignore Noah the rest of the meal. Sewall regarded Noah coolly, then Arick.

"I see nothing beneficial from sharing what we know with either of you," Zewal said with a sneer.

"I do, especially from the message we received this morning," Tariel said from where she sat.

"Oh? Pray tell, what message did you receive this morning, and who was it from?" Arick said with a friendly grin to Tariel.

Tariel said nothing, but a blush illuminated her whole face, turning her as red as a tomato.

It was Sewall who answered with a cruel gleam in his eye. "Your father, actually."

The smile faded instantly from Arick's face. He looked at Sewall with a solemn expression. "If you reply, do send my father my regards." A muscle tensed in his jaw as he forced a strained smile.

"What's the message?" Noah said, drawing everyone's attention. "What did the Arch Heads of Raziel and Michael say?"

"The message was an attack plan. Arch Mikael believes the demons have regrouped since reinforcements arrived.

They believe the best tactic is to attack while they have withdrawn."

"Strategic plan, as always," Arick said, sipping his water.

Sewall raised an eyebrow at him.

Arick continued, already knowing his father's plan. "If both of our joined forces attack from opposite sides of the mountains, it'll give us a heavy advantage in killing the demons and closing the largest hole that allows the demons through."

"Why should we help Arch Mikael?" Sewall said with venom.

Arick only shrugged. "It'll close the demon's doorway and possibly give us insight on who is leading the demons."

"And your father can't deal with them on his own?" Zewal jeered.

Arick didn't seem bothered by their tones. "He and his forces will probably bear the brunt of the demon assault. However, if he goes in alone, that'll merely force the demons back into your region and not into the hole," he argued with astounding logic.

Sewall regarded Arick, not in an unfriendly manner. Zewal saw his father's look and seemed to do a double take at Arick himself. Tariel simply blushed every time she looked at him, darting her eyes back and forth between him and her plate.

Noah might as well have faded into the background. He wondered how Arick won over the Azrael family so quickly.

"Am I that attractive that you males can't stop staring at me?" Arick said cockily.

Noah wanted to roll his eyes. Sewall chuckled quietly.

"Don't flatter yourself," Zewal retorted, his own lips twitching once again with amusement.

Noah and Arick laughed at his flat response.

"Do you not fear us?" Sewall said with a seriousness that drew Noah back instantly.

Arick thought for a moment before answering. "I have many fears, but not of you or your family, or even the demons."

"What do you fear then?" Tariel asked.

He gave her a gentle smile as if to not scare her away. "I fear the ones I love being hurt or tortured by the demons."

Tariel's eyes dropped to the ground, but Arick turned to Sewall now.

"I fear failing the clans, my people, and my family. Above all else, I fear loneliness."

Sewall regarded Arick once more. Neither one backed down from each other's gaze. Sewall blinked slowly before turning to Noah. "What do you fear, Heir of Raphael?"

"I fear . . . the guilt, I suppose. I fear failure as well, but only because the guilt that comes after failure will crush me," Noah answered honestly, his heart tightening in his chest as he thought of his family. Thinking of his father's expectations and his mother's strong reluctance of his position. He let it all show in his eyes.

Sewall regarded both him and Arick for a long time in tense silence before his face softened, and he offered a smile.

"I'm glad I got to meet both of you," Sewall said with warmth that sent Noah into a shock.

Arick was not so shocked. "Haha! I knew you were soft underneath it all."

"We can't have you thinking we're all smiles when new angels come into town," Zewal said, with a smirk of his own.

"Very well, Arick," Sewall said, raising his arm. "You've twisted my arm long enough. I'll send a reply to the Head Arch informing them we'll join them tonight in their attack on the demons in the Coal Mountains."

"Yeah!" Arick said with a clap, but Zewal was quick to cut his celebration.

"Our forces are weakened, tired, and not meant for fighting. Right now, Noah's troops outnumber ours."

Arick's eyes widened a little. Zewal seemed tense, unsure what Arick would say.

"How can a smaller force than ours defeat so many demons?" Arick said astonished.

"'Efficient' is the word I'd use," Noah murmured. He was mildly surprised. Their soldiers weren't meant for physical battle, but they were all the more deadly.

Zewal gave a gratuitous nod to both of them, while Sewall looked proud of his troops.

"Sunset it is then." Noah raised a toast, and all joined him. "To the joined battle and the last night these demons will see."

"At sunset," they all cheered.

Tariel cheered timidly next to Arick, but she caught his attention.

"Will you be joining us in battle?" Arick asked curiously.

Before she could answer, Sewall and Zewal gave a stern "No," looking in her direction.

Arick raised an eyebrow, but no one gave any other answers.

"Isn't it wise to use everyone we can?" Noah asked, wanting to know the reasoning behind their reaction.

"We've lost many females since the holes have opened up," Sewall said darkly. "We won't allow any of our females near them while we can." Noah started to protest, but Sewall waved him off. "All of our people are capable in battle. However, in battle the demons always target the females no matter how much we try to hide them or spread them out evenly in our lines."

Arick looked at Sewall for a long moment, fire burning in his eyes. Noah's eyes burned in anger as well.

"We'll get your females back from them. Every single one," Noah promised. He'd tear into the hole if he had to and make sure no female was left behind.

Sewall's gaze held a lot of emotion, but it was Zewal who spoke. "Thank you."

"Your wife?" Arick asked, looking at Sewall.

Sewall slowly nodded.

Noah's heart constricted for Sewall. If—no, when—they got all of their females back, the harder part would begin: the healing process. Getting them back would be the easy part, but many females would be forever changed. He looked away. His heart hurt, knowing some of the angels may be pregnant. The babies would be halflings of demons and angels. No halflings were allowed to live within the clans. It was a strict law that no one was allowed to break. If halflings weren't killed, then they were immediately sent back to the demon realm after birth. Early on in their history, any halflings that grew to maturation always wreaked havoc in their realm. The original Archangels tried to argue that halflings could be taught to love and obey laws. However, every halfling raised in the earlier times turned into a cruel, wicked being who enjoyed others' torment. The halflings became such terrorists that none of the Archangels could defend them against the law anymore. Since then, the law had been that no halflings were allowed to live in the Archangel realm.

Arick's gaze shifted to Tariel. "What do you fear, Tariel?" he asked gently.

Noah kicked Arick under the table, which did about as much good as kicking a brick wall. Why ask her such a question after what they'd just talked about?

However, Tariel didn't seem to mind. "I fear not seeing my mother again. I fear not being brave enough to fight for her as she fought for me," she said with a tremor in her voice.

"You're not going out there tonight," Zewal said softly.

"We'll leave some soldiers behind to watch over the city," Arick said.

Noah simply nodded. Not wise to leave the city completely defenseless, even if the females could handle their own.

"Thank you." Sewall looked from his daughter to Arick, and then to Noah last.

They ate the rest of their meal in somber silence. This would be their last moment of peace, and then they'd return to the camp to prepare for battle.

Tonight will be a long night, Noah thought.

Chapter 12

Atarah

This is going to be a long night, Atarah thought.

The rest of the day seemed long as they climbed through the mountain pass. They ventured along steep cliffs as they maneuvered around rocks to reach the crevasse. No one had spoken since they'd felt the tremors. Atarah told them the demon that awaited them was larger than any they'd faced before.

However, no matter how tired she was from the Head Tree, the constant strain on her powers to sense any oncoming threats, along with the rigorous flying trips through the mountain passes, she couldn't stop. Too many lives depended on them getting to the capital before nightfall.

They'd been flying through the cold mountains for several hours now. The brutal, frosty wind didn't match well for the others and their feathery wings. Even though Atarah also had feathery wings, she'd grown accustomed to the drag the frost and snow caused on her wings. She had instructed everyone to shake their wings vigorously to shake off any water from their fishing expedition. *Keep the feathers as dry as possible so less water will freeze and weigh your wings down. Also, use big flapping movements so the joints don't tighten up.* All the things she had done to adapt her wings for the mountain conditions. She gave as much encouragement as she could, but eventually gave the call that they should land.

Everyone, even Clarissa, gave her a grateful nod. They landed along a mountain ridge and started to scale the mountainside by foot. Frost still built up along their wings, but Atarah instructed them to vibrate their wings periodically to break up the ice. They weakly tried, exhausted from the flight, and their wings stiffened from the cold. It had been almost an hour now that they traveled by foot, and Atarah grew antsy as the time passed. She turned to look back to see how everyone was doing.

Clarissa and Isabella were huddled close together, trying to maintain what little heat they could. Poor Charlotte lost color in her lips and her nose, and showed early signs of frostbite. Ben was not much better off. He looked in better shape than the others, but his ears and nose showed signs of frostbite as well. He saw Atarah looking between them and gave the smallest shake of his head. They needed to completely stop for a moment and gather their strength.

Atarah thought back through her memories to find a little grove for them to settle down for a moment of two. She gave a small nod to Ben and led them to find shelter from the cold. It was a short trip, mercifully. She weaved her way through and found a dry cave for them to settle in. She took wood out from her pack she'd gathered before they went into the mountains and quickly started a fire for them. The fire gave light into the small space they had. The others gathered around the fire, murmuring their thanks. Atarah quickly wrapped her shawl around Charlotte, who was too cold and exhausted to argue.

Charlotte stuck her hands toward the fire. "How much farther do we have?"

Atarah debated not telling them the whole truth, but she knew they needed to get there as fast as possible. The stress of needing to get home as fast as possible was difficult to hide. Her heart raced and her limbs felt restless due to the urgency. Her head throbbed as she strained herself to use her powers. She needed them now more than ever to find the demon lurking in her region.

"We still have a long way to go," she said truthfully. To their credit, no one complained. Atarah grabbed at the frosty moss that grew in the corners and passed it around. "Here, eat this. It tastes worse than rotten fish, but it'll give you a little bit more energy."

The moss was the only green that grew up in the mountains naturally. It tasted disgustingly bitter and it left one's mouth dry, but it held a property that warmed one's belly when eaten. Atarah remembered eating tons of it when she was growing up. Even when she gagged and threw it up, she still ate more.

"How in the realm . . . do you live . . . like this?" Isabella shivered.

Atarah shrugged and couldn't help but grin as she thought about her homeland. It was indeed unnecessarily difficult to live here, but it was home. "There are a lot of reasons the Original Arch Michael chose this place. I can't remember them all though."

"I wonder what they were like, the Original Archangels," Ben said. Frost formed and fell as he spoke.

"We were taught Archangel Michael was a gentle soul. That he actually hated fighting, even though he was amazing at it."

Charlotte gave a shaky laugh at that. "We were told the Original Archangel Raphael hated the sight of blood and was very squeamish at the sight of any injury."

Atarah laughed with her. "It is strange how that can be sometimes."

"I think it's all done on purpose," Ben said, sticking his hands out. "We're always given weak attributes at first, but they always shine in the end."

"Well, my weakest attribute is dealing with the cold," Clarissa said irritably.

Isabella nodded earnestly.

"What elements do you control again?" Charlotte asked Clarissa and Isabella. "Fire would come in handy right now."

They both looked inclined to snap at her. While standing behind Charlotte, Atarah flared her wings in warning at them. They changed their demeanor before answering.

"My element is fire, and Isabella's element is air," Clarissa said as if bored.

The memory of when she first met the Uriel sisters came into her mind. Clarissa had always been feisty; fire was perfect for her. Her answer sparked more curiosity from Charlotte, who fired off more questions.

Every Uriel angel was different. They often sported different colored hair, clothes, and style, and controlled different elements. That was part of their illustrious nature. Uriel angels took pride in how diverse their region was compared to everywhere else. Clarissa answered each of them with the same bored tone, but a glow came into her eyes as she talked about her people.

Atarah turned to see how Ben was doing and came face-to-face with his soft brown eyes. *Uh-oh*, Atarah thought, suddenly stuck in his gaze.

Ben gave her a small grin, as if caught in her gaze too.

Atarah's heart rate sped up. Ben leaned in closer, as if drawn to her like a magnet. She held her breath for a moment as she gazed at him. Searching through his mysterious, chestnut-colored eyes, she tried to decipher him. He did the same. His eyes darted back and forth as if searching for answers.

"How are you holding up?" Ben said quietly beside Atarah. It took her a few seconds to process what he was truly asking.

"I'm fine," she said, a little breathlessly. "This is nothing I haven't faced before." Atarah tried to add more firmness to her voice.

Ben continued to hold her gaze, then broke off, only to grab something from one of the pockets of his tunic. "Here, take this."

He held out a small vial. The liquid in the vial was clear, but Atarah knew it wasn't water. She looked up at Ben, surprised, and started to shake her head. She couldn't accept it.

Ben grabbed her hand and stuck the vial in it. "You need this more than any of us. I know you're hiding a lot more than you let on. You can't hide the truth from me," he said the last part with a smirk.

Atarah held onto the vial and looked at Ben, knowing she shouldn't take it from him.

The vial contained a healing serum, which most other clans used to help them through battle. This serum wasn't easy to come by, and Ben needed all the strength he could get. She was about to force him to take it back, but Ben shook his head.

"There's no point in me having it, especially since I can't use my lightning inside a mountain," Ben reasoned. "Please, you've used up a lot of your strength, and you'll use up a lot more tonight."

"How do you know it'll be tonight?" Atarah tried to divert his attention away from herself.

Ben gave a small laugh. "Demons always strike at their strongest hour—when all of the light from the sun fades."

Atarah knew this, and he knew Atarah knew this, but

she wanted to challenge him anyway. She nodded in thanks and Ben sighed in relief. His hand lingered before letting go of hers.

Atarah quickly drank the contents of the vial. It had the same consistency as honey, but it tasted mineral-y, like mountain water. She watched as the vial crumbled into dust once the liquid was no longer there. Atarah turned back to where the others huddled around the fire, but Ben stopped her.

"Not everything's on your shoulders. I won't let everything be on your shoulders, Atarah." His eyes and his voice carried an intensity that hadn't been there before.

Her throat closed up and she shook her head. She felt too exposed, vulnerable. It was one thing if she lowered her own shield a little bit, but now it felt like there was no shield at all as he gazed at her. Ben stepped closer, which made her heart quicken and her wings hummed. Ben noticed, of course, and grinned.

"When everything is over, Atarah, I want to hear you say you trust me," Ben said almost mournfully.

"Not something cheesy like 'I love you'?" Atarah tried to laugh to keep the conversation light, but it came out as a gasp.

Ben shook his head. His face was still serious. "Love is too easy to earn. But trust is something else. I want to earn your love, trust, and friendship properly."

"I'd say you're doing it quite properly now," she replied breathlessly.

Ben's face shifted slightly, darkening. She cocked her head to the side confused by his reaction. She debated probing further, but decided against it. The intensity of their conversation was already enough for her. Since Ben said nothing more, neither would she. Atarah took the chance to escape to where the girls sat around the fire. No one seemed to notice their conversation other than Clarissa, who eyed her warily.

"We need to get going. Especially if we're going to get there by sunset."

Isabella and Charlotte groaned at the prospect of having to go back outside in the frigid cold, but Clarissa continued to look at her strangely. With some grumbling, they got up, put out their meager fire, and made their way toward the opening of the little cave. Atarah took the lead and launched herself into the sky. She could feel Ben's eyes following her closely. When she turned to look back, Isabella and Charlotte were close behind her, then Clarissa and Ben took up the rear. Despite him being in the back, his gaze was still on her.

Atarah faced the front again. She needed to focus on what was to come. She easily maneuvered through the mountain passes. She was used to the winds that blew against her wings and the frost that formed on them. She reminded herself to slow down, so they kept formation against the wind. Atarah wished she could decipher Ben's words, but she had to pay attention. Her mountains did indeed shift and change positions. Not that any being would notice. One could fly along the direct path to the capital, but then the passes suddenly shifted within a blink of an eye. Travelers would slow down to try to get their bearings on where they were and where they needed to be, but within that moment, the mountains would shift again. The shifts normally escalated confusion and frustration with anyone who dared to travel through Vivamus Montibus, the living mountains.

Only the ones who'd grown up in the mountains, who knew them intimately, could navigate them. Now the demons were trying to bypass the mountains and simply attack from underneath. Atarah knew every village and town between the forest and the capital city, Sanctum. While the other regions called all civilians to their capital cities for protection, in the Belli Causa Region, there was no need.

She sensed the citizens living deep within each mountain they passed. Every mountain had an underground space that allowed their villages and towns to flourish. The channels that connected the villages were large and vast, nothing like the tunnel they'd gone through from Chrysi Poli. The tunnels had elaborate carvings and large fire lanterns that illuminated light in every corner. All tunnels led into and away from Sanctum, allowing their citizens the chance to escape or quickly go to the city for protection.

Atarah quickly banked right, weaving through a pass before it shifted. The others kept up behind her. While there was no pattern to the shift, the natives learned about the mountains and recognized when the shifts were about to happen. It was hard to put into words, but once one knew their location, one could navigate the mountains. Atarah spotted another mountain she knew and banked right.

They flew for what felt like hours until Atarah saw a familiar mountain in the distance. Joy spread through her chest and even warmed her body. She signaled their final destination to the others. Charlotte tried to cheer, but her teeth chattered too much for any sound to come out. Ben, close to Charlotte, gave a tiny grin. Isabella and Clarissa flew faster, as if they could be the first to enter the mountain.

The mountain before them differed from the rest, due to its massive height and the amount of snow on its peak that stayed year around. Springtime made finding the mountain a little easier. During winter, Atarah and Arick often got lost in the mountains. Thinking of her family sent a jolt of excitement through Atarah. She could almost feel her mother's arms around her. She wondered if her father and brother were safe. Once they reached Sanctum, she would need to send out a message to them about the demon attack.

They neared the mountain before the guards grabbed ahold of each of them, appearing out of nowhere. In the rush to get there, Atarah had forgotten about the guards and to warn the others about them. Clarissa reared and fought like a hellcat, especially when one of the guards grabbed hold of Isabella. Charlotte was scared and looked as if she was about to cry. Ben had a cold look in his eyes that promised violence. Atarah flared her power out and pushed the guards back. They stilled, surprise on their faces, and regarded her for a moment. Really taking in who they dealt with. It wasn't every day that an angel could push back against a Michael angel.

With no other "small" Michael angels, she had always been easy to single out. She recognized the two guards as well: Ashear and Pahed. Both were good soldiers. Ashear and Pahed were muscular and tall warriors with curly dark hair, leathery wings, and golden eyes. Both immediately backed away from Isabella and Charlotte, and bowed their wings in respect to Atarah. Despite their stature, they regarded Atarah and her company reproachfully. While they said nothing to them, Atarah had no doubt they analyzed her companions.

"Take us to my mother." A single, firm command, and there was a moment of surprise on their faces, but they obeyed.

They flew into the wide opening for the mountain just behind the snowy peak. They landed on the top strip quickly; Clarissa and Isabella took up the rear. The snow crunched as Ashear and Pahed led them to the stairwell that led to the city. Around the snow encrusted bend, the stone stairwell started off small and gradually became wider as it descended into the mountain.

"Welcome to Sanctum," she called out to the others grimly, before she descended the stairs.

The large stairwell was brightly lit with lanterns along both sides. The stairs were carved out of the mountain many years ago and made smooth over time. While her team looked around in wonder and apprehension, Atarah tried to map out where the demon had gone. It would be sunset in an hour or so. They'd need to be quick in warning the citizens.

"Ashear. Pahed." Atarah caught the guards' attention. They looked at her, surprised yet again.

"There's going to be an attack soon in the capital." Their wings flared in surprise, but nothing else changed on their faces. Atarah continued, "Warn all of the other guards to move to battle stations and tell the citizens to move to the tunnels away from the city. I can go and find my mother."

They gave a salute before they quickly glided down the stairs. Atarah turned to the others, while the guards descended.

"Follow me."

Atarah flared her wings and glided down the stairs as well. She heard the others following behind her. They kept up with her better now that the frosty air didn't hinder them. The air grew warmer as they descended deeper into the mountain. She heard the ice and snow that had formed on their wings break off as they flew. She weaved down the stairs and then through the tunnels that would lead her home. They flew through each tunnel passage, and traveled downward for some time. Each tunnel grew larger than the last, the only indication of their changing position. She wished she could show off her stunning homeland and explain the elaborate carvings in the tunnel. How the carvings told the history of angels, demons, and even humans.

The start of the Michael Clan and how her customs and traditions originated.

But they had no time.

Finally, they entered the open underground city of Sanctum. The lights glistened so brightly Atarah almost stopped to take in the beauty. Elegant stone homes with elaborate statues, engravings, and designs were all over the city. Large and small lanterns gave the city its golden glow from the fires. A single large waterfall from the melted snow of the mountain peak gleamed in the far distance. The water glistened under the lights behind it and pooled into a deep well even deeper beneath the city. Atarah wanted to reminisce over the memories of her and Arick playing in the pool below, but something else caught her eye. The cobbled streets were busy as female and male angels moved into position. Atarah saw some children were already being gathered and led into bunkers all around the city, guided by several guardians.

Atarah breathed a sigh of relief as she spotted her mother on the massive balcony of their large estate. They all quickly landed on the balcony, and startled her mother. Her flared wings relaxed as soon as she saw Atarah. Her wings fluttered as she ran to embrace her daughter.

A sound came from Atarah as she embraced her mother; their wings encircled and warmed each other. Atarah hadn't realized how much she had missed her mother until now. Her heart ached with relief that she was safe for the time being.

After a while, her mother looked up to see who Atarah was with and her wings shook lightly in anxiety. Charlotte's face had gone completely pale; her wings shook as well. The two sisters stared at each other in uncertainty, while Ben struggled to stay as relaxed as possible in this tense situation. Clarissa and Isabella huddled together at the edge of the balcony, ready to take off if anything went amiss. Atarah wished she could give her mom a moment with Charlotte, but she needed to be quick.

"Mother, I can explain everything soon, but for now just know our city is in danger."

Ava whipped her head back to Atarah, immediately ready. "What do you know?"

All emotions reunion were put on hold for now. Atarah expanded her powers immediately, sensing all around her. "A demon is here. One of the largest demons I've ever felt. I think it is an Abaddon." Her voice trembled at the name.

Everyone behind her shuddered as well. They were told of this monster as a bedtime story, putting fear into them from a young age.

Her mother's eyes sharpened with an underlying emotion Atarah struggled to place. Atarah had never seen such a look from her mother before. An emotion between pure fear and pure determination.

"We need to evacuate," Ava said quietly; her hands shook severely. She flared her wings, and called one of the closest guards to her. Atarah stared at her in disbelief.

"Have everyone evacuate immediately. We'll exit through the southeast tunnels and make for Silva," Ava commanded in a stern voice. The guard gave a curt nod and was off.

"We're not leaving without a fight, Mother," Atarah said, as she grabbed onto her mother's wrist. She had never spoken this way to her mother, but shook off the thought. Her city was in danger, and she would defend it.

"Your father took the majority of his troops down south. We aren't adequately equipped to handle an Abaddon."

"We can—"

Ava cut her off. "I've seen Abaddons fight before, Atarah." Her voice held a tone that made Atarah pause.

Her mother trembled; her wings shuddered violently. Ava looked at her daughter with tears in her eyes.

Atarah realized now that her mother wasn't just scared but terrified. Truly terrified.

"Even your father has a hard time fighting them. They're demons of the void. They consume everything until there's only darkness. They can tear apart whole regions if left unchecked. This Abaddon is a strong enemy, and it's caught us off guard. We have no choice but to run." Tears streamed down her mother's face.

Atarah hadn't noticed she was shaking as well, until Charlotte came up behind her and put her hand on her shoulder. Ava looked at Charlotte with love and sorrow in her eyes.

"We only have a few minutes now before sunset. We need to get everyone out."

Atarah realized Ben had been by her side since she'd embraced her mother. By her side if she needed him, but giving her enough room to be on her own.

"I'll fight it. It won't be much of a fight, but I'll hold it off to give everyone more time to escape," Ben volunteered bravely.

"No," Atarah whispered. Even though it was a whisper, she knew Ben heard her. She grabbed his hand. He looked at her. "We'll fight it together."

"No!" Ava cried.

Charlotte grabbed Atarah's other hand. "Yes, I'll help with everything I've got."

"No!" Ava grabbed Atarah's face. She saw the tears in her mother's eyes, but saw the determination as well.

"We'll help as well," Clarissa said beside Ava. Clarissa and Isabella had odd looks on their faces as they regarded Ava.

Almost like compassion, Atarah thought.

"We fought for our land before. We know what it means," Isabella said softly. The hollowness came back into their eyes for a split second.

Ava sobbed, and clutched Atarah even tighter. Atarah embraced her hard and long once more before she pushed her away. Ava went to grab her again, but Atarah took flight. Ava made to go after her, but a guard Atarah had signaled earlier grabbed Ava. The guard gently pulled her mother into one of the tunnels as she wailed after Atarah.

Atarah forced herself to try to pull her emotions together. Ben's wings lightly tapped hers as they flew. Charlotte flanked her other side. Clarissa and Isabella made up the rear.

"I sense it," Atarah said, as she struggled to get her voice under control. "It'll come up from the waterfall. It traveled underground until it reached the water basin." Her voice became stronger as she spoke.

"I'm not overly fond of getting wet again," Charlotte said, as she tried to lighten Atarah's heart.

Atarah let out a short laugh, mostly just a release from the tension built up inside her. She'd heard stories of Abaddons. Her father had given an account of one of his battles with one. It always ended poorly. Ben flew closer to Atarah's side. His feathers brushed lightly against hers once more, in comfort. They would most likely die tonight. That reality sank in for Atarah.

They landed at the balcony edge that overlooked the waterfall. The city was breathtaking from their viewpoint. Yet Atarah looked at Ben with love and gratitude. She opened her mouth to speak, but Ben stopped her. He shook his head and simply held her hand. Atarah squeezed his hand as she turned back to look down at the waterfall and the city before them. Charlotte stood beside her. Beside Charlotte stood Clarissa and Isabella. Atarah moved to speak to them, but Clarissa lifted her wing to stop her.

"Save it for when we make it out of this alive."

Atarah grinned. "Just don't light me on fire again."

A tiny grin crossed Clarissa's face at the memory. Isabella released a small giggle that quickly stopped when they felt a tremor. All smiles faded from their faces.

"How long?" Ben asked. He looked at the civilians below scrambling to the tunnels to leave.

Atarah couldn't turn to look at them; tears swam in her eyes. If she looked now, she would start sobbing. Dread and fear made her stomach coil and her hands shake. Nonetheless, she kept her focus on the bottom of the waterfall before them.

"Few minutes. The sun's about to set over the horizon now."

She released Ben's hand as she widened her stance for battle. Charlotte backed away a few paces from all of them and stuck out her hands, ready. Atarah saw a bright light, then Clarissa's hands were engulfed in flames. Isabella gathered wind around her.

Ben took the same stance as Atarah, one of his daggers in his hand.

"I'm sorry you won't be able to reach your powers here," Atarah said truthfully.

Ben gave a little wave of his head. "Eh, it's all good. Lightning isn't my only power, anyway."

"Oh yeah? What are your other powers then?" Atarah said, happy for the small distraction Ben offered.

"I can read people."

Atarah paused. She looked at him with wide eyes. Ben chuckled as another tremor rocked the city, this time closer.

"But Noah said—"

"I can't read minds completely," he interjected. "I'm different from the rest of my family because of it, but I'm good at reading emotions, intentions, and motives. It comes in handy sometimes, especially in battle."

"That explains how you're able to fight so well."

"It's how I'm able to tell how you're truly doing."

"If we make it out of this, remind me to work on my poker face more."

Ben laughed, empty and short.

"Where do you get your lightning from?" she inquired. Her voice shook slightly with fear.

Ben took a moment to think before answering. "My mother is—was from the Elementa region. She came from a special family line that could manipulate lightning," he explained. "It seems I'm the only one who has inherited this ability."

"Your mom would be proud of you, Ben," she said softly.

Another tremor shook the balcony and the waterfall before them. The water cascaded down onto them, but they didn't break focus on the monster coming up from below.

A sound that was a mix between a roar and a shriek hit their ears so loudly, they all winced. It could have been the sound of a thousand snakes hissing or rusted metal scraping together. Either way, it made Atarah shudder. She expected the creature to explode out from the water basin below, but instead, it slowly crawled up toward them. Its pitch-black eyes, devoid of life or soul, filled Atarah with dread and fear. Its head was a skull with a thin layer of skin covering it. There were two black horns on top, and it had black, bat-like wings. It had four pale, clammy-looking appendages it used to crawl along the wall leading up to them. The appendages had claws that cut and latched onto the rock and made it shudder. The long limbs brought the creature up with ease. It looked like it enjoyed their fear.

Atarah couldn't shake off the feeling of despair spreading through her as she looked at its eyes, shuddering at the thought of the creature touching her. She and Ben backed up slowly as the creature reared its skull up above the balcony edge. It looked at them, then around the city. From what she remembered, Abaddons were technically blind but could sense life in any and all forms.

Atarah knew right when it locked onto the location of everyone escaping through the tunnels. The Abaddon shrieked and scrambled after them. Atarah flared her powers and launched after the creature. She drew her long dagger out and stabbed one of its limbs. The Abaddon whipped a limb around and swatted her away. Atarah rolled when she landed and quickly launched herself into the air once more. Clarissa and Isabella were already attacking it as a duo. Clarissa threw her fire at the demon, while Isabella used her wind to empower her sister's flame. Ben darted back and forth around the demon, and cut at each appendage to debilitate it.

More energy surged through Atarah and she remembered Charlotte. She turned to see Charlotte in deep concentration, trying to strengthen them through this battle; her bow and arrows laid beside her, forgotten. The look at Charlotte cost Atarah. She heard Clarissa scream in pain.

The creature grabbed a hold of her with its claws and pulled her close. Clarissa's face showed pure terror and the demon opened its mouth to devour her. Atarah flew to the Abaddon and dove under its stomach and cleaved through its abdomen. The creature paused for a moment. That was all Isabella needed to cut through its claw and free her sister. Ben moved to make another cut, but the demon turned to Ben and clawed him down to the ground.

Holding Ben, the Abaddon looked down at its wounds. The ones Atarah and Ben had caused to its limbs and abdomen healed within a few minutes, much to their despair. Atarah tried to think quickly about how to defeat this demon. She tried to remember how her father defeated one. He'd said the Abaddon could mimic every strength its opponent had by draining their power. Already, the demon mimicked Charlotte's healing ability and Ben's ability to read its opponent. Soon, it would master Clarissa's fire, and Isabella's wind.

Come on, think!

Atarah dove once more to attack. The demon saw her coming, even with its head turned away from her. Another limb came up and grabbed her in a crushing hold. She cried out in pain, and learned its claws were lined with sharp hooks. Even if she tried to fight her way out of its claws, the sharp hooks dug deeper into her skin.

The demon pulled Atarah closer, its eyes and mouth wide open. It wouldn't devour Atarah physically, but it would drain her life and soul from her body. Ben flew at its head and stabbed its eye. The demon was startled and loosened its grip enough for Atarah to kick herself out. She ground her teeth against the ripping of her skin and wings against the hooks. She landed sloppily and knew her wings were badly torn. She rose to her feet shakily, and gritted herself against the pain.

Ben had landed ungracefully. He quickly got up and moved to attack once more. Atarah saw this time—Ben attacked with his eyes closed and as unpredictably as possible so the demon couldn't read him as well. Clarissa and Isabella followed Ben's lead, and tried to make their attacks unpredictable. The creature roared in anger at the fire attack that came from Clarissa. It shot out one of the claws to grab her and clawed at her with a deadly quickness.

This gave Atarah an idea that she prayed worked, or else they were doomed. She signaled to Ben and Charlotte. They both gave a short nod before they moved. Atarah drew two daggers and flared her wings. Despite the pain, she managed to fly into the air with Ben, as they both raised their daggers to strike. Easily reading their movements, the Abaddon's claws latched onto them mercilessly. The other limbs grabbed onto Isabella and Clarissa with ease as they tried to make their escape.

Perfect.

Arrows soared through the air before they landed individually on each limb. The demon shrieked in pain, but more arrows came down all over its chest with amazing precision. She turned to see Charlotte firing her last arrow, while she flew toward them. Atarah dropped her second knife. The Abaddon's head whipped around to Charlotte's charging form; her open hand waited for the dagger. She flew with the swiftness Atarah had seen in her on their first day of training together and drove the dagger deep into the Abaddon's neck. All of its limbs were injured and occupied as it held onto them, which gave Charlotte a clear opening to attack. The demon let go of Atarah first to attack Charlotte.

Big mistake.

Atarah condensed all of her power within herself, giving her strength. She kicked off its limb and used the power to drag the dagger farther into its neck. The demon roared in anger and pain this time, then wrapped each of its claws around Atarah, and shredded her in blinding pain. However, the demon was a second too late.

Atarah shot her palm out with all of her power and cleaved its head off cleanly. The claws went rigid around Atarah, but she barely noticed. She started to lose consciousness and her body, bloody and battered, fell from the demon's grasp. The body and head fell down into the depths of the water basin below.

The last thing Atarah saw was Ben hobbling over to her, fear plain in his eyes.

She wanted to tell him not to worry, that for once she felt like she held her own, but darkness finally overtook her.

The accomplishment of defeating the Abaddon settled into her chest as a newfound confidence claimed her.

Ben tried to calm his roaring heart, but he couldn't stop seeing the image of Atarah's wings bent in odd directions, coated in blood. The same fear—no, fear wasn't a strong enough word—terror and panic he had felt back when they fought in Chrysi Poli entered his heart now. However, now a new emotion entered his heart: regret. To tell her how he truly felt, to tell her how much he loved her—he might not get his chance. Her abdomen was cut open and her insides hung out. The bone of her leg showed under the massive gash that circled down each leg. He shook as Charlotte worked quickly.

Slowly, her abdomen closed under Charlotte's gentle hands. Charlotte's eyebrows scrunched together as she concentrated on healing. Sweat dripped down her face in effort and her breathing became strained as she worked.

Ben silently pleaded for Charlotte to not let up and prayed that the Abaddon didn't completely exhaust her. He'd never seen Atarah look so pale before, so near death. He wanted to hold her, but he feared moving her.

"It's all right, Ben," Charlotte said once more.

No matter how many times she said that, a knife still went through his heart.

"We'll need to move quickly as well," Clarissa said. Blood was all over her face, as well as Isabella's.

All of them were badly injured. Charlotte was already tired from helping them in battle and the creature stealing her power to heal itself.

"Must we? Atarah will recover faster if we allow her to rest," Charlotte said, as she still concentrated on healing Atarah.

"We didn't kill the Abaddon," Ben said quietly.

Charlotte stiffened, but she continued to work.

A demon like the Abaddon couldn't be killed with just a severed head. The demon needed to be killed by an Arch Head. It would heal and crawl its way back up the water basin. In the meantime, they needed to escape while they could. Atarah's plan worked, but at too great a cost. They were all injured and tired, and if they fought again, they would all die.

"We saw an Abaddon back in Aquam Caput. It's why our city fell, even though we fought it with our father. It destroyed so much we had no choice but to retreat," Isabella said softly to Charlotte.

"We'll need to escape while it's down and healing itself," Clarissa said firmly.

Charlotte nodded and pulled away from Atarah. "I've healed her enough so that she's stable."

Ben's stomach clenched at what he was about to say next. "I know where we should escape to."

They all looked at him. Clarissa raised an eyebrow. He could tell she didn't fully trust him, but she was too scared to say anything else.

"We'll head southwest. The opposite direction of where everyone else escaped to."

Charlotte was quick to refute his direction. "If that demon goes after everyone else, we're dooming them."

"The demon will follow us out of anger that we injured it. Let's lead it elsewhere and give her clan more time to escape," Ben replied. Reading the monster's intention had been easy.

Charlotte quieted at his reasoning. Clarissa and Isabella exchanged a look. Ben could tell from their thoughts that they didn't like it but would go southwest. He sensed their resolve dissipating, and he took Atarah's hand once more. He said a silent prayer for her to be all right and lifted her, gently, into his arms. Charlotte worked on Ben's wings and aching muscles swiftly. Thanks to her healing hands, he could fly a good distance before the Abaddon caught up with them. Charlotte moved onto Clarissa's and Isabella's injuries, and gave Ben a moment with Atarah's unconscious body in his arms. He sensed her heartbeat and tightened his grip on her; he tucked in her wings carefully.

No matter how much he watched and read her, she always surprised him with her abilities. Lightly, he placed his lips on hers and sent up another silent prayer quickly before he moved away. He turned to see Clarissa and Isabella, almost completely healed, wave Charlotte off.

"This should last us a while. Save your strength for when we'll need it, Charlotte."

Ben thought Charlotte might protest, but she gave a grateful nod, and panted heavily. He could see the toll this battle had taken on her. They would definitely need her later on if the demon caught up to them before they reached safety.

"How do we know where to go?" Isabella asked, looking around the city.

"The city is faced like a compass. The waterfall is north. There's east and west." Ben indicated both sides of the city. "We need to go down that tunnel, and we need to go quickly."

As Ben spoke, a tremor came from the water basin beneath them. All of their faces paled. They all shot up into the air and made for the tunnel Ben pointed at. He took the lead, holding Atarah close to his chest. He hoped they'd have enough of a head start to get far away. Nonetheless, he didn't dare turn back to see if the demon had followed them. They veered through the tunnels with ease; everyone followed Ben as he led them farther and farther. He had read some of Atarah's mind when they navigated through the city. He prayed it was enough for the maze they were about to go through. From the roar and tremors that erupted around them, he knew who the demon had chosen to follow.

Dusk descended upon them so quickly Mikael didn't even register the change. He had been too focused on getting his men in position. Joshua had come to his camp setup an hour before to inform him of the Azraels' reply.

"Are you sure?" Mikael asked Joshua.

His wings were relaxed and his face expressionless. "Yes, they will go along with the plan." A smile formed on his lips. "Oh, and Arick sends his regards."

Mikael didn't bother looking up. Joshua and Arick were trying to get a reaction out of him. He didn't have the time or energy to give them a reaction. They would both be disappointed.

"We need to be up in the sky now. Let's hope they hold up their end of the bargain with this fight."

"Apparently, your son made quite the impression on Sewall and his heir," Joshua said, still looking at Mikael.

"Arick makes an impression on many angels. He's a natural born leader." Mikael's wings trembled for a second. Had he trained Arick enough for this moment? He had promised Ava that he would protect their son no matter what happened. He didn't intend to break his promise to her.

"Indeed," Joshua concurred. "Well, I'll mobilize my troops as well. We'll see each other in the sky."

With that, he took off into the evening.

Since then, Mikael had gathered his soldiers and they'd flown into the Coal Mountains, ready for battle. Joshua and his horde were on Mikael's right. Mikael's troops were in position on the left side. As they flew through the mountains, calm settled over his troops. This happened in every battle, the calm before the storm.

Mikael heard the rumblings and shrieks of the demons long before he saw them. The sky before them was black, and the wind roared around them as if an actual storm was forming. The sounds of screeches and metal clanging together grew louder and louder as they flew closer to where the hole was reported to be.

Mikael always despised this part of battle. He could handle the battle itself, but everything leading up to battle curled his insides; for he knew the chaos of battle. The stenches, the exhaustion, limbs flung in different directions—the cries of pain and of battle have never left Mikael's head. The anticipation and anxiety of knowing some of his soldiers wouldn't make it back home. The night before, he always wondered if there was more he could do, a better strategy he could have used. He wondered how many soldiers he'd lose. If he'd lose his life. Then the day of the battle, the normalcy of his morning routine always felt eerie to him. Waking up, getting dressed, eating, trying not to think it might be his last meal, trying to keep the food down. How normal and orderly it all seemed when chaos was on the horizon would never sit well with him.

The screams intensified as the demons came into view. The hole was a large rift that seemed to move as if it was a disturbance in the water flow. The unnatural ripple was one of the largest Mikael had seen. Thousands of demons poured out onto the land and raced toward them with abandonment. All of the demons varied in size and shape. Most had gray, gangly bodies with disgustingly long limbs with claws at the end. Some had twisted black horns, while others had extra limbs that poked out from their sides. The blackened mouths snarled and sneered at them. Arrows flew at them, even though they were well out of range. To

Mikael's relief, not all of the demons were fixated on their arrival. Some of the demons' attention was focused elsewhere. Mikael knew that meant Azrael and Noah's forces had indeed joined them for this battle. With the army they had now, they'd need all the help they could get against the thousands running toward them.

Let it be so, Mikael thought.

He released some of his power and dove toward the oncoming horde with a speed few could match. He heard a yell and knew his general had given the signal for all of them to dive into the fray. Mikael condensed then released his power and plowed through every demon in his path. He could've been a bull running through a herd of sheep. There was little fight these foot soldiers could put up for Mikael to feel any challenge. He plowed a path for his troops and a path toward the hole itself. The density of the demons that came at him increased the closer he got to the hole. Mikael had to slow his advance because of all the demons that swarmed him. They stabbed at his wings and grabbed onto his body to weigh him down. He flared his power once more, and knocked off all of the demons near him. This gave him a precious few seconds to look around to see how his men were. They were about a dozen meters behind him, and held their own against the onslaught charging at them. Mikael couldn't see Joshua in the fray, but he saw his own men. They were doing better than he'd expected. They cut down with precision and launched poisonous bombs at the demons. What was in those bombs? No one knew, except for the Raziel angels. The bombs did a good chunk of the work for them; they killed any demon within splashing distance and weakened them enough for one of the angels to finish the creatures.

Mikael felt the sting of demons attacking his wings and flapped it off, which knocked the demon into each other. He flared and swiped his wings, then attacked anything that came too close to him. He was saving his power for the rift up ahead. He gauged the distance and the number of demons before him.

While none of them were overly difficult to fight, the sheer number was an annoyance. As Mikael fought his way through, something seemed off and wrong about this whole battle. The battle was large, but not as strategic as the other battles had been. What was their play? Were there any key characters hiding? Mikael's stomach twisted. Something was too easy about this battle and almost lazy. He saw a flash to his left and saw Arick off in the distance fighting beside Noah. They were both surrounded, but they didn't seem fazed in the least. Noah's army was doing well against the demons.

Relief and pride filled Mikael as he saw Arick hold his own. *I hope it was all enough*, Mikael thought.

He gathered and released a good amount of power that launched him toward the hole. Joshua was surprisingly there already. Some demons tried to shoot him down with arrows, but Joshua easily shielded himself from them.

The hole was at one of the mountain's peaks. Like ants scurrying out of the nest, demons fell from the hole and slid from the mountaintop. Many tried to turn around and climb back up the mountain to attack Joshua and Mikael, all in vain.

"How do we close it?" Mikael yelled at Joshua, as he dodged arrows.

Joshua furrowed his brow. Sweat dripped along the sides of his face, and showed his exertion. "It's a long, ancient spell. I need to get closer, and I need you to keep them off me."

Mikael grunted in response. He cleaved through the demons, fired at them, then tucked and rolled, and cut off the demons that came in through the hole. The Archangel came behind Mikael, and encircled his hands around the opening itself. A flare of light shot through him and outlined the opening with light. Joshua came before the opening with glowing hands. The air around the opening seemed to condense and seal off the opening.

Mikael had been in the demon realm once before and never wanted to endure it again. The demon realm was dark, heavy, and enclosed. There was no real gravity, but the air clung in a way that was claustrophobic. Mikael had felt like he had aimlessly floated in darkness, while his insides and lungs were being crushed . . . suffocated. As if he wandered through an underwater cave. Eventually, one's eyes became used to the darkness enough to navigate, but the stifling never faded. Mikael glanced at the demon's realm now, and saw the same darkness as before. Gray arms and legs reached out from the darkness, trying to enter their realm and failing.

The demons were impeded from entering their world. Nonetheless, the roars and the squeals of demons could be heard. Demons pounded and hammered on the opening, demanding passage through. Joshua didn't relent. The hole was occluded significantly, but not completely. Forms on the other side wiggled and wormed their way through the smaller opening. Joshua was in close range, but he didn't flinch as a demon struggled to attack him. He stood firm and focused. His eyes were fixated upward as he murmured the words needed to close the opening for good.

Mikael continued to block and batter anything that came too close to them. Sweat stained his clothes, but he kept moving. Guarding Joshua from all sides took concentration. Demons made their way back up the mountaintop, attacking in a frenzy. The more Mikael cut through them, the more the demons were attracted by the violence. The dance continued for long minutes that turned into hours.

The darkness of night did nothing to aid Mikael and the soldiers on the battlefield. The clanging of swords, axes, and shields was the only indication of battle. With a lack of sight, Mikael changed to a more defensive attack style and prayed for his men to do the same. Nightfall was when demons had the advantage. Born out of darkness, the gloom embraced them and enhanced their senses. Whereas the lack of light caused panic within the angel troop, so they blindly stabbed anything that came too close. Terror closed in on many soldiers, and caused jerky, unsure motions and poor decision-making. Mikael exuded more power than necessary in order to give the soldiers more light for their battle. He created a white, flare-like light that fizzed out and released his power. The light he emanated shined, then faded out like smoke in the wind.

Nevertheless, screams of terror and dread became a chant all along the battlefield. Another light shot up and around, followed by another one closely behind. Mikael tore through all those around him and pushed those coming farther back to give himself a few seconds to look around. Farther down the mass, at the base of the mountain, were Arick and Noah. They still fought side by side, but they used their magic less conservatively as they fought. The beacon shining between them lessened the horrors for the soldiers, who used the light as guidance, calming their hearts.

Mikael maintained the strain of using his magic throughout the hours. Joshua's posture hadn't changed since he'd engaged the spell. He still emanated a light that lit the demons' opening and kept his head facing upward. Mikael didn't bother trying to decipher the words he murmured. It was in an ancient tongue. The listening, deciphering, and remembering how to close the portal was too much for Mikael to attempt. His concentration and usage of power had already caused other ailments. His head roared, and his wings quaked with weakness from the repeated attacks.

Mikael continued to fight, despite the exhaustion. He shined the light of his power brightly and hoped to endure until Joshua finished his part. Mikael chose not to notice the stench that came from battle, or the filth. The guts of angels and demons alike now soaked the grounds, which they stepped on. He knew the continuous swinging of their swords was the only thing present in the minds of the soldiers. Adrenaline slowed in their systems, leaving only determined preservation in their minds. Thoughts went as far as the breath before them. After the breath came the effort of earning another breath. Fighting and surviving was the back-and-forth dance every angel now participated in. One step out of focus, and the dance toppled.

Hours stretched on and on as the night sky before them. Mikael was only vaguely aware of the hours because of the shifting stars above them. There was no stopping; he tried to be conservative with his powers, knowing they would be in this battle for the long haul. There wasn't even an awareness of oneself during the night. Darkness shrouded any sense of injury or hunger. Knowledge of the light that would come with the dawn brought some awareness of fatigue to Mikael's mind. However, even he couldn't think that far ahead. The headache grew stronger as the hours moved on, and pushed its way to the forefront of his mind until he struggled to focus. While pain hindered his concentration, he prayed for patience to still his frustration with his body. Now was not the time to focus on the acute problem. Mikael continued his effort, despite the protests of his body.

He heard cries of pain all around him, but this time they were closer. The uphill battle was slowly gaining traction.

The gap between Mikael and the rest of the angels' forces had shrunk.

The sounds of mayhem reached his hearing. The sound of metal clanged louder. He heard the squelches of wounds created by demons and angels. The stench grew as more bodies slid down the mountain and piled at the base. The pulsating throng of soldiers forced more and more demons to be corralled. The frenzy of the demons became crazed with the confinement. The erratic movement, still in the shelter of the darkness, became harder to fight despite the Arches' best efforts.

A cry rang out, and jerked Mikael to its direction. He knew that cry. He feared ever hearing that cry. He pushed his power forcefully, as he turned to see Arick down on one knee in pain. Against the blinding pain, Mikael flung his power toward Arick, and incinerated all who stood in the path. Was that enough?

All too soon, the enemy swarmed Mikael. He struggled to maintain his stance as he blocked and countered other demons. He tried to resume his original dance, but the brief distraction had a cost. Something stabbed Mikael's left wing. He swung around and dislodged the knife and the demon. Demons clamored all around him and flung themselves high to attack from above. They tried to mount their offensive above Mikael, and dampened the light. He ducked and rolled, then used the momentum to spring into the air. He spotted Joshua and cut down the demon that made it past the craze. In all of the chaos, he could've sworn he saw the glimmer of a smile form on Joshua's face.

"Integrum."

The last word of Joshua's spell, Mikael heard clearly.

The word caused a ripple, and then light erupted. Mikael felt this tremendous power long ago in a previous battle and knew better than to go against it. He collapsed onto the ground by the force of the power that came from Joshua's spell. The light that erupted from Joshua was not from his own powers. The light, warm to the angels, burned the demons. Cries of agony could be heard all throughout the battlefield. Mikael kept his head down and allowed the light to carry around all of them. For the briefest of moments, everything felt weightless, as if he had no body and only his mind carried him. The vast abyss of weightlessness didn't last long, but the uncertainty that came with it lasted longer. Soon enough, Mikael felt his body once more and looked up.

The mountainsides were littered with thousands of demon and angel bodies. However, every demon was now an empty shell. Emaciated, hollowed, and crumbled demon bodies surrounded Mikael. A red glow shined brightly behind him. He turned to see the sunrise coming over the mountains as if in greeting. The demon opening was nowhere in sight. It had been completely closed off.

He took a few breaths as the sun's light grew and a new wind blew over them. Joshua was close by, but he had collapsed from the weight of the spell. *Unconscious but breathing*, Mikael thought. He turned and floated down to the cry he'd heard earlier; his mind raced with worry and guilt that he didn't do enough for his son. He spotted Arick instantly.

Arick had extensive wounds around his wings, which were expanded. By the looks of it, the demons had tried to cut off his wings or at least rip them to shreds.

Arick seemed to hover on the brink of consciousness; his body shook from the pain. Mikael's stomach twisted as he saw his son on the ground. Fear and guilt racked through his body. Fear that Arick was severely hurt and guilt that he didn't prepare Arick enough. Arick turned his eyes upwards, as Mikael flew down to his side. He said nothing. He simply used his arms to move Arick's body into a crouched position. Mikael was about to snap at Arick to not move, but he saw why he'd been injured.

Noah laid beneath Arick, and several stab wounds covered his chest. Arick must have been trying to protect him by covering him with his wings, Mikael mused. He gently moved Arick's wings into a fold to staunch the bleeding before he moved on to assess Noah. He felt a mixture of pride and fear. Proud that Arick saved another life, but scared that he didn't have enough sense of self-preservation for his own life. After so many years of training Arick to be ready for battle, this was the first battle where Mikael truly feared for Arick. All the other battles Arick had fought in, Mikael had always had someone watching over him. Not this battle. In this one, Arick was the one looking after someone else, which almost cost him the heavy price of his wings. *I will go over comrade recovery techniques with him when we get home,* Mikael thought. He wanted Arick safe.

Noah was mercifully unconscious, but still alive. The stab wounds had narrowly missed his heart. Mikael pulled out the vial he kept close by and poured it into Noah's mouth. He wrapped one hand around a knife in his chest and wrapped his other hand around Noah's arm, so he didn't unintentionally move the knife.

He will live, Mikael thought with some relief. Only a Raphael angel could have survived this attack. He withdrew the knife and quickly moved the wrappings into place over his wounds. The bleeding would slow soon for him. While he wasn't as gifted as Ava, Mikael knew the healing power was still strong in Noah. He looked over at Arick, who watched him. They said nothing for a few moments as Mikael assessed his injuries, and Arick seemed to wonder what to make of him. This was the first battle they'd ever fought together, the first time Arick had seen his father covered in filth from the battle. Mikael had no doubt he must look unsettling.

He gathered Noah up and heaved him over his shoulder. Arick didn't seem to be injured apart from his wings; nothing else was broken or torn. Arick's wings would heal well, Mikael determined. Arick tried to struggle to his feet, and Mikael promptly knocked him back down.

"Stay there," Mikael commanded in a harsher tone than he intended.

Arick's face morphed into anger, then crumbled in pain as his wings tried to flare. Mikael flew down the mountain and didn't turn back to look at his son. He quickly took in the damage done to his soldiers as he assessed the mountainside. Around half of them were standing, better than what he predicted. However, Joshua and the Azrael forces were far more scattered. He spotted Atticus among a rather large pile of demon bodies and landed beside him. Atticus had several gashes to his arms and legs, but nothing too threatening. He looked questioningly at Noah's body slung over Mikael's shoulder, but he said nothing.

"This is Arch Raphael's Heir, Noah. He's been wounded quite severely," Mikael answered Atticus's silent question. "Now comes the recovery process. We need to circle around to see if any Raphael angels have strength left to help heal the others. Use what few vials we have wisely."

"Very well. Jakob and Micah are alive somewhere. I saw them go down when the light came from the mountain." Atticus hesitated. "Will all of the holes have to be dealt with this way?"

Mikael thought for a moment. "I don't think so. From what I felt, I think many of the holes in the Southern Regions have closed, but we'll need to confirm as soon as possible."

Atticus nodded, then took off into the sky.

Mikael turned to see many able-bodied angels flying around, picking up bodies where they could. Maybe Jakob and Micah were already spreading the orders around. He laid Noah gently on the ground, miles away from the battle. He was still unconscious, but his bleeding had already slowed. The smaller cuts around his arms and face were closing.

Mikael turned and flew back to the mountaintop. He stopped where Joshua lay and crouched down.

"You need to be gentler with the boy," Joshua said, his eyes still closed.

Mikael grunted. "He's fine. He'll heal up nicely."

"Not the Raphael boy." Joshua now looked up at him. His eyes glowed brightly from the aftereffects of the power he'd used. Guilt and fear mixed together for Mikael. He knew Joshua was right.

Mikael offered him a hand, which Joshua took and stood. He quickly shook himself and looked around at the carnage.

"He's wounded just as badly and needs care," Joshua said, spotting Arick on the ground not far away.

The hair on the back of Mikael's neck stood up as he regarded Joshua. Joshua's focus on Arick didn't last long. He turned to the side of the mountain where Noah's and Sewall's forces came through. He descended over the ledge to aid with healing.

The effects of the spell would wear off soon, Mikael thought. Best to make the most of it while they could.

He flew down to Arick quickly and placed a vial into his hand—the last vial Mikael possessed. Arick's bewildered face mildly annoyed him, but he continued his work. He grabbed some wrappings he'd prepared and tended to Arick's wings. He heard a mumble of thanks and then a hiss of pain.

"Don't talk. Save your energy." Again, a simple and direct command. Mikael tried to keep his tone in check as he wrapped up his son's wings.

"Angry I'm alive?" Arick said, in a tone that was equally sarcastic as it was bitter.

Mikael tied off the wrapping tightly, and caused Arick to flinch in pain. Mikael thought back on Joshua's words. "I'm angry you got hurt," he said truthfully. "Be more careful next time." He struggled to soften his tone, "Please, son."

He could feel Arick's gaze on him, weighing what Mikael had said in his mind. Wordlessly, Arick drank the contents of the vial, then moved to his feet. This time, Mikael didn't stop him.

Arick moved to walk down the mountain slope, but was quickly lifted into the sky. Mikael held on tight, his arms around Arick's chest, and took care not to press on his wings. He flew to the other side of the mountain, and ignored Arick's protests.

"I need to check on my men," Arick hissed at Mikael.

He ignored him.

Arick used his arms to loosen Mikael's hold on him. "Put me down." Arick moved to jab him in the shoulder, but then saw where he was being flown. He finally stilled, and Mikael descended.

Mikael had gathered this was where the bulk of Noah's forces were, based on their green uniforms. He dropped Arick unceremoniously on the ground. Arick wasn't deterred. He quickly turned to land on his feet and glared up at him.

"Gather your men and return to Azrael. We'll notify you of the the new plans," Mikael commanded. His tone wasn't as harsh as before, but it was still firm.

He flew around the mountain without another look

back. He had no doubt Arick probably cursed him under his breath, but he had little time to deal with him. He needed to gather his own men and get them out of these mountains by nightfall. Something still didn't sit well in his stomach about this battle. The numbers had been plentiful, but the enemy itself had been fairly weak. He thought about who and what had planned these attacks and wondered what strategy they played into.

Mikael swooped low again; he gathered injured angels from his and Joshua's forces. While he tended to his own wounded, he played over the other battles that had happened in other regions. Joshua might have had an inkling of why the battle was the way it had been, but Mikael had lost him in the crowd already.

Soon, he thought. He'd need to get to the bottom of everything soon before the enemy played its true hand.

The sun had finally come up over the mountain peaks; it shone brightly on the passes, and guided them through. Mikael gave orders to his commanders to help the wounded. He passed off Noah's body to Brock, one of Arick's men. Noah had started to awaken as Brock lifted him. They spoke briefly. Mikael stated they'd be in contact soon. As they walked in the direction of his forces, Noah attempted to fly. Within a few paces, the two of them were able to lift into the sky.

"What will you tell them?" Joshua asked, as he appeared at his side. The glow in his eyes still hadn't receded.

"The truth. This battle was too easy."

"Will you tell him the truth?"

Mikael spun his head around and looked at Joshua. There was no judgment in his eyes, only sorrow. Mikael's heart sped up and his wings flared. He knew who Joshua referred to.

"Peace, Mikael. I mean no harm." Joshua's wings were down by his side.

Mikael relaxed his wings. He ran a hand through his hair in concern. "How do you know?"

"That no longer matters. What matters now is that the enemy knows as well," Joshua replied.

Panic spread throughout Mikael's body. His wings widened with alarm. "How do you know this?"

"I saw it as the hole was closing. I had my suspicions."

"What did you see?" Mikael demanded. He struggled to control his panic. His heart dropped in his chest. He knew what was behind the attacks. The organization and strategy gave Mikael an idea, but he hoped it wasn't so.

"That doesn't matter either. What will you do now, Mikael?"

Mikael roared in anger. He'd worked so hard to protect his family from this; he'd barely considered what would happen if the truth came out.

"What should I do?" he asked.

Joshua was calm beside him, which frustrated Mikael even more. How could he be calm when this could tear him and his family apart? Mikael resisted the urge to fly to Arick and take him back home immediately. *Hiding will do no good*, he thought. *It will only make things worse.*

"Mikael."

"What?" Mikael asked, irate. He'd begun pacing and stopped when Joshua called his attention.

"We know for those who love, all things work together for good."

"How can you say that?" Mikael said in a deadly quiet tone. "For what's about to happen, how could you say everything will work out?" His wings flared in anger.

"Because everyone in your family loves just as much as you love," Joshua said calmly, unfazed by Mikael's anger. "Those who love know the Trinity."

Mikael thought about Ava, Atarah, and Arick. How amazing they all were in their own ways. His heart constricted. He'd do anything to protect them if he could. He took a deep breath as he tried to calm his nerves. The aftereffects of the battle, his son being injured, and now news of what the enemy's motive might be had caused him to fray.

Now isn't the time to be unfocused, Mikael thought. He looked in the direction Noah had flown and wondered how long before they reached Mortem. He would get his men in order and then call them over. The news wouldn't be easy to share, but he needed to do it for all of their sakes.

"Please have mercy," Mikael murmured under his breath.

He turned back to where his men gathered the injured and threw himself into work.

Arick was in an irritable mood. It always took him a moment to shake off the feeling he got when he ran into his father. He found it helpful that so many soldiers needed his help, which was a welcome distraction from his thoughts. His wings sent sharp pains from the base of his head to all the way down his leg if he moved the wrong way. Arick welcomed the pain; it meant he was alive.

Speaking of the living, he'd sent Brock to grab Noah's body from wherever his father had put him. Noah had scared the mess out of Arick when he'd gone down on the battlefield. He'd looked so pale, Arick had feared he was dead. He hated to admit it, but his father's blast during the battle had saved them both.

His first time in a true battle with his father present. Arick had been excited to prove he could lead and handle the battle all on his own. He'd done great and had worked his way up to the top of the mountain where his father was, when Noah had gotten too far behind him. He'd heard

Noah cry out in pain and saw they were too far apart to watch each other's backs. He'd been too focused on gaining ground and left Noah behind. By the time he made it back to Noah, all he could do was shield him from any more attacks.

He knew now Noah would be all right, but he wondered where he and Brock were. Arick had been busy tending to the injured when Brock returned. Based off of Brock's green face, he was happy to do something else other than help the injured. Arick had almost laughed at the expression, but he thought better of it. He'd stopped being squeamish a long time ago. Arick was glad the companions he'd made survived this battle. His small team were the reason he and Noah were alive. When he'd gone down, trying to protect Noah, they were close enough to help keep too many demons from piling onto him. Brock and Jared had done well, but Galvin in particular surprised him. Galvin's fluidity while fighting was nearly frightening. While Brock and Jared were more brute strength, Galvin was smooth as he cut down his enemy. The way he killed was so blasé, it took demons by surprise.

I'll have to make sure I don't get on his bad side, Arick thought.

Most of the troops were on their way back to Mortem by the time Noah and Brock caught up to them.

"So glad you could finally join us," Jared said snidely to Brock, as he finished dressing a wound.

Galvin, who was close by, coughed to hide his laughter.

"I was helping the leader of our region, thank you very much," Brock jeered back.

Galvin helped the last of the injured onto a wagon that had been brought from Mortem. While Brock moved to help Galvin load the rest of them up, Arick took the time to talk to Noah, who'd walked over, very much alive and awake.

"Is this the last of them?" he asked, as he looked around. Dead bodies laid everywhere. Most of them were demons; Arick had tried to be thorough in his search.

"From what I've gathered. I was going to do one last search and let the others head back."

Noah still looked off into the distance as he nodded. "I'll look with you. Let's gather the dead too, while we can. They need a proper burial."

Arick started climbing back up the mountain. His wings were still in disrepair, so flying was out of the question until one of the healers looked at him. Arick felt eyes on him and turned to see Noah staring at his wings. He looked like he was going to say something, but Arick stopped him.

"You're the most stressful angel I've had to babysit in a battle," Arick teased.

Noah chuckled. "No more stressful than you. This is why I don't babysit."

They both laughed briefly, and released the tension that had built up before the battle.

"Thank you, anyway," Noah said.

"For what exactly?" Arick moved various demon limbs as he looked for fallen troops.

"For saving my life," Noah said quietly, as he looked through a different pile of bodies.

"Think nothing of it. I wandered too far, anyway. So, it was my fault you even got injured."

Noah laughed, which caught Arick off guard. "Even though you were just babysitting me, remember I'm older than you, and this was definitely not my first battle."

"Oh? What other battles have you been in?" Arick looked up briefly with a raised eyebrow.

"The Battle of the Springs, for one."

Arick's eyebrows shot up in amazement. The Battle of the Springs was known for its difficulties. The battle had taken place where the Dark River divided into several streams that led into the Silva and Lanua Regions. The streams were covered with trees and made an aerial attack difficult, so the soldiers had to go on foot. The slippery slopes were beautiful, but they were difficult to fight on. If he recalled correctly, they had fought against the aqua succubi demons. Arick stifled the laugh that built in his throat.

"This is a very inappropriate time to laugh, Arick," Noah said, as he chuckled too.

"You started it."

Their chuckles died down after a minute as they dug through the scattered demon bodies. The grim reality of what they needed to do set in fully. They searched for hours on end. The sun blazed on Arick's back and wings, which caused further discomfort. But it was nothing he couldn't shake off, at least in a few days. The sun was past high noon by the time he circled back with Noah; they carried a few angels who had passed on. They laid each body down with their arms crossed and wings out. The weight of each body was more burdensome on Arick's heart than his arms. Each body reminded Arick of how precious and short life could be. Arick wondered if there was more he could have done for the soldiers, if he could have spared more lives. All the bodies of the angels they gathered needed to be burned, as it was custom for every region.

"I covered every inch of the west side. Is there much left on your side?" Noah asked; sweat poured from him nearly in streams.

"I finished up not too long ago. All of the bodies are taken care of."

"We'll need to head back soon. Your father will be in contact, no doubt," Noah said.

He hadn't meant any harm, but Arick tensed anyway out of habit.

Noah seemed to notice. "It was your father who saved our lives, right?"

Arick gave a brisk nod; he wanted the subject to end.

"I guess we owe both our lives to that smug, overgrown bat," Noah said with a grin.

Arick couldn't help but return the grin.

"Let's move on." Noah moved closer to Arick; his hands buzzed mildly. "I'm not as good as either of my sisters, but I can heal enough for one person."

Noah was definitely not as good as the other healers. It took nearly an hour for Arick's wings to be prepared enough for flight, not fully healed, but enough to make it. The flight back to Mortem took them under an hour. When they landed, they were immediately approached by an Azrael soldier. Sewall requested their presence.

Noah nodded grimly to the soldier, who took off to relay the response. He groaned quietly as they walked toward their base.

"Something you want to talk about?" Arick asked as they walked. He spotted his trio almost immediately.

Brock and Jared struggled to get their armor off, while Galvin sat close by writing on a piece of paper.

"No more than you want to talk about your father," Noah grumbled.

Arick looked at Noah. "You don't like the Azrael family?"

"No! No. It's just . . ." Noah ran a hand through his hair. "I always say the wrong thing around them. I want to have a good, diplomatic relationship, but I seem to say things to make them loathe me."

"You're too scared of them."

"I've never been scared of them," Noah scoffed.

Arick shook his head. "That's not what I mean. You're scared of not having their approval. So much you ignore the fact they're people and get too focused on their titles." They reached Arick's tent, but he continued to speak. "You're too caught up in formalities and identities."

He stripped off his armor, eager to clean up. Cleansing his skin helped take away the pain, filth, sorrow, and guilt after a battle.

"Are you suggesting I speak to them like I talk to you?"

"I don't see how it could hurt." Arick moved to the wash basin and began his wash routine.

"But I hated you," Noah said honestly, as he shook his head. Arick laughed. "That could never work. I couldn't have cared less if you hated me."

"You don't hate me anymore? Ha! Then there's plenty of hope for you and Zewal," Arick replied.

Noah scoffed and ran his hand over his head once more as Arick finished washing his torso. "How do you find it so easy to converse with them? You'd never even met them, but they liked you almost instantly. How?"

So, that was the root of the problem. Why like him instead of Noah? Arick almost wanted to roll his eyes at the implication.

He reached for a fresh shirt. "I'm used to being disliked. I always think I have nothing to lose if I'm myself. If they do end up liking me after they get to know me, then I'll have gained something."

"Is Atarah like this?"

He looked at Noah. The question caught him off guard. He tried to think about how to explain what his sister was like.

"She's the complete opposite. Everyone usually instantly loves her, and she doesn't know that. She feels that she has something to prove because no one expected much from her when we were growing up. She's too hard on herself."

"I guess we have that in common," Noah said. He seemed to be in deep thought. "I'll meet you at the main house soon."

He walked through the tent flap, but Arick wasn't alone for long. Galvin entered his tent, followed by a bickering Jared and Brock.

"All I'm saying is that caltrops are way more useful than a battle ax," Jared countered Brock's argument.

"Caltrops are useful for a few seconds." Brock waved a dismissive hand. "Axes are useful the whole battle."

Jared went to argue back until he spotted Arick chuckling at them.

"What?" they both said in unison.

"Nothing, just not what I expected to hear from Raphael angels. I didn't know you have all this extensive weaponry knowledge."

Brock shrugged, as Jared answered, "Well, no one in this room is wholly a Raphael angel."

That was true. While marriages between clans did occur, they weren't common outside of the Archs. Average angels often stayed inside their home borders and didn't marry outside the clan. Marriages outside the clan were difficult and often split families apart. If two angels married and had children, they often moved to one region or the other. Whichever power trait was expressed the most in the children growing up determined where they lived.

Arick looked at Galvin. Galvin's mother was Raphael and his father was Azrael; however, he didn't express enough Azrael power to live there. So, Galvin had grown up with his mother in Silva. The children born between clans often lived close along the borders. Arick looked at Brock and Jared. They were the second generation between the Raphael and Gabriel Clans, so their parents were the ones who lived close to the border. However, their parents both married another Raphael angel—thus their traits of healing powers presented stronger than Galvin's.

His own mother was Raphael and his father Michael. But because he and Atarah were Archangels, they had been offered more privileges and leniencies. That was why when Atarah showed strong signs of Raphael traits, their parents could get away with keeping her in Belli Causa. Arick showed practically zero signs of Raphael power, so he was an easy choice.

"You'll need to get going soon, right?" Brock asked, pulling Arick from his thoughts.

"Yes. Apparently, the Azrael family wants to meet with Noah and I." Arick got up and noticed Galvin's stare. There was a look in his eye. Arick knew what he wanted. "Yes, you can, but stay vigilant."

Galvin gave a nod of gratitude toward Arick, while Brock and Jared waited.

"Galvin's going to visit his father tonight," Arick clarified.

"Why stay vigilant?" Jared asked. "Aren't the demons that came through here dead?"

"The power surge Joshua sent out seemed to take out many of them. Nonetheless, the females the demons took would have been dropped out of a different opening." Their faces darkened. "We should start seeing them soon, making their way back to their homes."

"How does that work?" Brock asked.

"The hole the demons came through was by their powers. They used their powers to hold the females in their realm as well. Now that the demons are gone, the females' natural powers from their Head Tree will open a portal that will lead them home."

Arick stepped out of the tent, but he looked back at their faces once more. "Stay vigilant and help any females you find wandering back into the city. If their families were killed by the demons and they have nowhere to go, create a tent for them, clothe them, and give them something to eat. No one else touches them except for that, understand?"

"Yes," Brock and Jared said in unison, while Galvin nodded with a hand to his heart.

With that, Arick took off into the sky. Dusk wasn't far away. The sun hung low in the sky as if reluctant to leave.

He made it to the front door of Sewall's home in minutes. Tariel greeted him at the front door and bowed. Arick grinned at her, which caused her to blush furiously. He was never sure why females outside of his clan always got flustered around him. Back in the mountains, the females were more direct about what they felt and wanted.

Zewal, mercifully, came to his rescue as he came around the corner. "Ah, Arick. Come on in."

He wasn't completely clean. Arick could tell by his hair that Zewal hadn't had a complete wash, but his face was clean, and he no longer wore his armor. His eyes seemed to be more sunken in.

"Any news?" Arick asked; hope sprinkled in his voice for his friend's sake.

Zewal's eyes darkened, and his fist clenched, but not at Arick. Death seemed to move in his eyes, and his powers swirled around him like dark shadows. "We found her, but . . ." He wasn't able to finish his sentence.

Arick nodded all the same. He put a hand on Zewal's shoulder. "I'm sorry."

Zewal nodded; too many emotions seemed to run through him to speak yet.

Arick spared him a moment as he walked farther into the house. He ventured back into the dining room where they had eaten . . . last night? So much had happened since then; time felt almost false.

Sewall knelt in front of a female who must have been his wife, holding her hands gently. She had the same pale, pointed wings and pale skin that made her navy hair stand out. Her eyes were what disturbed Arick the most. Vacant, unseeing, and red from tears, even though none were visible now. She was skinny—too skinny—as she turned to see Arick enter the room. Her eyes flashed, and she shook upon seeing him. She clutched Sewall's hand.

Sewall glanced at Arick hovering by the door. Arick turned away to give them another private moment.

"Wait," a raspy voice said. A voice that had been screaming.

Arick watched the female stand. She was wrapped in a dark blanket with a black tunic underneath. She walked over to him slowly. Sewall trailed her; he watched her every move, hands close by as if to catch her from falling. Zewal had joined them now, and stood beside Arick, even though he watched his mother intensely. Both Sewall and Zewal's wings flared slightly.

"This is my wife, Fatima." Sewall gave a quick introduction.

"I know you," she said to Arick.

Arick raised his eyebrows. "Well, that's a change. I promise anything you've heard so far is lies."

"What lies might those be?"

"I'm much more handsome in person."

A ghost of a smile formed on her face. "I heard something else."

"Oh? It must be that I'm funnier than Zewal here." Arick waved a hand over to Zewal, who looked bewildered. "Because that is one hundred percent true."

A definite grin formed on her face. Sewall and Zewal's wings relaxed. Tariel had now joined them. She tried to peek over Zewal's shoulder at her mother.

"You are Arick, the halfling who lived." Fatima spoke the words as if they weren't insulting.

Arick stiffened. Arick had been called many things, but to call someone a halfling was by far the worst. Halflings were seen as even worse than demons. Even his own father would never be that cruel.

"I assure you, I'm Arick, son of Ava and Mikael, the Arch Head of the Michael Clan."

She looked at him, confused, and shook her head. "No, they spoke about you," she insisted.

"Who spoke about him?" Sewall asked, as he looked rapidly between Arick and his wife.

"The demons."

Arick wanted to laugh at the absurdity of what she said, but Sewall's look stopped him. He looked at Arick with an expression of shock. Sewall turned to Fatima.

"Are you sure, my love?" Sewall asked earnestly.

"I'm sure," Fatima said vehemently. She clutched Sewall's hand. "They spoke of Arick by name."

Anger coiled in Arick's stomach. To be accused of being a halfling was not only disgusting, but it would mean certain death. Arick thought of how to retort but . . . he looked at Fatima's state. She had been tormented by demons. He wouldn't use angry words against her now. *She's been through enough already.*

"Listen, I'm not—" Arick started but was interrupted.

"Arick is a halfling?" The disgust was evident in Zewal's voice. His wings flared instantly. Zewal grabbed the dagger at his side.

Arick moved to a defensive position.

"Stop!"

They all looked behind them. Down the hallway stood Noah. He quickly walked toward them, and by his expression, he seemed to have heard everything.

"Mikael will be here soon with Joshua. He'll clear everything up. I'm sure it's a misunderstanding."

"Let's hope so." Sewall's voice was quiet, but filled with disgust. He had moved Fatima behind him, away from Arick.

Fatima looked to Arick with what could have been curiosity, but Arick wasn't sure.

"Let's move to the other room," Tariel said nervously behind them.

No one spoke as they moved rooms. Tariel and Fatima stood behind Zewal and Sewall, as far from Arick as possible. They eyed him distrustfully, but Zewal no longer had his hand on his dagger.

They entered a large, open area with a long, flat bench as seating. The bench curved around to form a large circle. There were minimal decorations on the bright white walls, which left few places Arick's eyes could wander. Tariel quickly scurried out of the room, and headed back toward the front door. Sewall had his wife sit, but he stood beside her. His wings had not yet relaxed. Arick took the seat opposite of her to put Sewall more at ease. Zewal sat on the other side of his mother.

Noah sat beside him, to Arick's surprise. His wings trembled ever so slightly—the only clue that his calm face was false.

They sat in silence for several long minutes, until they heard a noise at the front door. Heavy footsteps could be heard from where they sat. Arick knew without looking up when his father entered the room. He glanced up to see his father stroll over and take the other seat beside Arick. Arick stiffened out of habit, but said nothing. To Arick's surprise and horror, he felt relieved that his father was with him. Curious, he studied the Arch his father had walked in with, Joshua. His blond hair and striking features took

Arick aback a little. His silvery wings glistened against the white frame of the house, but his eyes caught Arick's attention. They were blue and seemed to have a faint glow about them. Based on the powerful incantation he'd given earlier, the power was still fading. He nodded briefly to Sewall and his family before he sat between Mikael and Zewal. Between both families.

Joshua chuckled and spoke first. "So much tension in the room, and we haven't even started yet."

Arick liked him just for that.

Sewall looked at Mikael. "Is there something we need to know about him?" He nodded his head toward Arick.

Arick started to be truly infuriated. How could they not see that her accusation was ridiculous? Hadn't they been friends a few minutes ago? He glanced at Sewall and Zewal. He was used to not being liked, but to be disliked by someone who was supposed to be a friend first hurt differently.

Arick glanced at Fatima, who stared at him. He had nothing against her, but he simply didn't believe her. How would the demons know his name? Why would she accuse him of being a halfling? Very few things added up to Arick. Nonetheless, nervousness brewed in his stomach as he wondered how to clear his name. Was she making this all up or did the demons truly mention his name?

"You shouldn't be quick to anger or judge, Sewall," Joshua said calmly.

"We weren't speaking to you," Zewal retorted harshly.

Sewall still stared at Mikael, and waited for an answer.

Mikael looked calm, but his wings were flared. Arick noticed he was seated in a strange way; he angled his body as if to jump in front of Arick.

"There's much you don't know or understand, Sewall." Mikael's tone was eerily calm. "But know this: Arick is my son, whom I love and will protect against anyone who tries to hurt him."

Arick stiffened. His father was never one to use words of love much, if ever. Despite Arick's best efforts, warmth spread throughout his chest at his father's words. He hated how much he cherished those words. He resisted the urge to look at his father, but glanced at Fatima instead. She still stared at him. Her eyes watered as she looked at Arick. He couldn't fathom why she regarded him with a strange look in her eyes. Did she think he was a halfling and it brought back memories of what the demons did? Was it anger? Resentment?

Zewal's wings relaxed the tiniest bit, but he looked uneasy. Sewall's wings relaxed more, but he looked between Joshua and Mikael with mistrust.

"Why did you ask for this meeting tonight?"

"There are a number of items to discuss. None of them are pleasant, but I need to voice it now in case we run out of time." Mikael paused and heaviness seemed to weigh on him. "Item one is that this battle didn't make enough sense, and I'm worried it was a mere distraction."

"I second this notion," Joshua said strongly. "I saw inside the opening and into the enemy's intent. Their objective was more to keep their enemy busy than to demolish."

"What can be done about it now? Other than wait?" Zewal asked. He leaned forward, his elbows on his knees.

"We need to send scouts out tonight to each region to see how they fare," Mikael said firmly. "The more information we have, the better."

Sewall scoffed. "Like any of my angels will be welcomed with open arms from the other self-righteous regions." He looked at Joshua, Mikael, and Noah. "I suggest sending your own men if you want information."

"I doubt my men will be welcomed either," Mikael said, as he looked at Sewall. "But they won't forget the effort we put in to help them, nor the lack of effort from you."

Zewal's wings flared even more at the last part. Sewall's face remained calm, but he kept a hard stare at Mikael.

"We only need one or two of your fastest fliers. We're not asking for much, Sewall," Joshua said coolly.

Sewall appeared to ignore him, but Arick guessed that Sewall weighed the words Joshua spoke.

"How many need to be sent out?" Noah asked, his face unreadable to Arick.

"Three to each region. Nine total. We need to check in with Selaphiel, Gabriel, and my own lands."

Noah raised an eyebrow. "Why your region? Isn't it already secure enough?"

"With the enemy we're dealing with, there's no such thing," Mikael answered.

Sewall's eyes narrowed on Mikael. "Who is this enemy, Mikael?"

Mikael looked grim, and his wings trembled a little. Arick turned to look at his father, and his stomach twisted at the sorrow in his eyes. His father didn't show emotion like this. Arick's nervousness grew. His father, who was always so sure and stern, now looked . . . shaken.

"Our enemy is a Luciferian." Mikael looked at Sewall. "My older brother, Matthew."

Noah whipped his head around. Ice entered his eyes. "Lies will get you nowhere, Mikael," he said in a voice that chilled Arick. "Your brother was killed long ago in battle. Many angels saw it."

"My brother did die," Mikael said, his voice full of emotion. "The brother I grew up with doesn't exist anymore. The demons took his body back to their realm. We all thought he was dead and in the heat of battle, no one could get close enough to him to retrieve his body. We saw him go through the opening and assumed."

Joshua put a hand on Mikael's shoulder. "I saw him beyond the opening," he said softly.

"That's one of the reasons why we needed to meet. Whatever they did to Matthew was bad enough to turn him into a Luciferian. It's been a long time since an Archangel Head was taken and turned. We can't take this lightly."

Arick almost fell out of his seat. His wings flared in uncertainty. What he knew of his uncle was very little, besides that Matthew had died long ago. Arick never wanted to be around his father long enough to ask further about it. He had no idea he'd been the Archangel Head of the House of Mikael. Arick looked at his father in disbelief. Mikael was never supposed to be the Arch Head.

Noah had stood up during Joshua's statement and now began to pace, outraged. "If an Archangel Head was turned, then why were none of us notified?"

"How could this have happened?" Zewal said, equally outraged.

Sewall also now stood from his seat. "Do either of you have any idea the dangers every region is in? An Archangel Head has all of the information of every region. Every weakness, blind spot, ally, and enemy. He would know almost everything about us. How did this happen?"

Sewall's questions were met with a brief silence. Everyone was in shock, except for Joshua, who looked at Mikael with sorrow.

Mikael stood slowly, followed by Joshua and Arick. "This brings me to item two." He looked at Arick.

Arick's legs started to shake; he sensed this had to do with Fatima's accusation. He was going to be sick.

"I found out about Matthew over twenty years ago. Ava was supposed to marry Joshua."

Noah seemed to tense at the mention of his sister. His wings flared more.

Mikael continued, "I was to be Joshua's best man at the wedding. I'd always been fond of Ava, but happy for both of them. We were in Gabriel's region wedding planning when Matthew reappeared." Mikael swallowed. "Ava was going to originally marry Matthew, but everyone had presumed him dead. He showed up to Ava first." His voice shook. "I was coming back from training when I heard her screaming." His wings trembled. "I busted through the locked door and saw him . . . Ava was on the floor naked, bleeding, and crying. Matthew looked at me and smiled. 'Long time, no see, brother,' is all he said, as if nothing was wrong.

"I covered Ava with my shirt and held her. 'Why?' I asked in outrage. I still thought he was my kind and thoughtful older brother. But he grinned and said because he could, that she already belonged to him. He said he intended to destroy each and every household. That he had long-term plans to destroy every region and breed out every angel. To get rid of our hierarchy. That we all needed to think for ourselves and not how we were programmed to be.

"I tried to reason with him. I tried to tell him evil acts would never bring the best outcome. He laughed and said he would come back for Ava, to use her as an example." Mikael struggled for control, for his hands to stop shaking. "I panicked, and I took Ava and flew back to Sanctum. Matthew is an Archangel from the Michael Clan. I knew of almost no angels other than myself who could take him in a fight if he came back for Ava. I took her and ran from there. She was so hurt and terrified. I was going to tell Joshua and her father, Elijah, but Ava begged me not to. She said she wanted to tell them herself when they came back from their regional summit meeting. Since Ava had already been through so much, I relented. I just wanted to help and protect her.

"I prepared the troops and strengthened our security measures. But by the time Joshua and Elijah came back from the summit meeting, nearly two and a half months went by. I went to check up on Ava again and found her crying on the floor. I'd seen her crying on the floor before, but this time was different. She looked up at me and said she was pregnant." A tear came to Mikael's eye. "I held her while she cried and begged me not to tell anyone. That it hurt enough without someone trying to take another decision away from her."

Arick fell; his legs could no longer hold him. No . . . he . . . truly . . . was . . . a . . .

Mikael turned and looked at him. "She said when she learned she was pregnant, it was the first time she felt hope and love bloom in her heart after what happened to her. Then, the thought of you being taken away from her felt like another decision being taken from her." He looked back up to Noah, who shook from the force of his wings vibrating behind him. "She and I knew that if we told anyone, Arick would be killed. So, I did what I thought was best at the time. I married Ava immediately and kept her away in Sanctum. Not because I wanted to control her, but because that was the only place where she felt safe. I married her because as soon as news spread of her pregnancy, I knew Matthew would come back and take not just Ava, but Arick as well. I married her to hide Arick as my own child and not Matthew's."

Joshua put his hand on Mikael's shoulder. "I came home from the summit to find my fiancée gone and a note saying 'farewell.' I learned later Mikael married her and felt so betrayed by my best friend. I've kept everyone at a distance since then. Once word of the marriage spread, no one wanted to be around Mikael and named him the Great Betrayer."

"My mistake was that I didn't trust enough people with the truth." Mikael looked at Joshua. "For that, I will always seek forgiveness."

"All is forgiven, my friend. You've had to suffer through enough already," Joshua said with kindness.

Mikael looked at Arick once more. Arick felt hot and cold as he shook with an array of emotions that overwhelmed him. He . . . was truly a monster . . . *No! Worse than a monster. A halfling!* Shock racked through Arick; his wings and body shook, his heart raced, and his chest felt tight with pain and self-disgust. He couldn't speak; he was sure he would throw up. His poor mother . . . Arick met Mikael's gaze and could feel true understanding for the first time toward him. Arick deserved his father's stern hand and upbringing. No, he deserved to be treated worse than that. Tears filled Arick's eyes, and blurred his vision.

Mikael crouched to where Arick sat, bewildered. "Even though you aren't biologically mine, I've never once thought of you as anything other than my son. I'll always protect you and Atarah from anyone who tries to hurt you. I thought if I was tough on you, and you resented me, then it would be easier to not love you. In case you ever were taken from me, it would be easier to not mourn you. But today, when you almost were taken in battle, I realized how stupid I've been. I won't make the same mistake twice."

No, Arick thought, *I don't deserve this.*

He turned to Sewall and Zewal; the latter looked at Mikael with uneasiness. "Matthew now knows Arick was supposed to be his child. The Head Tree that fell in Malachi's region didn't recognize Arick as the Heir to the Michael Clan, but as someone else."

Joshua spoke up. "Matthew will come to claim Arick soon enough, but we aren't sure when."

"We have a reasonable argument that this battle was a distraction. Matthew often favored using soldiers as distractions in battle tactics, which is why we need to send out our fliers immediately."

Sewall had watched Mikael with a grim expression the whole time; he weighed his words and his story. Sympathy seemed to swim in his eyes for a moment. "Then let us move out."

He turned; his wings flared, and he signaled for one of the guards. Two tall, thin guards with dark purple hair, dressed in black, walked over. Their spiny, pale wings were tucked by their sides; their forms exuded the personas of trained soldiers.

"This is Gaius and Claudius, my best soldiers in flight, stealth, and battle."

They both bowed briefly, and looked each of them in the eye. Arick thought he saw something familiar about Gaius when he glanced over at him, but he had a hard time focusing on anything. His body was still numb and tingling from what he'd learned. His body was in shock. He was still in shock.

His mother . . . How could she even look at him?

A hand on his shoulder pulled him from his thoughts.

"Come. We need to go through our own troops and decide," Noah said gently.

Arick could only muster up a nod, since most words escaped him. He moved through the halls in a blur. He sensed someone near him, but he had little capability to tell who. He knew he was in a fugue state, but he couldn't bring himself out of it.

He made his way for the door and took flight with no destination in mind.

Chapter 13

Mikael

"Give him some time," Mikael told Zewal.

The young Arch heir had followed Arick out of the door. Zewal didn't respond to Mikael but watched Arick dwindling in the sky. A moment passed, then Zewal took flight in the direction Arick took off, not looking back.

Mikael couldn't help but feel comforted at Zewal's fleeting form. He turned to see Sewall and Noah talking to each other. Noah, no doubt, had already named the soldiers he wanted to send on the mission.

Fatima appeared at Mikael's side. Her eyes were hollow but had clarity to them that gave him the impression she was far from broken.

"Arick's a good angel," she said it as a simple statement and not as a question.

Mikael's jaw tensed, but he said nothing. They both watched their sons' fly off in the distance until they disappeared.

"Do you know for sure?" Mikael asked softly.

"No one really knows for sure, but I have hope. No matter what happens, I decide. I have hope."

Mikael had that same hope. He believed in his son.

They fell into a natural silence; both felt comfort in their spirits, and let the moment happen. All too soon, Joshua, Noah, and Sewall came over with the plan.

"I've picked out my messengers. I'll talk with Arick on who he wants to send as well," Noah said hesitantly. No one objected.

"Joshua informed me of your picks, Mikael, as well as his own. We'll send them out now." Sewall looked at Noah. "We're sending my angels and Joshua's to Chrysi Poli, and Noah's picks to Urbs Antiqua, the capital city in Gabriel's region." Sewall glanced at Mikael. "Your angels are the only ones who know their way through Belli Causa. Arick has a team I'm sure he'll want to tag along with yours."

"I agree. While our flyers are out, I think it'd be wise to pack my men up and go home. I don't like to leave for long periods of time anyway."

"We understand," Noah said, and stood beside Sewall. He stuck his hand out. "You have my gratitude, Mikael, and an ally should you need it."

Mikael's throat closed up a little, but he kept his face neutral. It had been so long since his clan had allies. He reached out and shook Noah's hand.

"Should you need more than one ally," Sewall spoke up, and glanced at Joshua, "just ask anyone in the south. They'll extend their hospitality."

Mikael and Joshua chuckled quietly.

"Speaking of hospitality," Fatima said, "I must apologize for my husband's manners. Please feel free to fully wash off upstairs. The lingering scent of battle is on everyone in this room."

“Surely, I don’t smell that bad.” Sewall grinned at his wife; affection shone in his eyes.

Mikael’s heart ached to see Ava again.

“Thank you very much, but there’s a lot that needs to get done,” Noah declined politely.

Fatima raised her hand at him. “It shall be done after a good wash and a bite to eat. Come now.” She indicated with her wings where to go.

Noah looked inclined to refuse again, but with a hand on his arm, she led him out before he could say anything further. They all followed, as they quietly chuckled at Noah’s perplexed face.

Mikael looked back once through the front door in the direction Arick had flown off. He would give him his space now, but . . . Mikael was scared to let him wander off too far. He had enough regrets as it was. He wanted at least a chance to make things right for his family.

He made his way down the hall. He followed Sewall’s fading figure, and pushed his growing concern to the back of his mind.

It would be done.

Noah dove into the hot springs, eager to quickly wash off the day. He washed off the grime, blood, and filth with a rough scrub. He dipped and shook his wings, washed his hair, then jumped out. His mind raced too much to linger in the hot spring. He grabbed a towel and had dried off by the time Joshua walked in. Noah resisted the urge to move his wings. He moved to the adjacent room quickly to don new clothes. His thoughts turned to his family for a moment, traveling far enough that he didn’t notice Joshua until he tapped on his shoulder.

"I think you should contact your family," Joshua said quietly.

Noah bristled at first, then relaxed. Joshua was right. He needed to contact them; for he knew what was to come and he needed to stop it. Noah quickly suited up and walked out the door. He'd seen Zewal go after Arick and wondered when they'd be back. He hoped soon. He wanted to talk to Arick before they sent off their fliers and to see how he was doing.

Noah hadn't realized how much the overgrown bat had grown on him until he'd seen Sewall flare his wings at him. Noah had reacted like he would have if Charlotte or his mother had been threatened. He'd rushed over and realized how ridiculous he was as he tried to defend Arick, of all angels, from a fight. He would've laughed, but Arick's face had held none of its usual humor.

I'm used to being disliked, Arick had said to Noah earlier.

Noah grimaced at the memory. It didn't go unnoticed by him how Sewall grimaced when his son went after Arick. The disgust and sympathy on his face as he watched them fly away irked Noah. He knew Sewall wasn't the only angel who would have that reaction.

"Leaving so soon?"

A strong but soft voice stopped Noah in his tracks. He turned to see Tariel, Zewal's little sister. She looked similar to most of her family. Her navy hair hung in waves by her shoulders, framing her wiry figure. Her black eyes pinned him in place. All of the coyness from before was gone. She'd stayed mostly in the background during the confrontation of Arick's parentage. Noah wondered what she thought of Arick now.

"Yes. There are many things I need to get done before we send our unit out."

"I'm leaving with you." She reached for her light gray jacket.

Noah raised his hand to stop her. "I don't thin—"

"I know you know where they are," Tariel said, fiery. "I want to be there." Her jaw was set.

Noah doubted she'd listen to him anyway and gave up; he waved his hand for her to follow.

She quickly donned her jacket and walked swiftly to the door. As soon as Noah felt sunlight, he launched into the sky. He didn't need to look back to know she followed him. Azrael wings were often silent in flight. Death on swift and silent wings. Noah suppressed a shudder that built up in him and focused. He had a rough idea of where Arick might be and banked for the far west side of the camp. He saw one of his generals and landed next to him. All of the troops who were gathered around their makeshift fire stood when he landed.

"Good evening, sir. What can we do for you?" his general said with a bow.

"Get me a messenger immediately. I need to send word to my family. Also, bring Galvin, Brock, and Jared to me. I need them for a mission."

Without another word, his general left to complete his tasks. Noah moved to his own tent nearby and searched for something to write with. Tariel followed him and watched him from the corner of the doorway. His tent was small and fairly standard, like all of the other tents in the camps. The only difference was his tent had a small table that held all of his messages, maps, and plans. Noah scribbled a message for his family and read over it several times. He rolled up the message and sealed it as his general returned followed by Brock, Jared, and Galvin. He handed over the message to the general.

"Get this to the Arch Head of Raphael as soon as possible," Noah said.

The general bowed, then walked out of the tent quickly.

Noah turned to the trio of angels who stood before him. They were an odd bunch. One eccentric, one silent, and the other sarcastic. All were from a mixed familial line, which was rare among angels. They all stood in formation; their wings tucked by their sides. Brock and Jared had more common Raphael features, with dark brown hair, tan skin, and hazel eyes, while Galvin had paler skin, black hair, and shy gray eyes, which gave away his mixed heritage. Brock and Jared would be good picks for their destination to Urbs Antiqua, as both of their grandparents were from the Gabriel Clan.

"We need some fliers to scout the Lanua Region." Brock and Jared's wings twitched, but they showed no other outward emotion. "We need you to leave tonight."

"I'm going with them."

Noah looked past them to see Arick stood in front of the tent doorway. His large frame covered the entirety of the front of the tent.

"I don't think that's a good idea," Noah said gently.

"Oh? And pray tell, why not?" Arick walked farther into the tent. "I have no true reason to stay here, and I've trained with these angels extensively. As well, I know the Lanua Region very well because of its close borders to my ho—to Belli Causa. I'm a perfect fit to go with them."

Noah hesitated. Neither Arick's face nor wings gave away any emotion he might be going through, but Noah debated if this mission was something Arick needed.

"I'll join as well." Tariel stepped up from the back of the tent. It appeared no one had noticed her, for they all jumped when she spoke.

Only Arick didn't seem fazed by her appearance.

"Tariel, that's definitely unwise. I can't allow you to go with my team," Noah spoke.

"I can."

They all turned to see Zewal at the entrance of the tent. Arick was so large no one had seen him come in behind Arick. Tariel's eyes shone brightly at her brother's arrival. Noah sighed. Zewal's title as the ruling heir probably still wouldn't save Noah from the wrath of their father. Sewall had been adamant about keeping Tariel out of reach of any possible demons. There were no guarantees that demons weren't roaming free. There was still the army that had chased Malachi's entire population away, surrounding Chrysi Poli.

"There is no guarantee—"

"I can and will be able to take care of myself," Tariel said in a firm voice. "My father has just been on edge since our mother was taken."

"I doubt he'll spare me harm if that's all I can come up with. Even with Zewal's approval, it will be difficult."

"If there are demons"—Arick spoke up, and leaned forward onto Noah's desk—

"I doubt they'll handle me, an Azrael, and three mixed angels of the Raphael Clan. She'll be safest with us."

Noah sighed. He looked between the three of them and knew he was outnumbered. He gave a small nod and sent a prayer up for protection. "Very well. Pack now and leave after you've all eaten. Oh, Arick, wait for a moment."

They all filtered out of the tent, except for Arick. His eyes were hooded with emotions Noah couldn't decipher. The less Noah could read on his face, the more he worried. Noah knew Arick battled many strong emotions and tried to bury them. He knew because he tried to do the same when growing up in his torn household.

"I'd like to ask for your forgiveness, Arick."

Arick's eyes widened in surprise. His mouth opened as if to speak, but no words came out.

Noah continued, "I—my family judged you and your father. We were wrong. We've made mistakes, and I want to right the wrongs we've put both of you through."

"I—I, uh, Noah. I didn't expect that."

"Well, I didn't expect to hear what Mikael told us," Noah said with an empty laugh, but realized too late it was the wrong thing to say in front of Arick.

Arick's look of surprise turned to stone. His wings twitched once, then stilled. No humor.

Noah regarded him carefully. "What are you feeling?" he asked gently.

Arick looked down, his hands clenched by his sides. "So many things. Anger, shame, disgust with myself, and grief to start with. All the emotions are mixed in with one another. It's hard to tell what I'm feeling, exactly. I . . . don't like to sit with them for too long."

Noah stayed silent. Arick would need time to process everything and maybe this mission would give him the time he needed.

"Am I even an angel of the Michael Clan? Or a demon?"

"No one chooses what they are or where they're born, Arick. But everyone—humans, angels, demons—all decide who they're going to be. It's up to you, and not because of who you were born from," Noah said vehemently.

"Does this mean there are others like me? Halflings?"

"I don't know, honestly. Any other halflings in the record books were so full of obviously evil intent, they were killed immediately. Maybe it's different because Matthew was an Archangel Head, but I honestly don't know. I'm sure when everything dies down, there'll be an uproar."

Noah looked outside at the fading sunlight. Arick followed his eyes and stood up straighter to head toward the door.

"Arick."

Arick paused before he dropped the tent flap.

"No matter what happens or what you hear, I'm on your side."

Arick nodded and dropped the tent flap.

Noah listened to his fading footsteps and prayed he'd made a good judgment call. Noah sighed and ran his hand through his hair.

I'm getting too old for babysitting, he mused.

He wrote down one last note and called one of his soldiers back in.

"Please give this to Tariel."

Charlotte thought her heart would burst out of her chest, but she didn't dare stop. That thing still followed them. She could hear its claws scrape against the tunnel walls as they left. She shuddered, but not from the cold. The night sky seemed so dark. If it wasn't for Clarissa's tiny fire that glowed in her hand, Charlotte would have lost them by now. They had all expended a lot of power on the run. Charlotte tried to keep everyone refueled on power. Clarissa tried to light the way. Isabella kept the wind on their side, and Ben led the way, as he held Atarah.

Charlotte knew Atarah would be dead by now if it weren't for her powers. Hers were some of the most severe wounds Charlotte had ever had to heal before. She tried to send some of her healing power to Atarah, but her body dipped in the sky, once it reached its limits. This wasn't good.

Charlotte's small sound of distress caused Isabella to look back and see Charlotte start to fall from the sky. One minute, she was up in the sky, and in the next, she saw a tree coming right for her. Charlotte forced her trembling wings to expand, and she maneuvered around the branches. She got caught on one low branch and fell to the ground, breaking every branch in her path.

She stood on shaky legs by the time Ben landed beside her. Clarissa and Isabella followed. Charlotte struggled to get her breath under control. They'd just reached the forest outside the mountains, which was a miracle in itself, but Charlotte still groaned. They had flown at top speed for hours. She had hoped to be farther away by now. They'd gotten lost a few times, and now they had paid for it.

"Can you keep going?" Ben asked urgently.

The sincere yet frantic look in his eyes gave Charlotte enough strength to nod. Ben nodded and with shaking legs jumped weakly into the sky. They all followed. Everyone was at their limit, power exhausted, physically battered, and tired. The only thing that kept them going was the adrenaline and fear of fighting that monstrosity again.

Now that they were out of the mountain, more fear encased Charlotte. For at least in the mountain city, she could tell by the clawing sound where and how far away the demon was. However, now she had no clue where the demon would come from. Clarissa must have thought the same because she no longer kept her hand burning as brightly in case the demon saw them. Ben stayed low, just underneath the canopy of the trees to provide more coverage from the demon.

The sky turned from black to navy blue. She would have cried in relief at the fact that dawn approached, but a screech sounded off from somewhere close by.

They all gasped and darted through the branches, wild and frantic to get away from the demon. They moved quickly and didn't dare look back.

Suddenly, Charlotte fell forward slightly. They had reached a clearing. They all hovered over the green pasture in hesitation. Did they run on foot or fly up above and risk exposure?

Ben thought of the answer faster than the rest of them. He dropped to the ground and ran. They all followed suit. Charlotte realized his plan. She'd been in so much terror she hadn't realized where they were. The Dark River lay nearly right before them.

Ben dove into the water; his wings curled around Atarah. Up until that moment, Charlotte had been able to keep her mind off of the cold. But now, when she dove into the water, she wanted to scream and cry at the pain of the cold. She surfaced briefly, and tried to get her erratic breathing under control. Clarissa and Isabella pulled her close to them. They were all huddled together, and tried to share what meager heat they had. Ben looked off into the far trees as if he could see the beast. He raised a hand to indicate to stay still. They all stopped struggling against the current and watched him.

"We . . . are . . . going to let the river take us . . . to Urbs . . . Antiqua," Ben whispered through quivering blue lips.

"Are you . . . crazy?" Clarissa tried to hiss at him.

Ben shook his head. "There's . . . no . . . no . . . other way. We're . . . too exhausted to fly . . . and we can't outrun it . . . The river will take us there and hopefully . . . throw it off our trail for a bit."

Clarissa looked like she was about to say something else, but Ben's eyes widened. He put a finger to his lips and ducked down into the water; he kept Atarah's face barely above the surface. They all followed and looked to the trees they'd just emerged from. Fortunately, the river carried them downstream fast, or else Charlotte would have been frozen with fear.

The demon came through the trees. The pale, spider-like appendages crawled forward, while the black, empty eyes on the skull scanned the area for their life force. The Abaddon's wings were slightly damaged but healing. Probably why Charlotte felt even more drained. The closer that thing was to her, the more it stole her powers.

Isabella silently used her wind underwater to push them farther downstream. They turned the corner right as the Abaddon's skull turned in their direction. Ben pointed down to the water and indicated for them to follow. He clamped a hand on Atarah's nose and took a deep breath. Charlotte took a deep breath and ducked her head under water. She clasped her hand tightly around Isabella's, who held onto Clarissa's, who held onto Ben's shoulder. They tucked in their wings tightly, so they could move through the current more. Ben moved like a fish and tried to move around any obstacles in their path. The fish knocked against them as they swam upstream. The Dark River was so dark it was like swimming through blackness, and then suddenly, a large fish brushed against them.

Charlotte's lungs burned with the need to breathe. Ben whipped his head around to look at her. He gave an urgent shake of his head, but she could feel herself starting to convulse. Ben grabbed her quickly and maneuvered her around a large rock. They surfaced. Charlotte coughed up water and gasped eagerly for air. Clarissa and Isabella followed; they gasped and spewed water from their lungs. Ben raised a finger to his lips once more. They clung to one another, desperate for strength or warmth. Charlotte wasn't sure anymore at this point. A crunching sound of grass made them still. The sound was directly above them. They all froze; even their breathing stopped. They all stayed still in the freezing water, too scared to breathe or even chatter their teeth. Ben indicated they were going under water again. They all silently took a deep breath and slinked back into the water. This time, they sank deep into the river to swim beneath the fish. They all held onto one another, and trusted in where to swim.

They swam with the downstream current, and tried to keep from frantically swimming. It was better if they conserved their movements. After a minute or so, which felt like forever to Charlotte, they resurfaced again for air. This time, they did it as quietly as they could. Charlotte was about to ask Ben a question, but he shook his head. His eyes widened and he pointed upward; he conveyed they weren't alone. Charlotte shuddered unintentionally. Even though they were hidden beneath a rock, she felt eyes on her. Ben nodded to everyone and took a quiet deep breath once more. They all dove deep again. They repeated this pattern in silence many times. Charlotte lost track of time; for each time she resurfaced, she thought of the Abaddon grabbing her out of the water. A few more hours went by of this torture. The cold sealed off all feeling in her hands and feet. The fear forced her to move, and her lungs screamed for air. Despite it all, Charlotte kept going. Slowly, the sun crept up and lit the sky.

Ben gasped for breath as they resurfaced again; but this time, he swam outside of the protection of the foliage that concealed them.

"It's okay. You can come out now."

The words felt like a trick. Charlotte clung to the foliage that covered them from the river's edge, too scared to move. Clarissa was the first one to venture out, then Isabella, and last Charlotte.

Ben carefully cradled Atarah's bluish face above the water. He pointed to the other side. "We can get out now, but be quiet."

They slowly swam to the opposite side of the river. They scanned the area for any signs of movement. They each trudged out of the river as silently as they could.

Charlotte's arms were so weak from exhaustion and the frigid water that she needed help getting out. They all collapsed for a moment; their eyes still scanned the forest lining.

"This is the last stop before the river turns into rapids," Ben panted. "But we're close to the Gabriel border."

"The leaves are already different," Isabella observed.

Charlotte looked up at the trees. They were, in fact, different. They were no longer a deep green color, but more lime green, with hints of blue and purple.

"We're close to the springs?" Clarissa demanded.

Ben nodded, as he looked farther down the river. "We'll have to walk from here." He glanced at all of them and grinned. "Unless you want to fly from here?"

Their groans seemed to be enough for him. He hoisted Atarah close to his chest and walked farther downstream at a fast pace. They matched Ben's pace; they didn't want to linger. The sunrise came up above the mountains in the distance. The sky was an array of blue, pink, orange, and yellow as the night faded.

"Is the demon still after us?" Charlotte asked, needing to know. She was too scared to call it by name, as if speaking it aloud would cause the demon to appear.

Ben's face fell slightly as he nodded regretfully. "The demon's going deeper into the forest because of the sun coming up. But it has an idea of where we're going."

"Did it know we were in the water?" Isabella asked, terrified.

"The demon is blind, but it can sense life in form. Each time we surfaced, it could tell we weren't fish." Ben hesitated. "But demons don't usually like water, unless they're built for it."

"Then we need to move now," Clarissa said; her gaze on the far trees across the river.

They walked down the river. Charlotte stayed close to

Ben's side to monitor Atarah. While in the river, Charlotte didn't have a chance to check up on her. She wondered how she had fared in the frigid aquatic affair. She laid her hand on her head and scanned her vitals. Her blood pressure and pulse were weaker than normal but nothing life-threatening. There was surprisingly no water in her lungs. The surprise must have shown on her face because she heard someone respond.

"I kept a bubble around her face, so that water wouldn't get into her lungs," Isabella said.

Relief flooded Charlotte's heart. "Thank you," she said at the same time as Ben.

Ben looked away sheepishly; a blush seemed to climb up his neck. Isabella and Charlotte exchanged a look and resisted the urge to smile.

Within minutes, the river's current increased significantly. Charlotte heard the rapids in the distance. An hour passed as they walked along the edge of the river, and they looked out for any demons. Charlotte tried in her weakened state to strengthen the others, but failed. They were all too exhausted to gather any power, let alone fight off a demon. Charlotte prayed the rest of the journey was uneventful. The trees around them slowly transformed into beautiful spring trees with familiar bright colors, colors Charlotte had never known existed until she'd visited Lanua when she was a child.

If the trees and leaves are changing, then so is the climate, she thought excitedly.

The warmth of Lanua slowly thawed the ice in Charlotte's veins. The warmth alone was enough motivation for her to keep going.

The Dark River transformed into powerful rapids. Some of the trees' strong roots stretched across the river, and pulled nutrients from the water. The beauty of the rapids were the trees stretched across them; their iridescent, kaleidoscopic leaves fell gently into the rough current below. The mixed hues gave her the sense of fullness, peace, and a calming touch to the soul. Despite her best efforts, Charlotte relaxed, almost in a dream-like state of floating through the trees.

A hand brought her back to reality. Charlotte saw Ben standing in front of her, and realized he was worried.

"All of you have to stay alert. The trees give off a scent that's opioid-like and can make you lose touch with reality."

Charlotte blushed at her own weakness.

"Here, I can help." Isabella weakly lifted her hands and a small gust of wind whirled around them.

"Don't overdo yourself," Clarissa chided, as she stood close to her sister.

"We're close. We just need to make it through this part, and we'll be past the safe ward. Then the trees' scent won't be a threat," Ben said. He clutched Atarah tightly as he walked off down the now rocky terrain.

"Thank you," Charlotte said sincerely to Isabella.

Isabella shrugged like it was no big deal. However, Charlotte could sense everyone's health status, even in her weakened state. She saw how much strain and pain that small gust of wind caused Isabella. Charlotte glanced at Clarissa. Despite staying quiet, she knew Clarissa was the reason they hadn't frozen to death throughout this journey. Clarissa had saved everyone's lives. She strained herself as well to keep enough heat on everyone as they almost froze in the river. They wouldn't have survived without it. Their breaths were heavy with each step they took because of the strain. Charlotte sensed their bodies would go into a coma-like rest once they thought themselves safe from harm.

Last, she checked on Ben's health. She was taken aback that he could walk and carry Atarah. His physical health was completely drained, and his emotional and mental health were under stress. The stress level was so elevated, she presumed that was why he kept going.

She scrambled down the boulders to keep up with Ben's pace. They needed to rush to Urbs Antiqua. They were running on fumes out here and the threat was still present. They walked and walked, along the path of the river that expanded in size due to the rapids. The beauty of the rapids stunned Charlotte, even now in the midst of danger. The contrast of peace and danger whirled together in her heart.

Ben stopped in front of them and sharply held up a hand. He looked to their left, deep into the forest. He beckoned them forward. "There's a demon watching us."

They all froze at his words.

He slowly lowered his hand. "When I say run, run as fast as you can and keep your eyes down. This demon only takes form when you look at it. It's a Shedim demon."

Charlotte started to shake. Shedim demons craved to be seen and to consume others for companionship. Like how toddlers could be too rough with animals at first until they were taught differently, Shedim demons smothered and strangled their victims to death.

"The border is nearby. Maybe we'll get lucky."

They all nodded and lowered their eyes.

"Go," Ben whispered.

They all took off running.

Charlotte heard the leaves rattle behind her as something gave chase after them. Looking wasn't an option. They veered into the forest and farther away from the river. They hoped for coverage by the leaves and an easier surface to run on, instead of rocks. All the others ran ahead of Charlotte, and didn't look back. The demon closed in on her, and tried to get in her line of sight. She refused. She tried to expand her senses in the way Atarah taught her.

Move with every sense, and not the eyes.

She picked up the path of the others in front of her, but not well enough to close her eyes completely. Charlotte kept her gaze as unfocused as she could; she drew her focus inside her mind. She ran, and attempted to maintain the pace with the others.

They entered a small meadow with blooming red flowers. Upon entering, Clarissa let out a yell, along with her sister Isabella.

"Help!" they shouted in unison.

Something breathed heavily behind her, when an arrow shot out, hit the creature behind her, and caused a loud screech of pain to ring in her ear. She kept going. She sprinted as fast as she could, while everyone in front of her slowed, and came to a halt in front of a person. Charlotte couldn't stop, however. She couldn't control the momentum she gained as she ran. She spread out her arms to try to stop herself, but she ran right into the angel who'd saved them.

"Oof!"

She slammed into the hard chest of the angel before them, then dropped. Or she would have, but the angel caught her around the waist and lifted her. She weakly looked up to see Gabriel Fores Jr.

"Is this it?" Gabriel asked urgently, as he looked at Ben. Ben nodded weakly. Gabriel lifted her like a rag doll and turned into the forest. "Follow me."

The others followed, mercifully not for long. A few paces in front of them stood a large wooden wall made up of trees connected together. Vines wrapped around the wall tightly, as if it were a snake squeezing prey. They ventured through the wall with ease, as Gabriel commanded them to open. The vines loosened, and the tightly packed trees parted. The roots rippled underground as the trees moved back into place, and sealed the gate shut. No guards tried to pat them down, much to Charlotte's relief.

They followed Gabriel through the city on the cobblestone streets. Charlotte tried to admire the charming brick cottages, the picturesque river lined with golden lights that flowed gently through the city, and the litter of colorful flowers on the ground. But she was too tired to lift her head. They walked for a long while through the lovely city. No one spoke. From the exhaustion of fighting and running all night, sleep would be a most welcome friend.

Gabriel led them to a large brick house adorned with vines and flowers around the frame. They were quickly led inside and greeted by the Head Gabriel Sr. and his wife, Rachael. Charlotte could barely hear what was said, but saw Clarissa and Isabella escorted out by guards. Isabella wore a shocked expression and refused to leave. Charlotte wanted to mutter she was okay, but she failed to form the words. As they were roughly led out, Charlotte roused. She focused on the room and its occupants.

"It appears you got more out of the deal than we did, Mr. Benjamin," Gabriel Sr. said, as he looked at Atarah's still unconscious form.

She felt uneasy with how Gabriel Sr. looked at Atarah. He looked at her with dead eyes. It was unsettling to see such eyes, especially in Atarah's injured state. She wondered what deal he meant. Charlotte stiffened and tried to stand. The arms wrapped around her may as well have been the vines she'd seen outside along the wall. She looked at Ben, looking for help or clarity for Gabriel Sr.'s demeanor, then her confusion turned to apprehension. Ben's face was expressionless. Gone were the expressions of worry and love on his face. It was as if he didn't care about Atarah.

"What's going on?" Charlotte asked fearfully. She tried to get free from Gabriel Jr.'s arms, but he wouldn't loosen them.

"Let me go," she said, but to no avail. She struggled, and looked to Ben for help, but then she saw someone else. Someone that chilled her to her bone.

Her mother, Elizabeth, stepped forward, and stood next to Rachael Fores.

"It's all right, Charlotte dear." Her mother's voice didn't soothe her. Her voice was strong, stern, and calculated. It was the voice that she used at dinner on Atarah and Arick's first night at their home. It was her mother's way or the highway. The arms loosened a bit when she stepped into the room.

"What's going on, Mother?" Charlotte grew paler with fear.

"We made a deal. A deal that will let Mikael know of the pain we've felt for so many years."

"What did you do?" Charlotte asked incredulously.

Her mother looked at her frantic face with calm.

"They made a deal with us," Gabriel Sr. spoke up beside her. "To get Atarah away from Mikael's clutches."

Charlotte looked between them, confused for a moment, then her gaze landed on Ben. Her eyes widened and her heart dropped. "You knew," she whispered.

Ben flinched slightly, but he still held onto Atarah.

"She was supposed to marry sooner," her mother said, as she walked over to where Ben stood. "However, we had to modify the plan a little. We knew she would be suspicious. She caught on, of course—when you first arrived in Chrysi Poli and they fed you the lie that to work with the Head Tree, she needed to marry into the family. Once she knew, they knew she'd caught onto the plan. We knew over time she'd lower her guard. Then of course, Aesop passed on, which disturbed our plan a little. We weren't sure if Ben could still play the part anymore with the death of his father. To stay in character, even with your father's passing, would be difficult for anyone. Thankfully, you did, though."

"Everything was false?" Charlotte demanded. "Nothing was real?"

Ben's eyes never rose from the floor. His wings twitched with discomfort and his face tensed. She wasn't the only one to notice.

Elizabeth raised an eyebrow at him in mild surprise, and she clucked her tongue at him. "If you did develop feelings for Atarah, then I suppose that'll be a plus for your marriage."

"Marriage?" Charlotte asked weakly, as she became limp.

"Yes," Gabriel Sr. said; he drew her attention back to him. "Ben is to marry Atarah. It was supposed to be Amos, but Ben will do it. And you, my dear, will marry Gabriel."

Charlotte trembled. She'd always known she would marry whoever was most politically favorable. Nonetheless, she'd always thought her parents would take her opinion into consideration. Her opinion on who, when, and where she would be married. All of which had now been stripped from her. She felt a knife enter her heart. She looked to her mother.

"We're doing what's best," her mother said, her chin up. As if Charlotte was in the wrong for feeling betrayed.

She wanted to scream and rip the room apart. Surely, Mikael or Arick wouldn't stand for this.

Gabriel Sr. must have read her face. "This next part is the reason why your parents decided to approach us with this deal. My son will transport you, Ben, and Atarah into the human realm for a little while, until the Michael Clan cools down."

Panic clawed its way up her throat. The angels of the Gabriel Clan were the only ones who could move freely into the human realm. They would be trapped there for as long as Gabriel liked or until Mikael could gather enough power to break through the realm barrier, which could take days or weeks. Charlotte trembled as tears fell down her face at their situation and in anger at her own helplessness.

Her mother approached her and put a gentle hand on her face. "I can't wait to see you in your wedding dress, my dear. I do so wish your father could be here with us too."

Charlotte felt like a stranger was talking to her.

"I'm afraid we won't have time," Rachael said for the first time.

Elizabeth whirled on her in frustration. "Why is that?"

"A team was dispatched to every region to check on its demon status. It appears Arick, Mikael's son, is joining the one that's coming to Urbs Antiqua. They've been flying all night and could be here soon," Gabriel Sr. said regretfully.

Elizabeth made a sound of angry frustration. "Why are we just now finding out about this?"

"Our information was gathered as quickly as it could be, given the circumstances." Gabriel Sr. was unfazed by her attitude.

"How long do we have?" Elizabeth asked irritably.

"We have no idea."

She sighed. "Then we need to perform their ceremonies now, I suppose."

Charlotte trembled harder.

Ben looked at Elizabeth sharply. His grip on Atarah tightened. "Atarah is still unconscious and in need of medical care."

Elizabeth waved her hand over Atarah. "Charlotte did well. She's stable enough, and we'll only need her for the last part of the vows. We'll begin with Atarah's wedding."

"Absolutely not," Rachael said firmly. "We'll start with Charlotte to ensure you uphold your end of the bargain." Her tone was hard and non-negotiable.

Elizabeth winced slightly, but she nodded.

Charlotte would never see her mother the same.

The arms around her tightened slightly in surprise. They had loosened during the conversation, but now held tight. Gabriel Jr. might not have liked the suddenness of their wedding either. She wondered briefly if he had any choice in the matter.

However, he nodded and carried her deeper into the house. Everyone followed. Charlotte felt herself go numb with shock and hurt at her mother.

A priest stood at the other end of the house on a balcony. The balcony had a beautiful view of the trees and the river below. As good a scene as any for a wedding, even an unwilling one. The priest looked mildly surprised by their arrival, but he pulled in his composure quickly.

"Welcome. To what do I owe this visit?" the priest inquired. His gaze shifted to Atarah, then back to Gabriel Sr.

"We have to perform the wedding now. The plans have changed and the heirs need to be off soon."

The priest looked between her ragged form, Gabriel, and his vine-like arms. Then he turned to look at Ben and Atarah's injured, unconscious form. "Neither wedding will be possible, due to the physical states of the brides."

"It will be done. Right now." The harsh tone came from Elizabeth. She walked forward and stepped in front of the priest. "Their states will have to do, for our enemies are close."

The priest didn't look swayed by her tone. He shook his head. "I won't perform any weddings until they are cared for."

Elizabeth made a frustrated sound and stormed toward Ben. Ben tightened his hands around Atarah, as if to shield her from Elizabeth.

Elizabeth put her glowing hand roughly on Atarah's wings. The touch shocked Atarah awake, and caused her to cry out in pain and surprise. Ben's wings flared; he pushed Elizabeth back slightly.

Atarah was awake now; she stood and took in her surroundings. She relaxed a little when her eyes moved to Ben. But when her gaze met Charlotte's swollen, red eyes and Gabriel's arms around her, Atarah tensed.

"What's happened?" she asked; her wings flared.

"Come forward immediately," Elizabeth commanded in a cold voice.

Charlotte shook her head imploringly. "Ben betrayed us! It was my mother's plan from the start!" she cried.

Gabriel's arms tightened almost painfully around her.

Atarah took in the priest, Gabriel Sr., Elizabeth, and then lastly, Ben.

"Ben?" she asked steadily.

His wings trembled slightly; his eyes glued to the ground. Silence.

"You can't even look at me, can you?" she said. Her wings were flared and defensive. She stared hard at him.

For a moment no one, not even Elizabeth, spoke. Atarah turned away from Ben.

"What was your plan for this part? A . . . wedding?" Atarah said to Elizabeth, one eyebrow raised. "Surely, you knew I'd simply refuse to do the wedding."

"Yes, but I know you'll go through with it," Elizabeth said just as coolly.

"Oh? And why is that?" Atarah said.

"Because I know you want peace between families and power." Elizabeth replied, as she glanced at Ben. "He gave us good insight on what you want most in this world. If you want to make a change here, you have to do as I say, girl."

Atarah leveled a stare at her, but she didn't contest it.

"If you want to right the wrong your father caused my family, then this is the remuneration."

"You don't owe us anything, Atarah!" Charlotte cried.

Elizabeth waved her hand over Charlotte. She stilled all of her arytenoid muscles, which made speech difficult. Charlotte struggled to shake off her mother's affect. They continued like she had never spoken up.

"What will it be, Atarah? Will you bring peace between our families? Or do you not care enough?" Elizabeth said dispassionately.

Atarah glared at her, but she remained silent.

Rachael spoke up, which surprised them all. "Since Atarah is now awake, shall we move on to my son and Charlotte's wedding?" she said disparagingly to the priest.

The priest regarded Charlotte with a slight frown. "We can as long as the girl has the ability to speak," he said pointedly to Elizabeth.

Another wave of Elizabeth's hand, and Charlotte's speech was normal once more. She swallowed. She was too scared to speak up against her mother again. Not from any physical pain, but from what she would do behind closed doors. She couldn't stop trembling, but that didn't stop Gabriel from moving her forward. They both stood before the priest. Charlotte heard Atarah's voice behind her protesting.

"Charlotte, you don't have to marry anyone if you don't want to," Atarah said, as she moved closer.

Elizabeth cut her off. "While she is in our house, she will follow our rules. She will obey."

"Charlotte—"

"Will do as we say because I know what's best for her."

Charlotte wanted to tell Atarah her mother wouldn't listen. Her mother had always been this way with her. There was never any point in trying to reason with her.

She felt pressure on her right hand and looked down to see that Gabriel Jr. had grabbed her hand and given it a little squeeze. He tried to comfort her? *Why?*

The priest looked between them and nodded. "To start the wedding, we must recite the prayers that have been passed down from each household since the original Archangels."

This caught everyone's attention. Gabriel Sr. looked at the priest with a confused expression, while Elizabeth and Rachael looked mildly annoyed. Atarah looked between them, also confused.

"We haven't done those prayers in a long time. There's no need to—" Gabriel Sr. started, but the priest interrupted him.

"We will honor our calling and our ancestors to bless this wedding before anything else. Or else it will be out of the jurisdiction of the Trinity."

Everyone was silenced. Nothing went outside of the Trinity. There was no arguing against that reasoning, even if it did cause impatience. Charlotte understood why her mother didn't want the prayers to be recited. They were long and tiring. Back in the time of the original Archangels, each Archangel Head gave prayers to their clan to beseech the Trinity and live by it. The prayers were often recited at funerals, social events, or weddings. However, over the centuries, the prayers had been involved less and less within angels' lives. Now, they were mostly taught in school, but not applied to any other daily life activities.

The priest stretched out his hands. As they started to glow, a large, ragged book appeared in them. Within minutes, the book materialized into a solid form in the priest's hands. He waved his hand over the book and opened to the page to recite the groom's family household first, as was tradition.

Charlotte simply went numb and had a hard time focusing on anything the priest recited. Charlotte looked beyond the priest and out at the beautiful trees, leaves, and flowers. The leaves and flowers seemed to dance with each other in the wind, while they descended into the jerking motion of the river. She felt an odd similarity to the nature around her. The flowers drifted peacefully along the wind, like she and her friends had, until a cold, sudden current swept her away, and crashed over her. She dared a glance at Gabriel Jr. and wondered what he thought of everything. Was he like her and following orders? Or did he want this marriage?

His blue eyes gave nothing away. Neither did his black feathery wings, while her wings vibrated with anxiety and fear. Charlotte dared a glance back to Atarah. Atarah wasn't looking at her, but up into the sky. Her stomach twisted. Didn't Atarah care? After their wedding was done, it was her wedding that would be next.

Why isn't she putting up more of a fight? she wondered.

Charlotte didn't fool herself enough to try to fight against her own wedding. The repercussions would be severe and swift. *You've always known your wedding would be arranged*, she chided herself. She stupidly thought she would have a choice. Nonetheless, she didn't want her wedding to be part of a manipulative deal between houses that involved Atarah. She was her friend.

The priest continued to recite the prayer in long, drawn-out sentences. His voice was low and monotone and made Charlotte want to sleep right there at the altar. The vibrations of her wings and the adrenaline of the sudden marriage were the only reasons why Charlotte hadn't collapsed by now from exhaustion. She wasn't the only one tired from the recitation. Rachel and Elizabeth both stifled yawns. They shifted to stretch their wings as an effort to stay awake. Charlotte noticed the priest's eyes shifting upward and downward several times, but that might have been her imagination. She felt Gabriel Jr. also shifting in an effort to avoid nodding off. Only Charlotte, Atarah, and Ben seemed to be fully awake. Ben still hovered close by

Atarah. She would shoot him glares every now and then when she stopped looking at the sky. Why was she looking at the sky?

The priest's gaze was aimed upward and downward as he recited the prayer. He looked wide awake as well. Their eyes met briefly.

Atarah looked off into the sky and the priest continued the drawn-out prayers—they were stalling for time. Charlotte stiffened as she realized this. *Of course*, she thought. As soon as Atarah woke up, she would have used her powers to get a feel for the area. She probably sensed something. Charlotte glanced up at the sky as well. While Rachel and Elizabeth looked at the priest, she looked up and to her left. She saw six figures dive toward them. One figure in particular was larger than the rest. They started off small and quickly grew in size. They flew in fast. That must be the team they had mentioned earlier.

Just as Charlotte recognized the figures, everything happened all at once.

"Amen," the priest said with finality.

Arick landed forcefully right beside the altar where the priest stood.

"Hey, little cricket," Arick said, beside the priest. He smiled and bowed in greeting.

Up in the sky, farther behind were five more angels Charlotte had never seen before. It didn't matter, for Atarah sprinted to Arick and embraced him in a tight hug.

"What took you so long?" she murmured, then backed away and punched him on the shoulder.

Arick chuckled; his wings still flared and his gaze was on Elizabeth and Gabriel Sr. He was trying to piece together the situation he'd landed in.

Gabriel Jr. grabbed Charlotte once more and shifted her away from Arick and closer to the house. Charlotte tried to fight against him, but she was too weak and tired.

Everyone made small, subtle movements into defensive fighting positions.

"Well, what do we have here?" Arick asked, as he released Atarah and stepped forward slowly.

Everyone backed up for each step he took.

"It seems that Elijah and Elizabeth wanted to marry me off to the Selaphiel family as a way to make peace between our families," Atarah answered coolly.

Arick stiffened, as he looked at Elizabeth.

Elizabeth's wings were fully flared; her body half turned, ready to run. "Your father doesn't deserve a daughter. It's only appropriate for him to know what it's like to lose one," she hissed at Arick.

Something shifted in Arick's eyes. Charlotte could vaguely sense a lot of turmoil going on inside Arick, but she didn't focus on it. Gabriel shifted her farther away from Atarah and Arick. The other angels had caught up with them and landed around the balcony. For a moment, everyone stood still, as if predator and prey had fixed eyes on each other, ready to move.

"You don't have to do this," Atarah said quietly, as if afraid of triggering something.

Elizabeth shifted and looked to Gabriel Sr. "Now it's your turn, Gabriel."

Gabriel Sr. looked around at the new angels before them. His eyes shifted from Arick to another angel with dark hair and gray eyes. He seemed to be grimacing against what he was going to do. The angel with gray eyes came forward, and this was all the catalyst needed.

"Now," Gabriel Sr. said harshly to his son.

Gabriel Jr. spun Charlotte around and darted forward. Ben, who had fallen into the background, jumped out at Atarah, and snuck past Arick. Ben grabbed a hold of Atarah and sprinted forward as well. Arick moved to strike against Ben. All of the other angels moved to tackle one another. Fighting and chaos ensued along the balcony.

Gabriel Sr. called for guards. Charlotte never knew what happened, for Ben reached forward toward Gabriel's outstretched hand. Gabriel now held onto Charlotte. Ben held onto Atarah's fighting form.

Charlotte had a hard time putting into words what happened next. The closest thing she could equate it to was when she'd first learned how to fly—the weightlessness and yet heaviness of falling and nothing there to catch her.

She strained her back reflexively, but her wings felt like they were no longer on her back. Scared, she flailed her arms to catch herself, or tried to. Gabriel still tightly gripped her arm as the world swirled around them. Colors, lights, and visions streamed by in incoherent order that Charlotte was no longer sure was reality. Terror clawed its way through her.

Then it stopped.

They landed on bright green grass and toppled over. It was like she had spun fast and then suddenly stopped. Charlotte struggled to get her equilibrium in balance, as well as her other senses. She turned to look around her and saw Atarah. She froze at what she saw beyond Atarah.

Off in the far distance, cars drove along small, isolated highways.

Behind Charlotte, Gabriel and Ben started to get to their feet. Atarah easily knocked Gabriel back down, and pulled her dagger from her side to his neck.

"Why in the Holy Trinity did you bring us to the human realm?"

FOLLOW THE AUTHOR

WWW.GRACIEMITCHELL.COM

Instagram

@clanofarchsseries
@gmitchell505

TikTok

@gmitchell505

ACKNOWLEDGEMENTS

This story had been on my heart for a few years before I had the courage to write it. Starting was one of the hardest parts but that is what helped me grow into the author that I am today. I could not have done this alone, which is why I express immense gratitude to the people below.

I want to say thank you so much to my husband, Malcomn, for encouraging me that anything is possible. Thank you to my wonderful cat Zeus for cuddling by me while I burned through the candlelight, writing this book.

Thank you to my amazing family and friends for supporting me throughout this process! Love ya'll so much.

Thank you to my editors starting with Connie Dowell for developmental editing. Thank you Nichole Heydenburg both copy and developmental editing. The attention to detail is really appreciated! Thank you Anachal Jain for thoroughly proofreading. I am very grateful for all of the feedback you have given! Thank you Greg Rupel for formatting my book; it looks amazing! Thank you everyone for all of your amazing feedback and hard work! To the Team at Enchanted Ink Publishing, thank you for all of your hard work.

Thank you to Jessica Slater for all of the amazing work you have done for my book cover and design! Your work is amazing!

Lastly I want to thank- you, the reader. Thank you so much for reading my book and I truly hope you enjoyed this story! If you did please let me know by leaving a review- I would greatly appreciate it! Thank you again! :)

GRACIE MITCHELL is currently based in Atlanta working as an exercise physiologist by day, while writer by night. She always loved reading and writing since pre-adolescence. By 2018, She and her husband moved to Colorado Springs which gave her the opportunity to start writing her first book. On top of her love to read and write, Gracie enjoys going on adventurous hikes, painting, spending time with her cat and traveling to different countries.

www.ingramcontent.com/pod-product-compliance
Lightning Source LLC
Chambersburg PA
CBHW020340310726
48979CB00015B/2439/J

* 9 7 8 1 7 3 5 4 5 7 5 2 9 *